Advance Praise for *Tiger Lessons*

'*Tiger Lessons* is an intense adventure through the deciduous forests of Nallamala hills told with impeccable descriptive powers. It's a book you can open and walk into. It masterfully weaves tensions of caste, drought, smuggling, poverty, politics and human–wildlife conflict while narrating a coming-of-age story, honouring the shepherd's deep knowledge and respect for the wild. I wish every urbanite reads this novel.'

Yuvan Aves,
author of *Intertidal*

'By meticulously describing the hardship and intensity of a shepherd's life—a group of shepherds rove through the forest for over fifty days to keep their herds alive, with blood-curdling encounters with tigers and pythons and humans—Sannapureddy Venkatarami Reddy proves that all lives unfamiliar to us are as incredible as myths.'

Benyamin,
author of *Goat Days*

'What a story! Both heart-breaking and heart-warming, a testament to its amazing writer and translator. It's an epic about all the tigers of our country, apart from the real ones: casteism and community, the trials of "villagers" in our cities . . . and us "educated" types who are pathetically ignorant about people like shepherds and other providers of our food. We need to read it. Luckily for us, this is an enjoyable and gripping exercise, with a racy story, humour, memorable imagery and bold, relatable characters. I want more from Sannapureddy Venkatarami Reddy and Narasimha Kumar.'

Zai Whitaker,
author of *Kali and the Rat Snake*

Tiger Lessons

Tiger Lessons

SANNAPUREDDY VENKATARAMI REDDY

TRANSLATED BY
NARASIMHA KUMAR

BLOOMSBURY
NEW DELHI • LONDON • OXFORD • NEW YORK • SYDNEY

BLOOMSBURY INDIA
Bloomsbury Publishing India Pvt. Ltd
Second Floor, LSC Building No. 4, DDA Complex, Pocket C—6 & 7,
Vasant Kunj, New Delhi, 110070

BLOOMSBURY, BLOOMSBURY INDIA and the Diana logo
are trademarks of Bloomsbury Publishing Plc

Originally published in Telugu as *Kondapolam* by TANA
(Telugu Association of North America) Publications, 2019
First published in English in India 2025

ISBN: PB: 978-93-56402-29-4; eBook: 978-93-56402-22-5
2 4 6 8 10 9 7 5 3 1

Typeset in Adobe Caslon Pro by Manipal Technologies Limited
Printed and bound in India by Thomson Press India Ltd

To find out more about our authors and books visit www.bloomsbury.com and sign up for our newsletters

Contents

BOOK 1

Fear

1

IT WAS EARLY SUMMER, a few weeks after ugadi, the sun still in the constellation of Bharani. Peak summer, when it enters Rohini, was still a month away. That was when the grind stones were supposed to shatter in the heat. But they were already showing cracks.

It was searing hot well before breakfast time. By afternoon, the sun's horses were galloping hard and fast. Occasionally, a wave of hot air lashed the face, like steam from a hot pan.

The sheep were moving constantly, not letting the shepherd stand under the shadow of even a thorn tree for a few minutes. They pressed their mouths to the ground, trying to find dried leaves in the sunbaked fields where pulses were grown the past season. There was only stubble. Even the grass on the raised borders had withered completely. No green grass. No dry grass. No leaves anywhere. Not even dried leaves or stover. The flock roamed around the entire day to find a little feed or some water.

Walking behind them with a long stick on his shoulder, Gurappa felt distressed at the suffering of the sheep.

The water shortage was acute. All the water holes of Sagileru went bone-dry. The Vankamarri reservoir stood stark in its dryness. The shepherds were tending to the thirst of their herds by pleading with—no, begging—the landlords whose borewells still spat out some water. It was looking impossible to help the herds survive till the first rains.

Gurappa looked up at the Nallamala hills, some ten miles away in the distance, and thought, 'Hope it rains a little at least in those hills. Can take the herd there and save their lives.'

Similar thoughts were echoing in the minds of all the gollas in the village.

Gurappa's herd was big, with a hundred sheep. Even selling them wasn't viable, as they had lost fat and muscle and looked famished with their bones jutting out. Buyers would expect a bargain. After rearing them for years, selling them now would be like abandoning them to the mercy of wild animals. Already most of the old sheep had reached mutton shops. Some shepherds had started selling even the fertile sheep.

For a month they had been sustaining the sheep with extra feed. They were going to the villages downstream of the canals to buy stover from the groundnut crop and transporting it back in tractors. A tractor-load of feed cost around twenty thousand rupees. Even careful rationing could feed the flock for barely a month.

Rain was on everyone's mind. It would not rain here anyway. It would be enough if it rained in the Nallamala hills. If it rained just a little at a few places, from Raasala to Obulam, the dried-up grass beds would sprout green shoots. That could help the sheep survive the summer.

The herd moved through barren lands, parched fields, dry canals, rocky streambeds and thorny trails. Behind them, with a water bottle under his arm, a bamboo stick in his hand, clad in a dirty shirt and a gosi pancha, a handkerchief wrapped around the head, with rubber footwear, and skin tanned very dark, Gurappa walked under the hot sun.

The dirt-coloured sheep under the red-hot sun looked like rocks in a well-ploughed field. Iron balls in a furnace.

The herd turned towards the village after three in the afternoon. The sheep stopped looking at the ground and faced upwards as they became homeward bound. Gurappa could not have stopped them or changed direction. By four, they reached the barns and sheepfolds on the outskirts of the village. The herd stood under the shade of tamarind trees and began to clamour for the extra feed they expected at this time.

The little lambs inside the sheepfolds heard their mothers' voices and started bleating too, almost in unison. It was quite a cacophony.

Gurappa's sons brought two big baskets of groundnut husk and threw it all over the feeding area. Gurappa struggled to keep the sheep calm while they were doing it. The sheep then jumped into the feeding area and licked the husk off the ground, swallowing some soil too in the process.

Two more baskets of husk were strewn around. Within minutes, the sheep gobbled up the feed and looked up for more. Some were sneezing, while others were vigorously shaking their heads. The bleating for more feed didn't stop. It looked like they were not even half full.

It was not possible to actually rear sheep with bought feed. The only thing it could do was keep the sheep alive till the first rains.

The remaining half of the sheep's stomach had to be filled with water. Gurappa had a deal with the borewell owner, who wanted a ram instead of money.

Neither of Gurappa's sons came forward to take the sheep to the borewell. Gurappa directed the herd in the direction of the well, shouting at them, throwing stones and beating the ground with his stick.

The water from the borewell flowed into a small mud-banked canal. The sheep on either side of the canal was a sight worth watching. They almost attacked the water in desperation. Some tried drinking while standing, huffed in excitement, took a deep noisy breath, bent on their knees and then sipped and sucked the water with their lips. Watching them slake their thirst with such desperation made Gurappa's heart ache a bit. He felt as if his own thirst had been quenched. An inexplicable satisfaction spread through him.

In the saffron-red dusk, he thought of the sheep surrounding the canal as an army of red ants crowding over a crumb. Several sheep drank to their content, took a few steps back, and unable to leave the water, came back again for some more lazy gulps, before shaking their bodies. While the last of the sheep were lingering at the water, Gurappa too drank a few palmfuls and drove the herd homeward.

With two male goats leading the way, rams guarding on either side and the shepherd at the back, the herd headed towards the village without a care, its hunger satiated for the day.

On days when the sheep had had their fill, Gurappa did not mind if his own meal lacked spice. The satisfaction of the sheep being fed well made the food taste better, coming out as a burp. On such days, he would be all smiles at dinner.

When the sheep struggled to get enough food or water, his impatience during the short time spent at home was quite visible. The lady of the house would admonish him for being in a bad mood.

'When hundred lives are lying hungry in the backyard, how can I eat food here?' he would say with a lump in his throat.

The family found this reaction a bit extreme.

'Do all the other gollas behave the same?'

The herd was now approaching the fenced sheepfold built on a barren piece of land. Little lambs milled around in their enclosures, separated by bamboo wicket fences. The bleating grew in volume as they sensed their mothers coming towards the hold.

The mother sheep responded to the lambs and rushed towards the pens. They reached the shed's entrance but could not go inside as the iron gate was locked. Teats flapping they ran about trying to find a way in; watching them from the gaps between the wickets, impatient to suckle, the lambs almost began a small stampede.

Gurappa's elder son, Sankar, lifted the iron gate to allow the mothers to enter. Rush they did, like water breaking a dam. The cries of the lambs inside the pens reached a crescendo. The two young men went in and opened the gates of the pens too.

The little lambs came out of the dark almost blinded by excitement. They looked this way and that for a second or two, then leaped towards their mothers' teats with a primal, uncontrollable urge. The force of their mouths clasping shook the mothers' backsides for a moment before they could adjust and settle into a stable stance.

Once their babies' mouths settled properly on the teats, the mother sheep bent their heads to lick their offspring. By then, the excitement of the little lambs had subsided. Lifting their little tails up, they suckled milk, lost in tranquil immersion.

Some, unable to find their mother, were trying to suckle from a different sheep. A few mothers allowed such trespassers to feed, but others pushed them away. Some mothers did not allow even their own children to come close to suckle. A few lambs, unable to find a teat anywhere, stood around helplessly.

'Sankara, see to that one with the black-coloured mouth, she is nursing a lamb not her own,' shouted Gurappa.

Sankar pulled the lamb by its neck from the teat of the black-mouthed sheep and placed it near its own mother.

'See that little one there, feeding from the red with white spots. Bring it here to this sheep with red spots and make it feed from her.'

Gurappa continued instructing his elder son.

Sankar walked up to the reddish-brown sheep with white spots on its back and sides and lifted the little white one with red spots. He carried it in his arms to its mother, the one with big red spots, and squatted to ensure it was able to suckle properly.

With milk dribbling down their mouths, the children slaked their hunger by sucking as hard as they could from the paps of the mother sheep. To escape from the clasps of children sucking even after the last drop of milk was drained, some of the sheep lay down on the ground.

Cries and screams continued coming from the neighbouring cattle sheds.

Gurappa sat down on a bamboo cot outside their sheepfold.

While his elder son was working hard in the shed, the younger one, Ravi, sat in a corner, earphones on, listening to some music.

'Sinnoda!' called Gurappa.

'Ravi, nanna's calling you.' When Sankar tapped him on the shoulder, Ravi took the earphones out and went to his father.

'We can't rear these sheep any longer, sinnoda,' said Gurappa. 'These are cruel times. How can a man survive such hard times for long? I don't want to force peddoda as well to stay here . . . he wants to move to Bangalore with his brothers-in-law. I am fine with that. I will take care of these animals till I have the energy. My only worry is about you. It is giving me palpitations.'

'Why?'

'It has been four years since you graduated,' said Gurappa.

'Don't worry . . . I will land a job,' Ravi replied looking down.

'You have been sitting in Hyderabad, fighting to get a job for the past four years. I don't know about you, but I am feeling embarrassed in front of others, sinnoda. Once or twice is okay . . . but one shouldn't lose so many times, son. One should fight strongly like a ram and not retreat even if the head cracks. It doesn't seem to me you have ever been hurt that badly.'

Ravi's hand involuntarily removed the earphones hanging down his neck and put them in his pocket.

'Is getting a job a must? Can't we run a paying guest hostel in Bangalore and survive?' Sankar said.

'That is exactly my fear,' said Gurappa. 'You ran behind sheep to fund his education. My worry is that the buck that was to lead our family herd has fallen behind. If he grew like a big tree, I was hoping that you, me, all of us could live under his shade. It doesn't look good if he depends on you for shade, now and tomorrow, peddoda,' said Gurappa with sadness in his voice.

'Alright, alright . . .' said Sankar and headed home with his younger brother.

'You could have sent your father and stayed there. He could have washed up, eaten a little and gone back,' Guramma said to her sons.

'There are people in the neighbouring cattle sheds. He will come back with them,' answered Sankar. Both the brothers sat in front of the TV. Their sisters, Sasikala and Praveena, were playing with Ravi's phone.

Their grandfather placed his walking stick in the corner outside the door and came inside. He sat with his grandsons.

'Peddoda.'

'Thatha?'

'When did she go to her village?'

Sankar understood.

'One week yesterday,' he replied.

'Why don't you go visit? What will people think?'

'Which people?'

'Who else? Society. Not even three months since you got married. At least for the first six months, the husband should live with the wife.'

Ravi smiled. Sankar blushed a little. Guramma smiled to herself in the backyard.

'Don't talk about old traditions,' said Sankar.

The old man shot up like an arrow. 'No clumsy talk, peddoda! In my days . . .' he said and left mumbling something under his breath.

An old woman came inside. 'Peddoda, your grandfather went outside grumbling about something. What did you say?'

No one responded.

'What happened? Someone tell me!'

'He is not going to his in-laws' place,' said Ravi laughing.

'I thought so. The old man has lost all the hair on his head but won't stop grooming his moustache. And they won't stop teasing him. He needs to dump his spite some place, no?'

Sankar was watching TV, but the scenes did not sink in. He had been speaking with Swapna on the phone every morning and evening. He had wanted to go the day before yesterday but stayed back for Ravi's visit.

Sankar felt a little embarrassed at becoming the talk of the village and wanted to leave immediately to see Swapna. Her village was seventy kilometres away, on the banks of the Penna, near Siddavatam.

Gurappa came home.

'O'mme, draw some water for your father.'

Sasikala responded to her mother's call, gave the phone back to her brother and went to the backyard.

Gurappa bathed, had his dinner, put a rough blanket on his shoulder and went back to the sheep.

'Why don't you also have your meal?' called Guramma.

The brothers washed up and sat down for dinner. While Sasi served them, Praveena tried to help and also play with the phone at the same time.

The old couple came inside.

'Some of my wishes have been fulfilled. Some not . . .' said the old man looking at his grandsons.

No one responded.

But he didn't give up.

'I wanted to see peddoda getting married. I saw that. I also want to see peddayammi's wedding. If God allows, I will see that as well. I am not sure if I will be alive to see chinnayammi's,' he said.

'Don't you want to see my marriage?' asked Ravi.

'Aha . . . no . . .'

'Why not?'

'I want to see you bring bundles of currency. I wish to have you bring me a packet of thousand rupee notes every month . . . and then I would like to go into the street and shake the bundle in front of everyone . . . make people jealous by shoving it into my shirt pocket.'

'Enough of your dreams . . . are you not putting some big pots on the boil here?' said the old woman.

'Not me, your son put them long ago. I am just hoping for the rice to be cooked in those pots so I can eat,' said the old man and went into the backyard.

Ravi was silent.

Sleep eluded him for a long time that night.

He was being talked about in the village. The old man must have felt pained by the talk about his inability to get even a small job, after they spent a lot of money over the years to educate him.

He was the first engineering graduate among the yadavs in his village. For the past four years, he had been doing courses in the training centers at Hyderabad's Ameerpet. And yet, he had failed miserably in landing a job. Missing the merit list by a mark or half . . . the inability to answer questions asked in the interviews . . . the fear and sense of inadequacy common to all rural students . . . the lack of self-confidence that made him tongue-tied in group discussions when faced with the oratory of English-medium candidates . . . legs trembling even before he entered a room for an interview . . . the chill in his spine when facing company executives in the interview panels . . . the sweat that trickled down his face as soon as the questions began . . . the anguish at the inability to get rid of his fear and low self-esteem . . . the hesitancy that deprived him of the ability to make use of the layers and layers of knowledge acquired through much effort . . .

2

When Sankar left for his wife's village, he asked Ravi to come along. But Guramma would not permit it, because they needed Ravi's help.

The sheep would have to be managed when they were woken up at dawn and led out to graze, and in the evenings when they had to be herded back into the shed. Those with fever would need injections. During the day, when the sheep were out grazing, the little lambs in the pens would have to be given leafy twigs to munch. At night, Ravi would have to join the neighbours in climbing neem trees to gather bunches of leaves. Lambs that had grown a little big for the pens would have to be taken to the nearby fields for a while and brought back.

It was not as if Ravi would do all this work. But he could at least lend a hand to Guramma and the girls.

Just as Ravi got ready to take Sankar on the motorbike to Porumamilla to catch the bus, they heard a commotion and stepped out.

People came shouting from the direction of the kapu street. 'We need to find out who did this and tie him up,' they said loudly. 'It is the gollas who committed this deed,' others commented.

'Find out who did this and beat him with a slipper. But it is not acceptable if you accuse all the gollas,' replied some of the shepherds confronting the kapus. Other gollas joined them in solidarity.

There were pipes attached to the motor fitted to the borewell to supply water to the entire village. Individual houses got water when the motor was turned on. A windpipe ten-foot high had been set atop the large cement tank outside the village for the air in the pipes to escape and to channel excess water. The cement tank's purpose was to help wash the cattle, and it had been built by the government.

Someone had broken those pipes. All the water in the pipes had rushed out through the windpipe. After filling the tank, the water filled the holes on the ground and flowed towards the barren gutter by the cattle sheds. This meant the three streets on the upper part of the village would not get a single drop of water. Most of those houses belonged to the kapus.

They decreed that it was golla youth who had broken the pipes. They showed evidence to establish that none of the fields had water, and the gollas therefore broke the pipes to divert the water to the tank and make it available for the sheep to drink.

The borewell motor at best pumped out a thin stream of water, not more than one and half inches wide. And because of the broken pipes most of that water had seeped into the cattle ground to go to waste. The people in the upper streets did not know where to get water for their domestic use. Frustration led to anger and the anger was being directed at the gollas.

From dawn to dusk, you shepherds depend on our fields. It won't be good for you if you argue with us despite the evidence of your misdeed, was the refrain from the kapus.

The conflict about water was turning into a caste conflict. Some of the golla elders stepped in. Though gollas, they resided in the upper streets and faced the water problem too.

'Yes, this was done by gollas. It is they who broke the pipes and should fix them now,' declared an elder.

'Are you not a golla? Does that mean you were involved in breaking the pipes too?' questioned a fellow golla.

'Why link this issue with caste? A golla is one who rears sheep. See that guy Tiripal Reddy—he rears sheep. He is a kapu lad by caste, but he is a golla now. There we have muthraasu Pichchanna, a flower seller, and chakali Munayya, a washerman—they all own sheep. They are gollas too. Their sheep may have drunk the water too. You all know who broke the pipes,' admonished the elder.

That ended the confrontation and people headed back to their homes. Some of them went to fix the pipes.

'Even if they are fixed, will they let them be? You think the shepherds can keep quiet if the sheep die of thirst? The shepherd will go to jail but won't stop trying to provide water for his sheep,' said Gurappa sipping some water.

Ravi gave his father a strange look.

'If the rains don't show up, god knows how many such fights we might see.' Gurappa washed his hands, went into the backyard to look for something and came back into the house. 'By the way, peddoda, take Ravi with you,' he said.

Guramma did not object this time. She understood that her husband did not want the conflicts and tensions in the village to reach their sons.

Sankar was happy. The brothers decided to ride the bike all the way, and they reached Sankar's wife's village by afternoon.

They spent four days there, visiting the Siddavatam fort and the temples nearby. On the second day, they went to the Ontimitta Srirama temple, the Soumyanatha temple at Nandalur and the ruins of Buddhist monasteries. The next day, they spent time in the muskmelon orchards on the sandbanks of the rivulet.

Sankar's brothers-in-law became good friends with Ravi. They invited him to come to Bangalore along with Sankar. But he did not want to give up his job hunt just yet. '*I need to succeed . . . I must succeed.*'

They would have stayed a few more days, but their sister called from home. 'They are saying it rained in the Nallamala hills.'

They reached their village by evening.

Not a single drop of rain in the village though. Not even a brief drizzle.

Some villagers had gone to the Kasi Nayana ashram near Jyothi. They heard people at the ashram speaking about the rain in the hills and came back to the village with the news. Apparently, it rained a little in Varikuntla as well, but it was a good rain in the hills.

All the shepherds felt as if a weight had been removed from their heads.

Now they needed to find out where it had rained in the hills, locate the water bodies and decide on the trails to take the herds through. They needed to get ready for konda polam, hill-grazing: the practice of taking herds of cattle into the hills in search of water and grazing.

Two golla trackers, Gangayya and Pamuleti, went to do a recce of grazing spots and water sources. They got up before dawn, went to Narsapuram and rode the bus to Jyothi. The sun was up by the time they got down at Chelima Baavi, a wellspring in the middle of the forest.

From there, they made their way into the valley between the two hills. They reached Kurro's well through Murikomma's stream and the Grove of Teak Leaves. The well was dry. They climbed a nearby hillock, took some soil in their hands and tried to make a lump of it. The ease with which they could mould the soil showed there was enough moisture. It had rained a decent amount there, they reckoned.

They tested the soil again in Raasala meadow, and they investigated the Hidden Stream, after checking the Cloudy Stream and the Tiger Brook. Water was slowly coming up to the surface in the wellsprings. It would be enough to quench the thirst of men but not the sheep. Balappa's well had water though.

The trackers crossed Bopidevi rubble to reach Eguvootlu, where a tubular aquifer broke through the hard stone. A thin stream of water was flowing from under the roots of the mango trees. This could quench the thirst of the animals.

The two shepherds stopped briefly for lunch at the Garudadri ashram and continued their trek to reach the Pamuleti hill through Velpudari. From there, they climbed the Obulam hill. They covered the Grove of the Sacred Figs, the Alli stream, the Springs of the Immortals, Rommana's trench, the Mead of the Bald Oxen and other landmarks where water was likely to be found.

On top of one hill; near the tail of another; along the spine of hillocks; in the paths of streams and in valleys; on the plains and near the sandy tracts; on the mounds, pikes, ridges and fells; in the downlands, uplands, drumlins, knolls, banks and hogbacks; in the shrubs and under the grass heaps and in the crevices of rock beds they hunted for water. They bent down everywhere to pick up the soil and squeeze it for moisture. And where they found water, they tested it for quality—sipping a little or sometimes just smelling it or touching the surface. In most places there was no overflow of water. At some places, insects buzzed over rotten leaves covering up the water, making it quite dirty.

They did not rest anywhere for even a minute. Observing the lie of the land, memorizing the locations of the water bodies and by walking so briskly that it was almost a run, they covered over forty kilometres of the forest by evening.

Grass and shrubs on hills got burnt by the heat of summer and green shoots appeared within two to three days of rain. The scouts did not set foot on the few unburnt hills that were thick with vegetation. It would have been difficult to extricate themselves if they got stuck in the thorny bushes. The herds would be led only to those hills and forests that had been blazed dry, where fresh grass grew after rain drenched the soil.

They slept at the Jyothi ashram that night and returned to their village by the early bus next morning. The gollas would have enough information now to begin the preparations for hill-grazing.

3

THE RECCE REPORT CREATED a mild flutter among the shepherding families of the village. They decided to set out for the hills with the herds in two days.

Rations had to be prepared and the necessary ingredients were obtained. The womenfolk had already kept aside pearl millet for the purpose. They had to grind it to make flour for rotis. Only the golla women knew the art of preparing rotis for rations.

In the past, they had cooked the rotis on clay pans, with a light flame burning underneath. These days it was all iron. The flour is flattened into as thin a layer as possible and cooked red on both sides and left on the bricks of the oven to absorb the heat. The rotis are then dried in the sun on cloth spread on bedsteads.

After being properly cooked and properly dried, the roti becomes hard. Bite it with your front teeth and it breaks easily. And when you chew the piece, it softens and releases a lovely flavour.

The perfect roti requires an expert cook, one able to assess the rightness of the flame and the colour and sweet smell of well-cooked millet. When the golla women made the rotis, kapu women visited them to gossip and take home a few rotis.

The women then roasted groundnut and red chilli, added tamarind and some salt, ground the mixture by hand and rolled them into large balls. Dry coconut and garlic mixed with other spices were pounded to make another big ball. These were packed in a cloth bag along with two blocks of jaggery, ten onions and two sers of rice, completing the rations for one person.

Three sers of millet, in the hands of an experienced golla woman, would give thirty rotis. A somewhat inexperienced cook would end up with twenty rotis for the same amount of grain. The rotis would suffice for breakfast and dinner, eaten with jaggery and onion, for a single ration period of eight days. For lunch the men would cook the rice and have it with the tamarind and groundnut mixture. Two sers of rice would be enough for eight days. The other masala was handy for the rare occasion when they could cook a sheep that might have died of injuries after a tiger attack or due to an accidental fall.

*

During hill-grazing, a herd of fifty sheep requires one man. Sankar accompanied Gurappa every year to take care of their hundred sheep. And he got ready this time as well, but the elders asked him to stay back. The advice was firm—one should not go into the forested hills during the first year of marriage.

Newly married. He would need to move about in the forest amid tigers, leopards, pythons and bears. After escaping them, he would have to contend with the unseen tiger—chill fever, hill fever. If one catches that fever, no one knows how long it would take to recover.

That is why Sankar was left out of the plans this time.

Gurappa went around the village trying to find someone to accompany him. He was willing to pay a good amount for the work involved. But who offers their neck willingly to the fox?

He did not know what to do. For a moment, he thought of his younger son, Ravi. Ravi did not know the difference between an ash-coloured sheep and one with white streaks on top. He could not tell whether a ram was six months old or had crossed one year. He could not take a suckling lamb to its mother. Or find out that a lamb was feeding from a different one and take it away.

Ravi was sent away to study so that he did not have to do this hard work. He had proved himself in his studies and earned the plaudits of the golla community. To make him come back to a shepherd's job would be humiliating. Gurappa would not be able to walk around the village with dignity.

The girls were better than Ravi. They knew how to handle the sheep. But he couldn't possibly be so cruel and take them to the hills. They wouldn't get any marriage alliances if he did that.

Gurappa could not find a way out of the problem. He discussed it with his parents and shared his agony with his wife. He could not tarry. The sooner the herd was taken out of the village and into the hills, the better. If the sheep stayed in the village, it would lead to fights over water.

Guramma too went around the village, trying to find someone to accompany her husband. She got a call put through to her mother's house and spoke to her brother. No one came forward. Her husband's anguish entered her head too.

The old man saw the couple's anxiety. Around late afternoon, after eating some porridge with buttermilk, he called his younger grandson to his side.

'Why do you think you didn't get a job?' he asked.

Ravi gave him a startled look. It was a simple question, but the answer was complex. The old man wouldn't get it, even if he tried explaining.

'I think you are under an evil spell,' the old man added.

This time, Ravi gave him a questioning look.

'You earned a name that you are the smartest guy among all the local golla families. And that is true . . . but what does it mean if you still can't get a job?' Giving his grandson a thoughtful look, he continued, 'You need to get away from the curse.'

Ravi could not understand what the evil spell was and how he could get away from it.

'When people come and fall at his feet, the saint Kasi Nayana scolds them. "What will you get if you fall at my feet, son? Only dirt! Go provide food to that hungry man over there. You will get some good karma." It is not just humans; if you save the life of any living form by giving them a little food, I believe it will give you a lot of good karma . . . hundred lives . . . imagine how much punya you will accrue if you help a hundred lives to survive . . . think about it.'

Ravi half-understood the old man's words.

'All the negative forces and evil spells latching on to you will go away, sinnoda.'

'What should I do?'

'Go with your father on the hill-grazing trip. Sustain the lives of the sheep. Don't see my face again if you don't get a job within six months,' declared the old man as if he was making a vow.

Ravi understood fully.

'In that case, all the training centers in Ameerpet will have to be shut down. All the B. Tech students should sport tilaks and go round the temples chanting bhajans,' Ravi thought. He imagined the scene and smiled to himself.

The old man couldn't be faulted for his thinking. These beliefs have been handed down as tradition for generations. Even scientists sending rockets into space place the models at the feet of Goddess Chengalamma and Tirumala Sri Venkateswara Swamy to get their blessings. In any case, the old man managed to seed the idea of going into the forests in Ravi's mind.

How would it be if he goes with the sheep to the hills? Can he survive for a month? There won't be water to bathe. Leave alone bathing, just washing the feet with the water there might give you fever, he heard from others. Apparently, it is the nature of that water.

One must sleep on the bare ground without thinking of insects and worms. Wild animals might attack at any moment. One should not fear that. No shelter when it rains. One has to bear it in the open like the sheep do.

The family was in dire need. It was his responsibility to help. The old man's words—he liked the idea of saving the lives of the sheep. It was linked to the finances of the family, but still, it was a good deed to help quench the thirst and hunger of the sheep.

Guramma heard the old man's talk too. She was not happy with the idea of sending her youngest son to the forests. At the same time, she was anguished by the thought of her husband going alone and struggling with the unmanageable workload.

She did not know what to do. She finally asked her son at dusk, 'Will you go to the hills, sinnoda?'

'I will, if you ask me to,' he said.

'I am unable to ask you, sinnoda. Have I ever asked you to do any work?'

Ravi felt a tug deep in his heart.

He went into the street.

People were talking about the drought. In some neighbouring villages, drinking water was being supplied through tankers filled at borewells in farms. Almost entire villages had migrated to the city in search of livelihood.

Even in their village, half the reddy houses were empty. Unable to bear the cost of farm loans, they had shifted to cities like Bangalore, Hyderabad and Pune to do some business or the other. And now, half the gollas in the village were heading to the hills. Only women, children and old people would be left in the village.

Sankar told Ravi that two other young men of his age were also going hill-grazing. He suggested Ravi experience it as well.

*

Even if two people from the same house were going, each had to carry their own rations. The two sers of rice were placed at the bottom of the cloth bag and on top of it were arranged the rotis and pickles and a small vessel to cook rice. A blanket and a plastic covering on the shoulder, with the bundle tied to the stick of an axe, completed the attire. Gurappa added his necessities to the bundle—beedis, tobacco and lime, matchboxes.

Ravi did not want to have a bundle. He packed his rations in a shoulder bag along with an extra t-shirt and shorts. He thought of taking his mobile phone with him but dropped the idea because of the weak signal in the hills and the difficulty of charging the phone.

'The kapu woman Subbamma came and gave yellow lentils, despite my protests. She wants a teak spoon for mixing dal. Please bring it when you return,' Guramma told her husband.

Another kapu woman gave some butter to one of the trackers, asking him to bring a churning stick from the forest. Yet another gave millets, for a wooden ladle to mix porridge.

'Son, my daughter is almost due for delivery. Get us some seddi leaves, please. You will be a maternal uncle to the child. It is said the smoke from the seddi leaves brought by an uncle is good for the child. Please don't forget to bring them,' an old woman pleaded with one of the gollas and gave some palm oil as a gift to his household.

Many women were going to the houses of the gollas heading into the forest, with requests to bring what they needed and sealing the deal with a gift. Some people asked for herbal and aromatic roots that could only be found in those forests.

All the shepherds retired quite early that night. They had to leave before dawn. Excited and anxious about his impending journey, Ravi struggled to fall asleep. Till he completed high school, he used to go with his father to graze the sheep during school holidays. But he had never been to the hills. And it had been seven or eight years since he last accompanied sheep.

He was woken up at four in the morning. The water for his bath was bubbling hot already. Guramma had had her head bath, lit a lamp in front of the deity and broken a coconut. Father and son finished their head bath as well and prayed to the gods with folded hands. Guramma applied kumkuma on their foreheads.

The streets began to buzz. Men from around twenty families were going to the hills. They were more than twenty men and over a thousand sheep.

The women carried the rations and walked with the men till the sheepfolds. They adjusted the ration bags over the shoulders of their men and stood there with heavy hearts. Some farmers came too and bid farewell along with giving advice to keep safe. Konda Narayana spoke to each golla and walked with them till the edge of the village.

The herdsmen were walking ahead of their herds.

Despite asking them not to come, Ravi's sisters walked behind him carrying the ration bags. Guramma's eyes welled up with tears. She kept repeating safety precautions to her husband. 'Don't burden the little one too much, keep an eye on him, he is naive in the ways of the forest and can't sense the fox behind.'

The fox. The big fox. When they used the word, the shepherds meant the tiger, not the fox. They spoke of the tiger as the big fox or simply the fox. It is perhaps a way to stave off fear by thinking of it as a smaller wild animal.

Gurappa gave his wife a slightly surprised look. They did hill-grazing almost every year, but she never said such things. When Sankar went to the hills for the first time, she wept a few tears but had not uttered a word.

Her youngest son. The pampered one, who had never been made to do hard physical labour. Hence the mother's anxiety, he surmised and chuckled to himself.

4

THE HERDS WALKED ACROSS the fields, stomping on the dry stubble lying around. The herdsman at the front set at a brisk pace. He was followed by the big buck and then the older ram. Behind them, the herd moved urgently.

Except for the sheep sneezing and the sara sara sound of their hooves hitting the ground, there was silence. The sheep marched like a mile-long column of red ants, interspersed with human shapes.

The sky brightened beyond the eastern hills and dust swirled around them even though it was a cold dawn. They were joined by two dogs, who began walking beside Munayya and Pichchanna. Gurappa's dog had also followed him from home.

The herd had crossed the Poleramma temple near Errabatti by daybreak.

After a while, they ran into Ramulu from the yaanadi tribe. 'Be careful, brothers!' he said. 'The government has just released six big tigers. I heard they were sighted near the trails, moving about just like they used to in the past.'

Ravi's heart fluttered. He recalled the tigers he had seen on Discovery Channel.

As the herd approached the hills, they could no longer see fields and were instead surrounded by shrub forests.

There were no big trees along the first row of foothills. They saw only some small shrubs and bushes, interspersed with danthe, oodaga and some bandera and dadira trees. These lands had not been cultivated yet as they were in a forest reserve.

But some people had begun trying to occupy the hilly lands abutting the reserve. Bulldozers were being used to dig out the thorn trees and shrubs, changing the colour of the land from green to red. They had also diverted streams and uprooted big rocks to form boundaries.

As they were going down a hill, Ravi had a good look at the vast valley that lay ahead of them. He felt as if he had stepped into a new world. There were trees everywhere, no man-made construction anywhere.

When he had travelled in buses and trains across forest lands, only his eyes had experienced the forest. Now he felt his entire body—blood, muscles, bones, heart and senses—get closely acquainted with the trunks, branches, twigs and roots of the forest.

Ravi thought that it might not have been the best time to get to know the forest because it looked poverty-stricken and starving with barren trees and dry streams. Had they come after the first rains, there would have been a carpet of green grass covering the ground and leaves decorating the trees.

It was a rocky area with wide slabs of stone all around. There were smaller trails here and there, which were probably shortcuts to nearby watering holes. The sheep walked on a track once frequented by bullock-carts. There were two deep furrows made by their wheels, with stones and roots jutting out of the hard soil.

A horrific scene jolted Ravi near one of these trails. The large carcass of a buffalo calf lay across the track. The dry grass and leaves around it were covered with thick dark blood. The buffalo's neck had been gnawed away and the insides of its belly eaten. It was a terrible sight.

Ravi shuddered. Fear crawled up his spine like a snake. He looked around, almost paralysed with terror. He was scared that the tiger might come from behind any tree and pounce on him. He resumed walking, holding his breath.

No one talked about the dead animal. He wondered why, when they all must have seen it.

After a while, the sheep left the track and started up the hill. Once the herd reached the second row of hills, the shepherds rested for a while. Combining their herds, they allowed the sheep to graze. The grass and the shrubs were a bit greener there, and the excited sheep started feeding hungrily.

It was eleven, and the sun was high in the sky. Gurappa told Ravi to eat some roti. He wondered why they didn't eat on the way, and if there was a rule that a shepherd should not eat before the sheep started grazing. He took a roti from his bag and began eating it with a piece of jaggery. The fear of the tiger had still not left him, and he looked around as he ate.

After he finished his roti, he thought he'd have half of another one. He ended up eating the entire second roti and was surprised at his own appetite.

The sheep went towards the spine of the hill and then started going downhill, continuing to graze while walking. At one in the afternoon, the shepherds led the herds along the hill's edge and then down to a pond. The area was called Pulibeetlu, where there were two springs next to each other. The water in the pond was dark and muddy with rotting leaves. Flies buzzed thickly over the water.

Gurappa and the others herded the sheep to the water. It took an hour for the entire herd to slake its thirst, after which the animals were taken to rest under the trees. There they lay or stood chewing the cud.

In the meantime, some of the shepherds gathered stones to build a makeshift stove.

The water they had brought from home was enough for that day. But they needed to refill from the pond for the journey ahead. Ravi advised them all to boil the water and cool it and only then fill their cans. Thus the harmful germs would die, and they wouldn't run the risk of hill fever. He also warned them to stay away from the mosquitoes near the ponds. 'They seem quite dangerous.'

Pullayya laughed. He was the oldest and the most experienced in their group. 'Boy, you're so fastidious!' he said. 'Sometimes one finds just a handful of water at the bottom of a hole, with worms swimming in it. Put a cloth over the water, suck with your lips and stay alive. In the hills, one can't expect to have the same facilities you would get at home. As the saying goes, "Home today, on the pyre tomorrow." Nothing's permanent.'

'But what's wrong with boiling the water?' Ravi asked.

'Yes, do it,' said Pullayya. 'It is fine, just more work.' He went off to lie down under a tree.

Each person poured two fistfuls of their rice in a vessel. After it was cooked, they took a pinch of pickle and made a paste by adding some water. They mixed it with the hot rice and ate it off teak leaves. The meal was quite tasty. Everyone lay down to rest after they had eaten.

As they had walked over hilly terrain nonstop since the morning, Ravi felt his entire body ache. More than the pain, it was the fear of the tiger that was bothering him. He wondered if the shepherds could stop a tiger if it suddenly attacked the herd. What if it directly attacked a man?

'There was an animal lying on the track we came by,' said Ravi, loud enough for everyone to hear. 'Was it a buffalo?'

'It was an antelope,' Pullayya replied without opening his eyes. 'The big fox got to it.'

'Fox?'

'Yes, the big fox . . . with stripes.'

Ravi understood.

Although he had heard shepherds refer to the tiger as a fox many times before, it was only now he realised that they would never call the tiger by its name. They even sometimes referred to the sheep as 'them that are fox prey'.

'Heard there are many,' continued Ravi. 'What if one attacks the herd?'

Pullayya did not respond for some time. Then he said, 'What if it attacks? Can it take the entire herd? It will bite the neck of one sheep and satiate its hunger . . . that's all.'

Ravi gave him a strange look.

'It did not come to our home,' said Pullayya. 'We came here, to its home. We are able to save so many lives by coming here. Can't we pay a single sheep as a fee?' He laughed loudly.

Ravi did not reply. He tried to understand the meaning of Pullayya's words even as Gurappa milked a sheep nearby. He mixed the milk with some rice and placed the mixture on a flat stone for his dog, who ate it all and then licked the stone dry. Pullayya was snoring by then.

Pichchanna came over with Tiripalu. 'Why do you feed it a royal feast, mama?' he asked. 'Has it ever barked? Doesn't bark when it sees the fox. Doesn't bark even if there is another dog!'

'Don't worry, its day will come,' replied Gurappa.

'Whatever you say,' said Pichchanna. 'I haven't ever heard your dog bark . . . nor have I ever seen Pullayya sleep without snoring.' Everyone laughed.

'Dora, can you get me a garment like you are wearing?' Pichchanna asked, looking at Ravi's shorts. 'It looks stylish.'

'I will get one for you next time I go to the city, mama.'

'If one pisses or shits their pants after seeing the fox, it will remain above the knees, right?' he asked mockingly. 'It won't seep down, I hope . . . it would be embarrassing if everyone saw that!'

The others laughed louder.

'I will have elastic bands stitched, mama!' replied Ravi, equally sarcastic.

Such repartees and witty anecdotes lightened the mood for a while. However, even in the middle of the banter, Gurappa felt sad as he looked at his son. Ravi's education had been expensive, but he had not compromised in spending for his son's studies. Even though he was just a shepherd, Gurappa had sent his son to study at the big colleges in the city where the scions of rich reddy families go.

After spending so much to help him complete his engineering, Gurappa was unable to accept that his son might return to sheep-grazing. It had cost him a herd of sheep to pay for his son's education and to support his stay in Hyderabad for the past four years while he tried to get a job.

With these thoughts in mind, Gurappa propped his head against a stone and slept for a while.

At four, they started moving again and soon crossed the streambed known as the Village Creek. It got its name from the hamlets that used to be there long ago. Troubled by illnesses and wild animals, the villagers had migrated outside the forests.

The herds stopped and grazed wherever they could on the grassy and rocky terrain as they crossed the well of the Guy with Crooked Ears and circled around the Eagle's Nest hill. By the time they reached a tamarind grove, the sun was setting. The herds were settled on the spine of the hill.

Soon, the moon emerged. In four days, it would be a full moon. As darkness spread around them, the herdsmen could hear a variety of bird calls from the valley. They sounded like they were coming from the inside of a deep well. There were also the shrill screams of peacocks.

The sheep stood and chewed the cud for a while before clearing the ground with their hooves and squatting. It took the animals quite a while to get used to a new place to rest. Some of them tried to come out of the herd and walk past the shepherds. When shouted at, they slinked back into the herd. They stood up and then again lay down, sometimes changing places or rolling to a side. Once they were accustomed, they started ruminating peacefully.

The men ate rotis and drank some water before moving some rocks aside to make space for lying down close to their herds. Ravi hung his bag on a branch and spread a bedsheet under an axle wood tree. When he looked up, he could see the beautiful moon through the gaps between the branches. The silent forest was covered in white moonlight. The hills, valleys and streams seemed to be asleep under a blanket of trees.

However, neither the cool moonlight nor the beauty of the forest could help Ravi relax. His body ached all over. His calf muscles, thighs and waist throbbed with pain that would not subside. Unable to sleep, he sat up. It was not just the pain that was keeping him up but also the sliver of anxiety in his heart.

The fear had begun after he had seen that dead antelope, left half-eaten with its belly torn apart. He imagined a tiger biting the neck of a sheep and drinking its blood as a toll for allowing the herd to graze. The knowledge that the government had released several tigers in the area added to his jitters.

Ravi stood up and looked at the hills surrounding them. But instead of noticing the beauty of the trees bathing in moonlight, he was consumed by his fear of the creatures walking in the shadows of those trees. What if one emerged from behind the trees, pushed him down and then dragged him away by the neck?

He pulled out a torch from his bag and shone the light on the lumpy darkness near the trees before moving the beam across the herd. The eyes of the sheep glowed like LED bulbs.

There were hundreds of eyes, burning with a strange light. He recalled hearing that the eyes of the tiger burn bright like sparks of fire.

All the herdsmen were fast asleep. Some were snoring.

Ravi walked towards his father. His dog was standing beside him. Ravi thought that his father was also asleep, but just as he turned away, Gurappa asked, 'Are you unable to sleep, sinnoda?'

Startled, Ravi turned around. 'You're still awake?'

'Your footsteps woke me up,' replied Gurappa. 'This is a new place, right? That's probably why you are unable to sleep. Just lie down and close your eyes. You will soon fall asleep.'

Ravi returned to his spot by the tree, surprised that his soft tread had awoken his father.

He knew that he did not have to worry about worms or insects crawling among the leaves. The hooves of over a thousand sheep would have killed all such creatures in the evening. The only fear he had was of the tiger that would approach silently. His angst was preventing him from enjoying the pleasantness of the moonlight.

His fear began to take various animal shapes. Apart from tigers, he imagined leopards, bears and hyenas even when he closed his eyes. His exhaustion tried to overcome the fearful thoughts and eventually prevailed. By the time sleep washed over him, it was past midnight.

A spotted owl hooted intermittently from somewhere in the valley. The hoots increased in volume and could be heard in the hills too. Suddenly, a tiger's roar erupted from the whereabouts of Chelima Baavi. It reverberated in the hills, followed by another roar.

Munayya and Pichchanna's dogs perked up at the first roar. They reacted to the second roar by jumping in fear and hiding amid the herds of sheep. The sheep were startled by the sudden presence of the dogs in their midst. They panicked and ran. Without a signal, some of the sheep started running sideways.

The shepherds quickly awoke and recognised the danger immediately. They got up and grabbed their sticks, trying to calm the sheep by making familiar and reassuring sounds. Ravi could not react as fast as the other shepherds. By the time he got up, a herd of sheep had run past, stomping on him.

Unable to understand what was going on, he became fearful again.

Gurappa and Bhaskar drove the sheep back to the rest of the herd. 'These sheep and their cowardice,' complained Gurappa. 'Somewhere a fox shouts, and these creatures react as if their necks got bitten. This won't do at all.' He told Ravi to go back to sleep. 'Sheep getting scared is not unusual,' he said. 'We have seen this before.'

Ravi's heart was still beating hard. His body ached even more after being trod on by a hundred hooves, and he stank of the droppings that they had left on his body. His clothes were damp wherever he touched, but he was too exhausted to check the source of the wetness.

Weakness enveloped him completely, but his aching muscles did not allow him to roll on to his side. Ravi fell asleep without knowing what time it was.

The hill roosters started crowing from the valleys even before dawn. They were followed by the cries of other birds all the way from the valleys to the hilltops. The cries of peacocks joined in as well, as the eastern sky changed from dark to light. A cacophony of bird calls filled the air.

Elders like Pullayya and Gurappa were the first to wake. They mumbled their morning prayers to Rama and Krishna and then went into the forest to attend to their daily ablutions. The younger shepherds woke up at around five. Gurappa ensured that no one disturbed Ravi's sleep because he knew that his son had not slept well. Ravi got up at seven with bloodshot eyes.

He was asked to go finish his toilet but not to use water. 'Make do with leaves,' he was told by the other shepherds, who warned him that using water would lead to flu. Ravi looked at his clothes, which were covered in sheep droppings and hoofmarks. He felt odious. However, the others stopped him from cleaning himself. 'Once it dries, it will fall off by itself,' they said, 'but don't touch it with your hands.'

It was nine by the time they finished their breakfast and were ready to take the herds for another day of hill-grazing.

5

THE HERDS BUSTLED UP on to the hillocks, grazing while moving. The sun was getting stronger, but it did not bother them as they were walking in the shade of trees. The sal trees were showing off their blossoms, and other trees too seemed to be in bloom. Gurappa's herd waded into a streambed surrounded by tall sal and axlewood trees. The herdsmen tried to ensure that the sheep didn't go too deep into the streamlets.

Covered by sheep, the hillocks and streambeds looked like red anthills or like the red worms that cover the branches of mango trees.

They could see many barren sandalwood trees on the hillocks. Some had been felled and carted away, with only a few small, dry branches left on the ground. The sandalwood shavings that lay around in heaps indicated that the trunks were chipped with an axe or a chisel.

Soon, they found themselves in a bigger rocky streambed. The tangled branches of the trees on either side made it seem like a single large canopy. On the branches were hill roosters with long and colourful tailfeathers. It was a beautiful sight. They also saw black-mouthed Madras langurs hanging from the trees.

To prevent the sheep from going too far, Ravi had to step down into the streambed. He felt the place was dangerous. There were vast sheets of claystone sediments with dark cavities underneath and in some stretches the trees enveloped it in complete darkness.

The herdsmen suspected there were tigers resting under the cavernous rocks they could see in the distance.

A cold shiver rose in Ravi's spine. A tiger could jump into the sandy, dry stream from under the rocks and pounce on them. It might target a sheep but could attack a man as well. Trying not to make too much noise, Ravi threw stones at the sheep to get them back on to the hillock, while nervously looking all around.

None of the other shepherds looked harried. They ensured that the sheep didn't go deeper into the stream, but they were not herding them up the hill. Instead, they went down into the streambed and stood guard next to the sheep. Ravi wondered if they were doing it to protect the sheep from the tiger. He was unable to fathom their stubborn courage.

After herding his flock up the hill, Ravi tried to relax for a while. That was when he observed the rocks beneath his feet looked a little different. Some were the colour of dirt while others were dark, as if they had been burnt.

One of the shepherds told him that the sheets of rock in the streambed had iron. Ravi realised that these must be the stones that people in earlier times took to Akkemgundla, Bampaya Palli and Mudireddi Palli, where they had furnaces to melt them and make raw iron.

Watching Gurappa's dog walk beside him, Ravi thought of the previous night's disturbance. He had been a bit surprised that the dogs got so scared at hearing the faraway roar of a tiger. Did his father's dog jump into the herd as well? Or did it remain standing by his side? Ravi wondered why all the shepherds didn't bring their dogs with them. He asked Pullayya this question when they were preparing to cook that afternoon.

'If one has a king-like dog like your father's, they could bring it along,' Pullayya replied. 'Whether it's the fox or the big sister of the fox, that dog does not even lift its head. It will lie supine, rest its snout on the ground and watch impassively.'

'Mama!' cried Pichchanna. 'Is your dog really born to another dog or to a sheep?'

The others laughed at his attempt at humour.

'Rey Pichchiga!' retorted Pullayya. 'You always mock that dog; you are unable to see its strength!'

'What strength?' Pichchanna asked derisively. 'The ability to eat two lumps of porridge in one go?'

'Your smarts are limited to food,' Pullayya said. 'Did it shake even a bit when the fox was hollering so loudly? It did not get scared. It has no fear! As the saying goes, "The secrets of a man and the strength of a tree won't show on the outside." Just you watch, that dog will show its value some day!'

The endorsement Pullayya gave Gurappa's dog did not inspire confidence in any of them. There was even a suspicion that he was mocking it.

Ravi was told that normally the shepherds didn't bring their domestic dogs to the forest because tigers seemed to react with uncontrollable anger if a dog barked at them. If a tiger or a leopard attacked the herd and a shepherd's dog barked, the predator would pounce on the dog first and claw open its gut because it would see the dog as an enemy creating an obstacle in its hunt. If the dog tried to hide behind its master, then the tiger would target the man first. Shepherds therefore tied their dogs to a post at home or left them in the sheep pens before leaving for the forest.

Pichchanna and Munayya's dogs had somehow escaped from the pens and had unexpectedly joined their masters at the edge of the village. But Gurappa's dog had been with him right from when he left home.

Ravi boiled some water. After it had cooled, he filled his can. Then he boiled some more water in another vessel, dipped his kerchief in it and rubbed his body clean. He hadn't bathed in two days, and with the sheep stomping on him at night, he felt sticky. The others tried to stop him, but he wouldn't listen.

Ravi was warned that he would come down with fever by the evening. He replied there was no such danger as he had boiled the water thoroughly. He even planned to wash his clothes if it rained or if they found a lot of water somewhere. Gurappa worried about his son and wondered how he would get him home if he did get a fever.

While they rested after lunch, Pichchanna chatted with Pamuleti and Tiripalu. Suddenly, Ankayya spoke up. 'Oi Pichchi bava, answer this if you really are a man,' he said to Pichchanna. 'Does the water flow from Sagileti stream to Kapileddu stream or is it the other way round?'

Pichchanna was confused. 'Which stream is at a higher elevation?'

Ankayya got up in excitement and walked towards a swarthy red sanders tree a few metres away. Sitting down on its roots, he repeated the question, 'Tell me the answer, bava, if you are a man!'

Pichchanna didn't know the answer. 'You got me there, boy.'

Just then Ankayya felt the root move under his buttocks. Startled, he got up and looked behind him. The root was indeed moving under the dried leaves. He was surprised first, then confused. When he finally understood what it was, he was frozen in fear.

He tried to scream. 'Snake!' he wanted to yell. 'A python!' But he only thought that he had yelled. The scream had died in his throat. He was stuttering with a wide-open mouth. Pamuleti picked up his axe and moved quickly to where Ankayya was standing. He tried to hack the python, but it slithered away and vanished down the hill.

Ankayya took a while to calm down. He could still feel the snake's slithering movement on his buttocks. It had been waiting near the watering hole. If Ankayya had not disturbed it, the python would have swallowed at least one sheep. The shepherds felt the tremble of fear within and told each other to be careful.

A stunned Ravi watched it all.

He had earlier gone near that tree as well, thinking of taking a nap beneath it. If he had done that, the snake would have opened its mouth over him and gobbled his head. Scenes from all the *Anaconda* movies he had seen appeared before his eyes, and he broke into a cold sweat.

Pichchanna went over to Ankayya and looked at his legs. Ankayya knew that he intended to mock him.

'China bava!' cried Pichchanna. 'Looks like you leaked? Are you hiding it inside your pants?'

Bhaskar laughed and others joined in. The atmosphere became a bit lighter. But to Ravi, every root had started to look like a python.

Pullayya narrated a story about a big python that had grasped a man's legs and tried to swallow him. The man had taken a dagger and sliced through the python's insides to finally emerge out of its belly. 'If one is brave and spunky, one can escape from any danger,' said Pullayya. 'When your life is at stake, there is no point in being fearful. One needs to fight with calm courage.'

Munayya too narrated a similar story to help drive the snake's fear away. The shepherds then resumed walking with the herds, driving them up the hill.

*

Ravi's body pains had not subsided at all. He had had a disturbed sleep the previous night and no nap during the day because of the python scare. There was no sign of respite from the seemingly endless trek through the forest.

He knew that they had to continue hill-grazing and couldn't leave until the rains began. As they walked, Ravi remained cautious around tree roots covered with dirt and dried leaves and began throwing stones or prodding them with his axe to check for movement.

The herdsmen reckoned that it would be dusk by the time the herds climbed the Manti hill. They decided to find a relatively flat area on the hill and rest there for the night.

The sounds of the sheep and the shouts of the gollas disturbed the stillness. Ravi looked carefully at the sal and other trees that grew thickly on the soft soil of the watercourse. He watched the tree roots with suspicion, treading gingerly while holding his breath. The dry brook brought back the fear of the tiger.

Up ahead, he saw a few dark-coloured animals scramble up the Manti hill. He recognised them as wild pigs. There were more than ten of them. Ramachandra was shouting at them and trying to chase them away by throwing stones. The pigs climbed at a brisk pace, their feet dislodging stones that skidded down. They quickly went over the hill.

Sensing movement above him, Ravi looked up. A buck had climbed onto a stone slab about as tall as a man. As it tried to reach a creeper, it lost its footing. The animal skidded down the slab and landed in front of Ravi. Immediately, something shot up from the ground in front of the buck.

The creature had risen up through the dry leaves and now stood tall and straight. Ravi's heart flipped. He thought the creature would pounce on him and tried to scream. But panic had set in, and he was unable to utter anything beyond a hoarse cry. He dropped his shoulder bag there and ran to his father, scared beyond words.

Gurappa was worried when he saw his son. Ravi was shivering and repeating his weak cry for his father. 'What happened, sinnoda?' he asked. 'I am here, don't worry.' Gurappa wiped the cold sweat off his son's face with a kerchief and then washed Ravi's face with some water.

After Gurappa had made him drink a few sips of water, he looked around to see if the other gollas had seen them. Father and son were behind some thick trees.

'What is it, dear?' Gurappa gently asked Ravi.

'P-p-python . . .' Ravi managed to finally say.

'Where? Come and show me.' Gurappa grabbed his son by the arm and led him back to the spot where he had left his bag. He picked it up and gave it back to Ravi.

'No, it will attack us,' Ravi squealed and tried to resist as Gurappa dragged him forward. 'There, that's where the goat landed. The snake shot up from there.'

The soil there had the clear imprint of a goat landing on it. 'Is that the goat?' Gurappa asked, pointing to a male goat contentedly grazing a few metres away. Ravi nodded. Gurappa observed the nearby sheep for any signs of their usual reaction to a dangerous predator.

If they sensed danger, the sheep didn't munch the grass in their mouths. They stayed rooted, eyes bulging, ears pricked up, ready to flee in an instant. None of the sheep nearby exhibited any of these symptoms. They were grazing in a relaxed manner. Gurappa concluded that no snake had appeared in front of Ravi. He had just imagined something and panicked.

He looked around the area where Ravi said the snake had appeared. The dry leaves covering that area looked disturbed. He went and kicked around the place where the goat had fallen. A tall, dry branch shot up from the ground. It was bent and a little brittle. Stepping on one end made the other end rise up.

Gurappa looked at his son and asked, 'Is this your python?'

Ravi felt ashamed.

'This kind of fear won't do if you have to walk around in the hills, sinnoda!' Gurappa said. 'Even if a python actually appears, you should not be afraid.'

They resumed walking behind the sheep. Ravi felt very weak as they climbed the hill. Every part of his body seemed to cry out in pain.

The crest of the Manti hill was different from that of other hills. It was a vast expanse spread over ten acres, covered with axlewood, sal, satinwood and sandalwood trees. The herdsmen settled the sheep down and then set up their respective sleeping spots. They took out some rotis for dinner.

Gurappa took Pichchanna, Pamuleti, Bhaskar and Ramachandra with him to collect dry branches and twigs and then built a fire about ten metres from the sheep. Since it was summer, it was easy to kindle the fire. The thick branches ensured that it would burn through the night.

Ravi's sleeping spot was near the fire. Gurappa went and sat near his son. 'It will burn till morning,' he said. 'No fox will come here because of the fire, nor will any snakes or bears. Sleep without fear. You did not sleep well last night, so try to get some sleep tonight. Have you finished your roti?'

'No appetite,' Ravi replied.

'Do you have a fever?' Gurappa checked Ravi's pulse. 'Nothing. You are fine. Eat.'

'I don't feel like it.'

'If you don't eat, you won't be able to walk behind the sheep tomorrow,' said Gurappa. 'But you have to. We took an oath that we would do that and brought the sheep here. Your mother broke a coconut in front of the gods, performed a prayer and put the sacred red on our foreheads so that we return home safely with the sheep. We need to eat well in order to protect their lives.'

Ravi did not reply.

Gurappa got up. 'I understand that you can't handle this,' he said. 'Get up early. I will leave you near the wellspring. Catch the bus to Jyothi and go home. Ask your sister to join me with rations for two people. She is not afraid. Till she comes, I will manage on my own somehow.'

Ravi remained still for a while after his father left. Then he ate a roti with an onion and a piece of jaggery, drank some water and lay down to sleep.

His muscles continued to ache, but the fire helped him block out most of his fear. He slept soundly and did not get up even once during the night.

Ravi was awoken by a whisper before dawn. 'Sinnoda,' his father called. He felt a cool hand holding his elbow. 'There's no fever. The star is up. I can hear the Tiger brook on that side and the Cloudy stream on this side. Get up now.'

Ravi could not understand why his father was waking him up so early. He sat up, rubbing his eyes. It was still quite dark in the east, but a red star was rising in the sky. The birds in the valleys below started chirping. The sounds rose up the hills like fog.

The cool darkness was quite pleasant. The natural smells of all the plants blended to form a fragrance, and nature seemed to merge the various sounds made by the birds into one unique voice. The birds on the hills were joining the chorus of the birds down in the brooks.

Ravi stood up and stretched. His muscles and joints felt stiff.

'Come, son!' Gurappa urged. 'Let's go. It will be morning by the time I drop you at the wellspring and return.'

Ravi remembered then that his father had said he was to go home. His mind wavered for a moment. His first thought was that it was much better to go home than be scared all the time and suffer from body pain. Gurappa would give him company till the wellspring and then come back alone.

None of the other shepherds were awake yet. He realised that his father wanted to send him away quietly. Gurappa would use the excuse that Ravi had fever, but the shepherds would understand the truth and laugh behind his back. When they return to the village, this would become a topic for jokes. His sister, younger than him, would come here to support his father in grazing the sheep.

It would remain a disgrace for a lifetime in the village.

'Let's go, sinnoda.'

'No,' said Ravi. 'I will stay.'

'No one saw what happened yesterday,' Gurappa said in a low voice. 'But if you keep getting frightened by every little thing, we will become the butt of their jokes, son.'

Ravi just bowed his head in silence.

'We have not come this far into the hills just to get scared of foxes and snakes, sinnoda,' said his father. 'Why do we need to come so far searching for fear? We might as well stay comfortably at home, no? It's the sheep that are the prey of the fox . . . *they* need to be afraid. We need to drive their fear away and make them feed properly. If your fear is making you tremble at every tree and hillock, then how will you look after them?' Gurappa paused briefly before continuing, 'Sinnoda, your fear has stopped you from even seeing these hills properly. Look over there! Honeycombs hanging from the Raasala cliff, tall trees near the Cloudy stream, watering holes down in the Frolic springs, the hill roosters hopping from tree to tree, the dance of the peacocks near the Hidden spring . . . you haven't noticed any of this, right? If you only feel fear, you can't enjoy anything else. Get rid of the fear first.'

After saying this, Gurappa walked back to his resting spot. Ravi looked at him in wonder for a while. Then he noticed that the fire was still burning. He walked back to it and pushed the unburnt logs into the middle to stoke the flames, because the moon had set, and it had become darker.

Ravi looked around as he gathered his thoughts.

In the west, electric lamps glowed in the distance. He noticed similar lights in the southwest and northwest and fainter spots of light in the east. He could see all this as he was at the top of one of the tallest hills in the area. However, it was dark in the north as well as the south, where the Nallamala range towered.

Ravi surmised that the lights in the southwest were from Proddatur town, the ones in the west Chagalamarri, the northwestern Allagadda and the eastern Porumamilla.

The shepherds woke up at the crack of dawn. As they were having their breakfast, they could hear the echoing sound of axes hitting trees. People were felling trees somewhere in the hills.

The sheep were grazing on the flat top of the Manti hill, where the grass sported a few green shoots. It was mostly rottler grass. Shaking their tiny tails, the sheep ate to their heart's content.

'If they find rottler, they will ignore all other types of grass,' Gurappa explained to Ravi.

From their vantage point on the tall hill, they had a clear view of the surrounding ranges, valleys and streams. Raasala cliff was a frightening sight with its sheer rocky sides stained by rainwater. There were tree roots hanging from the cliff, and the big honeycombs on the edges of the rock slabs looked like dark goats. It was an awe-inspiring scene.

'Sinnoda, look at them,' Gurappa said, pointing at the honeycombs. 'The yaanadis extract honey from even those bee colonies.'

It would be a superhuman task to climb down to those honeycombs from the top of the hill or climb up the cliff to reach them. Secure even from bears, the honeycombs had a safe place to grow really big. Ravi wondered how the yaanadis got to them.

'Don't the bees sting?'

'If they sense a man, they will swarm and sting him all over his body. People shit down their legs and die of the poison.'

'Then how do the yaanadis extract honey from the hive?'

Gurappa explained that thorny bamboo shoots were gathered and cut into foot-long pieces, with which they made a ladder. On the night of the new moon, the topmost bamboo piece was tied securely to a tree and then the ladder was lowered to hang under the honeycombs. One yaanadi guarded the top while another descended the bamboo ladder and positioned himself under the colony. The man guarding was usually the brother-in-law of the man who lowered himself below the hives. Brothers did not pair up for this task.

The man who climbed down the ladder then lit a piece of leather on fire and placed it on the underside of the hive. The heat drove the bees away. After that, the honey could be extracted into pots or boxes lowered with a rope and pulled back up after they were full. Gurappa said that each hive yielded about two pots of honey.

Ravi spent a while visualising the entire process of extracting honey from those hives.

Manti hill had plants such as wild turmeric and hill pepper and varieties of jungle millet. The shepherds searched for them on the hill but could only find bare, dried-up stems. It was well past their harvest time.

*

In the afternoon, they went to the water source. There they found two bears near the apex. They were black and furry and kept disappearing behind the trees. Ravi looked at them in fear. After a while, they couldn't be seen anymore.

'They don't normally bother humans,' explained Pullayya, 'unless they are mothers of infants who are caught in a situation they can't escape. They will then counterattack ferociously to protect their children. If we don't disturb them, they won't come near us. They are the daughters of the forest.'

'Mama,' cried Pichchanna, 'you are speaking of the forest animals as if they are relatives. Who are the sons of the forest?'

'Who else? The tigers!'

'And the daughters-in-law?'

'Antelopes and deer.'

'Nice, nice,' said Gurappa. 'Then who are the sons-in-law?'

'Wild boars,' Pullayya answered without missing a beat, making Gurappa laugh.

'Then who are we? Distant relatives?' asked Ramachandra.

'That is correct,' replied Pullayya. 'We are like visiting relatives. We should come and stay for four days, eat our fill and leave. We shouldn't be doing things like cutting trees or killing animals. If we do such things, we lose our visiting rights.'

They liked his conclusion.

After a while, they began cooking rice for their lunch. Some of the sheep were lying down and chewing cud, while others were standing and moving their mouths with half-closed eyes.

'Orey Sreenu!' called Gurappa.

'Yes, mama,' replied Sreenu.

'See that white-legged one there? The one standing next to that black one. It has been limping since morning. Bring it here. I think it has a thorn stuck in its hoof.'

Sreenu walked casually towards the herd so that they wouldn't get startled. He held the limping sheep by the ear and dragged it to where Gurappa was seated. It looked like he was dragging a naughty kid by the ear.

'Shall I make it lie down?'

'No, hold it between your legs.'

Sreenu held it tight with his legs and grasped its head with his hands. Gurappa bent its right forelimb and looked at the hoof. He reached for the bunch of assorted tools tied to his waist and used a penknife to scrape the hoof.

Ravi went closer and watched with interest. 'Has it mated?' he asked, because his father had said that it was ready for mating.

'I don't know,' replied his father. 'I saw the ram follow this one around yesterday and day before. It may have . . .' He lifted its tail. 'Yes, it has opened up!' he declared. 'I think it mated.'

Gurappa spat out betel nut juice as he scraped all the dirt from the hoof, pressing an iron file at different spots. The sheep shook its leg when the iron pressed at a point in between the toes. Gurappa took the leg in his hands again and cleaned the gaps in the hoof. The sheep tried to pull its leg back if even a finger touched the spot. Gurappa applied some saliva there and examined it closely until he saw the dark spot of a thorn.

He used the penknife and the iron file to raise the thorn from the hoof and then tried to pull it out with a pair of tiny pliers. Unable to do it, he put the sheep's leg on his shoulder and peered closely at the spot, cleaning the remaining dirt with his headscarf.

Ravi thought that his father was attending to the sheep as if it were his own child. He showed affection and responsibility. It made no difference to Gurappa that it was an animal. This surprised him.

Pichchanna saw Gurappa's struggle.

'Come on, mama,' he said. 'Your eyesight won't help. Leave it to me.'

'You are right,' said Gurappa. 'My vision is a little blurry. It's almost as if there's a web in front of my eyes.' He stepped aside.

Pichchanna sat on his haunches in front of the sheep and peered closely at the hoof. He then brought the hoof to his mouth and pulled the thorn out with his front teeth. He spat it out and said, 'Get me some hot ash.'

Ash from the stove was spread on a stone slab. The sheep's hoof was pressed on the ash. As the heat from the ash singed the injured spot, the sheep tried to pull its leg back. But Pichchanna held its leg firmly, not allowing it to move. He let go after a minute. Sreenu finally let go of the sheep from between his legs. After limping for a couple of steps, the sheep walked normally.

The scene remained in Ravi's mind. He was not able to digest the fact of someone treating a sheep like their own child, even removing a thorn from its hoof with their teeth. The shepherds did not differentiate between man and animal. They showed no disgust at all when taking care of their herd, observing every stage of growth closely for each sheep, knowing their sexual lives and empathising with all of their experiences.

They made him realise that herding sheep was not just about walking behind them and managing their movements; it was also about recognising and responding to their needs.

6

THEY STAYED ON MANTI hill for two days. On the second day, they were cooking near the watering hole when they heard the sound of hooves coming up the hill from the stream below. It seemed like a large animal, because it was dislodging stones with each thudding step. And it was coming fast.

Ravi became excited and asked Bhaskar if he knew what kind of animal it was. Bhaskar had no clue. Soon an antelope crashed into their midst, panting and heaving. It was almost the size of a buffalo and had shiny dark skin and four-pronged horns.

The animal was trembling with fear. It had its ears pricked and kept looking back with dazed eyes. It came forward a few metres more and stood near Pullayya, who was at source of the stream.

'Chousingha, mama!' said Munayya, stepping forward as he lifted his axe. 'Let's have—'

Pullayya raised his hand to stop him. 'If it has come to us men without fear,' he said, 'it means that an even bigger danger is chasing it.'

Even the sound of their talking did not make the chousingha move. It was panting and looking downstream.

Then the shepherds heard some movement in the water below. They thought it was a tiger, but they were not scared as they were all together. From behind the bushes they heard whistling sounds. Then they saw the heads, which immediately slunk back at the sight of the men.

'Wild dogs!' shouted Pullayya. 'Muni, show them how the gollas can hurl stones!'

Immediately, Munayya picked up a couple of stones and hurled them at the shrubs. They heard the dogs howl in pain. Munayya and Pichchanna's dogs got excited and started barking loudly. There were over twenty wild dogs in the pack. Other gollas picked up stones and started throwing them at the creatures.

The sheep stopped chewing cud and stood up, looking at the scene with eyes opened wide. Faced with an onslaught of stones, the wild dogs ran away.

Munayya and Pichchanna's dogs were unable to control their excitement. They were barking as loudly as they could. However, they stayed beside the shepherds and did not give chase.

Pichchanna was looking at Gurappa's dog. It had lifted its head once and laid down again, uninterested. Smiling to himself, he threw a couple of stones at the retreating wild dogs.

During the commotion, the chousingha had made its way across the hill and vanished.

'If we had brought it down, we could have had tasty food for four days,' Munayya complained to Pullayya. 'You took the food away from our mouths.'

'Son of an idiot,' retorted Pullayya derisively. 'If an animal trusts us to save its life and we kill it for food, will we continue to be humans?'

Munayya did not bring up the topic again.

A surprised Ravi understood that something beyond jungle law had been enacted. He looked at the old man Pullayya with wonder. The incident with the chousingha kept coming back to him the whole day.

*

The herds climbed down the hill, and they found a meadow with lots of green grass. Looking at it, the shepherds' mouths watered. The sheep dug in with relish, their pleasure showing in the shake of their tiny tails. The gollas in turn found some fig trees and plucked fruit that resembled dark pearls.

They had planned to get the herds climb the Juvvi Tree rock—named after the lone and large fig tree atop a sheer hillock—that evening. But looking at the sheep grazing happily, they did not have the heart to move them.

Once dusk set in, they made the sheep climb a small hillock nearby. Its spine was not wide enough to accommodate all the animals comfortably, but they eventually adjusted and settled down.

The shepherds too found places to rest for the night. Gurappa showed Ravi a spot to the north of the herd, near the top of the hillock, and made space for Bhaskar and himself on the slopes below. Pullayya found a spot on the southern side. They were all so tired that they went to sleep quite early, as did their sheep.

That night, fires were lit in two spots. They were sleeping on a small hillock surrounded by fortress-like hills. It was another new experience for Ravi. Until then, they had been spending the nights on the tallest points of big hills looking down on the ranges below. The reverse perspective felt very different to Ravi. He felt he had lost some of his fear of the darkness and that he could sleep soundly instead of regularly waking up.

The moon would not cross the big hill to the east until about ten in the night. And though the moonlight was bright on the hills, they would be in darkness below on their smaller hillock.

The sheep slept without a care. Ravi thought that they only felt afraid when they saw a predator in front of them. Maybe they were conscious of only the present and had no memories of the past nor worries about the future.

Ravi's ears had become more sensitive. He heard Pullayya and others snoring. There was no other sound except for the occasional sneeze of a sheep or the cough of one of the shepherds. But then he heard something else and got up with a start. He looked up and saw that the moon was moving towards the west. The sound that he had heard was coming from a distant meadow in the southwest.

Ravi identified the noises as the angry cries of fighting animals. His heart shuddered as he listened to the guttural growls, the panting and the bloodcurdling screams. He heard the sounds made by animals rolling on the ground and breaking branches. The fighting animals seemed to be big and the sounds were horrific.

Ravi stood up and saw that Gurappa and Bhaskar were already standing. All the shepherds seemed to be awake. He went straight to his father.

'Did you get frightened, sinnoda?' Gurappa asked.

'Some animals are fighting, right?'

'I think the big fox met a wild boar by the meadow,' his father surmised. 'The boar seems to be an alpha male. It did not back down and counterattacked without fear. But the tiger is the king of the forest with a big ego . . . will it just back off? Sounds like both are fighting ferociously, neither will yield.'

'Does a boar have the strength to fight a tiger?' Ravi asked in surprise.

'If it is alpha and alone and old enough, it won't care for the tiger,' replied Gurappa. 'It too has long fangs, and if it hits with its lower jaw, even the tiger will see stars. But the tiger is very nimble and can jump around like a rubber ball. The boar does not have that speed nor the flexibility. It can't turn around in a flash but the tiger can. The tiger may not have the heft and blind aggression of the boar, but the boar does not have the strong claws, fangs and agility of the tiger. Eventually, the boar will lose and die. However, if they come close to us while fighting, we'd be in trouble. Both the creatures would be blind with rage and arrogance and will not care about the men nor the herd. If one of them swerves into the herd, the sheep will run helter-skelter all over the hills.'

Gurappa shouted for Pullayya. 'Ask them to light fires all around us,' he instructed.

Pullayya replied in the affirmative, and they all scrambled around gathering dry logs and branches. Then they built fires near each sleeping spot. The entire hillock was illuminated by the fires.

The fight increased in intensity. The tiger's roars resonated across the hills, but the boar's grunts were no less fierce. The shepherds listened to the thuds of their bodies hitting the ground and the thwacks when they bashed against tree trunks. They could see the trees shaking in the moonlight.

Gurappa's dog was standing next to him with his head cocked towards the direction of the sounds. Munayya and Pichchanna's dogs were hiding deep among the sheep with their tails between their legs. Ravi leaned against a tree and gazed in the direction of the fight. He had assumed that they would all stay awake until the fight ended and was surprised to hear Pullayya snoring. Ravi was amazed Pullayya could sleep in the midst of all this. He was unable to relax and walked over to his father.

'Just lie down and close your eyes,' said Gurappa. 'This kind of thing is all too common in the forest. It is new for you, but we experience this every year.'

'I am on the elevation, and you guys are down here,' said Ravi. 'If the fight reaches us, they will be on you first.'

'I don't see that happening,' said his father. 'They seem to be fighting quite fiercely, and it doesn't look like they'll stop till one of them dies. Though even the survivor will be close to death.'

Ravi slowly climbed back to his spot. The fight continued till the moon set. It ended after a huge roar from the tiger. It had probably won. Ravi's eyes closed in sleep after that. However, it was a disturbed sleep. The sounds of the animals fighting did not leave his mind even in sleep.

*

It was seven in the morning when he awoke.

The sun was not going to cross the eastern hills and shine on their hillock for another couple of hours. He got up and stretched. Then he folded his blanket and put it back in the bag. He looked around and saw that all the shepherds were busy checking on their herds.

Some were moving the sheep that had got mixed up in herds that were not their own. Others were tending to the hooves of sheep that showed signs of limping. Some of the animals had slipped from the rock slabs and hurt themselves. The gollas rubbed their legs and put on leaf bandages if required. Some of the sheep seemed unwell and had lost their appetite. The shepherds injected these sheep with medicine.

Ravi looked at the lambs drinking milk from their mothers. He did not have anything to do because Gurappa handled all of this work for their herd. He saw his father making reassuring noises while holding a black-and-white sheep.

'What happened to it?' asked Ravi.

'It wasn't eating well all of yesterday,' replied Gurappa. 'It kept lying on the ground, as if down with a fever.' He shouted for Tiripalu to bring Pullayya at once.

Pullayya walked through the herds and made his way over to them. He held the sheep's ears for a few moments and then placed his palm on the sheep's behind, closely observing it.

'It does have excess heat,' said Pullayya eventually. 'Running a slight fever. Did it mate?'

'Recently. Not even a week.'

'It's probably the pregnancy. Sometimes they have a fever for a couple of days. Just to be on the safe side, give it an injection. Do you have one?'

'Yes, I've brought some with me.' Gurappa shouted for Sreenu to come over.

While all the shepherds knew how to administer injections to the sheep, five or six of them were experts at the technique. The needle is inserted either in the thigh or the side of the neck. With the needle inside, the sheep is allowed to jump until it settles down. Then the syringe with the medicine is attached to the needle and the medicine is injected into the body. After removing the needle, the shepherd vigorously rubs the spot with his fist.

Ravi finished his ablutions and came back. He wanted to hear other's opinions on last night's fight, but no one was talking about it. They were all busy with their own work, as if nothing had happened.

Brushing his teeth with a neem twig, Ravi walked over to his father. 'Do you think the dead animal will still be there?'

'Where would it go?' replied Gurappa. 'If the tiger died, only the eagles or vultures would eat it. If the boar died, the tiger would have already eaten its testicles and soft muscles. It would have dragged the carcass to a nearby bush and covered it with leaves and twigs. If the tiger was also badly injured, it would have left the carcass there and walked away.'

Ravi was trying to imagine the aftermath of the fight between the two large animals. He wanted to go and see the place and asked Bhaskar and Ramachandra about it. They all went to seek Pullayya's advice.

'You were climbing up and down the rock the entire night,' said Pullayya with a smile when he saw Ravi. 'Did it leak down the legs?'

Ravi didn't know that Pullayya had been observing him.

'I am new to this!' he retorted. 'Why wouldn't I be afraid?'

'Fear won't work, my friend! When you come to the hill forest, the first thing you need to get rid of is the fear. Only if we are not scared will the sheep remain calm and settled. They are dumb animals that came to the forest trusting us to protect them.'

Ramachandra broached the subject. 'These guys want to go down to the meadow and see the place where the fox and the boar fought last night.'

'What do they want to see?' asked Pullayya.

'To see which one died.'

'Why do you need to see it? It is the boar that died. Our dogs were howling at dawn . . . didn't you all hear them? It's because the wild dogs were having a feast. They must have eaten the entire boar.' Pullayya talked as if he had been there and had seen the whole thing.

'Such a big fight happened so close to us,' said Ravi. 'Why shouldn't we go see it?'

Pullayya was silent for a minute. Then he lifted his head and said, 'This is not our place, son. We have come here begging for food. We should eat what we get, hide ourselves silently behind the rocks and trees during our stay and go back once we are done. If we bother about things that don't concern us, it will be like entangling ourselves in a creeper by the side of the road. We would not be able to move forward and will be twisting at the same spot. If you are all so keen, go and see it. But don't be greedy for the boar meat. It takes about a week of boiling to soften a wild boar's flesh.'

Ravi and five other youths went down the hill. They were all carrying strong sticks made of bamboo or satinwood. After walking a little, they found an acre's stretch of sandy soil that connected the bases of all the nearby hills. There were shrubs and bushes there and very few big trees. On one side was a rocky streambed. The two animals had fought on the bank of that stream.

They found the place without having to search for it, thanks to the racket that was being made by the wild dogs feasting on the dead animal's flesh. They were enjoying their communal eating so much that they did not notice the men approach.

Bhaskar shouted at the dogs and Sreenu put a bent finger in his mouth to sound a high-pitched, ear-splitting whistle. Tiripalu screamed and beat the trunk of a tree with his club. The dogs jumped up and ran into the stream. They emerged on the other side of the bank and watched them.

Ramachandra removed the sling tied to his waist and put a big stone in it. Swinging it a few times, he released the stone in the direction of the dogs. It hit a rock close to them, making a loud sound as it broke into pieces. That made the dogs retreat further. But after climbing to higher ground, they continued to watch the men.

The men understood that the dogs wouldn't leave their food so easily. Those dogs had the patience to chase an animal for miles, and the ability to use the power of their pack to hunt and eat their quarry. They might have looked small, but they survived on the basis of their pack-hunting methods.

They had eaten two-thirds of the boar already. Only the head remained intact. The rest of its body was just bones and some bloody tissue. The ground was wet with the boar's blood and fluids from its stomach. It was a horrific sight.

What startled the men and frightened them was the sight of the destroyed shrubs and bushes that stretched for about twenty yards from where the boar lay. They had been ripped out and the creepers torn. Even the branches of some trees were lying broken. The sandy soil looked as if it had been ploughed. There were streaks of blood on the ground and bushes at several spots.

Ravi's mind connected the sounds he heard last night with the sight in front of him. Imagining the battle made fear scramble up his spine. Both the animals had fought bravely. But it had been more than bravery—it had been a desperate battle for survival.

Tiripalu brought to their notice several broken branches lying on the ground some twenty yards ahead of them. The group walked over to the spot and found that a red sanders tree had been felled.

The people who did it cut off all the branches and left the ones that they did not want. The place was littered with chips of wood from the tree, which told them that the trunk and branches had been carved with an axe. The wood waste was still quite fresh, indicating that the tree had been felled less than two days ago.

The group walked around and found a few more stumps of red sanders trees with broken branches and chips in a heap. At one place, they found markings on the ground that seemed to be from something that had been dragged to the dry stream. They followed the trail and found several logs of red sanders arranged in a heap.

To Ravi it looked as if the trees had been skinned alive. He shuddered at the thought. Just then, someone from their group whistled from the hillock. Sreenu whistled back. They turned around and returned to the camp.

When they recounted what they had seen to Pullayya, he told them in a stern voice: 'Just forget it. You did not see anything. We are dumb shepherds who have come to the hills for our livelihood. That's all. No one should speak about those red logs.' He then added, 'We will see such logs not just here but at other spots throughout these hills.'

Ravi was surprised by Pullayya's response. He'd read about the illegal smuggling of red sanders wood in the newspapers and had now seen the handiwork of the smugglers with his own eyes. He had felt a certain anguish at the sight of those logs, the colour of blood. They had been arranged in heaps in the stream. Ravi likened them to children skinned alive, and the thought filled him with no less dread than the sight of the dead wild boar with its blood all over the shrubs and soil, muscles torn apart, only bare bones left.

Although the other shepherds talked a lot about the fate of the boar, they hardly spoke about the fate of the red sanders trees. No one expressed any sadness about the trees being felled. Ravi wondered why.

7

THE PARCHED LAND ON the hillock sported green shoots of grass, but the sheep weren't willing to eat them. Dabba grass has a thick shoot at the centre and the rest of the blades are soft, inviting the sheep to tuck into them.

The area surrounding the hillock they were on was abundant in rottler grass, a favourite of the sheep. They continued to graze there till the afternoon, while two of the gollas went in search of a water source.

When they found one, the shepherds moved the herds in that direction. They came across a hill with snake-like trails and crossed it to arrive at a streambed full of big rocks surrounded by dense vegetation.

Ravi thought that predators could be hiding behind those massive rocks. Some of the trees in that area had grown so huge that a man couldn't put his arms around their trunks. And they were so tall that if one looked up at the treetops, one's headscarf would fall off. Though the trees offered cool shade, they also made Ravi uneasy.

The herdsmen made the sheep drink water from the shallow spots without allowing them to get into the streambed. The ones in the front threw stones and thwacked the trees with their axe heads to scare away any animals hiding behind the rocks. Gurappa stopped Ravi from stepping into the stream because the noise being made by the gollas walking ahead could make any creature that was hiding step out towards the back of the herd. Ravi understood. He too picked up some stones and started throwing them on the rocks and trees.

The streambed resounded with the noise made by the shepherds. Their shouts echoed, resulting in a strange sound as multiple voices rebounded together.

The waves of noise made the langurs above them jump from tree to tree in fear. Ravi saw one jump from the wide branches of a booraga tree to a red-leaved Indian almond on the other side of the stream.

Ravi walked past another massive booraga tree with a trunk so large that if two men stood on either side of the trunk and put their arms around it, they wouldn't be able to touch fingers.

As he passed the tree, he saw a python hanging from a branch and jumped back in shock. After a moment, he recovered his poise and peeped at it from behind the tree. Yes, it was a snake.

The cobwebs in his mind cleared only when he looked at it for a third time. He realised that it was not a python, but a very thick creeper that had curved its way up the wide branch of the tree. As the langurs had used it to jump to another tree, it was swinging back and forth, which had made Ravi see it as something alive. It took a few minutes for Ravi's heartbeat to become normal again. He felt like laughing at his needless fear. He realised that his tendency to get scared easily in the hills wouldn't go away soon.

After all the sheep had drunk their fill of water, the shepherds moved them along the slope over to the side of the hill and settled them there. Fires were lit and they began cooking. Bhaskar came over to Ravi. 'Come with me.'

'Where to?'

'Just come,' he said and started walking away.

Ravi followed him along the streambank. After a while, they came across giant stone plates that curved into the stream. Moving slowly, Bhaskar cautioned Ravi to not make any noise. He stopped near a massive stone plate and, moving the tree branches aside, peeped through a crack. He then gestured for Ravi to take a look.

An unfamiliar tremor took hold of Ravi's heart. He did as Bhaskar asked. Once he understood what was under the stone plate, he shivered and moved away, closing the branches again over the crack.

Smiling silently, Bhaskar stopped Ravi as he walked backwards, away from the spot. 'You have never seen it before, right? Look at it properly. That, my dear, is the big tiger. Look at it without fear, because it can't hear you.'

'Why not?'

'Look again and you will understand.'

Ravi steadied his heart and stepped forward. Pushing the branches aside, he peered through the crack again.

The tiger was lying on the ground under the stone plate. Its big body was covered with stripes that were curved like the blade of a sickle. It shook its head every few seconds and suddenly opening its mouth, caught something and chewed on it. Observing more closely, Ravi saw that its head and mouth were covered with innumerable flies. Every time the tiger shook its head, they rose up with a loud buzz.

The flies had been attracted by the sticky blood on the tiger's jaws and body. They were landing on the tiger's face pulled by the smell of the bits of flesh stuck between its fangs. The tiger couldn't hear them—the persistent buzz of countless flies drowned out other sounds.

Unable to get rid of the flies, it was trying to catch them in its mouth and eat them. Ravi had heard the gollas remark that a tiger that had just eaten would be as deaf as an old dog. It had to bear the flies for about two days after a hunt. The buzz created by the flies may reduce the tiger's hearing, but it will not be completely deaf, he thought.

On the walk back to the camp, it sunk in that he had seen the tiger in its den. Probably no one in the city would believe his story. But he did see the tiger, and his fear of the beast was less than before he had seen it. He could not fathom why.

Once they reached, Bhaskar told the others about the tiger. 'Let us get the meal done with fast and take the flocks away.'

'Yes, those spots are the usual dens of big foxes,' said Pullayya. 'As the saying goes, "The pickle is greedy for salt and the prostitute is greedy for a hair bun." And so the fox is greedy for a hunt. There is water nearby and the stone plates are great for hiding. Some animal is bound to come for a drink of water every so often. At least once a week, the fox would find a prey.'

They did not rest after lunch. Pullayya told two herdsmen to stand guard facing the stream while the rest gathered the sheep and herded them up the hills.

Ever since they had seen Ravi wash himself using a wet cloth dipped in sterilised water, a few of the other shepherds had begun doing it too. But that day there was no time to boil the water and let it cool, so they filled the cans directly from the stream. As Ravi walked with the sheep, in his mind he could still see the visage of the tiger under the stone plates. Ramachandra found two ripe fruits that had fallen off a wood apple tree. He broke them open and offered the pulpy fruit around. Some of the shepherds did not eat the wood apple as they thought that it would make them thirsty or lead to a sore throat. However, Ravi and a few others ate the pulp.

It was still two hours to sunset. The herdsmen decided that they would cross two small ridges before camping on the higher part of the hill for the night.

The grazing sheep were spread from the foothills up along the slopes. Gurappa noticed that one of his sheep was just standing around and not grazing. He observed it closely and realised that it was struggling to walk properly. It kept lying down and getting up with much effort, looking balefully at the other sheep as it tried to keep up with the herd.

Gurappa examined the animal, which confirmed his suspicions—the sheep was ready to deliver a lamb. There was thick fluid oozing from its behind and its vulva was spreading open slowly. He sat next to it and started rubbing its back. The sheep stood up, but it was no longer able to walk fast enough to keep pace with the herd.

Gurappa asked Ravi and Bhaskar to stop the herd as he tended to the sheep carefully. He scratched its mouth, rubbed its neck and back and lightly massaged its hind legs. After struggling for half an hour, the sheep finally delivered its baby. The placenta was discharged as a thick fluid.

Gurappa dug a hole in the soil, buried the placenta and placed a rock on top of it. By the time he had finished, the mother had licked its baby clean. Gurappa took the still sticky lamb in his hands and began to walk ahead. The herd started moving again. The mother sheep kept walking between Gurappa's legs to try and trip him. It lifted its head up and cried softly, trying to reach its baby. Gurappa kept pushing it away as they climbed the hill.

Once they reached the top of the hill, Gurappa put the lamb down. It tried to get up and walk towards its mother, reaching for the teats. The mother stood at an angle that made it easy for the baby to reach them, and it licked the newborn's backside as it fed. It was a tender sight.

Ravi couldn't help but notice the affectionate way in which Gurappa watched over them, as if they were family members.

Pullayya left his herd and approached them.

'Did you not check this one before leaving?' he asked.

'I checked them all, but my calculations were wrong,' admitted Gurappa. 'I thought it would deliver after we returned. Did I not leave behind some old sheep and the mothers of young lambs? There are about ten such at home.'

'How did the calculation go wrong?'

'Its last baby had still not weaned off its milk when I saw it sniffing around a ram again,' explained Gurappa. 'I thought the deed did not happen, but it looks like the very first mating made it conceive again. This is the second time in twelve months that this one has delivered.' The happiness in his voice was unmissable.

'You sure are a lucky man!' exclaimed Pullayya. 'Your sheep conceive and deliver without a gap, your younger son becomes the most educated person in the village . . . you were whining about not being able to educate your elder son but even he is headed to Bangalore to start a hostel! Among us gollas, which family is as well off as yours?'

Ravi, who was listening to this exchange, felt something pull at him inside as he was reminded again of how much his community expected of him. But he knew that in just a year or two, the same people would berate him for being a failure. And his father would not be able to handle that. In his father's eyes, Ravi was not a sheep struggling to handle the pains of delivery or a lamb learning how to walk besides its mother. He was expected to be like a hill that could bear a heavy burden but still be stable or at least like a tree that gives cool shade and edible fruit.

Before he came to this forest, Ravi had seen a jungle in the city. He had experienced there the same fear that he felt here. In the city, the tigers, bears, pythons and wild boars were written exams, interviews, group discussions and people in suits. The executives who interviewed him saw him as a shepherd from the moment they reviewed his application. Worst of all, they thought that people like Ravi, who hailed from drought-prone villages, were uncivilised.

He felt his head heat up because of these thoughts. He had run away from the city to the village and from the village to this forest. There were no people, homes, roads or vehicles—and yet, the city kept haunting him. Shaking his head, Ravi looked around.

Gurappa was helping the infant lamb suckle. Nearby, Pichchanna was trying to pull down a creeper to feed its leaves to a ram. The other shepherds were busy with their chores. As the slope was not very steep, the herds were climbing up quite easily. However, the shepherds had to hold on to the tree branches and trunks to climb.

The hilltop was a wide space that was almost completely rocky with very few trees. If one faced south, it resembled a single, unbroken rock with no soil, no grass and no trees. The shepherds thought that it would be comfortable to lie down on this huge, clean rock slab. Bhaskar and Ramachandra were screaming and jumping around in excitement. 'Shall we play kabaddi?' asked Sreenu. The youngsters formed two teams of four each and played kabaddi for a while. Ravi forgot all his worries in that pleasant atmosphere and joined them in the games. He slept peacefully that night.

In the morning, Ravi found a few holes in the rocks. Each hole was about a metre wide.

'Those are water holes,' Bhaskar said. He picked up a small stone and hurled it inside. They could hear a splash from deep inside. 'During monsoon, these holes get filled and overflow down the rocks. They are the last resort if we don't find water anywhere.'

'How would you get water out of these holes?' asked Ravi.

Bhaskar took a small vessel from his carry bag and lay it down flat in front of the hole. Ramachandra held his legs. Bhaskar started crawling inside the hole. In a few moments, his head and body had disappeared into the hole, with Ramachandra still tightly holding on to his legs as he pushed him forward. After a moment, they heard him shout, 'That's enough!'

Ramachandra started pulling him out slowly. Bhaskar emerged with the vessel filled with water. The water was black and dirty.

If Ramachandra's hands had slipped, Bhaskar would have been fallen inside that narrow hole with no way to get out. What a risk to get a little water, thought Ravi.

If one didn't have a vessel, one would have to sip water from inside the hole. The inner walls of the holes were slippery and covered with moss. One slip, and it would be a very difficult task to come back out. Even after reaching the water, a cloth would have to be spread over it as a filter to avoid the worms crawling in it. Only then could one carefully take a few small sips. Shepherds turned to these holes for the sake of survival when they could find no water on the surface.

*

Eight days had passed since they had set out for the hills.

The shepherds who had been snacking on rotis between meals had run out of rations completely. The others had enough for another day or two. However, the women in the village had made fresh rotis by then and packed them along with other foodstuff, ready to be handed to the shepherds the following morning. After brushing their teeth, the men managed their meal by sharing the remaining food amongst themselves.

To get the fresh rations, some of the shepherds would leave for Kurro at the crack of dawn the next day. There, they would meet the party carrying the rations, who otherwise wouldn't be able to find them. The gollas believed that because of the auspicious time at which they had arrived at the forest, no one had gone down with hill fever, there had been no injuries and they had not struggled at all to find water. So, instead of going home early, they decided to stay in the hills for at least one more ration period of eight days. They hoped that the rains would begin by then.

They brought the herds down the hill. The sheep weren't stopping to graze as there was little grass on that slope. The shepherds noticed many wild palms along the brook. Those trees did not grow tall like they usually do but were spread low like bushes with bunches of black fruit hanging from their branches. It was a mouthwatering sight for the gollas, but they could not stop and pluck the fruit as the herds kept moving.

Some of the youngsters used their axe to cut off bunches of the palm fruit and hung them to the end of their sticks. As they hurried along beside their herds, they plucked the fruit, chewed the flesh and spat out the seeds. Ravi offered a bunch to his father, but Gurappa declined because he was chewing tobacco.

The newborn lamb was walking excitedly beside its mother. Whenever it faltered, the mother stopped to lick its body and push it forward. On steeper slopes, Gurappa carried the baby on his shoulders. They crossed another hill and began climbing a hillock with wide slopes. On the southern side of the hilltop, they saw a wall-like structure made of stones.

'In the past, bandits used to hide here with their loot,' said Gurappa to Ravi. 'Those are the walls of their hideouts.' Then he pointed towards the southwest. Ravi noticed a place with another wall-like structure with several trees near it. 'That is Onnuramma's fort, surrounded by tamarind trees. It is in ruins now.'

Ravi's eyes widened in surprise. He'd read about Onnuramma in a magazine. Seeing the ruins of her fort gave him goosebumps, and he wished he could go see the site. Stories of the valour of the woman had provided rich material for folk histories passed on through oral traditions.

Towards the end of the seventeenth century, the suzerainty of this area had been contested by the nawabs of Mysore, Golconda and Kadapa regions as well as the Matti Rajulu of Siddavatam. The battles fought by their armies devastated this region. It was then that Onnuramma emerged as a rebel force—a woman chieftain feared by all.

Onnuramma confronted the much larger forces of Hyder Ali of Mysore, Matti Venkatrama Raju and the Nawab of Kadapa and managed to maintain her independence. She was eventually overcome through trickery and deceit. Onnuramma was ambushed and executed in an inhuman manner. That episode remained a stain on local history.

It hadn't rained much in the area they were now in, and there was not enough grass for the sheep to graze. The animals were already showing their restlessness. The gollas were unhappy because the sheep hadn't been able to feed properly that day. Pullayya suggested they head northwest. They went downhill before climbing another hill to the west.

It was past noon when they found themselves in a large meadow full of big sal, axlewood and sandalwood trees.

Ravi's five-litre water can was empty by then. He usually didn't run out of water between refills. But that day, he had eaten too much palm fruit, which had made him thirsty. Others who had eaten a lot of palm fruit had also run out of water.

Gurappa gave some of his water to Ravi, who understood why the elders had refrained from eating the palm fruit.

A group of four young gollas decided to go in search of a water source and asked Ravi to join them. The five of them walked for a couple of kilometres among the trees before they came across an open patch of land. There, they found an old stepwell under some tamarind trees. Nearby were stone tubs used to store water drawn from the well.

'This is the one they call Balappa's well,' said Bhaskar. There was plenty of water in the well. They saw a few spots where stones had been arranged to build fire for cooking. The young men climbed down the stone steps into the well and first slaked their thirst. Then they filled their cans and poured the water into the tubs.

The cans were small, so it took them a while to fill the tubs. By then, the herds arrived and soon the sheep were crowding around the water tubs to quench their thirst. Struggling for space and unable to reach the water, some sheep climbed down into the well to drink. After all the sheep had finished drinking, they were settled down under the tamarind trees.

The shepherds found a cart track going south. The experienced ones knew that it led to the villages of Tippireddy Palle and Mudireddy Palle. Even tractors plied that route. They decided to cook and eat lunch at that spot.

After they had finished their meal, Pullayya said that since the sheep had not eaten enough grass that day, they should lead the herds towards a grassy area instead of resting for a while as they usually did after lunch. They got the herds moving again and decided to head towards the hills in the north.

However, the new mother did not move, because its infant remained lying on the ground. The mother was trying to make the baby get up by rubbing it with its forelimbs and head. Ravi looked on in amazement as the mother pushed its baby until it stood up. It shook its small body and was then ready to walk behind its mother.

A smiling Gurappa lifted the lamb into his arms and began walking. The sight reminded Ravi of the times when he would complain of leg pain while walking back from grazing in his childhood. His father would then carry him on his shoulders. With such memories flooding his mind, Ravi started walking beside the herd.

There was a tall hill towards the east. Towards the north, there was a hillock with a ramp-like elevation. In the distance was the range known as the Gopidevi hills. Nearby, there was a stream banked by a thickly wooded area. The vegetation was so thick on either side of the stream that it was almost like a dank, dark and deep cave.

The sheep began grazing on the grassy plain. The gollas stood on the bank of the stream, not allowing the sheep to step down into the streambed. Ravi looked down into the wooded creek, but it was so dark that he couldn't see anything. He thought that there could be wild animals behind those thick bushes and trees and that they should watch the sheep carefully while also being alert for any movements in the vegetation or from the streambed.

Bhaskar was walking about twenty metres behind Ravi. He was tapping his axe head against the trees and small rocks, the sounds ensuring that no sheep passed him and walked into the streambed. Gurappa was standing a further twenty metres away from Bhaskar. He was not only watching his side of the herd but also keeping an eye on Ravi's side.

Ravi did not like the situation. They all knew that some wild animal or the other could be in the stream. Why did they have to bring the sheep here and go through these anxious moments?

He realised then that the entire forest ecosystem operated on the basis of fear. While the shepherds had to take many precautions to protect their flocks, the predators had to come up with tricks and work extremely hard to secure their food. The only way to not go hungry was to risk life and limb. Ravi noticed the fear building inside him. He felt a slight tremble in his heart.

After a while, the herds began taking the bend along the higher bank of the stream. The sheep adjusted themselves to the new direction without any signal from their minders. There was a dense madder bush jutting from the streambank. A sheep drifted towards that bush. There, it suddenly stood still and stopped grazing. With half-eaten grass in its mouth, it froze and pricked up its ears, staring into the stream with bulging eyes.

Ravi did not understand its behaviour. Before he could go near the sheep, it urinated in two quick jets and suddenly jumped back into the herd. The sudden jump broke the herd's composure. Gurappa understood what was happening and immediately let out a loud cry.

That was when an animal leapt from the stream on to the bank, landing barely three feet from Ravi. Without even noticing what the animal was, he gave a shrill cry and started shaking in fear. The animal saw the axe slip out of his hand and could sense clear symptoms of fear. It stood up on its hind legs to its full height and opened its mouth wide to let out a loud cry, one of aggression.

With the animal so close and almost as tall as him, fear clouded all of Ravi's senses. He was unable to shriek or jump away. His hands and legs felt useless. The animal's eyes burnt like charcoals. It bared its sharp teeth and was about to strike Ravi with its paw when it sensed danger.

Gurappa was running towards them, howling at the top of his voice. Bhaskar rushed there too from the other side, screaming even louder and throwing fist-sized stones at the animal.

The other shepherds were hitting trees with their axes and shouting, creating a war-like cacophony.

The commotion was successful in scaring the animal. With a guttural cry, it jumped away and slipped back into the stream. Ravi began to feel faint. Gurappa reached just in time to prevent him from falling over. Slapping him on the back, Gurappa cried, 'Rey, sinnoda!' Bhaskar continued to throw stones into the stream at the spot where the animal had disappeared.

Gurappa sprinkled some water on Ravi's face and made him drink a little.

'Did it scratch him?' asked Bhaskar.

'No,' replied Gurappa. 'It never got close. He got scared, that's all.'

He saw Ramachandra and Munayya coming towards them and gestured them to remain at their positions. 'It was only a hyena. Don't relax now. It is still in the stream. You too carry on, Bhaskar.'

Once they heard that it was a hyena, the shepherds breathed a small sigh of relief and resumed their positions. Ravi sat up. He felt better, but the shiver of fear had not completely left him.

'It was a hyena that came upon you, not a tiger,' said Gurappa. 'A hyena does not have the power to attack a man. It will show its fangs and act threateningly. And when we get scared, it will seize the chance to drag away a sheep by the throat. If you'd screamed and spanked it with your axe handle, it would have whimpered and run away. You didn't know this and got scared.'

When he had seen the animal, Ravi's body had felt powerless. The animal had dark stripes on an ash-coloured body. Its bald head, red eyes, redder tongue and long canines had made for a truly frightful sight. At that moment, Ravi had felt as if death itself had leaped on to him with an open mouth. He'd never experienced fear like this before.

Ravi felt that it was not only fear but also fatigue. He walked slowly, his feet not moving in tandem with each other. Gurappa made him drink some more water. He felt sorry for his son's plight and had Ravi walk beside him. Even after such an incident, there was no question of stopping to rest. One had to carry one's load and keep moving. 'You keep an eye on the baby lamb,' Gurappa told Ravi. 'I will take care of the herd.'

Ravi looked at the baby lamb walking beside its mother.

Not even two days old, it was frail, with legs no thicker than his thumbs and only as tall as twice the length of his palm. It amazed him to see such a young creature trot behind its mother over hilly terrain. The lamb stopped when the mother stopped and moved when the mother moved. If it slipped, the adult sheep on either side helped it regain its balance and stand upright again.

Ravi felt some of his stress dissolve as he watched the baby lamb. He also felt an energy infuse into his body. Like a sheep shakes its body vigorously to get rid of raindrops in its fur, Ravi tried to shake his mind in an attempt to drive his fears away. He realised that he too had an axe with him like everyone else. And he could scream very loudly too. It was only his fear that stopped him from using these two weapons.

The sheep had to jump over a water gully that appeared in their path. The new mother sheep stood rooted at its spot. If its baby was a little bigger, it would have crossed the brook and then encouraged the child to jump over it too. But it knew the infant couldn't yet do that. Ravi picked the baby up and stepped over the gully. The mother followed him.

*

The abundance of good grass they found that day meant the sheep had eaten twice as much as they normally did. Because of the appearance of the hyena earlier, the shepherds suspected that there was a tiger in the vicinity. They herded the sheep over to a big hillock and built fires around the herd before lying down for the night.

They had walked a lot that day. The struggle to find proper grazing spots for the sheep had forced them to climb up and down several hills, and they had not even rested after lunch. Almost all of them retired early that night.

However, Gurappa found it hard to fall asleep. He was concerned about his son and wondered whether he had done the right thing in bringing him to the forest.

Instead of becoming tougher, Ravi had shown how weak-hearted he was. Gurappa was not only worried about his son but also about the inconvenience his behaviour could be causing to the rest of the group. He got up and went to where his son was lying down. On seeing his father, Ravi sat up.

'You were terrified today, sinnoda.'

'I had never before seen a wild animal from such close quarters, nanna,' replied Ravi.

'What would you have done, sinnoda, had we not been there? Would you have offered your neck to it?'

His head bowed, Ravi remained quiet for a moment. 'I don't know what I would have done,' he finally answered.

'You would have given your neck to the animal,' said Gurappa. He paused, trying to swallow the surge of emotions he was feeling.

Then he spoke again. 'Just remember one thing,' he said. 'Once you bring the sheep to the forest, you do not belong to yourself alone. You are a man of the herd. Your neck is not yours. It belongs to the sheep. If your neck is strong, the necks of all these sheep will be safe from the tiger's jaws. Only if you are brave will the sheep be able to graze without fear and sleep without care.'

Gurappa stopped chewing his tobacco and spit the juice out. 'Son, you can't continue to be like a young man from Hyderabad. You need to become a shepherd boy and should not get scared even if the tiger comes and grabs your neck. If you have an axe, swipe it at the tiger. Else bash its face with a stone. If you can't find anything to hit it with, punch its forehead with your bare fists. How can you give up without putting up a fight? My son, remember that those dumb animals are depending on you.'

Gurappa got up to leave but then sat back on his haunches as if he had forgotten something. 'It has been eight days since we left the village,' he said in a quiet voice. 'Have you thought of the sheep even once?'

Ravi could not understand the question. What was there to think about? He was doing his duty and watching over the sheep like everyone else.

'You saw a thick root, a foot long, and thought it was a snake,' said Gurappa. 'When you looked at a dark tree, you shivered thinking there was an animal behind it. You shuddered because you thought of the big tiger resting in the shadows of the rocks. You worry about some animal attacking from behind as you walk beside the sheep. You fear leading the herd from the front or being at the back. Are you even sleeping at night? You are afraid that if you fall asleep, a bear might attack you or a python might swallow you. Fear . . . always the fear. An all-consuming fear. You are not guarding the sheep, sinnoda! You are keeping watch over your fear, letting it graze as much as it wants. You are only thinking about yourself, not about the sheep. Dear son, you will know the truth only when you overcome this fear. And when you understand the truth and get to know the forest, you will be able to take care of the sheep. If you don't want to change, it is best you go back to the village with the people who bring us rations.'

Having said what he wanted to, Gurappa got up and went back to his sleeping spot. Ravi lay back down but could not fall sleep for a long time. He thought about the incident with the hyena and knew that his father was right. Without even a little protest, without even trying to run away like a sheep would, he had simply offered his neck to the animal. His fear had stunned him and made him inert.

Fear is necessary if one has to live. But why feel fear when facing death? How did such a simple truth escape him?

8

SOME OF THE SHEPHERDS went to meet the people from the village. They were to convene near Kurro's well to receive rations for the next eight days. Bhaskar asked Ravi to join them, but Ravi did not feel like going.

Seven people had arrived from the village. Sankar was among them. They walked to the camp together with the shepherds. Looking at the herds, they felt happy at how well fed the sheep were. Sankar heard about Ravi's troubles and went to speak with him.

'Looks like you've not been able to adjust here,' Sankar said to his brother. 'Let me stay for this ration period. You go home with these people.'

Ravi smiled a little and replied, 'No, I will stay.'

Sankar brought up the incident with the hyena.

'This is all new to me, right?' said Ravi. 'I need to get used to it.'

'With an axe in your hand, why fear the hyena?' asked Sankar. 'If you get scared by the hyena's growl, what would you do if the big fox comes across your path tomorrow? If you'd hit the hyena with the axe, it would have collapsed on the spot.'

Ravi bowed his head.

Pullayya, who was nearby, overheard this conversation. He guffawed and called, 'Ohoy Sankaroo! Swipe the hyena with the axe? Why? Just a holler would have been enough for it to run away in fear!' He continued, 'You know the saying, "The anger of a shepherd is a burden on the neck." Why do we need to use the axe in anger? Don't say such stuff. It won't work out for a shepherd. A golla may need to use his axe to cut a branch or pull down a creeper to feed his flock. He has no other use for the axe. It is just to keep our fears at bay. If he has to use it as a weapon, a shepherd should always swing the wooden handle of the axe and not its blade.'

'What you say is true,' said Sankar.

Pullayya addressed Ravi, 'Oye, my younger grandson! There's something I should have told you earlier. I will tell you now. None of the wild animals attack a man easily. Even the tiger does not confront a human directly. All animals fear humans.'

'Then what about man-eating tigers?' enquired Sankar.

'If a very old fox suddenly comes face to face with a man in a narrow space, it will risk its life and attack, fearing that the man would harm it,' explained Pullayya. 'It then realises that it is easier to kill a man than it is to hunt other animals. That tiger then becomes habituated to killing and eating humans. Some old tigers prey on humans when they get injured and lack the power and speed to hunt and kill other animals. But man won't allow a man-eating tiger to live long. He will feed it poisoned food as a bait and kill it.'

'Are there any man-eating tigers in this forest?' asked Ravi.

'I don't think so. I heard the forest officials released five or six tigers and two or three leopards in these forests recently. People say that around ten cows were eaten in recent weeks near the Jyothi ashram. Those must have been stray animals. But I wonder about the tiger that fought and killed the wild boar. It must have been an aged tiger. It suffered some injuries too, I reckon. If not right away, eventually it will become a man-eater. The sandalwood smugglers won't let it live that long though. They will kill it with their rifles.

'But don't get scared! One should not carry fear into the hills. That's not good at all. It is better to cohabit with the forest than live here with fear. Carrying fear will affect others in the group too.'

Pullayya paused for a moment and then said, 'What will happen if a tiger attacks our herd? It will grab a sheep by the neck and take it away. That's all! It can't take four sheep under one arm and four under another, right? Let it eat. It gets hungry too, it too needs to live. In any case, a tiger is not as bad as the famine in our village, right?'

The old man finished speaking and walked away, leaving Ravi to digest the import of his words.

Those who brought the rations ate lunch along with the hill-grazing group. Ankayya gave half a roti to Gurappa's dog. Because he often did that, the dog would get up and wag its tail whenever Ankayya approached it.

Pamuleti took Sankar aside and asked in a low voice, 'Did my son-in-law come to the village?'

'He came day before yesterday,' replied Sankar. 'I think he left yesterday.'

'Did he ask anything?'

'He asked when the sheep were taken to the hills and when they'd be brought back. There was a stranger who had come with him.'

Pamuleti did not say anything in response. He walked away muttering to himself . . . 'The bond will end . . . no more coming to the forest . . . or grazing the sheep . . .' Sankar half-understood the meaning of those words.

The ration-bearers stayed till it was time to move the sheep again. Gangayya gave them a pack of medicinal wicks and asked for it to be handed over to his family. Subbayya passed a heap of dried neddi leaves. When they left, the herds started moving.

The grass was quite green near the base of the hill. They found several palmyra trees along the stream that had small blueberry-like fruits hanging down in bunches. The youngsters grabbed them and ate with relish. Even the elders chewed a fruit or two. They also found and ate a local fruit called tooky.

Plucking fruit while herding sheep was not easy. One had to not only keep a lookout and also keep an eye on the herd and simultaneously pluck the fruit without halting for more than a few seconds at a place. It wasn't possible to stand and eat leisurely. They had to eat while walking alongside the sheep.

Ravi was walking with a heightened sense of alertness. He was trying hard not to let any thoughts distract him from observing his surroundings. He had earned a reputation for being the most cowardly person in the group and now burnt with a desire to change that perception.

Pichchanna's and Munayya's dogs were walking in the middle of the herd. Ravi noticed that they never walked at the edges. However, as always, Gurappa's dog was walking beside its master.

Ravi was quite miffed at Gurappa's dog. When the hyena was about to attack him, Gurappa came running and screaming, but his dog did not follow him. Since then, Ravi felt angry every time he saw the dog being fed sheep milk and rice by Gurappa.

In the afternoon, they scouted for water sources nearby and returned to Balappa's well again.

While they were resting after lunch, a group of ten men came to the well. They were clad in half-dhotis with kerchiefs tied around their heads. All of them had cloth bags hanging from their axe handles.

'Which village are you from, brother?' one of them asked.

'We are from a village near Porumamilla,' replied Gurappa. 'Where are you from?'

They did not reply immediately. Putting down their bags and axes, they wiped their faces with the kerchiefs. 'We are from villages near Vanipenta,' one of them eventually responded.

Gurappa did not ask them the purpose of their visit. It was obvious what their work entailed. But Munayya could not hide his curiosity and asked, 'Are you hill-grazers?'

'We came to work for the forest officials,' one of the men replied. 'We have to cut and trim the bamboo plants.'

The shepherds knew that the noise they had been hearing every day was not the sound of bamboo shoots being cut. Munayya was about to say something again when Pullayya stopped him by gesturing with his hand and instead asked the newcomers whether they had eaten lunch.

'No,' they replied. 'We need to cook.'

'Do you have rice?'

The men said that they did and then started cooking. They made a curry of dried fish to go with the rice and invited the shepherds to join them. 'We already ate our lunch,' one of the shepherds replied. 'You go ahead.'

After their meal, one of the men asked Pullayya, 'Can you spare a thin sheep for us? We have been eating bland food.'

'We don't sell any sheep that we bring to the hills, son,' replied Pullayya.

'Even a ram is fine,' the man said. 'We will give you whatever you ask.'

'Each herd has only one ram, son. The ram is the leader of the herd, no?'

At that, the other group retired to a spot under a big tree and lay down.

The shepherds got up after a while. Gurappa went to Pullayya to discuss their plans. It had been almost a week since the sheep had eaten the grass towards the east. Gurappa thought fresh rottler grass would have grown back by now and they should head back in that direction again.

Pullayya agreed but felt they couldn't travel that far if the sheep grazed and moved slowly. They could cover the distance only if they rushed the herds. That made sense to everyone. The sheep were herded towards the eastern rim of the hill ranges instead of climbing in the north direction.

The sheep moved briskly without stopping to graze. The shepherds spotted fruit on parika trees. This fruit gave off a musky odour and even its soft pulp-like seed could be eaten along with the flesh. But one had to be careful to avoid the thorns while picking the fruit.

The hills were silent. Even if a small bird sang in the valleys, the sound echoed over a great distance. Only in the forests could one get to hear sounds so clearly. One could not see the birds on the treetops and the peaks of the hills, but their presence could be discerned through the sounds coming from the brooks and streams.

Where big rock sheets had risen through the valley floors, even faint sounds were amplified by echoes, causing a strange sensation. In normal life, sounds are constant, featuring silence only once in a while. In the forest, it was silence that was constant, only occasionally disrupted.

As fear started leaving Ravi's mind, he could better experience the wondrous beauties of the forest. A peacock whooped in a brook somewhere in the distance. Ravi imitated its cry. He thought it almost magical that the sound he made echoed in those valleys and came back to his own ears in waves. He repeated his rendition of the peacock's call repeatedly until Bhaskar turned around to give him a look.

They were on the curve of a hill. From there, the stream looked very deep. The sheep munched on the grass quietly. Bhaskar and Ravi talked about the strangers they had met at the well. Both had the same suspicion that those people had come for the heap of the red sanders logs they had seen along the streambed a few days ago.

Ravi criticised the cold-hearted loggers, the evil designs of the ones who made them cut the trees and the selfish greed of the merchants who dealt in sanders timber. As Bhaskar concurred with Ravi's arguments, he suddenly noticed a sheep standing near a rock plate. It was trying to pull its leg from behind the rock.

They saw the sheep jump and jerk its body, straining to pull its leg free. Bhaskar thought it probably had its foot stuck in a crevice. 'Dumb creature,' he said. 'It doesn't know where to put its leg.' He was about to go and help free it when he saw that four other sheep on either side stood frozen to the spot. They had stopped grazing.

Suddenly, they turned around and jumped aside, all four urinating in fear. Realisation dawned on Bhaskar. 'It has got the sheep!' he shouted loudly. He did not know what kind of animal had the sheep by its leg, but it was obvious that some fanged creature was under the rock plate.

Bhaskar threw his bag down and lifted his axe high. He moved towards the sheep screaming, 'Thoi! Thoi!'

Ravi felt his feet tremble. But he ignored the sensation and threw his shoulder bag down as well. He followed Bhaskar, holding his axe stiffly. He was sweating, and his heart was beating fast, but the sight of another man ahead gave him just enough courage to continue.

Gurappa ran towards them just as the sheep pulled its leg free. Right under the rock, they could see a python's head trying to drag the sheep back. It was a konda sila, an Indian rock python.

Bhaskar took a couple of steps forward when the python suddenly emerged from the rock and twisted itself tightly around the sheep. The sheep let out a shrill cry and fell down. Bhaskar swiped his axe at the python but missed. By the time Ravi had lifted his axe, it had already made two blindingly fast rolls on the downward sloping rocky terrain, moving further away to avoid a second blow.

The konda sila slithered down the slope like a stone wheel and dropped into the streambed below. 'Rey Ramachandra, Munayya, Sreenu!' Bhaskar yelled. 'Come here! The konda sila took the sheep away!' He started to follow the python into the valley.

Excitement and fear merged with a desperate urge to save the sheep surged through Ravi. It was different from the pure fear that he had felt earlier. He started to follow Bhaskar down the slope.

Pullayya shouted, 'Don't climb down! Stop there! What will you do by going down there?'

'We will cut the snake into pieces and bring back the sheep!' replied Bhaskar.

'Orey, clasped by the big snake and having fallen from this height into the streambed below, do you think the poor sheep would have survived?' cried Pullayya. 'The python would have dragged it behind some stone by now. It would have bitten the sheep all over and broken its bones by squeezing it. Even if you go down there and kill the snake, you will bring back a dead sheep or one about to die. What will we do with it? Can we eat one bitten by a snake? Why make all this effort, sons? You will get into trouble if there is a tiger or leopard behind those stone plates below. As the saying goes, "Bother the dog, and lose your beauty." Why go after the python now? Come back!'

Pullayya's words convinced them to return to their positions alongside the herds. The herd had had its first casualty. Despite all their precautions, they couldn't stop death coming in the form of a python. That sheep had belonged to Bhaskar. He was full of grief and struggled to accept that he couldn't prevent it from being taken away. He knew that such things happened during hill-grazing, but he couldn't stop mourning the sheep that he had reared for several years. He thought about the time it was born, the times it gave birth and the time when it escaped a hyena during the previous year's hill-grazing. These recollections brought tears to Bhaskar's eyes, and he did not speak to anyone for a long time.

The tension and excitement of the incident stayed in Ravi's heart for a while. He walked quietly beside the herd. Bhaskar stopped every now and then and looked back into the streambed. He was still in denial about the incident. During their afternoon stop near a water source, the shepherds were all silent. They went about their routine work without any wisecracks and guffaws.

Pullayya consulted with Gurappa for a few minutes and called for everyone's attention. 'It is normal to lose our animals when we come to the hills,' he said. 'The one who lost a sheep will grieve. The one next to him will be fearful, for he knows it could be his herd's turn next. We have all come to the hills to survive. If today the snake claimed Bhaskar's sheep, it means the Hill Goddess took it as a sacrifice on behalf of the entire group. The benefit of the sacrifice will accrue to all our herds. What I am trying to say here is—as the saying goes, "Whichever leg slips, the butt will be in danger"—any loss should be a loss for the entire group. Let us assess the cost of the sheep taken by the snake, divide that among us all and compensate Bhaskar for his loss. It should never be the case that only one person ends up losing. What do you all say?'

They liked the idea of sharing the loss equally and agreed to his proposal. They also agreed on the rate. But it was not the market rate for a sheep. It was the cost of the mutton.

Whenever a ram is sold, it is always at the rate of mutton. A sheep is usually never sold at the rate of mutton because it is a productive resource for the herd. Its pricing model therefore had to be special. For a sheep, the price is based on the stage of its life. It is valued differently when it is fertile, when it has had lambs and after it becomes incapable of breeding.

*

The newborn lamb happily ran behind its mother, nibbling at the fresh grass shoots. It tried to get close to the grazing rams. Young sheep rubbed their heads against the little one, almost making it topple over. Sheep that hadn't ever mated seemed to want to have the baby close to them.

Each of the herds had rams of various ages. Some were only six months old and a few were over a year old. At the front of his herd each shepherd had a mature ram that was at least three years old. When a tiger or leopard attacked the herd, they mainly targeted the rams because the necks of rams have more flesh and muscle.

The gollas took special care of the rams. They fed the head rams with grass and tamed them. The head rams became habituated to walking just behind the master. It was common to see the shepherd leading the herd from the front with the head ram walking proudly behind him, in turn followed by the rest of the herd.

When the shepherd had to walk behind the herd, it was the buck—the male goat—that led the way. Bucks always tried to move forward and stay at a distance from the group. Even at night, a buck would attempt to leave the herd and sleep separately. It was common for the shepherds to have to hustle the buck back into the herd at least a couple of times every night.

Ravi was slowly learning all these aspects of the shepherd's life. As he lost his fears, he gained more knowledge about the profession, the forest and the animals. But he wondered what was the use of this knowledge. Would it help him crack a competitive exam or make it easier to ace a group discussion or an interview? Where exactly could he utilise this knowledge? Ravi smiled at his own thoughts.The sheep reached the top of a mound of soapstone plates. The place had a few wood apple trees that were laden with fruit. The fruit looked like white balls hung from the top branches.

'Orey Pichchanna!' called Pullayya. 'See that white-spotted sheep there? I have been observing it since late afternoon. It has not eaten even a blade of grass. Get a hold of it and see what's wrong.'

'Perhaps it overate?' said Pichchanna.

'Stop joking, Pichchigaa!' reprimanded Pullayya. 'You are like a guy who compliments the quality of the voice of a drowning person screaming for help!'

Pichchanna went over to the sheep Pullayya had pointed out. He felt the sheep's belly and then declared, 'You are right, it has gone a bit soft.'

They treated the animal the best they could as the evening sky darkened. Sreenu held it tight while Pichchanna made a scratch behind the sheep's left ear and put a drop of its own blood in its eye. Then they settled all the sheep down for the night before it became completely dark.

The stars in the night sky looked like white sorghum grains spread out for drying. A small dot appeared in the northeast and moved towards the southeast. Ravi guessed that it was a manmade satellite. An aircraft flew overhead with its red lights blinking. The air was a little warm.

The shepherds retired for the night after lighting fires in all four directions. Apart from the sneezing of the sheep and the occasional sounds made by animals in the valley below, the forest was silent. In the dark, a calm silence prevailed, one in which even a faint rustle of the wind was clearly audible.

Suddenly, Ravi heard something crash into the ground a few feet away from him. He opened his eyes immediately and looked around to see what it was. He couldn't see anything. Something seemed to rush through the air and fall down. Ravi felt a slight tremble in his heart. He sat up and looked around. He wondered whether he should alert the others.

Then he saw the wood apple tree above him. Maybe it was just the sound of falling fruit. Ravi smiled. He would have become the butt of jokes again if he'd woken up the others. He looked at the moon shining at the top edge of the hill. Bright moonlight spread everywhere except on the western slopes, which were in shadow. It was darker still in the valleys.

Ravi checked his torch once and was about to lie down when he heard the same noise again. This time it came from near where Bhaskar was sleeping. Whatever it was, it fell on a sheep, which frightened the animal and made it jump into the herd. This made a few sheep stand up and start whimpering.

The noise awoke Bhaskar, who shushed the sheep.

'What happened?' called Pichchanna from where he was sleeping. 'The sheep seem scared!'

Before Bhaskar could respond, it happened again—the sound of something falling. This time it was near Gurappa, who immediately understood what it was. He whistled loudly, which woke everyone up. He then shouted, 'Thieves, thieves!'

Palm-sized stones started falling on the sheep right then. Some people were throwing stones at the herd from the valley. The shepherds tried to stand firm at their positions to drive the frightened sheep back into the herd. They started whistling loudly, shouting and throwing stones back blindly into the darkness below.

'Orey!' shouted Pullayya. 'Those on the other side, come here. Don't switch on your torches.'

'Don't let them get away,' called another shepherd. 'Attack them!'

The gollas continued to shout and hurl stones. Many of them whirled their catapults.

'Come on, you bastards! We will break your skulls!'

'We grew up drinking raw milk, and we will drink your blood!'

They launched stones using their catapults. The stones flew into the darkness with a buzzing noise. They could hear them hit rocks and tree trunks. Screaming and shouting cuss words, they stopped the frightened sheep from running into the valley.

For over an hour, the gollas fought by hurling stones using catapults or their hands. The thieves threw stones back at them. The surrounding hills echoed with the noise. Instead of a tremble in his heart, Ravi felt excitement. There was an adrenaline rush, a desperation in their fight. Battle frenzy drove fear away from him completely. Like the others, he too found himself using cuss words liberally while throwing stones using his catapult.

The moon rose further up in the sky and the moonlight spread to the western slopes too. In that light, they could make out the movement of the thieves and launched more stones in their direction. The barrage of stones hurled by the thieves reduced. It seemed as if they were retreating.

'Come on!' yelled Bhaskar, moving forward while swinging his catapult. 'Let's catch and deal with them!'

Ravi joined the makeshift assault team along with Sreenu, Pichchanna, Ramachandra and a few other youngsters.

'Rey! Stop there!' shouted Pullayya. He ran over to them. 'Where the hell do you think you're going?' he asked in a low voice once he was near them. 'You wanted to scare them away. And you managed it. That's enough. Now go back to your positions.'

'What if they come back?' asked Bhaskar.

'Why will they come? To sit under our legs? The stones would have hurt at least a couple of them. They won't bother us again. You all did a great job in not allowing the herd to disperse in all directions. That's enough. Their plan was to lift one sheep each. Because the herd did not get down to the valley, it did not work.'

The young men were not convinced.

'Don't behave like children,' rebuked Gurappa, joining the conversation. He spoke in a low but firm voice. 'Listen to what we say. If those were Chenchu or Sugali tribals, they would be carrying bows. If you go closer, they will shoot their arrows at you. If they were the sanders smugglers, they would be carrying country rifles. We have done enough. Just stay here without a fuss.'

Ravi twitched a little.

They all went back to their sleeping spots, but none of them could sleep properly that night. They sat in pairs and discussed the fight.

In the morning, the youngsters went down the hillock and found the damage caused by the stones they had hurled. There were broken twigs and branches and marks on tree trunks and rock slabs. They took it as testimony of the power in their arms, and it made them happy.

Bhaskar twirled his moustache and let out a war cry. Ramachandra too broke into victory whoops and threw a large stone hard against a rock. It splintered into pieces. Their loud celebration resounded in the valley. The elders, who had stayed at the top of the hillock, could not understand what was happening there and figured that the yelling was just youthful exuberance.

As they ate rotis for breakfast, Pullayya called the younger shepherds over. 'Rey Pichchigaa,' he said. 'If you don't slam your thigh, twirl your 'stache, shout till you're hoarse and hit a rock with a stone, you would not be able to shit and pee?'

Pichchanna laughed and retorted, 'Are we doing it every day?'

'Then why do it today?'

'Didn't we drive the thieves away last night? Wouldn't there be some excitement?'

'Yes, but what if they had hid on the other side of the hill and heard your celebrations?'

'What if they heard us?' asked Sreenu.

'What if they want to twirl their moustaches as well?'

Sreenu was about to retort when Gurappa cut in. 'Orey, stop this childish behaviour and listen,' he said.

'All of you should listen,' declared Pullayya, raising both his hands. 'As the saying goes, "One should not play football while carrying a water pot on one's head." Our sheep are the pots of water, and we are carrying them on our heads. The other side has no such burden. They can play any game they like. We should simply stay out of our enemy's sight and move on. There are tigers around, right? We should avoid their path but not think of killing them to save our herd. There will be pythons and leopards. We should protect our herd by escaping from them. Each one of us came here with fifty lives to protect and to sustain ourselves. We are only here temporarily, so we should not think of chasing away those that live here throughout the year. Even the thieves are like foxes. We should chase them away from the herd. That's our job. If we provoke them, they'd want to take revenge. You don't know how much loss we would bear then. Just focus on the job we came for.' Casting aside the sternness in his words, Pullayya then said, 'Oye Gurappa, you mentioned yesterday that the grass would have grown again. Tell me about it.'

'The place where we grazed last week, it had rottler grass in abundance,' explained Gurappa. 'The grass would have grown back and greened by now. There will be water in the streams nearby, and the springs would also have water. If we climb the hill and go down the eastern slope, there will be water in the Belum and Donla streams as well.'

Pullayya felt that the sooner they headed back to the east, the better it would be. He said so to Gurappa. And they got the herd up and moving again.

Gurappa saw Ankayya feed half a roti to his dog again and asked, 'Did your rotis get spoilt? Or did your old mother burn it black because she couldn't see properly? Do you want a roti from my ration?'

'No,' replied Ankayya, still feeding the dog. 'I just didn't feel like eating.'

*

The shepherds walked along the eastern ranges and reached their destination by afternoon. Gurappa had guessed correctly. The grass had grown back.

They reached the water source, where they cooked and ate lunch. They were all feeling quite sleepy, and most of them took a nap. Four of the elderly shepherds stayed awake guarding the herds.

In the evening, the sheep started climbing the hill while grazing on the fresh rottler grass. Pullayya discussed with Gurappa their plans for the next week. They decided to move around the iron rock circuit, use the water from the Belum stream and camp on the upper hills.

The bucks and rams were leading the way along the rocks by the stream. The sheep were following their lead. Sreenu was standing on the bank of the stream to ensure that the sheep didn't go into the streambed. He hit the rocks with his stick and directed the sheep away from the streambed by making the usual shepherd sounds of 'jjjo', 'tsst' and 'ppptch'.

Ankayya was on the other side picking and eating palmyra fruit.

'Didn't you have a roti earlier?' asked Pichchanna.

Ankayya did not respond and remained standing near the palmyra bush. Just then, a bent-eared sheep tried to jump over a rock outcrop and twisted its leg. It slipped down the rock and hit the ground on its back with a thud. It flailed its legs in the air and managed to stand up. But after taking four steps, it collapsed.

Sreenu waited for it to get up. It could not. It kicked its legs and cried out in pain with tears rolling down its face. He tried to help it stand up. It was unable to stand. Sreenu then checked it all over but couldn't see any sign of blood anywhere. But when his hand brushed against its back, it jerked and wailed louder. Sreenu knew then that its spine was fractured.

'O Pichchi mama!' he called. Pichchanna came by, repeated the examination and declared that it was a spinal injury. 'If this happened at home, we would have bandaged it and given it support on a cot,' he said. 'It would have recovered in a month. We can't do anything in the hills. Carry it to the top of the hill. We will look at it tonight.'

Sreenu lifted the sheep on to his shoulders, held its spindly legs on either side and started climbing up the hill. Pichchanna answered the concerned enquiries from the other shepherds. Sreenu found a soft grassy spot and gently laid the bent-eared sheep down. It was shivering. It had broken into a cold sweat, and its legs were trembling.

Sreenu pulled up a few fistfuls of grass and tried to make it eat. The sheep tried to chew on the grass blades, but unable to handle the pain, gave up midway. The grass blades remained in its half-open mouth. Its pitiful look stirred Sreenu's heart. He couldn't control his tears and wept a little, before wiping his eyes and looking to see if the others were watching.

The herds had not yet reached the top. Sreenu could hear the shouts of the climbing gollas. He tried to control his anguish. Once the other sheep had been settled down, the shepherds came one by one to have a look at the stricken animal. They all walked away with a resigned look.

'This one delivered twins at each calving and always had plenty of milk,' Ramayya reminisced. 'Its udder would be so full and heavy that they'd hang low. I remember wondering how it could bear such heavy udder. Finally, fate had this in store for her.'

A heavy sadness grew inside Sreenu. He knew that if he opened his mouth, he would start weeping and wailing. He therefore kept silent. Sreenu's silence was well understood by the others, who began to discuss what to do with the sheep. That sheep would never be able to walk. But they couldn't leave it there nor carry it around.

'Let us set a price for it and carve it,' suggested Tiripalu. In this such a situation, it seemed to be the only recourse. It was not uncommon to resort to such measures.

'We have never gone through a single ration period without eating mutton,' reminisced Pullayya. 'This time it has been different. There were times when two sheep would die when wild animals attacked the herd before being chased away. There was more mutton than we could eat.'

No one noticed Sreenu in the darkness, but his eyes were completely wet. Before Pullayya could announce the decision that they would carve the sheep in the morning, Sreenu stepped up and said, 'No, the sheep won't be carved.'

'Then what will you do, son?' asked Pullayya. 'Will you carry it around?'

'I will take it home and get a cast bandage done.'

They all knew that it was a special sheep but did not realise how much Sreenu loved it. No one spoke for a while.

'Okay then,' Pullayya said. 'How will you get it home?'

'I will take it till Nayanapalle and leave it at my uncle's. They will take care of it.'

Pullayya nodded and walked away.

Sreenu took the injured sheep to his herd. The other sheep sensed the predicament of their comrade. Some of them came close to the bent-eared one and put their mouth near its face or tried to rub it with their knees. Even the shepherds were moved by the sight.

Before retiring that night, Pullayya said to Gurappa, 'What is this crazy behaviour? We all love these animals, but this is overdoing it. No one knows when a sheep becomes fodder for a fox . . . such is their life.'

'Yes, the prey of the tiger lives without a guarantee,' agreed Gurappa.

'For that matter, where is the guarantee for anyone's life in the hills? If an aged tiger confronts us, it will take its share . . . someone or the other will end up as its food, right?'

'Do you think there are aged tigers around?'

'Since that wild boar's fight with the big fox, I have had my suspicions,' replied Pullayya. 'It might attack a man now by waylaying him. If some idiot ends up in its path, it may get used to the taste of human blood. Things will become difficult for us then.'

Gurappa understood the old man's reasoning. He got up and slowly walked to his sleeping spot.

The next day, Sreenu got ready to leave before dawn, but Pullayya stopped him and asked him to leave after sunrise.

Sreenu wanted only Bhaskar to accompany him, but Bhaskar asked Ravi to join them too. The three of them left once the sun was up, with Sreenu carrying the sheep across his shoulders.

They walked on a track in a valley between two big hills. It was a track that had seen ox cart traffic in the past. The wooden wheels of the carts had made two clear tracks, which had become water gullies over a period of disuse. Grass and other vegetation mostly covered the tracks, and the branches of big trees intertwined to form a canopy over the path. The bent-eared sheep occasionally squealed in pain or because it was separated from the herd.

As they walked beside streambeds and dry brooks, they heard various peculiar sounds made by colourful birds that were hopping from branch to branch. The jungle fowls and cocks were putting up quite a show. They saw big squirrels scampering up the branches of trees. The sandy surface near the streams looked clean. There were no other footprints besides the ones made by the two jungle cocks walking in front of them. Their prancing walk created unique patterns on the smooth and moist sand.

Once they had gone past the curve of the hill, they started along the bank of another stream. That was when Bhaskar sensed a movement in the bushes. He did not stop walking but kept looking out from the corner of his eye.

He saw the bushes move again. Perhaps it was a bear or an antelope that had seen them and was moving away, he thought.

The path took two more turns before the soft soil became hard. The stream turned southwards, away from their path. The movement of animals in the streambed was now clear. Bhaskar thought it likely that those animals were following them. If his suspicions were true, once the stream turned away from the path, the animals should step into the open ground.

He kept looking back as he moved forward. He focused on the area where he had seen the bushes shake the last time. Within a few seconds, the animals stepped out from behind the bushes. Two tigers. Bhaskar was startled. Fear surged through his body.

They must have heard the sheep cry and started following them. Bhaskar's heart sank, but he controlled his emotions immediately. He knew what would happen if he showed fear. Even if one among the three got scared and started to run away, he knew the situation would go from very bad to fatal within moments.

They passed a hillock by the side of the path. It was covered in sandra, oil cake and satinwood trees.

'Orey!' he called quickly to the others in a loud voice. 'Run on to that hillock!'

'Why?' asked Sreenu and Ravi.

'Just go!' Bhaskar spoke with such urgency that they all rushed to climb the hillock.

'Put the sheep down,' Bhaskar ordered.

Sreenu put the sheep down and looked at him in confusion.

'There!' Bhaskar said. From between the two hills, they could see the two tigers coming their way, calmly walking through the trees.

Sweat trickled down their backs. Ravi felt his feet tremble.

'Don't be scared,' said Bhaskar, removing the sling tied around his waist. 'These seem to be young tigers. They are not fully grown yet. They are walking side by side but did not have the courage to attack us directly. Get your catapults ready.'

Sreenu took out his sling. Ravi was not carrying his.

Bhaskar and Sreenu stepped away from each other, put stones in the slings and, after whirring them a few times, released them with a feral cry. Ravi screamed along with them.

One of the stones hit one of the tigers straight in its gut. It uttered a guttural growl, jumped a couple of feet in the air and ran back into the bushes by the stream.

The second tiger looked surprised. The stones hit the pebbles near its legs with a loud noise. The splinters from the broken stones rained on its body. It too jumped and ran into the bushes.

The shepherds did not stop. They kept screaming, whistling, shouting and throwing palm-sized stones towards the stream. The stones hit the tree branches and bushes with loud sounds. They could see movement in the vegetation, away from them.

Ravi's fear slowly disappeared, but it took some time for him to calm down. He could still feel his heart beating fast, and there was a slight tremor at the base of his throat. Chasing tigers away as if they were common dogs . . . he was amazed at how they did it.

Bhaskar offered to carry the sheep now, but Sreenu refused. The sheep kept crying till it was settled across his shoulders. They resumed walking on the trail, staying alert and looking closely around the forest. After crossing two more hills, they reached the area known as Tiger Beat. It was a place where tigers usually crossed the main trail.

The rocky terrain changed into plain clay soil. The heavy growth of trees on either side of the path made them anxious. After walking for a while, they observed the birds making agitated sounds from the treetops. Bhaskar found it a bit unnatural and made a sign asking the other two to stop. Walking carefully without making a sound, he looked around the bend at about twenty metres, where the path curved away.

A huge tiger was standing in the middle of the path. It was a mature tiger, fully grown and muscular. Bhaskar gulped. The tiger was about two hundred metres away. He composed himself and signalled to the others to start retreating. They were right behind him. Sreenu understood but tried to peep around the bend.

'It is a big tiger,' hissed Bhaskar. 'If it sees the sheep, it will come straight at us. Make sure that the sheep doesn't make any noise.'

By then, Ravi had taken a look at the tiger. His heartbeat increased. He indicated for Sreenu's catapult to be handed to him.

'It is an adult,' said Bhaskar. 'It won't get scared and will counter-attack.'

They had no clue what to do and were worried that the sheep would make a sound and give them away. All three were sweating profusely. Bhaskar took another look and jumped back. The tiger was walking slowly in their direction. It was a cool, majestic walk.

Without a word, the three turned around and started running. Sreenu fell behind within moments. The other two stopped for him and offered to carry the sheep. But they also feared that if they moved the sheep, it might wail in agony. After running for a little while, they stopped to look behind them. The tiger was not to be seen.

They decided that they should step away from the path in any case. They found a sheet of rock outcrop towards the west and climbed it quickly. From the elevation, they could see the tiger take the bend in the path. Escaping from the tiger seemed impossible unless they left the sheep there and ran away.

Sreenu suggested that they place the sheep on the path and leave. Bhaskar asked him to put the sheep down where they stood. He helped Sreenu lower the animal from his shoulders. If the tiger attacked them, they could leave the sheep there as a distraction.

Then they collected as many big stones as they could. Keeping their axes ready, they hid themselves and the sheep behind a big bush on the outcrop. Ravi knew that if there was no way out, they would have to fight the tiger. He found himself mentally prepared to do it.

They watched the path from their hideout behind the bush. The tiger did not deviate from the path after the bend. Its body glistened under the mild rays of the sun. Despite their predicament, they noticed its proud and kingly gait and beautifully shaped body. It was over two metres long with black-coloured stripes, like the curve of a sickle, on its reddish skin and on its face, like the vermilion stripes worn by devotees of Shiva.

Suddenly, the sheep let out a cry, startling the three of them. It was the one thing that they had hoped would not happen. The tiger seemed to have heard the sheep's cry in that cold silence. It stopped and looked at the outcrop. The sheep cried again.

The tiger resumed walking with the same gait. It did not increase its pace and continued ambling along the path. The three shepherds held their breath and sat tight behind the bush.

The tiger stopped on the path directly in front of the outcrop. It would have to climb over a hundred metres to reach the top of the outcrop where they lay hidden.

Suppressing the fear that gripped them, Sreenu and Bhaskar put stones in their slings. They were determined that whatever may happen, the first stone should hit the tiger squarely. The tiger did not move. It kept looking at the rocky outcrop. Then, quite slowly, it turned towards the outcrop.

As it was about to move forward, they heard some voices. A group of people were coming down the hill to their west. They were on a trail to the east of the outcrop that would meet the path. They could hear voices of men, women and children engaged in loud conversation.

The sheep let out another cry, and the tiger began to move faster. The people on the trail were coming closer to the hillock.

'Who is there?' Bhaskar called. 'There's a tiger on the path! Get on the hillock!'

The newcomers all rushed up the outcrop immediately. There were ten people in the group. The shepherds counted four men, four women and two children. They had dark skin, flat noses and curly hair. The gollas knew that they were yaanadis.

The tiger slowed its walk. The yaanadis saw it too. 'That tiger is in its prime,' said one of the yaanadi men. 'It has been trying to waylay passersby for the past ten days. Two days ago, it stood in the middle of the road near Jyothi. Traffic came to a standstill for about an hour, and the cars and motorcycles had to wait for it to leave the road.'

The sheep gave another plaintive cry. The tiger moved forward steadily. Bhaskar started winding up his sling. He was two whirs from releasing the stone when one of the yaanadi men signalled for him to stop by raising his hand.

The men took some bunches of the sticks the women were carrying. Each stick was only as thick as a finger, but they were bunched together tightly by the dozen. The ends of the sticks were beaten flat. They heaped the dry leaves that they were carrying and lit a fire. The men then dipped the stick-bunches in the flames. They immediately caught fire and started burning like torches.

'As soon as we start down the hillock, you guys start throwing stones,' one of the tribals told the shepherds.

The tiger was approaching them slowly.

Letting out feral cries and brandishing the burning torches wildly, two of the yaanadi men began to walk in the direction of the tiger. The rest of the yaanadis started screaming. Sreenu and Bhaskar joined them while firing heavy stones at the tiger with their catapults. Both found their mark, hitting the tiger on its gut and torso.

The tiger jumped sideways. With an angry glare, it let out a tremendous roar. It was a fearsome sound that echoed in the hills. They released another volley of stones. One whizzed past the tiger's head and crashed into the ground. The other stone smacked straight into its ribs. The yaanadi men began throwing flaming sticks at the tiger as they continued to scream and move forward.

More than the courage of the yaanadis or the nerve of his fellow shepherds, it was the calm surrender of the yaanadi women in sending their men to face the tiger that chased away any remnant of fear in Ravi's heart. He picked up two big stones and ran down the outcrop screaming loudly. The two other yaanadi men followed suit. With bloodcurdling cries, the secondary assault team attacked the tiger with stones.

The painful hits from the rocks, the sight of the flaming torches and the fearsome noises made by the humans scared the tiger a little. It took a backward step. However, it did not go back to the path, and instead began climbing up the hillock to the east. The group chased it, hurling stones by hand and with slings. The tiger jumped off the hillock and disappeared.

The tribals and shepherds celebrated the victory over the tiger with enthusiasm. The women and children also came down and joined in. The two groups then introduced themselves to each other. The yaanadis were from the tribal settlement near Varikuntla. They scoured the forests to gather gum, honey, tuber and nannari roots for a livelihood.

The yaanadis may have faced such incidents before, but for the three young shepherds, it was a completely new experience. They already knew that it was an incident that they would never forget for the rest of their lives. For Ravi, it was no less than a rebirth. Fear slipped out of him, and in its place, he found courage to even face a tiger. Ravi felt surprised at the change in himself.

Engaged in happy conversation, the group failed to notice the movement in the bushes around them until Narsimhulu, one of the yaanadi men, shouted, 'The animal has gone for the sheep!'

The tiger had been hiding behind the trees and bushes and now climbed up the hillock very rapidly. They all started shouting again, throwing stones and running with the torches alight. But before they could move even a few paces, they heard the death cry of the sheep. The stones from the slings hit the bushes nearby.

The group recreated the scary sounds and barrage of stones as they once again climbed up the hillock. But when they reached the top, there was no sign of the sheep nor of the tiger that had dragged it away.

'If you chase it, you will find your sheep,' said Narsimhulu. 'But you won't find it alive. However, the tiger will be furious and likely attack you.'

'It's okay,' said Sreenu. 'That sheep was destined for the tiger's mouth. I took it from the mouths of our people and carried it here for the tiger . . .'

The two groups bade goodbye to each other and headed off in different directions.

They had carried the sheep over such a long distance and risked their lives to fight the tiger only to have to let it become the tiger's meal. The three golla men felt bad. In a way, they also felt that what had happened was natural justice. Like Pullayya kept saying, the jungle would take some form of a toll for allowing them to graze their herds in the hills. In any case, the incident left them richer with a new experience which, while frightening, was also valuable.

When they reached their camp, the rest of the shepherds could scarcely believe the story. The yaanadis were praised by all. With the grass being abundant, the sheep had eaten their fill by the time the three young shepherds returned. The herds descended into the iron stone circuit to drink water.

While cooking near the water source, Pullayya called the three of them to his side. 'I have been a shepherd all my life,' said the old man. 'My father was a shepherd too, as was my grandfather and his father and his grandfather . . . for many generations, grazing sheep has been our livelihood. If the sheep do not eat well, we find it difficult to sleep that night. If an animal bites the neck of one of our sheep, we may not show it, but we will grieve for at least two days.'

He pointed to Ravi and said, 'See, this man's father won't eat if his sheep are starving. If his family request him to eat, he will shout at them. If they shout back, he will cry. As a shepherd, one should love one's animals. No doubt about it. But there should be a limit to that love. Sometimes you have to give up, because your love for a sheep should not become a risk to your life. What if the yaanadis had not shown up at that moment?'

The young men understood the meaning of his words. Gurappa joined them, and old Pullayya started chatting with him. The youngsters went off to eat.

'Whatever it may be,' said Gurappa, sounding happy and excited, 'this has toughened them up, mama! I thought that my son is a coward . . . still can't believe that he rushed at the big fox!'

'Oye oye, pipe down a bit,' Pullayya said quietly. 'If you praise them, they will think no end of themselves. They will then want to throw stones to chase away a tiger that is just passing by and attract its unwanted attention. Our lives are like clay pots being carried on a potter's cart. If the wheel of the cart slips on a stone, the pots will break. If someone throws a stone at the cart, then too the pots will break.'

Gurappa nodded in agreement.

BOOK 2

Community

9

THE HERD MOVED TO the top of the hill as darkness fell. The gollas cleared pebbles from the ground with their feet so that it would be comfortable to lie down later. They were yet to settle the sheep down and open their ration bags for rotis when the dogs started barking as they looked towards the northeast.

The shepherds became alert. A couple of them moved their torchlight in that direction and saw a group of people walking up the hill towards them.

'Who is it?' shouted Gurappa. 'Stop right there!'

As some of the shepherds got ready to go and stop them before they reached the camp, a male voice answered from the group: 'We are the yaanadis, swamy!'

Bhaskar recognised the voice. 'Narsimhulu?' he called. 'Is that you? Come on here.'

Ravi too welcomed them.

'Why are they coming here?' asked Pichchanna. 'At this hour of the night . . .'

The yaanadis stopped at a distance from the herd. Pullayya went over to them.

'We have been roaming around the hill too, swamy,' said Narsimhulu. 'It has been two weeks. We have women and children with us. If we could stay near you, we could sleep properly for at least one night.'

'Didn't you people settle down as watchmen for the orchards in your village?' asked Pullayya.

'Yes, swamy! The government built a colony for us near the Shiva temple. We live in that colony.'

Pullayya asked them a few questions about their parents and grandparents, whom he knew as cowherders. Their answers satisfied him; they were indeed the yaanadis from Varikuntla.

The yaanadis began clearing stones and pebbles away to make their sleeping area.

'Did you all eat anything?' Pullayya asked them.

'We did, swamy!'

'Rice or rotis?'

'Neither . . .'

'Then?'

'We ate the fruit we could gather.'

'What do you mean?'

'Fruit, swamy! Tooky fruit, palmyra, wood apple, palm fruit . . . whatever we could find.'

Some of the shepherds stopped biting into their rotis and looked at the yaanadis in surprise.

'Oh, my goodness!' cried Pullayya. 'Food, my son! Don't you have rice or rotis?'

'We ran out of rations two days ago, swamy,' said one of the women. 'We've been surviving on shoots and fruits.'

The shepherds did not ask any more questions. Each member of the yaanadi group was given one roti, a piece of jaggery and an onion, which they accepted gratefully. They ate without making any sound and then built a fire before lying down.

The gollas could not fathom how the yaanadis had subsisted on small fruits for two days. They could have gone back to procure more rations. Varikuntla was not too far off. Or they could have gone to Jyothi and eaten at the Kasi Nayana ashram. They could have also packed some food from the ashram. The yaanadis did not have the burden of sheep, they wondered, so why make the children starve?

That night, they could hear the roar of the tiger intermittently from the valley below. The cowardly dogs made themselves safe in the middle of the herd.

When they woke up in the morning, the yaanadis were gone. They seemed to have left quite early, well before dawn. The sheep got up enthusiastically. The younger sheep were gambolling around.

Even the baby lamb was in high spirits. It ran around before coming back to its mother. Long-winged and small-bodied birds dominated the sky that morning.

The pleasant weather made even the harsh task of running behind the sheep on rough ground seem like light work. The sky was soon decorated by thin clouds. If it were a cyclone caused by a depression in the Bay of Bengal, the clouds would travel eastward. No such movements could be noticed. One possibility was that of a thermal low formed on the land surface due to heavy water vapor condensation. That could cause rain in some areas. The shepherds' hope was that those rains would fall on their village, allowing them to go back home soon. By afternoon, the clouds had darkened.

'Thank you, dear god, for such a lovely day,' said Gurappa as part of his silent prayers. 'Keep showing us this compassion, father.'

He saw the head ram following a dirt-black sheep. Spitting out the areca nut he was chewing, Gurappa paid attention to the mating ritual. The ram was trying to mount the sheep, but the sheep was not allowing it. It was moving its body around to make it impossible for the ram to mount. Gurappa wondered if the sheep was not ready. But the ram would have smelled the sheep's backside to confirm its readiness and only then attempted the mount.

The ram ignored the grazing and kept up its pursuit of the dark-coloured sheep. For some reason, the sheep kept rebuffing the advances. It hid its tail, constricted itself at the back or moved within the densely packed herd to stay out of the ram's reach. The head ram eventually gave up but continued to stare at the sheep from a distance.

At four years of age, the ram was in its prime. It had long curved horns, a strong body with furry thighs, shining hooves and dew claws. Its forehead was broad and looked hard enough to break a hill rock. It zealously guarded its right to copulate with and impregnate the sheep in its herd.

Gurappa was confused. Either the sheep did not want to be mounted by the ram, or it was simply not ready for intercourse. 'It's just had the one calving so far,' he said to himself. 'Still very young. It will accept the ram's overtures by evening . . . or perhaps tomorrow.'

When they reached a water source, they found the yaanadis resting under the trees by the stream. Narsimhulu greeted them.

'You left quite early?' Bhaskar said, asking the obvious question.

'Yes, swamy . . . our work demands that we rise and move before the birds get up.'

'What did you eat at that hour?'

'Ate the usual fruits and shoots, and licked some honey! One proper meal a day is enough for us.' Narsimhulu produced a rabbit from his gunny bag. 'We set some traps at a watering hole on a nearby hillock and caught three of these. You were the kings who fed us rotis to sake our hunger. If you can cook these rabbits, we would like to eat with you again.'

The shepherds were happy with the proposal.

'It has been ten days since we came into the hills,' said Pamuleti. 'Our taste buds have gone bland. The air, heat and water have made our bodies a bit dull. I have never gone so long without eating meat. Especially on a cloudy day, it would be great to have some meat to bite into, Narsimhulu.'

The yaanadis quickly and efficiently cut the three rabbits into pieces and handed the flesh over to the gollas. Tiripalu and Munayya took on the responsibility of cooking the meat.

'Orey Munayya!' said Pullayya. 'Your father is a very good cook. He even used to cook for small wedding parties. Did you inherit the talent from him?'

'I am not that good,' Munayya replied. 'I have just come to assist this reddy here.' He pointed at Tiripalu.

'He is a good cook indeed,' Gurappa said. 'Oye Tiripalu, one month ago, a relative of yours visited your home, right?'

'Yes, my cousin from Kalsapadu. He is the son of my mother's elder sister. Why?'

'He and I travelled together till Narsapuram. He told me that you cooked a very nice chicken curry for him.'

'Who? Me? I don't even go in the direction of the kitchen at home!'

'Your cousin praised your cooking a lot . . .'

It dawned on all of them that Gurappa was just jesting with Tiripalu.

'You mean at your home, all the chores—washing the utensils, cleaning and swabbing the floor, kitchen work—are done by my brother-in-law?' asked Ankayya.

'That is what it looks like.'

They all laughed lightly.

'I eat at home and step out, that's all,' said Tiripalu as he mixed the masala for the curry. 'I don't ever touch a pot or a pan.'

'Why so?'

'If we go near the stove just once, it will become a lifelong duty.'

'It is not a wrong thing to do, brother,' said Bhaskar.

Tiripalu gave him a considered look and then said, 'Don't be naive. If you bend down for the stove after you get married, your wife will climb on your back. By the time you get free, you would have become an old man.'

'It doesn't matter to us,' remarked Pullayya. 'We are gollas anyway. You need to be careful though, being a reddy and all that.'

'Don't jest with me, ayya,' protested Tiripalu. 'Did I ever claim to be a reddy? Narayya is my father's name. Ramayya is my grandfather's name. I am Tiripalu . . . only those with a lot of money and land call themselves reddy. I am just a kapu, same as you all.'

'How can we be the same, Tiripalu Reddy?' said Gurappa with a smile. 'During election time, don't you wear a white shirt and white dhoti, comb your oiled hair with a side parting and join the other reddys to come and bully us? How can you say we are all the same?'

'Don't bring up that topic, bava! They called me uncle, mama, anna, bava and all that . . . got me high on alcohol and brought me with them. But for that day, have I ever raised my voice with any of you?'

'Then why the aggression that day? What was the problem if we cast our votes for whomever we like?'

'I am in the same boat as you, ayya!' cried Tiripalu. 'If I don't go with them, there would be problems on the road and at home, issues with the extended family . . . too many things to list. What about you guys? You vote as per the diktats of Ramanayya anyway. Having said that, I didn't even cast my vote this year . . .' He stirred the curry with the ladle and then picked out a piece of meat. He offered it to Pullayya and said, 'Let's set aside this useless talk. Taste this piece and tell me.'

Pullayya blew on the meat chunk and then put it in his mouth. 'Excellent!' he declared. 'The bangled hands of women have nothing on your cooking.'

'They say he is an expert at making curry,' Gurappa said, beginning to tease him again. 'He doesn't admit it, but I hear no dish gets cooked at his home without his involvement.'

Tiripalu refocussed on the cooking pot with a smile on his face.

To feed the yaanadis, they each put some extra grain into the rice pot. As they were about to sit down for the meal, served on teak leaves, they heard a voice call from the hill above them. The group lifted their heads to see who it was.

'We are gollas,' Gurappa shouted back. 'Who are you?'

'We need to speak with you,' came the reply from above. 'Should we come down there, or will you come here?'

The shepherds could now see the other group from between the gaps in the trees. It was a ten-member group. The yaanadis saw them too and quickly hid behind the trees. They looked anxious.

Hearing no response, a couple of the newcomers started making their way down the hill.

'Don't let them come here, swamy!' pleaded Narsimhulu. 'Please go and meet them there.'

Pullayya thought that the yaanadis were perhaps worried about sharing the food with the other group. The curry wasn't enough for all of them.

'Oye Gurappa,' he called. 'Go over there and speak to them.'

The yaanadis went into the stream even as Bhaskar and Ravi joined Gurappa in climbing the hill to meet the other group. When they saw the gollas climbing up towards them, the two people walking downhill stopped. Both of them were carrying axes on their shoulders. These were not the slim tools used to cut small branches and creepers but were big and sturdy axes used to cut trees.

The shepherds noticed that all the others in their group were carrying similar axes. Two of them were dressed in shirts and trousers. One of them had a rifle.

'Need to go to Jyothi,' said one of the men. 'Can you tell us a shortcut?'

'Where are you guys coming from?' asked Gurappa.

'From the west.'

'If you'd taken the Manti hill route,' said Gurappa, 'it would have led you directly to Jyothi. You came the wrong way. But okay, come on . . .' He showed them the approach along the hill ranges and explained the route to the wellsprings.

The two men started to climb back up the hill, but after taking a couple of steps, one of them turned around and asked, 'Did you come across a group of yaanadis? Around ten, including women.'

Before Bhaskar could reply, Gurappa quickly said, 'No, we didn't.'

They left, and the three shepherds climbed back down.

'These people have come to cut the red sanders trees too, like the group we met near Balappa's well,' Gurappa told them.

It was not clear why they asked about the yaanadis.

Once they sat back down to eat, Tiripalu looked around for the yaanadis. 'Where have they gone?'

They looked in the streambed and behind the trees. They were nowhere to be found.

'O Narsimhulu!' shouted Bhaskar, but there was no response.

'Must've found a deer or some other small animal,' said Pamuleti, but Ravi suspected they were hiding somewhere in fear of the men from the hill above.

Bhaskar and Ravi started looking for the yaanadis and found them hiding in the bushes behind a rock outcrop. They came out when they heard Bhaskar and Ravi call for them.

'They are demons, swamy!' cried Narsimhulu. 'They are the ones who threw stones at you the other night.'

'How do you know?' Bhaskar asked in surprise.

'We were on the hillock next to where you were that night and saw it all.'

'Okay . . . now come join us for the meal.'

The yaanadi group had fear writ large on their faces. Once they were back with the other shepherds, they all enjoyed a hearty meal. After lunch, when they decided to leave, Gurappa told them that the wood smugglers had left for Jyothi. He told the yaanadis they could stay if they wished.

'They will come back, swamy!'

'No, they won't.'

'They can't even set foot in Jyothi,' said Narsimhulu. 'The area is teeming with police. Near Obulam on one side and near Mudireddypalle on the other. And also near Sovisettipalle and Ambaaram . . . the police have camped all around after they heard that these wood thieves are in the hills.'

The yaanadis left, walking along the streambank.

The gollas now understood why the yaanadis did not go back home and were roaming around the hills, even if it meant not being able to eat properly.

'But will the police ever catch these people by waiting on the roads?' asked Pamuleti. 'There are so many shortcuts and trails. They should come into the hills and catch the smugglers.'

A discussion ensued on the topic for a while, until Pullayya interrupted. 'Orey, listen to me,' said the old shepherd. 'We should not be concerned about all these things. Our group and our herds—that is all we should care about. Why get into all these issues that are irrelevant to us?'

With that, the talk about the smugglers and the police ended. Some of them lay down to rest, while others gathered in groups and conversed quietly.

Gurappa observed his herd. They were peacefully chewing the cud. The dirt-black sheep was standing up. A two-year-old ram was standing right next to the black sheep, and the two were engaged in typical mating rituals such as rubbing their heads against each other and pushing and bumping their bodies together. It is the after play, surmised Gurappa, with the coupling having been consummated a little while ago.

Usually, the head ram would mount the herd sheep that are ready for mating. If the head ram found younger rams trying to mate, it would chase them away. However, it is the younger rams that would engage in foreplay to excite a sheep and get it into the mood for intercourse. Then the head ram would chase the young ram away and mount the sheep. Although, if five to six sheep were ready for mating on the same day, the bigger ones among the younger rams also had a chance, which they would have to take when the head ram was not looking. Gurappa found it amazing that the dirt-black sheep had avoided the much stronger head ram and chosen the younger ram instead. He sat leaning against a tree trunk, lost in thought.

Ravi was in deep discussion with Bhaskar about the people who were cutting down the sandalwood trees. The red sanders trunks with their bark removed had seemed to them like human bodies bleeding red. They were unable to accept the greed-driven destruction of the forest and the inability of the police to come into the hills and apprehend the culprits.

The two young shepherds wondered how these criminals could operate so casually and without fear. They thought it was because they knew that the politicians and even the police were on their side. The two talked about the topic till the sheep had to start moving again.

The herds separated and moved forward, grazing along the brooks and rock-beds. By four in the evening, the clouds darkened further and a slight drizzle began. The raindrops were like fine grains of finger millet pouring from the sky. The herdsmen enjoyed its pleasant sensation as it cooled off their warm bodies. Though hidden by the dark clouds, the sun was still strong enough to evaporate the drizzle before it reached the ground.

The sparrows looked quite busy as they flew hither and thither. They spotted four peacocks with their plumage fully spread on a small hillock near the Berry Tree hill in the west. They were enjoying the delicate sensation of the water sprayed from the sky as they made their dance-like movements. Ravi found the scene magical.

Gurappa walked in front of the herd. Behind him to the right was Bhaskar, with Ravi bringing up the rear. The shepherds had decided to camp that night on the nearby hillock, and from the neighbouring streams and rock plates, the herds were being made to converge on to the hillock.

Gurappa was tapping the ground with his axe head and making the typical sounds to prevent the sheep from straying away from the path or falling over each other's legs. The other two joined him and whistled as the sheep slowed down. The drizzle had stopped by then. One of the bucks tried to rush forward while shaking its head. Gurappa made rapid sounds with his lips and thwacked the nearest tree with the handle of his axe to get the animal back in line.

The male goat suddenly shivered and stepped back. A dark animal stepped out from behind the tree. From the corner of his eye, Gurappa initially mistook it as the goat. But just then Bhaskar shouted, 'Mama, mama!' and startled him. He turned to look at the animal in the darkness that was fast enveloping them. It was an ugly adult bear with dark fur.

The creature bared its teeth and raised its claws as it tried to stand up on its hind legs. Gurappa deftly stepped sideways just as the growling bear was about to jump on him. He noticed two cubs waddling behind it. It was a mother bear.

Ravi and Bhaskar ran towards Gurappa, axes held aloft. Gurappa tried to threaten the bear by shouting and brandishing his axe. While the bear didn't come forward, it did not take a backward step either. It kept growling and remained ready to attack.

All of a sudden, Gurappa's dog swung into action. Looking murderously at the bear, it stretched like a strung bow and gave out a ferocious and fear-inducing war cry. Then it barked loudly and started lunging at the bear. Gurappa held it back, holding on to its waist with difficulty. He shouted at the two young men running towards him to stop.

The bear took two steps back, drawing its children closer. The three of them understood that its fear and aggression were for the sake of its cubs.

'Let us move away,' said Gurappa, stepping back. 'She will leave by herself.'

The bear gently pushed its cubs in front of it and went down the hill. It looked back a few times to ensure no one was following them. The cubs were very young and struggled to keep up with the mother.

Gurappa went to the tree and peered carefully through the branches. Honeybees were buzzing around a spot on a branch. The honeycomb on the ground explained the situation to Gurappa. The mother bear had broken the hive on the branch and was feeding honey to its cubs when their presence had scared it.

It was completely dark by the time all the sheep reached the hilltop and settled down. Ravi reflected on his father's behaviour. If he hadn't stopped the two of them, Bhaskar and Ravi would have surely hacked at the bear with their axes. The infant bears would have been orphaned.

The bear might be a wild animal from a human's perspective. But it was a mother to the cubs. His father understood the bear's situation, and that's why he restrained his dog too. Ravi saluted Gurappa in his thoughts.

At the same time, Gurappa was wondering about his dog's behaviour. He found it strange as it had never acted like that before. It reacted immediately when the bear was about to attack him. What a scary and powerful cry it had! It had shown no fear in lunging at a much bigger animal. It had proved wrong all those shepherds who called it cowardly and lazy. It acted only when it needed to, perhaps showing its gratitude for the good food it was fed.

The conversation at dinner drifted to the yaanadis, as they had not come back to the golla camp. The shepherds figured that they must have found a cosy spot somewhere for the night, because they knew the hills very well.

10

THE SHEPHERDS ATE ROTI for breakfast after completing the morning inspection of the flock. Gurappa leaned back against a tree as he ate. His dog watched him eat. Gurappa tore half a roti and fed it to the dog. It chomped noisily. In the mornings, Gurappa's dog ate a full roti, the same as any man in the group. At lunch, it ate more than a man, relishing the rice mixed with sheep milk that Gurappa served it lovingly. But it didn't touch a morsel at night and stayed awake till dawn.

The shepherds felt hungry all the time during hill-grazing. They needed to eat two full rotis per meal to satisfy their appetite. But eating two rotis for every meal would mean running out of rotis before the next ration period. So they had to make do with one and a half rotis for each meal.

Three sers of bajra flour would usually yield thirty rotis, but some golla women made twenty thick rotis from it. One and a half portions of the thicker roti was enough for a meal, but the gollas who received thick rotis had to subsist on just one such roti per meal. Thus, the men almost never felt full.

The toughest part was to survive on only five litres of water for every twenty-four-hour period, using only that quantity for all their bodily needs. Sometimes, the water they found to replenish their stores would be dirty with worms crawling inside. After spending a day under a hot sun, running behind the sheep up and down the hills, unable to stop and rest for even a few minutes while trying to survive with such little water, sometimes the shepherds felt as if they were being punished for sins they had committed in a previous life. One could bring more food and water along, but it was not possible to walk the hills carrying heavy loads.

Ankayya gave half a roti to Gurappa's dog. Gurappa asked him, 'What did you eat? Just the other half? Will that be enough for the whole day?'

'I didn't feel like eating,' replied Ankayya.

The yaanadis again showed up at their camp. The gollas offered them some rotis but they declined, citing lack of hunger. 'Yesterday's lunch was quite filling,' they said. 'We ate a lot, so we won't feel hungry till lunchtime today.'

Ravi found their statement interesting. Even if one didn't do any work, one felt the pangs of hunger every few hours. How could these yaanadis say that one full meal would suffice for twenty-four hours? He wondered if these tribal people had habituated their bodies to survive on one meal a day like other jungle creatures that ate only occasionally. A python could lie idle for a couple of weeks after swallowing an animal, and a tiger could stay without food for a few days after a hunt and a hearty meal.

However, Ravi could see the hunger in the children's eyes. They looked as if they would readily accept the rotis on offer. Ravi offered one roti each to the two children. They looked at their parents and initially refused but relented when he forced the roti into their hands. They immediately started munching with eager mouths.

'Where did you all sleep last night?' asked Bhaskar.

The yaanadi named Obulesu pointed out a hillock below. 'There, it's known as Tortoise hill.' From their elevation, the hillock did indeed resemble a tortoise.

No one asked the yaanadis why they didn't come to the golla camp to sleep. It was assumed that they didn't come because of the women. The four dark-complexioned tribal women were thin, with not much flesh on their bones. They were all young and easy on the eye but seemed to lack any of the delicate feminine qualities of women their age. They wore faded sarees and worn-out blouses, and their short hair was reddened by the sun and had broken ends due to a lack of nourishment. They walked barefoot and looked famished, an overall pitiable condition.

The gollas still didn't know why these people ran away when they saw the wood smugglers.

'You said there is police watching the roads,' said Pullayya. 'But the men who were headed to Jyothi seem to have reached their homes?'

'No, swamy, they have all returned, right?' replied Narsimhulu.

'Returned? No, not this way.'

'Maybe the police chased them. They climbed over the twin hillocks until Eagle Nest hill and walked past Siddappa's heaps. Then, from the Gopidevi trough, they took the path towards Balappa's well. We saw them at dusk yesterday, hurrying away.'

Pullayya thought that it was quite possible that the yaanadis were correct.

The gollas forced the tribals to take a roti and an onion each. The yaanadis accepted the food and folded their hands in gratitude. After they had eaten the rotis and drunk some water, Ravi and Bhaskar took Narsimhulu aside.

'Why were you scared of them the other day, when you all ran away?' asked Ravi.

'Our lives will get destroyed if they catch hold of us, swamy!' said Narsimhulu, his voice fearful.

'What will they do?'

'Our young men have had their lives ruined by them. Many are now rotting in jails.'

'Why?'

'Smuggling cases of red sanders, swamy. Non-bailable offenses!'

'What do you have to do with red sanders?'

Narsimhulu was quiet for a while. Then, with a deep sigh, he opened up. 'Our home is no longer the yaanadi colony, swamy. It is deemed the abode of wood thieves. Irrespective of where the police find sandalwood logs, they find the thieves only in our colony. It is true that some of our youth went to cut the red sanders trees out of greed for money. And they were later used to transport the logs. Our people saw money. They got new motorbikes, TVs, dish antennas, stoves and mixer-grinders. The women started wearing fancy sarees and blouses.'

Narsimhulu told them that they had depended on the gum from the trees and the fruits, roots and tubers they found in the forest. There had been no dearth of food, but money only started coming in after the trees were cut. Their people did not realise that along with the trees, the tigers and leopards that depend on the forest would also enter their homes. And they first came in the form of the police.

In a colony where poverty was prevalent, the sudden affluence ensured the police didn't have to look elsewhere for the culprits. All the youngsters were sent to jail. After that, even the older men were carted off to prison. Someone would arrange for a bail and release . . . but after a few days, the police would find sandalwood somewhere and raid the colony again, arresting whomever they could find.

The yaanadis became the sacrificial lambs in the game played between the smugglers and the police. Even if the smugglers were caught red-handed, at the police station they were replaced by some yaanadis. And when people like Narsimhulu's group left the colony and began living in the forests, they became the target of police searches.

'We have left our homes, swamy,' said Narsimhulu in a voice hoarse with sadness. 'We live in the forest now. We don't have any fear in these forests, because no one can catch us here. Yes, we struggle to find food sometimes, but the forest is our mother, swamy!'

'If the police catch us, they will lock us up and foist some case or the other on us,' said Obulesu. 'If the wood smugglers catch us, our women and children will be held ransom and we will have to do their bidding. It has become a curse that we know every inch of these hills. We know where the trees are, and the routes to bring the wood out of the forest. They won't leave us at all if they catch hold of us, swamy!' He was in tears. 'The trees are like our own children, and they made us cut down so many trees with our own hands.'

Ravi and Bhaskar felt their hearts melt. They were at a loss for words. It was not a problem they could solve. The issue wouldn't be resolved until the red sanders thieves left the forest. Even the government was unable to chase them away.

'Come to the water source in the afternoon,' Bhaskar finally said. 'Have some lunch with us.'

'No, swamy,' said Narsimhulu. 'You will starve if your rations run out.'

'Don't worry, we can always get rations delivered.'

'Where do you go during the day?' asked Ravi. 'How do you pass the time?'

'We don't ever sit around, swamy! We keep gathering roots, tubers, gum or honey all the time.'

'Where? I always see you all empty-handed!'

'We have a place where we stash all the things we gather. It is under the rock plates. We cover the opening with thorny bushes and branches tightly tied together.'

The shepherds didn't ask for the location of their stash nor did Narsimhulu volunteer that information.

'When the time and weather are conducive,' continued Narsimhulu, 'we use secret trails and reach Varikuntla. There is someone there who buys our stuff. We sell it for whatever price we get and buy rations with that money. Fearing the police, we haven't ventured out that way for the past two weeks.'

With heavy hearts, Ravi and Bhaskar watched the yaanadis leave. Ravi briefed the rest of the group about the conversation. The shepherds all said that they would be happy to provide lunch to those forest dwellers, should they return.

The entire morning, Ravi was haunted by the travails of the yaanadis. A searing anger at the red sanders smugglers took root in him and grew. When he could, he shared his anguish with Bhaskar.

When they brought the herds to the water source, they saw the yaanadis camped atop the rocks on one side of the brook. The four yaanadi men were huddled near a big stone slab and were busy with something. The children were trying to meddle in the matter. The women were seated under the trees a little distance away, picking lice off each other's hair and grooming themselves.

The shepherds filled water in their cans first and then allowed the sheep to drink in batches. The sheep stood on the bank and bent their knees to reach the water. Gurappa went over to the stone slab.

'You seem to have caught some animal?'

'Yes, swamy,' replied Narsimhulu. 'A kura pandi.'

It meant a 'small pig', but it wasn't really a pig. Bigger than a rabbit and tipping the scales at four kilograms on average, the kura pandi had a mouth shaped like a wild sheep but the ears and teeth of a pig. It had spots on its body like an antelope and lived under stone plates or in dense bushes. Usually, the meat of a wild animal is tough, but the flesh of the kura pandi was soft. Its nourishing, oily meat melted in the mouth with a heavenly flavour.

'We found it near the tandra tree by the stream, swamy. It saw us and scurried under the rock plates. We surrounded it but couldn't make it come out. This little boy of mine then squeezed himself in, under the rocks. The animal was sprightly . . . it threatened the boy, but he pulled it out by its leg. It will make a tasty curry, swamy!' Narsimhulu ruffled his son's hair.

Gurappa looked at the little boy. These yaanadi kids were apprenticing with their parents and learning how to find food at such a young age. No schooling or literacy for them, no proper path to survive and thrive. Leave alone these children in the hills, Gurappa thought, even in the villages people like him did not get an education until recently. His generation of shepherds did not attend school though there was one in their village.

Among the kapus though, many went to school and got jobs. After seeing them lead a comfortable life and being spoken about respectfully as 'reddy garu', a change occurred in the mindset of the gollas. Gurappa was the first of the gollas to send his children to school. Because his younger son did so well in his studies, he thought of making him a salaried employee. He invested beyond his capabilities in Ravi's education to try and ensure that Ravi never had to run behind sheep or do any shepherd work—which he hadn't, till now.

As some of the other gollas walked over to the rocks, Gurappa made a conscious effort to get rid of the thoughts buzzing in his mind. He turned around and saw that his son was engaged in a serious conversation with Bhaskar, Ramachandra and Sreenu.

When Ravi had returned from Hyderabad, he was all shiny skin and handsome looks. But his real complexion had come out in the jungle. In the two weeks of hill-grazing, his body had attained the same dark and sun-beaten complexion as the rest of the gollas.

Gurappa could not see any difference between Ravi and the other golla youth gathered around him. There was nothing special about him. He was just a golla like the others. Even after his father spent lakhs on his education, Ravi eventually turned out to be a shepherd. His learnings had vanished into the streams and the truncheon stick used to herd the sheep had appeared in his hands.

Gurappa could not bear the anguish of his disappointment and sat down under an axlewood tree. He tried to lie down on the ground with his head on the tree's roots but had to hurriedly get up as Pullayya approached. He wiped his tears off with his headscarf.

Pullayya squatted on his haunches next to Gurappa and asked, 'Do you reckon we'll get into trouble with these yaanadi folk?'

'Trouble?' Gurappa said. He thought for a moment and then replied, 'They don't strike me as troublesome folk, mama.'

'These are good folk all right, if somewhat naive,' said Pullayya. 'But don't you see the traps laid all around for these people? If they step out of the hills, the police are waiting to catch them. And the red sanders smugglers are looking for them inside the forest. Two groups of "wild animals" lying in wait for them on both sides. If we take them under our wing, might one of these animals attack us too? As you know, we are not alone. Each one of us is responsible for fifty lives. Why do we have to add to our existing burden?'

Gurappa did not say anything for a while. With his mind clouded by the despair about his son, he could not find it in him to respond properly. 'Yes, I don't know,' he said finally. 'Maybe you are right . . .'

'These kids seem to respect no limits,' said Pullayya, gesturing at the golla youth. 'They are hatchlings unaware of the hunter's arrow. Only if they get bruised will they learn to be vigilant. They are like the one who would claim a thorn bush by the roadside by covering it with a towel. You should warn them. Don't make me get involved.'

Gurappa took a while to compose himself. He spat out his well-chewed tobacco leaf and then said, 'What do I tell them, mama? It is the hot blood of youth. Even if the trail is full of stones, they would stomp on them and move ahead. Youthful exuberance.'

'Your son has joined them too.'

'My son! Did you not see him faint when the hyena showed up the other day?'

'It is not his mistake,' retorted Pullayya. 'Have you ever assigned a task to him? Ever made him walk behind the herd for a day? The palms and feet have to get hardened, only then will the heart toughen. I sometimes wonder . . . this boy is so shy even among his own people in the village. How will he get on in the big strange city?'

Gurappa quietly lifted his head and looked at Pullayya.

'Before one sends a man to a strange place, how should one train him? You did not teach him the strength of a monitor lizard nor the fighting style of an eagle. Your boy is confident as long as he is amid books. I used to think that he kept himself to books because he didn't know how to face the outside world. In any case, I think he is no longer a softie. Not a chick from the poultry farm any more—he has become a fighting cock.'

Gurappa did not reply. Pullayya left him to his thoughts.

*

They cooked and ate the kura pandi for lunch. Those who'd never eaten its meat before found its taste a little different from what they were used to.

After lunch, the younger shepherds gathered for a meeting at a spot a little removed from the camp. The yaanadi men joined them. They were discussing some topic quite intensely.

The young gollas often stole glances at old Pullayya. They also noticed that Gurappa was observing their discussion. Pullayya assumed that they were just chatting casually to kill time, while Gurappa's mind was still occupied with thoughts about his son. Pullayya's words had created a new bother. Gurappa couldn't tell whether the old man was criticising him or giving him a compliment.

Gurappa had wanted to avoid these hardships for his son. He had kept him away from shepherding so that he could focus on his studies. The herd had helped to pay for the cost of educating Ravi. Even after Ravi had completed his degree and was searching for a job, Gurappa had managed to meet his expenses by selling a ram or a sheep every month.

What could he teach his son now? Should he train him in the core skills again? Wasn't that the purpose of education? Gurappa was lost in his thoughts.

Later, even as the herds were moving about and grazing, the golla youngsters huddled together whenever there was an opportunity. Some of the others, like Pichchanna, even overheard some of their words. The young gollas seemed to be agitated that it was the sandalwood smugglers who had attacked their herds. Pichchanna felt the same anger too.

'We should give a proper spanking to those sons of bitches,' Pichchanna heard Bhaskar saying.

The yaanadis met them again on the hilltop at night. They arranged their sleeping area to the north of the shepherds' camp.

11

IT WAS PAST NINE. Under the faint light of the distant stars, the forest seemed to have wrapped itself in a blanket of dark trees and fallen into a deep sleep. A cool silence enveloped the surroundings. Even the sound of a leaf falling could be heard clearly. An animal cried somewhere down in the valley and in the distance a bird flapped its wings.

The animals that roamed around the forest through the day foraging for food, rested now in safe nooks on branches, inside thick bushes or in rock crevices. Other animals that were active at night, hunted for food, creating ripples of noise here and there in the forest.

The shepherds were in deep slumber after another tiring day. One of the yaanadi men sat up and stirred the other three men awake. They moved silently and woke six of the golla youth. Meanwhile, the two yaanadi children also got up.

The group melted into the darkness wordlessly and began descending the hill. They were walking briskly. The gollas saw the two children running behind, trying to catch up with the adults.

'Why are they coming?' asked Bhaskar.

'They won't get caught, swamy!' said Obulesu. 'Let them come . . . might be useful.'

Ravi was surprised to see one of the children carrying a bow and arrows. They said that the weapon had belonged to some from the sugaali tribe, who may have misplaced it.

'Did you ask them to bring bows and arrows?' asked Bhaskar. 'Or is it their idea?'

'We did not even wake them up, swamy! Entirely their idea.'

Ravi was confused and fascinated by those children. They had probably prepared themselves after they had overheard the discussion between the tribal men and the young shepherds at lunchtime, when they had agreed upon the course of action. The children seemed to be around thirteen or fourteen years old. There wasn't much muscle on their bodies due to lack of nutrition, but they looked sharp and alert like snakes.

The group walked through the valley for about an hour, after which they reached plain ground surrounded by rolling hills. The men divided themselves into three groups and climbed up the slopes. They could now see the ground below clearly, and spotted the light from a campfire burning near a group of trees. They decided that a circle with a radius of about ten yards around the campfire would be the target of their attack.

Ravi and Bhaskar were on the western slope. Two yaanadis were with them. On the northern slope, one yaanadi accompanied Ramachandra and Sreenu. Jayaramulu and Mohan readied themselves on the eastern slope, along with the fourth yaanadi. They'd left the southern side open.

As the western slope was the farthest, they decided to wait for a signal from Ravi and Bhaskar once they had reached their position. The two yaanadi children also went with them. The shepherds removed the slings from their waists and collected a heap of stones.

Upon getting a nod from an adult, one of the yaanadi boys placed fingers in his mouth and produced a cry exactly like that of a jungle fowl. His thin and sharp scream ascended in waves and resounded through the valley. The boy made the sound again and again. It was met with answering calls from the other slopes.

From the eastern side, three stones were released simultaneously from the slings. They flew through the air and hit the ground near the campfire. It was followed by three more stones each from the northern and western slopes, crashing into the branches and the ground near the fire. There were thudding sounds and sparks rose from the fire.

Chaos engulfed the area surrounding the fire. People started to yell.

'Who is that?'

'Rey! Get up you all! Some bastards are throwing stones!'

'We will kill you sons of bitches!'

There was more screaming and swearing as they alerted each other.

'Take the rifle . . . shoot the bastards!'

Ignoring their shouts, the shepherds and yaanadis kept at their attack. The stones continued to rain on the wood thieves. The two children were really quick at collecting stones and handing them over to the adults. The men showed their expertise in slinging precisely targeted stone missiles.

They heard a loud scream. One of the stones seemed to have found its mark, hitting someone. It excited the gollas and the yaanadis even more, and they increased the ferocity of the attack. Suddenly, a rifle shot pierced the air, and the sound echoed through the hills and valleys. The stone throwing stopped for almost a minute. And then it started again.

The sandalwood smugglers fired two more rounds from the rifle, but they soon realised that none of the stone throwers were within range. None of the smugglers had the guts to walk closer to the elevation to shoot the rifle. They also observed that the stones were coming from three sides and none from the south. Some more of them were hit. There were no big trees around to provide cover.

The attackers seemed to have an inexhaustible supply of stones. The stone throwing intensified. The thieves could not fathom who they were, and why they were attacking. They even screamed to reveal their identity and clarify that they were not shepherds and didn't have any sheep. Some still shouted threats in a loud voice even as the stones continued to rain down on them.

More thieves got injured by the barrage of stones, which also crashed into the burning logs, making them scatter and thus weakening the fire. Some heavier stones thwacked into thinner rock plates, and broken rock fragments flew into the air. A few stones hit the bags of the thieves and made a clanging sound when they hit a vessel. Some bags broke open, and their utensils got dented badly by the rock missiles.

There was no respite from the stoning for the thieves to even gather their belongings. By then, most of them had received injuries, but no one seemed to have been hit on the head so far. It was clear to the thieves that they needed to run away to save their lives. The group immediately started running towards the southern side. The stones kept chasing them.

'Rey!' screamed one of the thieves. 'We will hunt you down tomorrow during the day! We will not leave you alive, wherever you might hide in the hills.' This attracted a few stones in his direction. Two of the thieves received serious injuries, while a third fell down. When the man next to him tried to shout and help him up, he was warned by the others not to make any noise lest more stones were hurled at them.

The attackers on the eastern slope stayed in position. The teams from the western and northern slopes walked down to the flat ground. They found ten bags of rations near the fire. It seemed to be a big group of sandalwood thieves. The shepherds and yaanadis had prevailed, and their anger was sated. They had managed to attack and chase away the enemies.

'Let's get out of here quickly,' urged Bhaskar. 'Maybe they will return since the attack has stopped.'

Ravi agreed with him. They had attacked as a group, so he felt no fear, though there was a slight tremble within. 'Come on, let's go!' he said.

'They won't come back now,' said Narsimhulu. 'But they will probably search the hills tomorrow morning.'

A sliver of fear entered their minds. No one showed it openly, but they were all apprehensive of the smugglers' vengeance. The yaanadis quickly tied the ration bags from the camp on both sides of two long wooden poles. They all wanted to leave the place as soon as possible.

Narsimhulu took two arrows from the boy carrying the bow. He planted one at the base of a tree and another on the ground nearby. No one understood why he did that nor did they have the time to ask him about it.

They started walking along the trail silently, with their hearts in their mouths. They walked as fast as their legs would allow and finally reached the hill where their herds were camped. The moon was high above them and there was faint lightning in the sky in the east. It was around midnight.

The men slithered into the camp, making no noise as they reached their respective stations beside the herds. With no master guarding the boundary of the herd, some of the sheep had shoved their way through, crossed the line and descended a few yards. The returning shepherds quickly prodded those sheep in the guts and pushed them back into the herd. A smell unnatural for that time of the night spread in the air. It was the smell that arises in the morning when the herd is made to stand up.

A few moments after they had all lain back down, someone started talking in their sleep.

'I am feeling ashamed, Subhadra! Come home, dear. Let us attend the wedding together. I will walk behind you . . . or walk holding your hand . . . or carry me like you would carry a child!'

It was Ankayya. Bhaskar and Ravi were close by. They suppressed their laughter.

It took them quite a while to fall asleep after the thrill of their adventure. They had done something out of the ordinary. The events of the past few hours kept flitting behind their closed eyes. They eventually drifted off to sleep sometime in the wee hours.

The yaanadis woke up at the crack of dawn and vanished into the hills along with the ration bags captured from the thieves. The gollas too got up. The ones who had joined the attack got up along with the others, but their lack of sleep was evident in their eyes. Even after they had sprinkled some water on their faces, the dull look of sleeplessness did not leave them. It stood out the way a dog's red tongue lolls out as it pants.

There was a sense of excitement. It had been a new kind of experience. At the same time, they were worried about the sandalwood thieves crossing their path as they searched for their attackers.

'You were shoving the sheep back into the herd at midnight,' Pullayya asked Jayaramulu. 'What happened?'

The old man seemed to have sensed something. But Jayaramulu did not miss a beat in his reply. 'They were the dumb ones that sneeze and bleat at night,' he said. 'A couple of them came and fell on me. I had packed them a little too tight last night, I guess.'

Pullayya looked at him suspiciously.

'There was such a racket last night,' he said. 'Did you not stir even a little? Was it such a sound sleep?'

'Yes,' replied Jayaramulu. 'I was dead like a log and did not realise what had happened until the sheep went past me. Probably the effect of the kura pandi curry . . .'

Pullayya's questions seeded some doubts in Gurappa's mind too.

'Bhaskar, you don't seem to have slept at all last night,' he said. 'Did you all go somewhere?'

'Where would we go without your knowledge, mama!'

'I think there was a clash last night at some distance. I could hear some rifle shots as well. I wonder if the cops ambushed the smugglers. Did you all get scared?'

Gurappa provided enough content for the young shepherds to frame an answer to his question.

'How could we not be?' said Bhaskar. 'We were shit scared that the fight might spill over to our side. Could not sleep a wink the whole night.'

'Why were you so scared?' asked Gurappa, who found their fear a bit amusing. 'No one would bother with stupid shepherds like us. Everyone knows that we don't harm the trees nor the animals in the hills. At worst, they might ask us for a sheep to feed their craving for mutton. That is all.'

The shepherds then went to check on their herds as they went about their usual morning chores.

The six young shepherds gathered when they stepped away for their ablutions and again while having their rotis for breakfast. They reminded each other about the need for caution and carefully observed the surrounding peaks and valleys. What if the smugglers, smarting from last night's attack, combed the hills and decided that it was the gollas who stoned them? The sandalwood thieves cut the trees in the forest for money. They would go to any lengths to remove obstacles to their business.

It had been five days since they received fresh rations, so they had three days to go before the next supply. However, they had been sharing their rations with the yaanadis and had only a day's worth of rice and rotis left. At least the yaanadis wouldn't starve for the next ten days, now that they had the rations of the smugglers. They wouldn't need anything from the gollas.

The golla youth had taken an enormous risk for the sake of the yaanadis. They were fortunate to have prevailed over the smugglers. If their plan had backfired, the gollas would have had to abandon their flocks and run away. Ravi wondered silently if they had made a big mistake.

The idea was to chase the smugglers away from the hills to give the yaanadis some respite. They had also felt grief for the red sanders trees being felled by the smugglers. That emotion, together with the desire to take revenge for their earlier attack, had spurred the gollas. Why fear the consequences now, Ravi asked himself, after the deed was done? Hadn't they agreed they would mount another night-time attack if needed?

Ravi thought the sheep were the reason for their fear, weakness and cowardice. If a tiger confronted the sheep, they would simply offer their neck instead of running away. Even if a small fox grasps at the neck of a sheep, instead of fighting, it would simply submit. We are the masters of these sheep, thought Ravi, masters of a bunch of cowardly sheep. And hence, we share their fear.

Ravi spoke with Bhaskar again as the herds grazed. The yaanadis would observe the movements of the smugglers and alert the gollas of any impending danger, they reassured themselves.

The grass was not as soft as it had been a week ago. The bases had toughened. The sheep were biting fresh grass shoots as they moved forward. Ravi observed the antics of the little lamb with some amusement and affection. It would run beside the mother for a while, lie down while the mother sheep stopped to graze and then jump up to run and catch up with the mother again. And where it could, the lamb tried to eat the soft grass.

The lamb was now used to Ravi and halted when he called it. It didn't run away when he came close. When Ravi picked it up, the lamb seemed to like it. Some of the herds were climbing up the hillocks on either side, while the others were grazing the dry grass on the harder ground below.

The elevation was covered by sandra, a tree that doesn't grow straight. Both the trunk and the branches bend and grow crooked. But it is hard to find a more resilient wood. It is considered the best wood for the pillars of a hut. It can last a generation and beyond without rotting at the base. Even worms cannot infect it. It is wood like iron.

Between the sandra trees, they could see some oilcake and satinwood trees. Beyond the trees, there was a further stretch of hard ground along with sheet rock.

'Don't let them go on to the hard ground,' shouted Gurappa. 'Drive them back!'

'Why?' asked Ravi.

'All sheer rock. Not a single blade of grass . . . see that one with the tiny ears has wandered there. Drive it back!'

Surprised by the impatience and anger in his father's voice, Ravi herded the sheep back. On the other side of the rocky ground, some cuckoo-like birds rose up into the sky making excited noises. Ravi had not noticed them till now.

'There could be tigers around those rock banks,' Gurappa screamed again. 'You come back too!'

The warning did not sink into Ravi's brain right away. When he understood, he felt his legs shake a little. About two hundred metres from him, an animal had jumped from the bank on the other side on to the hard ground. It was an adult tiger.

The tiger took four steps forward and stood majestically, looking straight ahead at Ravi. Gurappa had sensed its presence from the cries of the birds and alerted Ravi, but his reaction had not been quick enough. Now his whole body trembled and his hands and legs were paralysed with fear.

The tiger had sickle-curve stripes, its body almost three metres in length, its head the size of a big pot. It was gazing steadily in their direction. If it started to run, it would take only a few seconds to reach Ravi. He was unable to slink away into the trees beside the rocky ground. The axe started to slip from his hands.

Gurappa appeared next to him, held his arm and pulled him back. Bhaskar showed up too. 'Rey, take the sling out,' he said to Ravi as Sreenu arrived there as well and took out his sling. Bhaskar and Sreenu both picked up heavy stones and readied their slings. Ravi tried to remove his sling too, but his hands were unwilling to cooperate. However, he was feeling calmer than before.

'Orey orey, stop now,' whispered Gurappa. 'The tiger's standing on an elevation. We are down here. We won't be able to handle it if it lunges at us nor would we be able to escape. It is a fully grown animal. Don't tangle with it. It is still fearful of us humans. See, it has not taken a step forward. Don't excite it and make it lose its fear of men.'

Gurappa's words managed to briefly hold their slings back until four more gollas joined them. Ramachandra gave out a wild scream and banged his axe head against the trunk of a sandra tree. The tree swayed with the impact and some leaves fluttered down. The others followed suit, thumping the trees and rocks with their sticks and axes while screaming at the top of their voices and creating a sense of mayhem.

Bhaskar and Sreenu gathered the courage to hurl stones from their slings. The stones flew on either side of the tiger and hit some rocks close to it. The tiger was not perturbed at all. It roared loudly and turned its neck to look at them sideways. Then it disappeared into the trees.

The gollas continued making threatening noises and hurling stones for a few more minutes. After that they deftly moved the herds and took them a fair distance away in a short time. The intensity of Ravi's fear reduced and the beating of his heart quietened. The vestiges of the fright remained in his body for some time though, and he felt weak. He sensed that being with a crowd melted his fears away faster.

Later, while cooking their lunch at a water source, Gurappa said to Pullayya, 'Did you see it, mama? What steel in its eyes! Arrogance seeping through every pore of its body . . . the recklessness of brute power! So many of us hollered at it but not a single hair moved on its body. If cornered, it would surely bite a man!'

Pullayya replied, 'Don't do stupid things. What does it need? A little food for its belly. Let the tiger have its prey. Maybe it will eat one sheep, that's all. The tiger has hunger too . . . let him eat. We should not make it learn a new taste—which we will, if we stop it from having its due.'

They all understood what he meant by the tiger acquiring a new taste.

'And you,' said Pullayya, turning to Ravi. 'I believe you peed in your pants?'

'Yes, I did get shit scared,' Ravi admitted.

'Didn't you confront a tiger near the hillock besides the Tiger Beat area a few days back? The fear must have vanished, right? Why did it come again?'

'I was with a lot of people then . . . and that gave me the courage to throw stones along with them. This time it was just me, all alone! The way it stood there looking at me, my hands and legs froze.'

Pullayya laughed lightly. 'At the Tiger Beat you had lost your fear and hence challenged the tiger with your bare hands by throwing stones at it,' he said. 'Here, you brought your fear back and peed down your legs. But you are the same person now as you were then. Fear is the only factor that was different. A golla needs to get rid of his fear first.'

Pullayya went on to enumerate the benefits of handling one's fear and the disadvantages of allowing it to cling to one. Gurappa too listened to him intently, gesturing at the others to not interrupt the old man.

'I have a question,' said Ravi when Pullayya had finished speaking. 'Even with so many of us creating a ruckus and throwing stones, why did the big tiger not show any fear? It walked away as if it was generously allowing us to escape today. Before that, the tiger and I were standing face to face. Even the axe had slipped out of my hand, and I was rooted to the spot . . . and yet, the tiger did not lunge at me. Why? It just stood there looking at me but did not take a step forward.'

Pullayya scratched his head for a few moments.

'Any fanged animal fears humans, son,' he eventually said. 'It is habituated to hunt four-legged animals. Those animals have their head lowered towards the ground. The tiger's gaze is only on the neck and the throat. It knows that grabbing the throat would take the life out of its prey. We are different. We are not bent towards the ground. We stand straight. The tiger does not know where to attack us. It doesn't know where our throat is.'

The old man paused and then continued, 'A cornered tiger doesn't find it easy to lunge at a man,' he said. 'If it has to, it will come at him and wrestle him, and then bite him all over the body. When the man bends down or falls to the ground, it susses out his anatomy and locates the throat. That's when it grabs hold of the throat to kill the man. And once a tiger figures out how to attack and kill a man, it stops fearing humans.'

'Such a big animal fearing humans is so strange,' said Ravi.

'Don't we run away from a snake that is hardly as thick as a finger?' replied Pullayya. 'Yet we are not afraid of a bigger animal like a buffalo or an ox. Why do men fear snakes? Even the ones without venom? Like the snake is to us humans, we are to the tiger. In the tiger's eyes we are a venomous creature that might pose some danger to it.'

All of them felt it was a reasonable explanation.

'Be careful,' Pullayya added. 'It is a mature tiger, reigning over this area like a king. We are in its kingdom. At some point, it will attack the flocks. Scare it away but do not confront it directly. If it stands on the trail, get off it and take another route. It is the king here and it will take its toll from us in the form of a sheep or two. Let us be sensible, pay our dues and go away to another hill. As the saying goes, "The reddy of one village could be a servant in another."'

Ravi found Pullayya's way of thinking quite novel. To assume a kingdom for an animal, accept its suzerainty and be ready to pay tax . . . maybe that is what the law of the jungle was, he thought.

12

BY THE TIME THE herds reached the top of the hillock, the evening shadows had darkened into twilight. The calls of a wide array of birds ascended up the hill as they returned to their nests in the trees down in the valley. Ravi had never seen so many types of birds or heard such sounds. He could not match the calls to the birds.

The shepherds checked on their flocks and attended to the sheep that had thorns stuck in their hooves or had fallen and twisted an ankle. The ones that looked dull or had slowed down were closely inspected. During the day, some of the sheep had got stuck between rocks or in thorny bushes and had scraped their hide in the struggle to extricate themselves. The shepherds treated the wounds that were oozing blood. Three to four gollas assessed an injured sheep together, identified the problem and decided on an immediate solution.

Slipping away from the herds and their busy elders, with the excuse of relieving themselves, the group that had gone on the night expedition went to the very edge of the hill. They squatted on the rocks there and deliberated their next course of action. It was a matter of some concern that the yaanadis had not showed up that day. They were supposed to provide an update.

The young men decided that it would be fine as long as the sandalwood thieves did not suspect the gollas. They had moved quite a distance away from the area of attack, but the thieves were unlikely to give up their pursuit so easily. The trees they felled gave the sandalwood smugglers their money and power; they would not permit hindrances to their operations.

The action of the gollas and the yaanadis had posed a grave challenge to the smugglers. Usually, their challenges came from the outside world—the police, the forest department and the government—not from within the forest. They were not going to let any opposition survive in the jungle and would seek to obliterate it at any cost.

Grasping the complexity of their situation, the young men felt danger approaching them. They all felt a flutter in their hearts and their legs trembling as they silently retreated to their camp.

A hot breeze was blowing, but it was so light that even the leaves barely moved. The ground and the rocks wouldn't cool down till midnight. Only then would the breeze offer any relief. Far away, beyond the hills, the electric lights from the villages and towns were flickering like earthen lamps. Stars crowded the sky.

Exhausted after a hard day's trek, the tired bodies of the gollas cried for rest. They ate their rotis, drank some water and lay down at their respective places. Most did not have time for passing conversations and were asleep by eight.

Ravi ate his roti with an onion and then walked into the herd. The one-week-old lamb was lying next to its mother, who was chewing the cud. The baby had put on some weight. In the last couple of days, it had started biting the tips of fresh grass and mingling within the herd. It did not show any tiredness through the day. By the time the herd got back to the village, it would be independent and able to survive without its mother.

Pullayya called Ravi over to him. 'Thanks to the yaanadis, we are running out of rations two days ahead of time,' said the old shepherd. 'Not sure if we even have enough for tomorrow. We need to call home and ask for fresh rations to be sent by the morning of the day after; so we have to go to Nayanapalle or Varikuntla tomorrow morning to make the phone call.'

Ravi told him that he would do that. As he was heading back towards his flock, Ankayya stopped him. 'I will accompany you,' he said. 'I need to make a phone call too.' Ravi nodded and went to his sleeping spot. But he could not fall asleep. He thought of his friends in Hyderabad.

After some time, he got up and walked for a while through the trees. He wanted to sit on a rock in the forest, but fear entered his mind before he could reach the spot that he had thought of. All around him were cutch, satinwood and sandra trees whose branches did not allow the moonlight to reach the ground. Spread over the rolling hills, the forest was like a crowd of dark shapes with dangers lurking everywhere.

Ravi heard a sound behind him and froze. He could not take another step forward. It was some kind of animal. He turned his head in the direction of the sound, fear springing like a snake from his trembling spine . . . until he realised that the animal was his father's dog. He exhaled a deep sigh of relief.

Weakly, Ravi took a couple of steps forward and sat down on the rock. The dog came closer, stood next to him and looked around. Ravi's breathing returned to normal, and he looked at the dog in wonder. He had never shown any affection towards it, but it had come to give him company. He bent down and rubbed its head affectionately, taking in the courage the dog's presence gave him.

It was a strange feeling to sit alone on that rock and gaze at the hills all around. The silence was magical. Ravi wondered if the people of early civilisations had gone about their lives with a domesticated dog for a companion. Facing fear and danger at every step, it may have lived a life of fright and fight. Even though the way we look might have changed over the centuries, our fears have remained the same.

Cities might have been built with impregnable security, but even there, every step was a game of survival. One had to save themselves from the humans who had become predators with their greed and nepotism, their desire for power, their discrimination based on caste, religion and economic disparities . . . Ravi was soon lost in his thoughts.

The dog paced around him till he slowly got up and started walking towards his sleeping spot by the flock. The dog followed him and stayed by his side until he fell asleep. Then it went and lay down next to Gurappa.

*

Ankayya woke Ravi up before dawn. The moon had covered three-fourths of the sky by then. The shepherds calculated the moon's movements using the jaamu, a unit of two hours and twenty-four minutes. Ankayya estimated that it would take another jaamu for the moon to reach its apogee, so he knew that it was around four in the morning.

Ravi and Ankayya informed old Pullayya that they were headed to the village and started walking down the hill carrying their axes on their shoulders. Ankayya led the way through the foot trails, taking shortcuts wherever possible. He was conscious that tigers usually hid by water sources or cart trails. They walked quickly and silently, not reducing their speed even when the rocky trail went uphill. The cold of the dawn could not prevent a film of sweat breaking out on their bodies.

Once they reached flatter land, their young bodies reacted to the easier terrain by almost breaking into a run. They arrived at Varikuntla village at the crack of dawn and immediately headed to the dosa shop next to the temple by the village square. The woman at the shop had not yet started making dosas, but she had already lit the stove and brewed some tea. When the two young shepherds arrived at her shop, she was mixing the batter.

Nearby, there was a telephone booth with a coinbox. The woman exchanged a ten-rupee note for coins for the gollas. A rupee coin allowed one to speak for a minute, after which one had to drop another coin into the box to continue the call. Ravi called home and informed Sankar about the rations. His brother told him that the next batch of rotis had been made and was being dried in the sun. Ravi asked him to ensure that the rations reached the hills by the morning of the next day.

After finishing his conversation, Ravi turned to Ankayya.

'Anna, you wanted to make a call, right? Where to?'

'To my in-laws' place. Will it connect?'

'Why wouldn't it connect? Tell me the number.'

'It is a village near Badvel.'

'Tell me the number, anna!'

'The number, yes,' Ankayya mumbled, scratching his head. 'Ninety-four, forty-six . . .'

'Don't remember it?'

'Wait . . . white . . . sheep . . . tanned. Yeah . . . twelve . . . teak brown, thirty-seven . . . fawn, forty-five . . . yeah, that's it!'

Ravi could not help but smile at the way Ankayya had created a mnemonic to memorise the phone number. He counted the numbers. Yes, there were ten. He dialled the number and dropped a coin into the box once it started ringing.

The dosa maker looked up at Ankayya. Her eyes flashed a mocking smile, which spread on to her thin lips and then vanished.

Someone answered the phone. 'Ankanna, here, a male voice is speaking on the other side,' said Ravi and handed the receiver to Ankayya.

'Who?' said Ankayya in confusion. 'Oh, the brother-in-law . . . hey, orey Santebbi, everyone's fine, right? OK, OK . . . give the phone to your sister,' Ankayya spoke excitedly. It took a while for his wife to come on the line. In the meantime, they needed to put one more coin into the box. 'Where the hell is she?' Ankayya wondered aloud.

The dosa woman smiled again.

The wife seemed to have come on the line, because Ankayya said loudly, 'Who is this? Didn't that half-eared fellow tell you? This is your husband! You didn't recognise my voice? How is my son?'

He listened to her speak and then responded, 'Where? Where else would we be at this time of the year? We are in the hills. I came down to Varikuntla to speak with you from the one-rupee phone . . . yeah . . . the rations, we ran out of them. The next set is coming tomorrow . . . I was hoping that at least this time I would get rotis made by you, but you are still at your mother's place. Is this fair on your part?'

'. . .'

'Will you remain there, Subhadra?'

'. . .'

'I mean, for the rest of your life. Will you remain there?'

'. . .'

'Why would you live there? You are my wife . . . my girl . . . the mother of my son!' Ankayya was shouting now. He was gesturing with his free hand and expressing his emotions into the phone, oblivious of his surroundings. Ravi kept dropping rupee coins into the box as the counter ticked down.

'Ammi . . . what did I do wrong? Did I ever say or do anything to hurt you?'

'. . .'

'Yes, I am a golla, a shepherd! A dumb golla who doesn't know anything other than his sheep! That's why I married you, a high school graduate . . . I hoped you would teach me about the world!'

The dosa woman could not control her laughter at Ankayya's performance. She hid her face behind her saree pallu and smiled into it. Soon, three other men appeared. They looked inside the phone booth and decided to wait outside and listen to Ankayya's conversation.

He was nodding and saying 'hm' as his wife spoke. When it was his turn to speak, there was a sadness in Ankayya's voice. 'Ammi,' he said. 'Ammi . . . how much you have changed, Subhadra! Earlier, when I returned home, you would keep hot water ready for my bath and wouldn't let me sit down for dinner or go to bed with you without first having a bath. You wouldn't let me go out if my hair was not combed properly. You would embarrass me on special occasions by rubbing scented talcum powder on my face. You would treat me just the way you bedeck your son and keep him by your side. For the big festival, when the entire village followed the procession of the mother goddess to the outskirts, you made me wear the shirt and trousers that you got stitched especially for the occasion. Your makeover almost made me look like a reddy boy going to town for higher studies! When you held my hand and made me walk by your side, I almost died from shyness. Ammi, this year too the procession was held, but you were not around. I couldn't leave the flock and go to the village. What did I do wrong, ammi? Tell me why you won't leave your mother's house and come back to our village!'

There was only one coin left. Ravi went over to the dosa shop and exchanged another ten-rupee note for coins. Four more people gathered near the dosa shop, but Ankayya was not in a position to notice that they were all listening to his conversation.

His wife seemed to have said something hurtful on the phone, because Ankayya wailed, 'Ammi . . . ammi . . . don't say such words! Don't talk like that . . . should I come over to take you back? We have been married for two years now. Did I ever object if you wanted to visit your mother's place? And you would always return before I asked you to. Tell me this . . . whose writ runs in our home? All the decision-making is in your hands, right? Because you are educated and know how to do calculations and all . . . didn't I agree before we were married that you would manage everything at home?'

The dosa woman was serving tea to the waiting customers. She looked up and gazed at Ankayya for a few moments. There was no mocking smile in her eyes now.

' . . . '

'My mother can't see properly. My father can't move around on his own. Neither of them would interfere with your management of the house. Maybe they grumble now and then, but you should be a little patient and adjust to such things.'

' . . . '

'What, what did I do wrong, ever?'

She said something to which Ankayya nodded. 'True, I agree,' he said. 'I should have come along with you . . . should have bought new clothes . . . but what could I do? I couldn't find water anywhere . . . I had to herd the flock to Vankamarri dam. There was some muddy water there that we let the sheep drink. Did I have the leisure to come shopping with you? Didn't I tell you the very next day of our wedding that you will have to deal with all such activities? You know better than I do what kind of clothes suit me well. Ammi . . . you can't stay at your mother's place for such a long time and give such flimsy excuses! What kind of injustice is this, ammi!'

From their conversation, Ravi understood that Ankayya had not visited his in-laws' place to accept a gift of new clothes and wear them for the festival.

' . . . '

'I agree, Subhadra!' Ankayya responded after his wife had spoken for a while. 'It would have been nice to go. I should have gone with you for your cousin's wedding. I understand that it would have been embarrassing for you that your husband did not show up for the function. But what could I do? The situation was such. And you know it all, right?'

' . . . '

'The damned famine,' said Ankayya in despair. 'There were days when even one proper feed for the sheep was difficult. We were only allowed to graze in farms owned by reddys, and there too only the sheep of those who had helped with their harvest were allowed. We had to pluck their toor dal plants, pile them in heaps and move them to the neighbouring plot. Only then could we bring in our flocks to graze. I had no option but to go for harvesting, to save the lives of our sheep . . . what else could I have done? I agree the mistake was mine. But I committed the mistake only to save the lives of the sheep . . .'

Ankayya's voice was hoarse and heavy with sadness. Ravi felt sympathy for him. But on the phone, his wife seemed to continue reminding Ankayya of his other mistakes.

'Yes, ammi,' he said, 'even that time, I was at fault. I should have been there as the son-in-law of the house, when your brother's marriage was being arranged. But I couldn't come with you then either . . .'

She kept talking, and they were running out of coins again. Ravi was about to take out another ten-rupee note when the dosa woman came over with a palmful of coins, heaped them on top of the coin box and silently returned to her dosa pan.

'Yes, but you know the reason,' Ankayya was saying, 'the dusty black sheep struggled to deliver. The infant had turned inside, and the sheep suffered through an entire day . . . ammi, when they cut your tummy at the hospital and delivered our boy through the caesarean procedure, you were looking pale and not in your senses due to the anaesthesia. I was so worried for you that I did not feel like seeing my first child—I wanted to see you first. My eyes welled up when I saw you in that situation . . . I cried in front of everyone at the hospital. I wailed, beating my chest. I could not control my tears even when the folks at the hospital were giving me strange looks. You know, some of my aunts still tease me about that incident. But we had hospitals and doctors who operated on you and saved you and our child. The sheep don't have any doctors or hospitals, Subhadra! It wailed in agony till evening and then died. Its baby died in its womb. And I cried the whole day, just like the day I cried in the hospital for you . . . that's why I couldn't come . . .'

Ankayya's voice was laden with grief. Subhadra spoke a little.

'Ammi!' Ankayya cried when she had finished speaking. 'Without you around, my life has become pathetic. You showed me how wretched and miserable a shepherd's life could become if there is no woman to do the prayers, prepare his rations and come along to see him off as he heads to the hills with the flock. Did I commit such a serious sin, Subhadra? My almost-blind mother could not make the rotis properly for my ration . . . they were burnt to a cinder on one side but were uncooked on the other. When I ate them, my belly ached from indigestion, but if I didn't eat, it would ache from hunger . . . I gave away half the rotis to the dogs. During the day I have been foraging for wild fruit to stay alive, ammi! Did I make such big mistakes that I should suffer like this, Subhadra? Even assuming I made those mistakes, I have borne more punishment than I deserved. Come home at least now, Subhadra, at least for the third ration . . .'

Ankayya was wiping his tears away as he spoke into the phone. Ravi was stunned. All these days, a man in their group was living on a half-full stomach, and they hadn't even noticed. He felt ashamed. The customers of the dosa shop watched Ankayya silently. No one moved. The dosa woman's face had an anguished expression.

'Ammi!' Ankayya said, 'When the rains begin and we return to the village, if you are not there, I won't even be able to step into our home. I won't. You at least have your mother's place. What do I have, tell me? Before coming to the hills, on several nights I didn't feel like going into a house without you in it; I slept on an empty stomach with the sheep. I would drink some sheep milk to wet my intestines a bit, that's all. It's your wish . . . if you don't come, I won't go home either.'

With that, Ankayya handed the receiver to Ravi and stepped out of the booth. He sat on a bench and wiped his tears with a scarf. Ravi held the receiver to his ear. Subhadra was still on the phone. He heard a woman's voice, crying and hiccuping. He disconnected the line with a heavy heart.

The dosa woman refused to take the ten-rupee note Ravi offered her. When he took Ankayya's hand and started walking away, she called out, 'Have some dosas and leave, anna!'

Ravi sensed that she was tearful. 'No, sister,' he replied. 'We'll go to the hills and have roti.'

'You eat the rotis every day, anyway,' she shot back. 'Today, have some dosas before you go.' It sounded almost like an order.

The shepherds sat back down again. Ankayya covered his head with his scarf and sat glumly. The woman served some dosas on a banana leaf, but Ankayya refused it saying that he was not feeling hungry. She packed the dosas and told them to eat them on the way. She also handed over two water sachets and refused the money Ravi offered her.

'I have always taken money for my dosas,' she said. 'Let me serve some food for free at least today, anna. I will count it as my offering to Kasi Nayana . . . please eat them, anna!' She wiped her eyes as she spoke.

The two gollas started their journey back to the herds. On the way, they sat under the trees near the Mittaboti pond and ate the dosas. After drinking the water they had been given, the two young men found that it was an easy and brisk walk with the sun on their backs. It still took them another half an hour to reach the golla camp. The other shepherds were ready to set out for the day.

On their way back, Ravi had walked behind Ankayya and had not looked at his face. He could now see that Ankayya was looking better than he had after the call. Maybe he had cried during the walk. Ravi thought that his wife too would have cried for a long time after their conversation. Maybe, he hoped, she would find an auspicious day to return to their home with the little boy in tow. And then, for the third round of rations, Ankayya might finally receive rotis made by her.

*

The shepherds cooked the remaining rice for lunch. It barely sufficed for the men, leaving nothing for the dogs. But Gurappa ate a roti and gave away his share of rice to his dog.

Old Pullayya was trying to shoo away two young sheep that were trying to lick the grains of pickle-rice from his hands. 'Oye Gurappa!' he said. 'Look at these animals falling all over me!'

'Aren't you the king here?' joked Gurappa. 'No need to wash your hands.'

'Leave the jokes aside. Why are they doing this?'

'It is obvious,' replied Gurappa. 'The tastebuds of the sheep have gone bland from all the grass they have been eating. Many of them haven't been grazing properly for the last two days. I think they will send some rock salt with the rations. If we make them lick the salt, they will start craving the grass again.'

Pullayya nodded in agreement. Even in the village, eating grass every day numbed the sheep's sensation of taste. They had to be taken to the salty sands at least once a fortnight. If they licked the salty, loamy soil, it got rid of the problem. However, the salty soil upset their stomachs for a day or two, making the sheep and their pens stink. To avoid this, the shepherds poured lines of salt on flat stones and let the sheep lick it off them.

13

Ravi woke up at five o'clock. Usually, even with the loud birdsong rising up from the stream, he was reluctant to get out of bed. The coolness before dawn was so pleasant that he liked to snuggle tight and sleep for a while longer. He tried to remember why he had awoken at this hour. He had gone to bed at nine the previous night so that he could do so.

Then he remembered. Last night, Ravi had given Ankayya's roti to Gurappa's dog and had instead shared one of his rotis with Ankayya. The man was too shy to ask, but he had accepted the trade. However, Ravi feared that Ankayya would crunch up one of his undercooked rotis before anyone could offer an exchange this morning. That was why he had woken up earlier than usual—to ensure that Ankayya ate a properly cooked roti with some jaggery.

How deep the pain of separation was, thought Ravi. If both sides were proud and obstinate, their differences could become a stout wall between them. But since both Ankayya and his wife were the type to cry and wail over the separation, their differences could melt away. Ravi admired the way Ankayya opened up his heart and laid it bare to his wife. It was also heartening for him to see Subhadra's response to the outpouring of her husband's grief and love.

While the shepherds completed their morning rituals, the baby lamb ran around with a belly full of milk from its mother. It would run to Gurappa, go back to its mother and then run to where Ravi was standing. Sometimes it would leave the herd and try to go into the trees. Then Gurappa's dog would give chase and drive it back into the herd. Ravi noticed that the baby lamb had white streaks on the head like the ram that had mated with its dark-headed mother.

The fresh rations were scheduled to arrive by the time they got the herds up and moving. The last few rotis they had left had to suffice for breakfast, leaving no rice nor rotis for lunch. Ravi found one roti in his bag and one and a half rotis in his father's cloth satchel. The dog needed to eat one full roti, which meant that Gurappa would have to make do with just half a roti.

Ravi suspected that even the previous night his father had only eaten half a roti. When he asked Gurappa about it, he replied, 'We can eat a fruit or a root to satisfy our hunger. But the dog can't do that. And it can't even tell us when it is hungry. It has come along trusting us to take care of its needs. So, it doesn't matter if we starve, but we need to ensure that it has food.' Ravi looked at his father with a new understanding. He was starving himself for the sake of his dog, ensuring that his son and his pet had a proper meal before thinking about himself.

'Ankanna!' hailed Ravi. 'Give me a roti if you have one left.'

Ankayya looked at him. 'For you or for the dog?' he asked.

'Just bring it here, anna!'

Ankayya came over with his bag. There were three rotis in there. Ravi gave him the roti from his bag and took two from him. He broke one into pieces and threw them in front of the dog. He started eating the other roti. It was like biting into a broken piece of a clay pot. The undercooked roti had become hard as a bone over time.

'How did you eat these rotis, anna?' he asked.

'If you dip it in water, it softens,' explained Ankayya.

Ravi looked at him in disbelief. Gurappa took a piece of Ankayya's roti and tried it. 'This can be quite tasty if soaked in sheep milk for some time and eaten with a piece of jaggery. Ankayya just did not know how to eat such rotis.'

Ankayya picked up a small vessel and ran towards his sheep. He returned with some milk and threw the roti pieces into the vessel along with two pieces of jaggery that he crushed on a stone. He let the roti soak in the sweetened milk for an hour. The hard bread absorbed the milk and softened a bit.

After an hour, Ankayya popped a piece of soaked roti into his mouth. The morsel tasted sweet and melted on his tongue. Ankayya shared the dish with Ravi while cursing himself for having missed out on this trick.

There was no sign of the rations when it was time to get the herds moving.

'Oye Gurappa,' shouted old Pullayya. 'The ration-bearers should have arrived by now. I wonder why they haven't.' He expressed the thought that was on everyone's minds.

'I don't think they will come today, if they haven't shown up till now,' replied Gurappa. 'There might be some problem.'

'Two among us could go to Kasi Nayana ashram and beg them for enough rice to sustain us for two meals,' said Pullayya. 'If we plead with Gangapalle Chenna Reddy, he will oblige.'

'Why beg?' questioned Tiripalu. 'We have been donating a sack or two of rice every year to that ashram, right?'

'So what if we donate?' shot back Pullayya. 'Once we give it to the ashram, we don't have any right over a single grain! We only get the punyam, the virtue from doing a charitable deed. However rich a person is and even if he has donated hundreds of thousands to an ashram, he needs to request food with open palms when he visits the ashram. One should visit an ashram as a pauper, only then will the visit have any meaning!'

They all laughed at Pullayya's animated expressions. Tiripalu and Pamuleti got ready and left for the ashram.

When the shepherds reached the water source in the afternoon, Tiripalu and Pamuleti were seated on a stone there with a bag of rice by their side. There were two others with them.

'Oye Pulla mama! Oho Guranna!' shouted one of the newcomers, waving a scarf in their direction. The shepherds recognised them as Chinnayya and Nagayya, gollas from Nayanapalle. They were related to gollas from their village.

'You gollas have it all sorted, mama!' said Chinnayya. 'Though you are in the middle of the forest, you get rice from the ashram and from Nayanapalle! And full rations will come tomorrow from your village.'

'Aren't you gollas too?' asked Gurappa.

'We are not gollas anymore,' said Nagayya teasingly. 'We dug borewells and ploughed our lands and are now engaged in agriculture. We are farmers, bava!'

'But you are still gollas by caste!' countered Gurappa.

'By caste, we are yadavs now,' said Nagayya, grinning. Everyone laughed, except for Pamuleti and Tiripalu. The latter had a distressed look on his face, and his eyes were red.

After the sheep had finished drinking water and were settled down, Tiripalu broke down in sobs.

'What is wrong?' asked a concerned Pullayya.

It was Chinnayya who explained. 'Your rations were ready on time,' he said. 'But someone from your village called me last night and said the rations can't leave the village while a body is awaiting a funeral. So, they asked me to deliver enough rice for two days. That's why Nagayya and I came over.'

'A funeral? Who is it?'

'Konda Narayana. He drank poison in the hut next to the motor on his farm . . .'

The news shook them all. Sadness enveloped the group immediately. No one uttered a word.

'Too many debts, I believe . . .' Chinnayya was saying, but none of the shepherds were paying attention to him anymore. They were thinking of Narayana.

'Chho chho chho,' cried Pullayya. He was in tears. 'What an injustice! Such a good soul, never a harsh word or deed . . . where will we find such a person again? Will our village ever give birth to such a kind human being again? Impossible!'

Wiping the tears away with his headscarf, the old shepherd continued his eulogy. 'He used to be at the forefront of any activity intended for public good,' he said. 'People used to follow his words, which cut across caste barriers.'

'When we were leaving the village with the flocks, he had come to the sheep pens to bid farewell to us all, mama,' said Gurappa. 'Not sure if you remember, but he said something that day . . .'

Pullayya struggled to recall what it was.

'When I asked why he came by at such an early hour,' said Gurappa, 'he said, "I don't know when I will see you all again or if I will ever see you again . . . this life is like a water bubble." I had wondered why he was saying such inauspicious words just as we were about to leave. I now realise that he was talking about himself. He must have already made up his mind . . .'

Pullayya started to remember. 'Yes, he had said something else as well that day,' said the old man. 'He had said, "You gollas are all pious souls! Braving the heat and rain, struggling for water and shelter, surviving on very little food, you roam around the hills and forests and keep these dumb animals alive. You are like gods!" The depth of his words . . . he was hiding something inside.'

'He had sowed chickpea over ten acres,' said Pichchanna. 'The rain was enough to make it sprout but not enough for the crop to survive. The entire crop dried up, and he left it to us to graze the sheep there and pay him whatever we could afford. But what could we give him? Hardly anything. Even by a conservative estimate, he lost around fifteen thousand rupees per acre . . . I believe he already had debts of five or six lakhs. Now, another one and a half lakhs were added to that. The debtors were doing rounds to his house for repayment. I guess he was unable to handle the stress and decided to end his life.'

The shepherds were deeply affected by the news. Nearly all of them felt like going back to the village to get one last sight of Narayana. Tiripalu was still in tears and said that he would go home. The elder gollas advised against it, as the funeral rites would get over by the time he would reach.

Tiripalu spat in disgust. 'It took us a day to get the news!' he shouted. 'Even those in a far-off place like Kuwait would have got the message sooner than us!'

A feeling of despair and listlessness spread among the group.

'As the saying goes, "Today at home and hearth, tomorrow on the funeral pyre,"' said Pullayya. 'As long as we are alive, we should be doing the work given to us by God. That is all.' He pointed at the sky and added, 'It is the one above who will pay us for our labour.'

They all reluctantly ate a little and then rested for a long time. The Nayanapalle gollas were asked to take their rice back with them as the fresh rations were going to arrive in the morning.

When they resumed moving with the herds, Ravi felt as though the hills were covered in a layer of sadness.

'I used to feel so energetic every day in spite of the scorching sun,' he said to Pullayya. 'But today I feel dull and lethargic. I wonder why.'

'The hills too seem to have heard about the death of the farmer,' replied Pullayya. 'Without the hills, we can't have farms or farming. Only if it rains here can we see our streams flowing. Only when the trees grow strong here can we get ploughs to till the fields. A farmer does not just belong to the farms—he is a child of the hills too. Why wouldn't the hills feel sad at his demise? It will grieve the whole day today.' Pullayya spoke as if in a trance.

The herds were dividing themselves into small groups wherever they could find some grass, whether it was near the stone plates, the streambeds, the napes of small hillocks, the dried-up ponds and gullies or the flat and elevated lands.

In the village, the funeral rites would have been completed for the dead farmer. The grief-stricken villagers were like fish in a pond, where the water has drained away through a breach in the bund. They could manage to move about but were short on hope and energy.

Tiripalu was hit the hardest by the news because Konda Narayana was a close relative and had helped him out many a time. The young golla was quite upset that he couldn't go see Narayana for one last time, console his family or attend the funeral. There was no one who could placate him.

Gurappa saw that Tiripalu was unable to focus on his flock and had taken to leaning against a rock or a tree whenever the sheep stopped for a minute or two to graze. He sent Bhaskar to help him out. Bhaskar's absence made it tough for Ravi to manage the herd because now he had to either lead from the front or bring up the rear of the flock instead of just limiting himself to walking along on the side.

The shepherd at the front needed to lead the flock forward and give it direction. In addition, at certain times—while entering a streambed or passing by one, or where there was thick vegetation or a group of huge trees, and even at the bend of a brook or near marshy areas—the lead shepherd had to keep throwing stones while shouting at the top of his voice to scare away any animals and snakes that might be hiding there.

The role of the shepherd at the back of the herd was different. He needed to be alert and keep an eye on all sides, ready to spring to the defence of the sheep while protecting his own life during any surprise attack. Even a momentary loss of focus could lead to irreparable damage.

Ravi took the lead position. Walking in the front, he sweated profusely out of fear while stepping down into the streambeds. He felt as if needles were piercing his head as he trudged forward with difficulty. The others were yelling and throwing stones. Gurappa, who was at the rear, was doing it too, especially when they passed through a narrow trail. Ravi struggled to shout. As the clutches of fear grew tighter, he became more stiff and silent, always keeping an ear out for any sounds from the bushes or from behind the rocks. However, the concept of shouting and throwing stones was to scare the danger away. If the animal was close enough for you to hear it, all bets were off.

As daylight began fading into the western hills, Gurappa's flock was on one side of the hillock by the stream, slowly climbing while grazing. Pichchanna's flock was moving up the hill on the other side. That was when a sudden cry came from below them.

It was Ramachandra. He was shouting, 'Fox! Big fox! Coming this way!'

Venkanna's cracking yell followed immediately and then Ganganna's scream echoed around them. After a loud whistle from someone, the shepherds started screaming, whistling and hurling stones in turn. After Gurappa shouted when his turn came, a feral cry issued from Ravi's throat as well. It was an involuntary reaction and he felt goosebumps when he finished screaming and someone else started. The adrenaline rush had done its job of chasing his fear away.

Ravi understood then the dual purpose of the screams when the lead shepherd hurls stones into the forest. He also figured that it was for a similar reason that a lone traveller at night sings puranic drama poems at the top of his voice.

The hills resounded with the continuous hollering of the shepherds. Suddenly, from behind a rocky outcrop, two animals came running at them at top speed. They were young antelopes with horns shaped like tree branches. They were running so fast that they seemed to be flying off the rocks with their hooves barely touching the ground. The tiger was probably pursuing them.

The antelopes ran straight into Gurappa's flock and stopped amongst the sheep, upper bodies heaving. Their nostrils were flared and their eyes full of fear as they kept looking back at from where they had emerged. The sheep quickly adjusted to the presence of the new animals and turned to stare at the scared antelopes while absorbing and expressing their fear.

The gollas began hurling stones in the direction the antelopes came from while keeping up their loud shouting. The hills kept echoing and amplifying the sounds. The frightful cacophony seemed to have affected the chasing predator. They could not tell if it was a tiger or a leopard because it did not come out from behind the outcrop. The antelopes eventually made their way out of the flock and started climbing up the hill.

The gollas watched them move steadily up the hill under the low sun. They first walked one behind the other and then side by side. They seemed to be a couple. If one of them were to be captured by the tiger, the other would have to survive alone. The mad run for life by the antelopes and the way they managed to survive stayed in Ravi's mind for a long time. It was an unforgettable sight for him.

By the time the gollas had slowly brought all their herds up to the hilltop while helping each other to ensure that the sheep don't go towards the stream, the sun had almost set. Ravi felt that he was the only one still under the spell of fear. The others seemed to be merely alert and cautious. He also thought that his fellow shepherds seemed to be experts at making the flock move forward while hurling big stones on all sides and keeping wild animals at bay.

Without even turning around, a seasoned shepherd could hurl a stone backwards with the same speed as he could throw it forwards or sideways. The stone would invariably hit the intended target. And they could do both underarm and overarm throws.

Once he reached the top of the hill, Ravi looked back down and traced the path taken by the antelopes. In his mind's eye he saw the animals running wildly through the shortcut from behind the outcrop, passing by the flocks of sheep and then charging up the side of the hill. It was as if fear took the shape of a big deer and ran to survive. His fear made him one with the antelopes for a few moments. He felt that he could sense his legs bend like theirs as they scampered across the hard earth and stones. It was a strange sensation.

Jerking back into reality, Ravi felt ashamed for identifying so intensely with the fear of the antelopes. He then tried to imagine himself screaming and throwing stones at the tiger and chasing the predator away. But he couldn't. The sight of the antelopes running for dear life refused to budge from his mind. Ravi struggled to replace that image with one where he was chasing the tiger away.

For dinner, the gollas ate the rice that they had cooked for lunch. They sat around in groups of two or three and discussed the death of Konda Narayana. Before lying down for the night, Ravi walked over to Ankayya.

'Anna, do you think she would have come home by now?' he asked.

Ankayya thought for a couple of seconds and then his eyes lit up. 'It is likely,' he said. 'Narayana was affectionate towards her. He used to bring her newspapers and books to read from the town and advise her on various matters. Yes, she would have returned for sure. Narayana said about her: "My daughter is like gold." Once she got the news, she would have undoubtedly returned to the village weeping and wailing.'

There was a new hope and happiness in Ankayya's voice. His eyes shone and enthusiasm seemed to spread through him. Ravi noticed the change. Feeling satisfied, he went back to his spot.

As he was adjusting his bedding, he saw Ankayya get up and move about. He first went to his flock and rubbed the body of the ash-black sheep affectionately. He then caressed the heads and horns of the rams. Not satisfied, Ankayya then walked to Gurappa's flock, picked up the baby lamb and petted it for a while, before showering affection on his dog.

'Rey, what are you doing at this time of the night?' enquired a puzzled Gurappa. Ankayya did not reply and silently went back to his sleeping spot. Ravi understood the meaning of Ankayya's actions. He was sharing his happiness with the animals through touch. He drifted into sleep thinking about Ankayya's emotions.

The ration-bearers arrived before seven the following morning. They must have started quite early. The shepherds surrounded them eagerly and quickly relieved them of the ration bags. Then they started asking questions about Konda Narayana's death.

The story was that Narayana went to his farm at night, ostensibly for guard duty. He sat in the motor room, drank a bellyful of pesticide and lay down on the cot. His wife went to the farm at ten the next morning to find him dead. It was only later that the villagers understood that Narayana had been making preparations for his death for almost a week before committing suicide.

He had given an old photo of his to a studio and asked them to enlarge and frame it. It was for his funeral. To avoid causing any inconvenience to his family, he had also bought a white cloth to cover his body, a garland of marigold flowers and all the other stuff needed for the funeral rites. Narayana had kept them ready in the room where he died. They even found the money required for the funeral in his shirt pocket.

There was also a note in which he had written a list of all the things he had prepared. It included the names of his debtors and the amounts he owed to each of them. He killed himself only after completing all his preparations. The reason for the suicide was his inability to bear the burden of debt.

Narayana had been the go-to man for advice for many people in the village. He was the person they would call upon to resolve any dispute. After his creditors started visiting his home and threatening him, he decided to end his life before the entire village could start talking about his situation.

It is said that there were only six reasons for Karna's death in the Mahabharata. But there were usually many more reasons for a farmer's death. It could be the lack of rains, the drying up of borewells or the government not executing irrigation projects. Or, it could be inadequate crop prices, greedy middlemen, delayed loan waivers or adulterated seeds, fertilisers and pesticides.

The shepherds reflected on the sad story of Narayana with heavy hearts. After a while, old Pullayya reminded their visitors of the time and asked them to have some food before their journey back home. They opened the ration bags and started eating rotis with jaggery.

Ankayya was impatient to know whether his wife had come back to the village yet. If she had indeed returned, it would show in the rations he received. He opened the bag with some excitement and trepidation. But the sight of the same old half-burnt rotis told him that his wife had not come back home. He had received only four rotis, a single block of jaggery and two onions. But there was enough rice to last until the next ration period.

Ravi was observing Ankayya and quietly handed him one of his rotis. He took Ankayya's roti, broke it into pieces and thew them in front of the salivating dog. Ankayya was confused about whether Subhadra had returned home or not. Maybe she had come back, but not in time to make proper rotis for his ration. His mind was not willing to accept that she had still not returned. After all, he had cried his heart out to her over the phone.

He had accepted that he had made mistakes and had pleaded with her. And then there was also the matter of Narayana's unfortunate demise. She would have definitely come back, Ankayya thought, his hopes very much alive. But as he walked around the herd eating the roti Ravi gave him, his doubts persisted.

Ankayya opened the bag again and found a thread dyed with turmeric paste on top of the rice. He pulled it out to find an amulet with the image of Hanuman. 'She has come, Subhadra has come,' his heart screamed silently. A new excitement spread through him as he recognised it as the amulet of Gandi Anjaneya Swamy. Last year, she had tied a similar amulet to his right wrist when he was heading out for hill-grazing.

Ankayya went to Ravi and asked him to tie the amulet on his forearm. He whispered to Ravi that Subhadra had sent this amulet as a sign that she had returned.

'Anka bava, what are you whispering about?' Pichchanna asked him in a teasing tone. 'No need to whisper. I heard my sister has come back.'

Ankayya looked at him in surprise.

'I completely forgot,' said Sankar suddenly in a loud voice. 'She had asked me to tell you about the amulet in the rice. Wear it!'

Ankayya blushed. He should have asked them about her right away instead of fretting, he told himself.

'I believe the rotis are not good,' continued Sankar. 'They weren't cooked well as the old lady couldn't see clearly. But she is sending a man to Jyothi tomorrow with properly made rotis. Asked me to tell you. Go to Jyothi in the morning and collect them.'

Ankayya quietly took it all in.

'Sankar, did my son-in-law come by in the last week?' asked Pamuleti.

'I think he visited twice.'

'Did he talk to you about anything?'

'Yes, he enquired about when the sheep would return from the hills. Asked whether the sheep looked famished or had put on any weight. He said that he had found a middleman who would arrange for buyers as soon as your flock returns from the hills. I believe he needs the money for the new business he is starting?'

'Maybe,' said Pamuleti. 'Who knows!'

He walked over to Pullayya and sat next to the old man. Pamuleti remained silent for a while, scratching the ground with a twig. Then he began talking.

'If I had settled the matter at the time of the wedding, I would have lost only half the flock, ayya!' he cried. 'I thought I would just give him the dowry money later but did not realise that he would charge me interest on it! It's like I've taken out a loan—two rupees interest, compounded every year . . . charging interest on interest! The amount has ballooned over these four years. Now I doubt if the dowry debt would be cleared fully even if I sell off the entire flock. This interest . . . it is a lifeless creature that keeps growing. If it was a living thing, it would at least fall sick sometimes or wouldn't grow so fast. But it doesn't need to be watered nor does it suffer from pests . . . come rain or sunshine, it keeps growing silently.'

He sighed deeply and, pointing at his sheep, continued, 'These animals though . . . they need food and water. They get sick and need treatment. They cannot grow fast enough to keep up with the interest.' His eyes welled up with tears.

Pullayya tried to console him. 'At least you are giving them to your daughter,' he said.

'But then how will my son eke out a livelihood?' Pamuleti almost screamed. 'Should I ask him to take a bowl and become a beggar?'

He then stood up and addressed them all. 'Listen, I am telling this to all of you,' he said. 'Pullayya, you have a granddaughter. Orey Pichchanna, Tiripalu, Munayya, Ramayya . . . you all have daughters. Don't think of offering a big dowry and getting them married to businessmen or salaried employees. Find them husbands who earn their livelihood through physical labour, like you do. You will be happy, and your daughter's life will be peaceful too. She will value whatever clothes you gift her and will relish the food you serve her. When you visit her home, she will receive you at the doorstep in delight. In short, your daughter shall remain your daughter!'

The shepherds gaped at him in amazement.

Pamuleti turned his gaze to the bachelors among them, and once he caught Ravi's attention, he addressed him directly. 'Oho dora!' he cried. 'I am telling you this because you will be a company employee anyway. Marry someone of the same status as you—another such employee. Don't marry a girl from a shepherd's family. The moment you are married, she will become the wife of an official. You don't have to do anything—the women of the neighbourhood will give her that status immediately. But her parents shall remain gollas and won't transform into the in-laws of an official. After that, the dresses and gifts given to her by her golla parents will appear to be of low quality to her eyes and the food they serve will seem coarse and rustic to her mouth. When they visit their daughter once in a while, she will strive to keep them away from the eyes of her neighbours, not wanting them to see the cheap clothes and rustic nature of her parents. Why cause all these troubles for her? You get married to the daughter of an officer with high status . . . or the child of a businessman who will pay the dowry in full. If there is a little shortfall in the dowry amount, ensure that he pays you the remainder on the day of your wedding!'

Pamuleti finished speaking and briskly walked back towards his flock.

They all understood his anguish. Pichchanna began discussing something with Sankar. Ramayya whispered something to another young shepherd.

'We are late,' yelled Pullayya suddenly. 'Get the sheep moving!'

Along with the rations, each shepherd had received two small bags of salt. They spread the salt in lines on flat rock slabs and the sheep licked them clean with their coarse tongues. Seetharamayya, Mohan and Ramachandra were to be replaced by Bala Rangayya, Sudhakar and Veerayya who had arrived from the village. The former group took their leave and began their journey home.

The herds then started to walk down the hillock. With their tastebuds rejuvenated, the sheep munched on bunches of grass at a time. The little lamb excitedly walked besides its mother. They reached a water source by one in the afternoon and began cooking rice for lunch. They broke a small piece off the balls of freshly made tamarind chutney and added a little water to make it into a paste which they mixed with the piping hot rice. They sat in the shade of a tree, enjoying the slight breeze as they ate.

At three, they got the herds moving again. Having sensed the tiger's movements nearby the other day, they were doubly cautious. The tiger would be incensed as the gollas had denied it its prey. If it had not been able to hunt any other animal since, its hunger would be driving it crazy. It would definitely be looking for a chance to attack the herd.

The gollas carefully watched over their flocks to ensure the sheep didn't stray too close to the big stone plates, to the sides of ravines and into deep streambeds. There was a spot of loamy soil between the hills where the sheep were allowed to graze for some time before they were herded uphill in a straight line nearly two kilometres long.

A deep ravine had split the hill at a right angle. Gurappa's herd walked ahead while grazing slowly along one side of the ravine. Pichchanna's flock was on the other side. The ravine was thickly wooded, with the vegetation making the ravine's bottom appear pitch black.

'Be careful,' cautioned Gurappa. 'Big snakes usually live in such deep crevices.'

Bhaskar stood at the edge of the ravine, hustling away any sheep that approached the gap. Ravi stayed at the rear of the flock, standing close to the crevice, which was about twenty metres deep and ten metres wide at that point.

Gushing rainwater from the hill had silted away the soft soil, leaving stones that jutted out from the ground. It was a geological formation locally called a loddi. It was impossible to climb up to the opening from below as the rocks protruded sharp and straight. The trees on the sides had extended their thick roots below. Some of them hung from the stone plates and covered up the opening.

'This one is called Budda Reddy's loddi,' shouted Gurappa to Ravi and Bhaskar. 'I was told that long ago, a guy named Budda Reddy slipped and fell into this ravine. Hence the name.'

Every hill, stream, brook and ravine had been given a name, but only those who had a close relationship with the forest knew those names. Gurappa continued to explain something in a loud voice. Bhaskar nodded his head while keeping an eye on Ravi behind him.

'My bava is telling stories today,' said Pichchanna with a laugh.

Suddenly, like a bolt of lightning, a tiger jumped on the sheep right next to Bhaskar. It had long black stripes on an orange-green body, red eyes and white fangs. Its forelegs clasped the sheep's body, pinning it down. It gave a casual and relaxed little tilt of the head to grab the sheep's neck in its mouth.

It was just a metre from Bhaskar, who stood stunned. His eyes bulged at the scene right in front of them. His frozen vocal muscles did not let the desperate cry out that his mind wanted to release. Fear clouded his heart, making his body go weak and stiff like a dried-up bamboo pole.

Gurappa screamed first, a feral high-decibel cry that shook the surroundings. Pichchanna followed suit immediately. They shouted 'Thoi! Thoi!' at the top of their voices. Behind them, Ravi joined in the shouting too.

The tiger ignored the cries of the humans. It did not move nor drag the sheep away. Instead, it grabbed its neck in its wide mouth and took a neat leap backwards from where it stood. Like those itinerant Dommari gymnasts do a reverse cartwheel and land on their feet, the tiger jumped backwards and landed somewhere in the stream below.

It all happened in a flash. The onlookers took a few moments to recover from the shock and awe of that wonderful feat. They all had seen with their own eyes the confidence and courage in the tiger's eyes, the strength of its upper body and the velocity of its movement.

Bhaskar was whimpering. He was still unable to loosen his constricted throat muscles. Ravi could relate to his helplessness. Gurappa continued to yell. Ravi looked down into the ravine. He walked down along the edge and peered inside.

Somewhere towards his side of the streambed, he observed a movement in the trees. It was the sheep. It was stuck between the rocky edge and a tree, less than a couple of metres below him. The sheep was trying to wriggle free but was unable to do so. Blood was flowing from its neck.

The tiger had failed to land properly. It should have landed with the sheep covering its fall, its neck still clutched between the tiger's jaws. But the narrow space made the tiger hit a branch midway, causing the sheep to fall on one side and the tiger on the other.

There was just a couple of metres between the ground and where the sheep was stuck. It was possible for the tiger to lunge upwards and reach the prey. Suddenly, Pichchanna shouted, 'There, there!' Ravi saw the tiger walking up the narrow gully. Four gollas arrived and started pelting stones at it. The tiger avoided the stones and kept looking up at the sheep.

Ravi then heard the baby lamb's cries and realised that the sheep the tiger took away was its mother. Sadness engulfed him when he thought about the pitiful life that awaited the bereaved lamb. He looked down into the ravine again.

The sheep was still trying to move. Ravi thought that maybe it could still survive if they rescued it now. Then the baby lamb wouldn't be orphaned. Ravi did not think twice and quickly slithered down the ravine using the tree trunk, branches and thick roots.

The others yelled, 'No, don't go!' But the tiger was deep inside the ravine and that gave Ravi courage. He was driven by the hope that if he could drag the sheep back up, the baby lamb would still have its mother.

The sheep was stuck in a tiny gap between the tree trunk and the stone wall of the ravine. When it shook its head to free itself, blood oozed from the wounds caused by the tiger's fangs. Ravi looked down into the streambed again. The tiger sat inside, bracing itself against the wall, its forelegs primed to jump. Its gaze was steady. It did not blink at all. The bloodstains around its mouth added to its frightful appearance.

The shepherds kept throwing stones into the ravine, hoping to hit the tiger. The barrage of rock missiles broke a branch, allowing Ravi a small opening. He bent down and grabbed the hind legs of the sheep. Seeing this, the tiger roared. It could not tolerate someone stealing its prey right from its mouth. It jumped, almost reaching the sheep's head, but missed by inches, falling back down to the ground.

Ravi shivered in fear seeing the tiger at such close quarters. Its open jaws, its sharp teeth and its fearsome eyes made his legs tremble. He knew that his sweaty palms could slip and let go of the sheep, leading him to fall in front of the tiger along with it. Instead of the sheep, the tiger would be feasting upon him.

Ravi made a conscious effort to control his fears and steady his hold. He told himself that the tiger wouldn't be able to jump so high nor could it climb up the sheer incline of the ravine's rocky walls. He suddenly unleashed the loudest scream he had ever managed. Ravi did not even realise that he was screaming. But scream he did; an animal-like scream that felt like the nerves in his throat would burst open.

His body shook involuntarily, and he felt a strange sensation crawling up his spine. It was as if he had been given an injection, and he could feel the medicine work its way upwards. Then, Ravi's legs stopped shivering, his feet became firmly balanced against the tree trunk and his hands turned steady as they held on to the branch. He was suffused with courage.

Ravi reckoned that if he needed to, he could simply climb up the ravine and get to safety on the top. At the same time, he sensed that the tiger was about to make another leap. Without thinking about it, Ravi pulled out a big stone from the ravine's wall and held it up with both hands. Just as the tiger jumped, he hurled the stone at it with all his might.

The stone hit the tiger squarely in the gut and knocked it back to the ground. The tiger got up and moved behind the cover of the stone plates. It stood there quietly. Ravi did not wait anymore and used both his hands to pull the sheep free and held it against his shoulders. He then lifted the sheep up over his head, which allowed the shepherds to grab it and pull it up.

Down in the loddi, the tiger had started growling. It was almost panting in anger. The gollas continued to hurl stones while urging Ravi to come back up quickly. Ravi turned to throw one last stone at it. The stone missed its mark, but the incensed tiger gathered all its power and made a leap in one powerful motion. The jump was accompanied with a huge roar. Ravi clambered up, holding on to the roots of the tree. He reached the top in two strides, and strong arms pulled him to safety.

For the next ten minutes, the shepherds continued to throw stones into the ravine and even rolled down some boulders. The stone attack backed by their shrill cries and whistles eventually succeeded in driving the tiger away from the area.

Some of the shepherds congratulated Ravi for his bravery, while others castigated him for his foolhardy behaviour. Gurappa was upset at his son's actions and scolded him in a choked voice.

'Help the sheep,' responded Ravi. 'It is the little one's mother.'

Pichchanna examined the sheep. 'The fangs have cut deep,' he declared. 'It's lost a lot of blood. It seems to have hit the hard wall of the ravine when it fell. The impact has broken its thighs into two. Even its ribs seem to have fractured. I doubt it will survive . . .'

The sheep's throat was punctured. Blood bubbled up through the holes. Ravi could not stand the sight of the innocent little lamb staring at its mother. He held it to his chest, hoping it would feel reassured, while he felt anguish about the lamb's bleak future as an orphan.

'But where are the dogs?' asked Munayya suddenly. They all looked around for the dogs.

Gurappa's dog was right by its master's side, scratching the earth in front of it. The other two dogs were nowhere to be seen.

'Have they started back to the village on their own?' someone wondered out loud.

'Hold on, my fellow,' interjected Pichchanna. 'When even brave men are pissing their pants, do you think those dogs would hang around here after they have smelled the tiger?'

'Then why is our Gurappa's dog still here?'

'This one? Is it really a dog? It is a clay model of a dog. No show of fear or anxiety nor does it bother to do anything. It chills out as if it is resting on the stone bench outside Gurappa's house and doesn't make any effort to move.'

Gurappa caressed his dog. Even when the tiger was roaring loudly and jumping, the dog had simply observed. It did not fold its tail and scamper away. It kept circling Gurappa but did not leave his side. Once Ravi had emerged from the ravine, it went to him and sniffed him before returning to its master.

Pichchanna carried the wounded sheep on his shoulders. They all moved up the hill where the flocks were waiting. They found the other two dogs there, hiding behind the sheep with their tails firmly tucked between their legs. They were walking around as if they were sheep too. Those who noticed the dogs laughed silently and pointed them out to the others.

The wounded sheep breathed its last after a while. Pichchanna declared it dead at five in the evening, an hour from sunset. The group agreed to camp for the night on the flat surface of the hilltop. The dead sheep would be cut up and a curry cooked with its mutton. Some of the shepherds went back down to fetch water for cooking. A few others took the sheep a fair distance away from the herd to carve it.

They threw away the unwanted parts into the streambed. If the skin were intact, they could have sold it at Varikuntla. But the claws and fangs of the tiger had sheared it off in bits and pieces. No one would buy it. They brought the mutton back to the camp.

Three stone stoves were arranged to cook the mutton and fires lit in each. They had to use all the vessels to cook the meat. Bonfires were lit all around the campsite to ensure that the smell of the cooking mutton did not carry to the wild animals in the vicinity. The shepherds took as much meat as they wanted and ate it with rotis until they were full. They knew that the hill winds would help with digestion and that they would all feel hungry again in the morning.

A lot of meat was leftover even after they had all eaten more than their fill. They packed the remaining meat in the pots, closed the lids tightly and hung them up on the branches of trees. The only one who didn't eat the mutton was Ravi. They all entreated him to have some but to no avail. Even when Gurappa gently asked him to eat at least a small piece, he refused to touch it.

Instead, he took the baby lamb to another sheep and helped it feed from its udder. He kept holding the lamb in his lap. The little one would always gambol for a while after having milk. But that night it remained still and quiet, probably having realised its mother was no more. Ravi felt it would be obscene to eat its mother's flesh. Even the sight of the meat made him feel nauseous.

Gurappa and other shepherds ate the meat without any qualms, because they had witnessed many such deaths. Though each death pained him, Gurappa had long ago rationalised it as a natural occurrence, something that was bound to happen every now and then. His attitude was the same as that of the farmer who, during famine, would cut down his crop while it was still green instead of letting it go dry. It was fodder to save the lives of the farmer's cattle.

A tiger killing a sheep was a natural phenomenon. And it was just as natural for humans to eat a dead sheep's meat. Properly rearing the motherless baby lamb was a separate duty. The gollas knew that all such actions proceeded as per a natural cycle and rhythm. But Ravi thought differently.

It was completely unnatural for him to climb down into the ravine. If he was being honest with himself, he knew he wasn't that brave. He did it only because of the lamb. He wanted to rescue the lamb's mother, even if it was a natural phenomenon for it to die.

Ravi knew that some strange magic had happened there. Even when the tiger was leaping at him, the cold fear coursing through him like a chill fever had suddenly transformed into courage.

Instead of offering his body to the tiger without a fight, he was able to save himself and even rescue the sheep from the tiger.

He was still not valorous enough to fight a tiger, but at least he now had the mental strength to escape it. Even if it gave chase, he was now confident that he could climb a tree or a hill to evade its claws. He would no longer passively surrender to fate.

Keeping the little lily-white lamb by his side, Ravi fell into a deep sleep.

14

The shepherds woke up at the crack of dawn and immediately brought down the curry pots tied to the branches. There were big red ants crowding the rims of some of the pots. But once the pots were lowered to the ground, the ants went away.

On the way to their daily ablutions, the gollas passed the small mound of bones from the previous night's feast. But the dogs did not go over there even in the morning. It seemed like the two cowardly dogs were still scared from the encounter with the tiger. If they'd been a little braver, they could have feasted on the bones.

The baby lamb went to seek out the udder of the sheep it had drank from the previous night. But that sheep did not allow it to come near. It kicked the little one and pushed it away with its head. Undaunted, the little lamb tried again but was rebuffed a second time. It was standing around looking forlorn when Ravi, who was observing this, walked over to the sheep, held its head between his legs and made the baby lamb drink milk from its udder.

Pichchanna and Munayya's dogs ran to the edge of the hill, hid themselves behind a bamboo bush and started barking. No one could figure out why they were barking so vehemently. Two of the shepherds went over there and looked down into the valley but found nothing.

'They have finally lost their fear from last night,' remarked Pullayya. 'They're feeling brave now! Or perhaps the smell of the bones and the mutton curry has reminded them of the tiger again.'

The barking continued incessantly until an irritated Munayya threw a big stone in their direction. One of the dogs hid itself immediately with a whimper. The other ran towards the herd and lay down there. Smiling to himself, Munayya went to the dog that was hiding in the grass by the bamboo bush. He lifted it up by the ears and legs and held it aloft, before dropping it. It jumped a couple of times before lying down again and playing dead. Munayya could not control his laughter.

The dogs recovered from their fright only after some water was sprinkled on their faces and they had received the reassuring attention of their masters. Gurappa's dog watched quietly with a bored look on its face.

Around seven, the yaanadis Narsimhulu and Obulesu appeared as if from nowhere. No one saw them coming. The two kids accompanied them.

'Namaste, swamy!' said Narsimhulu. 'Last night, we camped on Belum hill over there. And this morning we heard your dogs barking. So we climbed down to come meet you.'

Ravi took him aside and enquired about the sandalwood thieves. He explained his fear and anxiety as they had not received any updates from the yaanadis for the past few days.

'If there was any danger, we would have come and alerted you, swamy,' said Narsimhulu. 'Our deed was not traced back to us.'

'Then?'

'The smugglers suspect the Kothakota sugaalis.'

'Why is that?'

'Didn't we plant the arrows, swamy? You don't use such arrows nor do we. An archery attack would only mean the sugaalis, right?' Narsimhulu gave him a sideways glance.

Ravi now understood why Narsimhulu took the arrows from the children and pushed them into a tree and the ground. He had assumed the yaanadis were naive, but they seemed to be quite crafty.

'Did they attack the sugaalis?' he asked.

'Not possible. These wood thieves are from the Mydukur area. The sugaalis are from the Giddalur range. Too much of a distance to cover. The smugglers are basically going crazy as they try to figure out why the sugaalis would attack them. They are wondering if any big shots were behind the attack. This time they are coming fully prepared. They are bringing lots of firepower and people to launch a raid into the hills. All the sandalwood logs they felled are still lying around and need to be transported. There is probably a full lorryload of logs lying in heaps.'

Ravi felt relieved that the danger had passed. He invited the yaanadis to join them for a breakfast of rotis and leftover mutton curry. The two silly dogs fought with each other over the bones that were being discarded by the shepherds. Gurappa served some mutton to his dog along with its daily roti. Ravi still did not touch the meat.

The dumb sheep, which of course did not understand that one of them had been cooked and served as a curry, were lost in a world of their own.

Ankayya came by and asked Ravi, 'We should be going to Jyothi tomorrow, right?'

'Yes, for your new rations,' replied Ravi. 'But let's send Narsimhulu instead.'

Ankayya was silent for a few moments but then suggested that they go themselves.

'We don't know these shortcuts well, anna!' Ravi protested. 'Narsimhulu will recognise the ration-bearer and bring the rations to us. Why make the extra effort?'

Ankayya was again silent for a moment. Then he said in a low voice, 'She might bring the rations, Ravi.'

Ravi was not sure if he had heard him right. 'Why worry?' he said. 'She did say she would send the rations with someone, right?'

'Maybe Subhadra herself will come, Ravi!' explained Ankayya. He scratched his head.

Ravi looked at him in surprise. Was he expecting too much, he wondered.

'You will be blessed, my little brother,' pleaded Ankayya, holding Ravi's hands. 'Please accompany me.'

Ravi briefly stared at Ankayya before agreeing to his request. As they didn't know the safe shortcuts through the jungle, he asked Narsimhulu to join them at dawn and be their guide.

*

The gollas had the flocks moving. The little lamb had not yet found an adult to walk with. The white-streaked sheep that it fed from again that morning did not allow the lamb to come close to it, repeatedly shoving it away with its head whenever the little one approached. Ravi eventually carried the baby in his arm. Wherever they found soft grass, he put the lamb down and helped it bite the tips of grass blades with its tiny teeth.

The lamb was just ten days old. When it used to walk with its mother, it would lie down for a while whenever it got tired of all the jumping around. Then the mother would walk back and scratch the baby with its foreleg, indicating that it should get up and walk again. Anytime it felt hungry, the lamb would rush to its mother's udder. When the herds lay down to rest, the lamb would snuggle and rub its head against the mother's belly. The mother would lick the baby's body with its coarse tongue, sending the little one into raptures.

Sometimes the baby would convey its happiness to the mother by rapidly twitching its short tail. If it was separated from its mother even for a few minutes, the lamb would screech in a shrill voice. Hearing its call, the mother would come rushing to the child. When the flock needed to cross a small brook or water gully, the lamb would be unable to jump across like the adult sheep. The mother would wait for one of the shepherds to pick up the baby and only then cross the stream while still keeping its eye on its child.

The baby lamb's little world comprised only itself and its mother. The mother reciprocated its love in full measure. Now, with the mother dying well before the child was ready to face the world on its own, the little lamb found itself in a desolate situation.

Ravi understood the little one's fears and uncertainty and lavished attention on it. He carried it around and kept a close eye on it like a mother would whenever he let it walk by itself. He often patted it and helped it eat the fresh grass stalks. He found himself worrying about the lamb slipping and falling whenever it did its tiny jumps on the rocks.

Having faced a tiger, Ravi found that he was no longer troubled by the bushes and thick woods. The deep water gullies and streambeds did not frighten him anymore, and the hanging roots of huge trees stopped looking like pythons to him. He also lost his fear of stone plates concealing tigers and the thick vegetation surrounding the streambanks having hidden hyenas. Discretion had replaced his sense of fear and foreboding, and he walked ahead while throwing stones at any suspicious-looking spot and yelling loudly.

They walked through a grove of yepe trees, the lush green leaves of which formed a canopy over the trail. The recent rains had changed the shoots on the tree branches into leaves. The red polika and white polika trees too sported green leaves. While the shoots and buds were just about making an appearance on some of the trees, their branches and twigs still looked like dry sticks. The birds perched on those trees were like unripe fruit that never fell down.

The rains had washed away some of the ashes of the burned grass, but not all of it. The ripe leaves that fell off the trees covered the remaining black soot. From between the leaves, one could see grass shoots popping out like thin green tongues. It was nature in its varied hues and forms.

With the various small bushes and dry grass fields having burned down during the harsh summer, only the trees were left standing around proudly. The forest land looked strangely empty at places. The stones bore the marks of the forest fires, as did the tree trunks. It seemed like it was the job of the green grass shoots to cover up the black burn marks and make the forest floor look more presentable until the heavy rains could come down and wash it all away.

The yepe did not bother itself with all these changes and bloomed well before the other trees. It grew as tall as twenty-five metres and in full bloom; it made one wonder if the green of the grass had been absorbed by the tree and made its way to the top, greening the leaves on the few drooping branches.

When he was still under the hold of his fear, Ravi was oblivious to the charm of the green shoots, the birds on the trees, the formations of the hill ranges, the calls of birds and little animals, the unlimited expanse of the blue sky and the silence of the forest. He simply did not have the mental space to think about these things. Once the fear and its bodily symptoms went away, and the trepidation he had felt at every step became a distant memory, Ravi was able to see the real form of the forest clearly.

He found the sight of the hills and forests cleansing his eyes, and its silence enhancing his hearing. The plants and stones were like warm scrubs for his body, and the breeze felt like it was purifying his lungs. The cornucopia of smells and fragrances from the leaves, flowers, roots and soil flushed the toxins out of him. As he carried the little lamb on his shoulders or under his armpit, Ravi felt like a tree branch offering the birds to perch on it.

'Sinnoda, put the lamb down,' instructed Gurappa. 'It will forget how to walk if you carry it all day long. Its legs and joints need to become stronger. Let it walk with the flock!'

Ravi put the lamb down with a smile. It stood still for a few moments, shook its body, looked around and then started walking slowly behind the last of the flock's sheep. Ravi kept an eye on the little one.

They came across a narrow stream that traversed the length of the hill and then merged with a brook in the valley. As Gurappa stood on the bank of the stream and herded the sheep away, he called out to his son. Ravi looked up at him from behind the flock.

'Konda Narayana's children,' said Gurappa, 'what are they studying?'

'The son is studying engineering,' replied Ravi. 'The daughter is in high school.'

With the distance between them and the noise made by the sheep, Gurappa could not hear Ravi clearly. He repeated the question. Ravi walked a few steps forward and shouted the answer again. They all knew that taking loans for his children's education was one of the main reasons Narayana fell into a debt trap. Gurappa moved a few steps towards Ravi and asked, 'Is there a way we can help them?'

'If I had a job, we could have helped them . . .'

'We owe them, sinnoda!' said Gurappa. 'When we had the dispute with Subba Reddy, Narayana kept his family relationships aside and supported us. He was firm about our claim being just and fair. Such help cannot be forgotten, ever. Get a job, sinnoda . . . if not for yourself, then at least for them.'

Gurappa suddenly threw his arms up and started shouting, 'Thoi! Thoi!' Ravi turned around in surprise. The sheep at the back of the flock were flustered. They were running around and dispersing.

Then he noticed it. A large head, black stripes on its ash-coloured body, mouth wide open, fangs showing—a panther. It had been lying in wait. Vaulting out from its hiding spot, it stood on the bank of the stream.

The lamb seemed to instinctively understand the behaviour of the adult sheep. Its ears pricked up and it froze, holding its breath with eyes wide open. It knew the smell of fear. As the other sheep had sprung away, the panther only had the little lamb to pounce on. And pounce it did. The lamb helplessly squeaked in fear seeing the strange wild animal lunge at it.

Ravi suddenly screamed at the top of his voice and ran towards the panther with his axe held high. He was determined to not let the wildcat take the lamb. The panther stopped just before its final lunge and turned around at the sound of Ravi's approach. It bared its fangs and rose up on its hind legs, readying itself to attack Ravi with its forelegs.

Without a break in his step, Ravi thwacked the panther on its ribs with the eye of the axe. Just the one thump was enough. The panther lost its nerve and jumped into the streambed with a visceral cry emanating from its throat. It ran away swiftly, not giving Ravi any chance to chase it. Gurappa and Bhaskar threw stones after it and kept yelling in the direction it disappeared.

Ravi lifted the little lamb into his arms. It was shivering uncontrollably. Ravi caressed its body and rubbed its back. In a few minutes, it had calmed down. Gurappa looked at Ravi with an expression of equal surprise and happiness.

Exactly one week ago, Ravi had become numb with fear at the sight of a hyena and had quietly offered his neck. It was nothing short of magical to see such a transformation in just a week. Yesterday, he had dared to confront a tiger to rescue a wounded sheep. And now, he attacked a panther and dealt with it as if it were a common dog . . . To Gurappa, it was unbelievable. He kept stealing glances at his son as they resumed walking.

Ravi did not put the lamb down till they arrived at the water source. While they were resting after lunch, Tiripalu brought up the topic of Narayana again. He was in tears reminiscing his relationship with the deceased.

One of the shepherds suggested that they relocate the herds to a different area of the Nallamala forest ranges. The small and large predators in their vicinity had all become aware of the flocks by then. Some animal or the other attacked the herd every day, and deer, antelopes and wild sheep tried to use the flocks as a cover to escape the predators. The predators must naturally be frustrated by those escapes, and their anger and desperate hunger could lead to more attacks on the herd. There was nothing to do but shift to a different zone of the hills. The proposal was accepted unanimously.

Crossing a certain hill to the southeast of the iron plates allowed one to reach the Donla sub-stream area. If one travelled south from the sub-stream, one reached Belum hill and the nearby Belum stream. Going further south, one would find the Banyan with the Big Props and the Banyan with the Small Props—both impenetrable forests.

Every Monday of the holy month of Karthika, at the onset of winter, devotees travelled to the Belum caves to worship Muneeswara, a mendicant form of Shiva. They also did some sightseeing of the Belum cave system while on pilgrimage. The shepherds thought about travelling towards those caves but dropped the plan when the yaanadis informed them the grass there was not enough given the poor rains.

Pamuleti and Gangayya had scouted the entire forest range before the group set off for hill-grazing. They confirmed that there was an abundance of rains and grass in the region of Pedda Ootla water springs. They decided the herds would travel in that direction.

The advantage of heading towards Pedda Ootla was that they could find multiple water sources on the way. Many of those springs were perennial and would always have sufficient water for both the sheep and the men. The disadvantage was that it would be more challenging for the ration-bearers to reach them because of the narrower trails and the lack of shortcuts. However, the group would be quite close to the Garudadri ashram of Kasi Nayana, which could help them in case of any delay with the rations.

*

Narsimhulu joined the group at nightfall and slept with the herds. He roused Ankayya at four the next morning. Ankayya in turn woke Ravi up.

'You guys go ahead, anna!' suggested a sleepy-eyed Ravi.

'Please come along, Ravi!' pleaded Ankayya.

Ravi got up and got ready to head out. The moon was at its apex in the sky. It was a Dasami moon, and the faint moonlight filled the forest. Narsimhulu avoided the cart trails because tigers would typically lie in wait around the area at that time. He led them across the hills into the forest.

Aided by the cool weather, they walked fast. Passing under the trees, they moved along the streambanks and climbed up and down some steep hills. They were soon sweating heavily despite the breeze. They rejoined the forest road again near the wellspring and reached Jyothi around six, just as the sun emerged from behind the eastern hills.

The Kasi Nayana ashram was already buzzing with the usual activities of the residents. The fires had been lit in the kitchen. The brisk walk—almost a run—had soaked their clothes in sweat. Ankayya proceeded straight to the bathhouse, turned on a tap and sat directly under it without removing his clothes.

Ravi stared in surprise. Where was the fear of disease that made Ankayya avoid even wetting his feet in the forest? Probably the hope that his wife would show up had made him discard the rules of the forest. Ravi wondered if he was cleaning himself to look presentable to his wife. Perhaps he did not want the stink, of not having taken a bath in two weeks, to disgust his wife. However, that stench of sweat and dirt mingled with the dried urine and dung of the sheep was difficult to get rid of. At least he was making an effort.

Ravi bought soap from the ashram shop and handed it to Ankayya. It seemed to Ravi that Ankayya had cleansed the dirt from his mind a few days ago over the phone and was now scrubbing away the dirt from his body. Like Ankayya, Ravi too sat under a tap with clothes on. They used the soap to wash their bodies and their clothes too.

Once done, they tried to squeeze their dripping clothes dry as much as possible before walking to the bus stop. By then, Narsimhulu had asked around and found out that the bus had broken down somewhere and was not expected to arrive that day. Two autorickshaws had arrived earlier, but no one had alighted with a ration bag.

Ravi felt disappointed at the update, but Ankayya's eyes kept searching the spot where the autorickshaws were parked. He then looked near the dining hall, by the temple, near the amla tree and finally headed to the stone platform surrounding the old tamarind tree. A woman was standing there with a cloth bag placed on the platform. With her was a child about a year old. Her gaze was on them.

'There she is!' cried Ankayya and walked towards her immediately taking long, brisk strides. Ravi looked disbelievingly as Ankayya went near the woman and spread his arms wide. She handed him the child. Ankayya lifted the boy up, kissed him on the forehead and then handed him back to his mother. She silently took out a set of clothes from the bag and handed them to Ankayya, who changed into the fresh clothes right there.

He took the boy again, held him close to his chest and patted his head. He began uttering gibberish to make the boy smile while his wife spread his wet clothes out to dry on the stone slabs near the tree. Ravi was still finding it difficult to believe what he was seeing. She must have started her journey at midnight and walked three kilometres with the heavy bag and the little boy in tow to reach the bus stop. And then she had had to catch an autorickshaw but still managed to arrive early.

It was amazing for Ravi to see a woman with so much love for her husband. How did she manage to stay away from him for such a long time? Ravi had heard many tales of men braving the odds and suffering hardships just to go see the women who had their heart. But this was the first time he had seen a woman do that.

What was even more surprising for Ravi was that Ankayya had been able to guess that she would come to meet him. He was so confident that she would be there. How could he be so sure? Ravi had heard the ration-bearers say that she would send the rations with someone. How did she manage to imply that she would be coming herself? It was inexplicable to Ravi.

He guessed that maybe only when he was married and truly in love with his wife would he be able to relate to such things. It was probably a waste of time to even try and understand such a bond while he was single.

Ravi went to the dining hall along with Narsimhulu. They relished the hot meal that was being served there. Stomachs full, they sat under the amla tree to talk and kill time until Ankayya was ready to head back.

From the intelligence gathered by Narsimhulu, the game plan of the sandalwood thieves had become clear. The thieves were confident that the government was too negligent to catch them and were preparing to smuggle the red sanders logs out of the forest to safe warehouses in the city. The wood would then be sent off for interstate or international trade.

The smugglers had hidden piles of logs at several places in the forest according to Narsimhulu. The yaanadis had come across these hiding spots as they roamed around gathering honey, resin gum and medicinal roots. Ravi ended up having a long conversation with Narsimhulu while waiting for Ankayya, who returned after spending an hour with his wife and son.

Ankayya kept turning around to look at his wife and son as the shepherds set off again into the jungle. They arrived back at their camp at ten.

'Did she come, my daughter-in-law?' asked Gurappa.

'Yes,' replied Ankayya.

'She brought the little boy as well?'

'Yes, she did.'

'Both are fine, right?' asked Gurappa, before continuing in an admonishing tone, 'That woman is gold. You are the senseless fellow. At least now learn to properly engage with your relatives. Would anyone else offer sheep as an excuse to avoid attending the marriage of his wife's brother?'

Ankayya was touched that nearly all the shepherds enquired about the well-being of his wife and infant son. His eyes welled up.

15

THE LITTLE LAMB DID not walk with the sheep and instead kept itself by Ravi's side all the time. It wouldn't stay by the white-streaked foster mother from whom it fed; it kept coming back to Ravi. It even slept by Ravi's side one night.

When Gurappa got up in the morning, he saw the lamb cuddled like a ball near Ravi's feet. He pointed out the scene to Pullayya. 'Yes, it is like that once you pamper a creature, be it human or animal,' remarked Pullayya, laughing. Gurappa picked the lamb up and left it near the white-streaked one. But the lamb got up, shook its body, looked around at the sleeping sheep and hopped over to Ravi, who had just woken up.

Pullayya coughed a dry cough and said to Ravi, 'Orey, what is it you think you are doing? It doesn't matter how much you pamper an animal at home, but it won't work in the hills. If we keep an eye on only one life here, there will be trouble for the other hundred lives. As the saying goes, "The cattle should be tied near the grass mound." The lamb should be with the sheep. What is the use of it being with you?'

Pichchanna laughed. Ravi was silent.

'When we are hill-grazing, the problem of one person becomes the problem of the entire group,' continued Pullayya. 'That's why everyone should be watchful all the time. Can't let up the vigilance. You are no longer a young ram, wet behind the ears. You have gone beyond that and are now an alpha ram. One who handles a herd should not have these little indulgences.' He finished by instructing Gurappa to take care of the little lamb.

Ravi silently gazed at Pullayya for a few moments.

The white-streaked sheep was still not allowing the little lamb to come near its udder. Gurappa came by as Ravi was struggling to force it to let the little one have its milk.

'Why doesn't it allow that one to drink?' wondered Gurappa. 'Let's take a look. Let go of it for a moment.'

Ravi moved away from the sheep and Gurappa sat on his haunches in front of the white-streaked mother sheep. He scratched its forehead lightly with his nail and rubbed it affectionately under its neck while making calming noises to steady the sheep's restless movements. That way, he ensured that it would not kick or headbutt the little one. The sheep's own child was a little red lamb that was born while they were in the village. It still stayed close to its mother and drank from its udder.

Because the red one was older than the orphaned lamb, it tried to establish its ownership rights over its mother by shoving the smaller one away. Gurappa left them to their antics and watched as the little one fell twice when the red lamb pushed it. The second time, the little lamb just lay there, legs up in the air. It did not try to get up. The mother sheep looked at it blandly with no reaction whatsoever.

Along with Gurappa, Ravi and Pullayya also kept an eye on their interaction. After a few minutes, magic happened. The red one pushed the little lamb down for the third time. It was about to charge again as the little one tried to get up when the mother suddenly stopped its own child, pushing it away with its head.

Gurappa smiled at Pullayya. Ravi was amazed.

*

The group had to cover a longer distance to reach a different part of the forest, so they left early. The goal was to reach a water source by noon. Whether they aimed for the head ponds or the big springs, they needed to cover roughly fifteen kilometres to reach it.

The herds formed marching lines atop the Manti hill and grazed without stopping their march. They were eating, urinating, defecating, sneezing, whimpering and screaming, all while continuing to walk. Some sheep would rub themselves against a rock or tree to shed a bit of fur before jumping back into their place in the marching column. A shepherd could track the path taken by a flock even a week later. He would notice the fur stuck on the trees and rocks and smell the faint whiff of sheep droppings and urine across the path.

As the herds marched along the western edges of tall hill ranges, they could see the forest extend from Balappa's well till the Gopidevi stream. The trees that completely covered the hills below had fresh buds and leaves of a light green colour. The green of the leaves was interspersed with the dirt colour of twigs and branches. Here and there, yepe trees appeared in full green regalia.

Suddenly, they heard the sound of axes hitting tree trunks. In the distance, the shepherds could discern the shapes of men, who appeared no bigger than their thumbs. They saw a man lifting his axe and bringing it down on to a tree trunk. The sound of metal hitting wood came to them a second later. The lack of sync between sight and sound seemed strange.

Ravi knew that they were the sandalwood thieves. They seemed to have begun their activities again. The smugglers knew neither the police nor the forest officials would dare to come into the deep forests, and hence continued their brazen felling of red sanders trees. The tree fellers were hired labour who seemed unable to get by on honest work and were greedy for the attractive pay and bonuses offered by the smugglers.

Ravi thought that the forest department employees probably earned salaries that were twice or thrice of what the illegal woodcutters made. Why couldn't they go into the hills to do their job, which was to protect the forest? If the forest was lost, would they still have their salaried jobs?

The forest officers knew a great deal about the kingpins who ran the wood-smuggling gangs. Their dereliction of duty was allowing smugglers to eventually become politicians and lawmakers. Ravi felt anguish over the situation.

The straight route north led to Garudadri. From Garudadri, they would have to go downhill and around Siddappa's heaps to reach the Big springs. Alternatively, they could descend now to reach the Upper springs by walking past Gopidevi stream. Or they could continue north towards Garudadri and halt for lunch near Head ponds, a large pond fed by subterranean springs. They opted to proceed towards the Big springs.

Over two weeks, the shepherds and their flocks had traversed all the hills and forests within the radius of thirty kilometres. They had stopped at or passed well-known landmarks or features such as the Village brook, the well of the Guy with Crooked Ears, the Eagle Colony hill, the tamarind grove, the iron ore plates, the Berry Tree hill, the windy pile of rocks, the Thornwood Tree spine, the Cloudy stream, the Raasala pasture, the Tiger brook, the Hidden spring, the Frolic springs, Jivvi Tree cliff, Onnuramma's fort and Balappa's well.

As the herds headed towards the western corridor of the Nallamala hill forests, the shepherds were a bit apprehensive. Not because of tigers and other wild animals; they feared the sugaalis, who were capable of stealing away entire herds of sheep. If the shepherds were even a little negligent, the tribals could divert the head ram and have it lead the herd in a different direction. The sheep stealers were supposedly all from a single sugaali hamlet. That was the only thing they did. The reputation of the entire sugaali community was tainted because of that one small hamlet.

Experienced shepherds knew that one should be strong-willed enough to not get shaken by their attacks. Pullayya instructed the shepherds not to spread their herds thin along the hill ranges. They had to ensure the flocks remained in view at all times.

They left the hilly terrain, crossed two large rock outcrops and arrived at the Big springs. There were several tall and wide mango trees, and a brook flowed through the centre of the mango grove. One could discern the lilting sound of the water flowing beneath the roots of the mango trees as well.

It was mid-afternoon and the sheep's throats were parched. Within minutes, the brook was covered in sheep desperate to quench their enormous thirst. Ravi gazed upon the flow of the stream both above and below the surface. He felt a sense of wonder at how the water had pierced the black soil beneath the tree roots and created dark tunnel-like channels to flow underground too.

Suddenly, he felt the wet touch of a sheep's tongue on his heel. It was the little lamb again, licking his feet to get his attention. Ravi picked it up, placed it under his arm and continued to enjoy the pleasant ambience of the spot. The rains had been abundant there and had made the forest floor a veritable green carpet. The trees were heavy with leaves. It was the forest at its most beautiful.

'The forest here looks like a bride wearing new clothes and flowers in her hair,' quipped old Pullayya.

It certainly was lovely, almost achingly beautiful to look at. The continuous flow of water had made the mango trees grow tall and lush. Hidden under the leaves were green mangoes that had not yet ripened. Monkeys had probably plucked some of the fruit and thrown it down. Gurappa picked up a green mango from the ground and gave it to his son. It looked slightly ripe. Ravi bit into it. Fleshy and sour, to him it tasted more like a lemon.

In the water were dark-coloured fish the size of human fingers. Gurappa said that they were known as raati kolukulu, or stone fish. They were found near the black stone slabs in the water. Swallowing one of these fish alive did wonders for asthmatic people, added Gurappa before plucking one out of the water. Holding its head between two fingers, he opened his mouth wide and popped the fish inside.

Eating a fish while it was still alive seemed like a novel experience to Ravi, who wanted to try it too. He used his headscarf to catch a fish the size of his little finger and then pushed it all the way into his throat. He closed his eyes and swallowed it whole. He could feel the fish beating its tiny fins as it travelled down his gullet. And then it was still.

There was a mossy smell to the fish and a slightly oily sensation when one swallowed it. It wasn't a feeling he wanted to experience a second time. He cleared twigs and leaves from under one of the big mango trees and spread out his headscarf. He then lay down, using the thick roots for a pillow. The little white lamb snuggled close to him.

Above him was a green canopy that covered the sky. Ravi looked up at branches so wide and thick that a man could not put his arms around them. They grew upwards and sideways and were completely covered with leaves. Suddenly, he noticed black-faced grey monkeys perched on the branches, their tails dangling as they groomed each other's hair. They were all langurs. Ravi couldn't see any common Indian monkeys.

Strange-looking jungle birds sat quietly or flew between the trees. With some, Ravi could only hear their calls, as they were hidden behind the thick leaf cover. Then he sensed a movement on a branch. Up there something was scrabbling swiftly. He rubbed his eyes and peered again but could not spot the animal. A few moments later, it came into view again, now scarpering in the opposite direction. It was an Indian palm squirrel.

It had brown fur the colour of an areca nut and a tail with mixed black and red stripes. Its head moved in jerky sideways motion. It stayed rock-still one moment and moved forward rapidly the next, almost as if it was a remote-controlled toy being piloted by a child. Ravi realised that there were two of them. One squirrel would run across the branch lightning fast while the other stayed still until it suddenly jerked away and moved to the further ends of the branch. The first one would then chase it but stop at a distance and just observe its mate. It was probably a courting ritual between the male and the female.

The first squirrel moved quickly, hugging the underside of a branch. It jumped without changing position—with its back facing the ground—but somehow landed on a branch to the side, seemingly defying gravity. The second squirrel followed suit immediately. They kept their heads straight and held their tails stiff and aloft as they jumped from the underside of one branch to the other. With the blue sky in the background, the squirrels appeared like flying kites. Ravi could not take his eyes off them. He had never imagined that these dainty little dirt-coloured creatures could be so fine-looking and perform such amazing acrobatic feats.

The palm squirrels eventually moved their courtship ritual to another tree. In the meantime, the shepherds had finished cooking lunch. They used teak leaves as plates and sat down for the afternoon meal. They were eating under the cool shade of the trees surrounded by various birds and animals with a brook flowing beside them. To Ravi, it felt like a picnic in the jungle.

After the late lunch, some of the shepherds sat near their flocks and chatted while others lay down under the trees for a nap. Tiripalu sat leaning against a tree near his flock, smoking a beedi. Pullayya called him over.

'I hear you refused to give your daughter's hand to the boy from Varikuntla,' said the old shepherd.

'That is right,' replied Tiripalu. 'I decided not to proceed with that alliance.'

'I believe that boy owns four acres of land with a very steady income. Why are you being foolhardy and refusing the alliance?'

'Because it won't work out.'

'I also heard that the boy has no avocation other than his farm and home. Rare to find such a boy, son.'

'It doesn't matter.'

'They are financially secure and aren't even asking for a dowry!' said Pullayya, but Tiripalu remained silent.

'He even owns a pair of oxen,' Pullayya continued, still not giving up.

Tiripalu sat on his haunches in front of Pullayya. Looking into the old man's eyes, he said, 'Do you know of any youngster these days who uses oxen to plough his fields?'

Pullayya caught the sarcasm in Tiripalu's voice.

'It is not a wrong thing to do, son.'

'There was no other option when you were a young man. This is the time of your grandchildren now. The generation of tractors.'

'So, you say it is wrong to use cattle? But I have heard that he is a good farmer!'

'I am a farmer too. What is good about it?'

'What do you lack?'

'I am able to survive because of the sheep. Had I remained only a farmer, my life would have been a disaster,' said Tiripalu, his voice bitter.

'What are you trying to say, son?'

'I won't give my daughter's hand to a farmer!' said Tiripalu vehemently.

Pullayya was dumbstruck by the rash statement.

Ravi could overhear this conversation and was following it with some interest.

'I have been to their home,' added Tiripalu. 'I met the boy and his parents. He has a younger sister. I saw her too.'

'So? What about them?'

'You will understand if you see them.'

'I asked around,' said Pullayya. 'They are known to be good people who don't interfere in other people's lives.'

'Have you seen the boy's mother?'

'No . . . what about her?'

Tiripalu pinched the skin on old Pullayya's shoulder and said, 'She does not have an ounce of flesh anywhere on her body! Just leathery skin over bones, that is all . . . like dried fish.'

'What else will hardworking people look like? You are making too much of it! Some people just have bodies like that. They are naturally thin—'

'Okay, forget the mother,' cut in Tiripalu. 'At least the young girl should look good, right? She's of a marriageable age.'

'Even the daughter is like that?'

'Oh, compared to her, the mother is all right.'

'Maybe it is in their genes, then.'

'The men look fine though. Aren't they from the same gene pool?'

'Rey, what do you mean to say?' cried Pullayya, who seemed to be in an argumentative mood. 'Isn't it enough if the groom looks fine? The groom's mother, sisters, relatives—should they all look good? You are talking as if you are the only one looking to get a girl married. As the saying goes, "Your bragging words match my brass ear studs." You are putting yourself on a high horse, son!'

'Old man, is it enough if the boy looks good? Is it enough?' Tiripalu suddenly stood and loomed over Pullayya. 'Why wouldn't I worry that my daughter's fate would be the same as the other women in that family?'

'Why would it be like that?'

'The men in that family seem to be leaving the household and farmwork to the women while they roam around the streets playing puli joodam and bara katta and other gambling games,' Tiripalu finally explained. 'Haven't we seen many men like that? Yes, they come across as good people. But the reality is different.'

'Okay then,' conceded Pullayya. 'Are you looking elsewhere for a suitable alliance?'

'Yes, I must.'

'What kind of an alliance?'

'Anyone but a farmer,' replied Tiripalu firmly. 'It could be someone running a small shop, a construction worker or someone selling vegetables on a pushcart in the town. Even a casual labourer is fine . . . I swear, even if he is a watchman, it is fine with me!'

Pullayya looked at him in silence.

'I don't want a future where my daughter marries a farmer and then he dies by consuming pesticide and she returns home a widow,' Tiripalu declared. 'I won't be able to bear her burden for the rest of my life. Her husband does not need to own land or other property. It is fine as long as they earn enough to live, even if it is a daily wage. No debt traps for the sake of farming, and no suicides in my daughter's life.' Having said that, Tiripalu walked back to his spot.

There was nothing Pullayya could say to that. Ravi understood the harsh reality of Tiripalu's words. He was thinking of Konda Narayana's life and untimely death.

*

After resting for a while, they got the herds up and moving again. There was plenty of grass thanks to the rains in that part of the range. The sheep gorged on the fresh grass and were full by the evening. That night, they camped on the flat and wide elevation near the head springs area.

As soon as they were herded together for the night, the sheep lay down and started chewing the cud. Seeing the sheep so well fed made Gurappa happy, and he went to bed a content soul. Ravi lay down and looked at the starlit sky. The surrounding hills stood like the walls of an ancient fortress. Ravi found himself thinking how that same sky had frightened him so much just a few days ago. He thought the night sky resembled a blue saree studded with pearls all over and wondered if he could see a sky like this in the village.

He suddenly thought about the sky in Hyderabad. Ravi could not remember ever having even seen the sky in the city. It was just an overhead void filled with dust, dirt, smoke and the reflection of haze. One couldn't see a starlit sky in the city.

Out in the jungle, the sky exhibited itself from varied perspectives. The sky that appeared and disappeared in the gaps between branches and twigs. The sky that seemed to bend within touching distance from the steep incline of the hill when one looked up at it. The sky that shook with a start when a wild animal suddenly bellowed. The sky that spoke the language of silence in the darkness.

Ravi was lost in a pleasant reverie as such thoughts crossed his mind under the twinkling stars. Occasionally, he heard the cries of some nocturnal birds or the noises of animals in the valleys below. Suddenly, he thought he could hear another sound that was quite distinct from the usual sounds of the forest night. It was a continuous thrum from quite afar that spread across the hills through the cold night.

No, he then thought, it was coming from within the hills, from somewhere along the valley. It was emanating from the edge of the valley bed extending to the south, from behind Balappa's well—the sound of a motor engine. It sounded like a heavily loaded tractor, its engine struggling to carry its load up an incline. It seemed to be moving slowly between the big rocks, its hum distinct enough but faint. One had to really listen for it to be able to hear it.

Ravi sat up. He suspected that the tractor was transporting the illegally felled red sanders logs from their hiding places in the forest. Even after their big attack, the wood thieves had calmly resumed their activities without any fear and continued to destroy this magnificent natural ecosystem with their beastly and demonic greed.

Ravi struggled to sleep well after that. He kept having horrifying visions of the entire forest being cut down, with just rocks and pebbles remaining and nothing for his sheep to graze on. His nightmares woke him up twice during that night, and each time his ears searched for the tractor's sound. The engine continued to hum for most of the night. When he finally awoke to the bird calls at dawn, he tried to make out the sound of the tractor. The birdsong was quite loud and perhaps drowned it out.

Dawn was lit up by the sounds of birds. There was a perennial water source and trees that offered plenty of edible fruit, which made it a haven for many species of birds. That morning, it seemed as if thousands of birds were holding a concert, filling the forest with many different sounds, creating a magical atmosphere. No musician could ever imagine or compose such a wondrous performance.

Some birds were crying at the top of their voices as if they wished to streamline the noise and establish some sort of an order. Even the peacocks joined in the chorus with their shrill cries. It seemed like the celestial Gandharvas were expressing themselves through the birds' throats. The rushing stream, the wind and the rocks added tonal properties to the sounds even as they echoed them. Every now and then, a tiger would roar in the valley and the birds would suddenly go deathly quiet, almost holding their breath.

The rest of the shepherds woke up around five. By the time they were done with their morning ablutions, Narsimhulu had arrived at the camp. He told them that the yaanadis had travelled overnight to reach Garudadri, but they did not feel like staying in the southern forest due to an inexplicable fear.

After breakfast, Ravi and Bhaskar walked towards the water springs with Narsimhulu in tow. Ravi told them about the sound of the tractor he heard at night. That was when Narsimhulu said that he had come to alert them about the smugglers using a tractor to move their illegal stashes of logs. So Ravi's assumptions had been correct.

According to Narsimhulu's intelligence, the tractor's carriage had been overloaded with red sanders logs and was going up an incline when the wheels got stuck in the deep grooves of a cart trail that ran through a dried-up streambed. As they tried to rev the engine, the wheels sank further into the loose soil, getting stuck deeper into the stony grooves. The smugglers' crew struggled through the night to free the tractor but gave up around dawn and left it there. Narsimhulu said that they would return either that night or the next with a Poclain excavator to pull the tractor out.

For a while after that, Ravi, Bhaskar and Narsimhulu discussed their next course of action. Narsimhulu was in favour of another attack. He said that most of his fellow yaanadis were still in jail despite having done nothing wrong, and as long as the wood thieves were active in the forest, there was no hope for their release.

Though apprehensive about the plan, the two shepherds decided to continue on the path on which they had already embarked. However, from the group that had participated in the attack the previous week, Mohan and Ramachandra had already returned home. Ravi and Bhaskar discussed the idea with Sreenu and Tiripalu to see if they would like to replace them and were glad to find that they were enthusiastic. Narsimhulu left to do a recce of the area and ready the plan of attack.

The herds started moving again. That day, they set out on the trail to the rocky plain west of Garudadri. Pamuleti had told them that if they travelled north from that plain and crossed Rama Gundala, they could easily find enough grazing spots for four days on the wide hills there.

On the way to Garudadri, they saw two heaps of rocks to the left of the trail. The heaps did not look like natural formations. It was as if people had picked up all the hand-sized stones in the area and piled them up. It was known as Siddappa Nayani Guttalu, or the Siddappa heaps.

Pullayya told them that during the annual fair at the Ahobilam temple during the month of Phalguni, pilgrims from Porumamilla and other towns took this route. When returning from the temple fair, the tradition was for each pilgrim to pick up a stone and throw it in one of the heaps. The belief was that adding a stone to the heap would help ward off evil spirits, reduce the strain of the journey and, most importantly, protect them from wild animals. Thus, the stone heaps had grown larger every year. The old shepherd then went on to narrate a fantastic story about the legend behind the Siddappa heaps.

A long time ago, during the time of the Vijayanagara kings or even before that, in the western edges of the Nallamala forest lived a sugaali chieftain by the name of Siddappa Nayaka. He found his lady love in a tribal hamlet near the village of Ankalamma Peta, under the overhang of a big hill on the eastern edges of the forest.

After sunset, Siddappa Nayaka would walk across the hills to spend the night with his lover. He would return to his hamlet in the morning. The couple were so deeply in love that even the thick forest couldn't be an obstacle to their rendezvous. Siddappa walked through the forest taking long strides, carrying his giant battle axe on his shoulder. It was said that even the tigers would give him way.

Once, due to some unavoidable reason, Siddappa could not visit his paramour for about a week. She could not tolerate the lengthy wait; she burned with the fires of passion and worried if any evil mishap had befallen her lover. She wondered if he was down with some illness or facing some trouble . . . or if a wild animal had attacked him? She could not sit quietly in her hut anymore.

Meanwhile, Siddappa Nayaka was finally free to make his nightly visit and was desperate for the sun to set. His mind was full of thoughts about his lady love. If only he had wings, he would fly to her right away. Soon, it became dark and the household retired after dinner. Siddappa put his battle axe on his shoulder, a dagger in his waist cloth and stepped out.

At the same time, his lover decided to go find Siddappa herself. Once everyone else in her household had gone to bed, she put a stove of burning coals on her head and started walking through the forest by the light of the flames. The dense forest did not scare her as her mind was full of anxiety. She wanted to rest her head on her lover's chest and dissolve in passion. Seeing the burning stove on her head, the tigers and leopards did not cross her path. She moved like wind on that dark night.

Siddappa Nayaka had crossed the Matti Palle tank, the Enkalaboti pasture and the Big springs when he saw an apparition coming his way on the route from Garudadri. It was walking briskly with flames over its head. He could tell that the figure was a woman, moving like rough wind on the walking trail.

Siddappa thought that only a demon would walk through the forest in the shape of a woman at this time of the night, that too with flames over its head. Siddappa was a brave warrior and did not think twice. He swiped under the stove with his giant axe.

'Nayaka!' cried the woman as she fell down. The stove rolled over and the flames burned brighter as the coals littered on the ground.

The woman's neck was sliced clean by the axe. She lay there, gasping for breath. Siddappa recognised her and realised what he had done.

He had killed his lover with his own hands. He was stunned into silence. He decided it was only proper and just for him to join her in death. Siddappa plunged the dagger into his heart. They were found later by the sugaalis, who built two graves for the lovers.

People travelling through this route would stop at the graves and reflect on their tragic love story. They would then put a stone near the graves as a mark of remembrance. Over time, the custom became a ritual, and the graves eventually became huge heaps of stone over hundreds of years.

Ravi found the story of Siddappa Nayaka and his lady love fascinating. He thought it amazing that even in this dense jungle, amid these wild animals, a great story of everlasting love could survive over many generations with the help of a ritual. The lovers had not been derided for their lust or for their secret extramarital dalliance. Instead, they were seen as representatives of true and pure love, and a custom was begun to ensure that their story lived on for posterity.

*

The sheep climbed up the elevation near Rama Gundala. The place was full of wild palm trees. Even after the bears in the area had eaten their fill, the trees were still groaning under the weight of mouth-watering palm fruit. The shepherds could not resist the sight. They plucked bunches of fruit and hung them on the handles of their axes.

Walking behind the sheep, the shepherds would drop a fruit into their mouth, chew the flesh and the skin and then spit out the seed. The proximity of a water source meant that they did not have to worry about the thirst that followed eating the fruit. There was plenty of water in the Rama Gundala spring stream and the Pamuleti brook.

Narsimhulu found them in the evening and spoke to Ravi in secret. He had trekked past Raasala Petu, the pillow rock of the

Manti hill, Balappa's well, Onnuramma's fort and the Juvvi Tree hillock, and he informed them that the tractor was still stuck at the same place. It needed a big machine to pull it out, but it was not easy to bring such a machine into the forest without bringing it to the notice of the forest office.

There were no guards near the tractor, but around twenty members of the smugglers' group were camped on a hillock a couple of kilometres away. Apart from the logs in the tractor wagon, there were piles of red sanders logs hidden at six other places in dry streambeds or behind rock plates.

Ravi discussed the plan in detail with Narsimhulu before he left.

16

THE GOLLAS HAD DRIFTED off into a deep sleep by eight that night. Half an hour later, a strange new bird call was heard from somewhere near Garudadri. Four of the shepherds sat up. They checked the slings around their waists and silently left the camp to join the yaanadis who were signalling them.

The four shepherds were nervous about their plan for two reasons. The main source of tension was the fear that what they were about to do would land them in big trouble. The secondary fear was about the flocks they were leaving behind unguarded at certain spots, allowing for openings through which a wild animal could attack.

However, they were urged forward by the excitement of the adventure and their sense of optimism—of serving their dharma by engaging in an activity beneficial to the forest. All their fears and apprehensions soon vanished as they marched forth on the jungle trail with the yaanadis leading the way. Not caring about the light film of sweat on their backs and confident about the strength of their group, four gollas and four yaanadis moved silently and swiftly like a pack of leopards.

Despite walking as fast as they could, it took them two hours to reach the tractor. Once there, they closely observed their surroundings without making a sound. The tractor's wheels were stuck in the ruts that had formed by fast-flowing water repeatedly cutting through the rocky ground of the streambed. It had sunk so deep that the belly of the tractor was touching the ground.

The group did not delay any further and set to work. They gathered dry twigs and placed them between the sanders logs. The yaanadis had brought along a tin of kerosene, which they poured over the logs and the tractor. Then they lit a match and threw it on the logs, which immediately burst into flames.

The group ran into the forest without looking back, their hearts beating fast. The light behind them told them that the fire was now raging and growing in size every minute. The group walked briskly for a couple of kilometres and then climbed up to some elevated ground to look at the fire. They were anxious about what would happen next.

The tractor was ablaze with red tongues of fire leaping up into the sky. Soon, a commotion began in the smugglers' camp atop the hillock. They could hear the thieves shouting and whistling loudly as they ran towards the tractor, showering abuses on their invisible enemy.

Ravi's group did not waste any more time watching the fire. The yaanadis led them to the six other spots where the red sanders logs were stored. Moving quickly, they set fire to the logs at each location and turned to dash across the forest through shortcuts. The yaanadis escaped to Jyothi via Garudadri, while the shepherds came back to their camp a little after two in the morning.

None of the adventurers slept properly that night. What they had accomplished was extraordinary, something that they could never imagine doing but were able to execute easily thanks to the yaanadis. Though they felt a light pang of guilt for burning the tractor, the crimes committed by the smugglers justified it.

Destroying the property of others by means of stealth was not the right thing to do. However, even with no one watering them or feeding them fertiliser, the trees had been growing in the forest minding their own business and providing the gift of oxygen and rains to the world. But some people cut down those trees secretly, illegally and cruelly to satisfy their own greed and caused the destruction of the ecosystem.

The shepherds and the yaanadis were powerless to stop such ghastly deeds directly, but for once they had done what was possible to stop the atrocity being inflicted on nature. As responsible citizens, it was a virtuous deed that they had accomplished. In fact, it would have been wrong to not do it. By the time this self-justification allowed them to drift off to sleep, the night had almost come to its end.

The four young gollas woke up along with everyone else in their camp and did not show any telltale signs of their adventure. It seemed that no one had noticed their absence either. During the day, the group of four could not stop thinking about the events of the previous night and used every opportunity to huddle together and review their actions and talk about what to expect going forward. Their long afternoon rest the previous day had certainly helped, because they did not feel any ill effects of the lack of sleep.

The 'big people' behind the smuggling gangs would have learned about the incident by then. It was probably the very first time that they had faced any resistance of this sort. The attack would have resulted in a huge financial loss for them and they would find it difficult to digest it. The kingpins would definitely take some action in response. Whatever they decided to do, the outcome was not going to be pleasant.

Narsimhulu and Obulesu joined the moving flocks and their shepherds early that afternoon. 'We were on our way to the Om valley area to collect edible roots,' they told the gollas, but Ravi knew that that was just an excuse. The yaanadis had come by to soothe their frayed nerves; they pulled them aside to caution them. 'Till the dust settles on this one, do not venture into the areas where the logs were hidden, not even for honey or roots,' he warned. 'Be careful to not speak of what we did—with anyone.'

As evening approached, the herds were brought down to the flat land near the Pamuleti Narasimha Swamy temple. The Pamuleti stream offered a steady supply of water. The shepherds set up camp there and started cooking dinner.

The flow of the stream had eroded the bank at several places and thick roots had emerged from the ground in those spots. The roots intertwined and climbed upwards reaching for the branches. Some of them looked like pythons. The shepherds had lots of fun sitting on the roots and creepers, using them as hammocks or dangling from them.

The watercourse on the right side of the trail led to a temple nestled amid the trees. It looked ancient and was dedicated to Narasimha Swamy, the deity of the area. The cart trail from the temple led south. Bloodstains and other telltale signs of animal sacrifice were visible on either side of the trail.

A goat, sheep or hen was sacrificed to the deity at the temple every Saturday. Devotees showed up in tractors, cooked the sacrificed animal and ate a hearty meal. They were not supposed to take home even an ounce of meat. They could eat as much as they wanted but had to leave behind any leftover meat. No one was to remain at that place after sunset.

The gollas did not take the sheep near the temple nor did they camp there for the night. They just prayed with folded hands for the welfare of their flocks and for a safe passage. However, they did this without coming down from the rocky mounds on which they were herding the sheep. Normally, they would wash their hands, feet and face before praying. But when taking care of the sheep, they had to let go of such rituals and count on the deity's understanding of their situation.

There was no scarcity of grass on the mounds around Rama Gundala. Now and then, a panther or some wildcat would appear at a distance, but the shepherds chased it away. For the next two days, the sheep grazed happily near the Squirrel hill, slowly moving towards Bayakka mound.

They set up camp near a rivulet below Bayakka mound. The shepherds then took turns to hike to the top of a nearby hill to visit the temple at Upper Ahobilam and offer prayers to the Ahobilam Narasimha Swamy. A few shepherds took their flocks around the valley to let the sheep graze near the Iron Pillar area. During the annual temple fair, this place teemed with pilgrims, the hills resounding with their commotion. The group also took the herds towards Potagiri hills and all the way to Prahlada's rock. From there they could see the vista of the Upper Ahobilam temple.

The new moon passed, which meant that they had completed three weeks in the hill forests. For the past few days, they had been drinking water directly from the streams without boiling it first. Abundant rains in that area meant the water was flowing and not stagnant.

They assumed that such flowing water would not have impurities and therefore could be safely consumed. But it's only when the water jets down the hills that it cleanses the accumulated compost in the streambeds and carries it downstream, leaving a continuous supply of fresh water in the brooks and rivulets.

Ramachandra's uncle Veerayya had arrived the previous week as a replacement for his nephew. He started feeling a chill one night, and the shivers and trembles began shortly afterwards. By morning, he was shaking even when covered with two thick woollen blankets. Soon, Veerayya was muttering gibberish in a delirium.

It was the hill fever. They knew that he had to be sent back to the village right away or the fever could prove fatal. Veerayya was covered from head to toe in a blanket and a headscarf was tied around his ears to hold the blanket in position. The left edge of the blanket was kept on his right shoulder and the right edge on the left shoulder, which gave the person on either side a handhold to support the ill man as he walked.

Bhaskar and Gangayya were nominated as the escorts and Ravi was asked to accompany the group. They started for Jyothi right away. They were anyway scheduled to meet the ration-bearers that day for fresh rations and would hand over Veerayya to those who had come from their village.

Veerayya was burning with fever and groaning loudly. He struggled to walk and kept asking his escorts to let him lie down every few steps. They resolutely kept him moving though they could feel the heat radiating from his body through the blanket.

'This isn't working,' said Gangayya finally. Grabbing Veerayya by the waist, he lifted the sick man on to his shoulder. But Veerayya was a heavyset man, and after carrying him for just half a kilometre, Gangayya had to put him down, exhausted from the exertion. Bhaskar took over the load and then it was Ravi's turn.

Some mendicants stopped them near Garudadri. They applied the paste of some medicinal leaves and herbs on Veerayya and made him drink some hot lemon tea. They finally reached Jyothi, where the ration-bearers were waiting for them. At the Jyothi ashram, the residents treated Veerayya with some herbal medicines.

Ravi looked around for the yaanadis but could not find them. Leaving Veerayya in the care of the ration-bearers, the three young men made their way back with heavy ration bags. It proved difficult for three people to carry the twenty-one ration bags that had been brought for the entire hill-grazing group. That day, the three young shepherds had already accomplished one extraordinary feat of carrying a heavy man over a long distance through forest trails and that too at a brisk pace. Now, another demand was made on their youthful energy.

It would have been easier to carry their load if they had taken three gunny sacks and put seven bags into each of them and carried one sack each. Carrying seven ration bags slung over their shoulders was tricky. As they walked, the bags swayed with the movement and dashed against their backs and stomachs. It became quite a task to walk with such inconvenient loads through the uneven trails. They stopped every now and then, encouraged each other and then started moving again after a few moments of rest.

Avoiding the longer Garudadri route, they took the trail that went past Devarakonda and Velpudari and hiked along the streambed to the north of the Anantarayani hill. This was a shorter but tougher route as they had to traverse the hills to get back to Bayakka mound.

The guttural barks of wild dogs reached them as they climbed up the hill. Without stopping, they looked down into the valley. A pack of wild dogs had clustered like an army of ants around the body of a big animal. Either they had hunted as a pack to kill the animal or they were fighting over the remains of a tiger's kill. In any case, the dogs were having a feast. The shepherds felt there was no need nor time to observe the scene closely and understand what had happened.

They finally made it to the camp, sighing with relief as they put down their loads. They were breathing heavily and sweat trickled down their bodies. Each shepherd came by and received their respective ration bags. With their task done, Bhaskar sat down next to Pullayya and ate some roti, mentioning the wild dogs that they had seen.

Pullayya nodded his head. 'Oh yeah . . . just after sunset yesterday, I had heard a cow's death screams,' he said. 'My ears have become a bit dull so I was not able to place the noise properly. I could not tell if it was near the Obulam stream or down below towards the east. The area is filled with ringing rocks that make all the sounds echo. I assumed a tiger had made a kill.'

'Probably a mature adult tiger, if it killed a cow,' said Gurappa. 'We should be a bit watchful.'

'If it is an old tiger, it won't even fear us,' said Pullayya. 'If it attacks the herd, it would grab a sheep by the neck and drag it away before we can even open our mouths to yell. We can't stop it from taking at least one sheep. The tiger won't hesitate to jump at us if we try to deny it its prey. We should just ensure that it doesn't take a second one. If we scare it enough and make it run away with just one sheep, we would have done well.'

His listeners became thoughtful after hearing his advice.

*

The white-streaked sheep had become a full-fledged foster mother to the orphaned white lamb. It was feeding milk to that lamb along with its own offspring. Both the lambs were walking beside or behind the mother all the time. When the white lamb struggled to cross a brook or got tired under the harsh sun, its foster mother licked and nudged it, making a low sound and urging it to move forward. Ravi found their interaction endearing.

Summer had truly set in by then and daytime heat had increased in intensity. When the sheep reached a water source, they were reluctant to get up until the heat started dissipating around dusk. The rocks under the trees had become too hot for anyone to sit on them during the day. The shepherds squatted on the grass instead. Even the water sources had started drying up.

Pullayya reckoned that it marked the arrival of the Rohini Karti period. Afternoons were characterised by sweltering heat and humidity and nature went into silent mode, struggling to breathe. It was the middle of May.

The shepherds sweated profusely, their bodies sticky and damp. Old Pullayya likened the steaming weather to rice coming to a boil. 'So much heat and humidity can only mean that the rains are not far away,' he said with a touch of hope. As if to prove him right, dark clouds covered the evening sky, and it thundered a couple of times. But it did not rain.

A corner of Ravi's mind remained occupied with thoughts about the wood smugglers. They had received no further intelligence about their movements. It seemed even the yaanadis did not dare venture close to them. They were now in a dense part of the forest. There were no cart tracks, only foot trails. That could be the reason the smugglers were not to be seen on this side of the forest even though the place had an abundance of valuable trees.

Sandra, satinwood, teak, oil wood and yepe jostled for space with arjuna, sirimanu and polike. Bamboo thickets were abundant too. Each thicket seemed a source of danger because they allowed wild animals to camouflage themselves in the dense undergrowth.

The gollas kept moving through the forest as they always did, throwing stones and hollering constantly to scare away any hiding animals. Peacocks would come out of the bamboo at times. It was quite lovely to look at a peafowl appear followed by five or six little ones. The bevy would be on the search for their primary food source—termite colonies that build a thin layer of soil around the bases of trees. The termites preferred green trees to dead ones, and there the peahens looked for their food.

The little bit of rain in the hills helped the ecosystem survive, but the rainwater did not leave the forest. The streams and rivulets did not become full enough to flow out of the forest into the human habitats. Even the pleasant and cool weather remained within the forest, as if stuck to the trees there. The continuum of tree life that acted as a channel to pass on the cool air from the forests to the trees near the villages did not exist anymore as it had been snapped off by the greed of the humans.

If it rained heavily and continuously for two days, the streams would rejuvenate and rush down the hills, cross the valleys and the forests to flow beside the villages. The shepherds longed for heavy rains. Their troubles would end. The constant walking had made their legs stiff like dried wood. Their bodies had become numb to pain, like termite-infested tree trunks. What remained was a silent acceptance of suffering.

Old shepherds like Pullayya found their emotions drying up. They turned into barren tree trunks. Heavy rain or severe heat, they covered their heads with a blanket and sat like obelisks. They had no sense of fear even if a tiger appeared near the herd, only a stoic resignation to fate. 'Let it come,' they thought. 'It will take a sheep . . . that is all it can do, right?' This emotional detachment did not let them react even when a sheep received fatal injuries from a tiger's claws. It allowed them to look at a dying sheep and calmly instruct the others to 'carve it and make a curry'.

Ravi wished for the rains for the villages and towns too. Fields soaked in rainwater would turn green with fresh grass and the gollas could be released from their exile in the jungle. He knew that he had to get out of the forest before his body became dull and his heart a stone. He wanted to leave before he became like the other shepherds whose hopes for a good life had died away completely.

For the past few days, the shepherds had not been able to bathe. Their skin felt abrasive and mucky and their clothes, drenched in sweat multiple times during the day, were stuck to their bodies, stiff and stinking. Their scalps were itchy, and they scratched at it with dirty fingernails. If they rubbed their skin, dirt peeled off in layers.

Ravi thought of his friends at the coaching centres in Hyderabad. They would be wrestling with English and preparing for interviews, correcting body language and expressions by practising in front of the mirror over and over without knowing how long it would take to land a job. He then looked around at the surrounding hills. The wind had changed direction. This westerly breeze would be unbearably hot in the village. But in the hills, it was cooled by the trees.

The sheep had spread over five or six hills. The shepherds kept moving behind them constantly, shouting and throwing stones into the streambed. Some of the flocks had gone to the other side of the hills to graze. It was from over there that there was a sudden yell from a shepherd, followed by screams from other shepherds. Ravi thought that they must have sighted a wild animal and were using their chorus of cries to scare it away. Perhaps a hyena or a panther or maybe even a tiger.

Ravi joined in the screaming. Theirs was the last flock of sheep. If they could let the sheep graze peacefully for a while, they could then lead the flock to the water. The swooshing sounds of the wind increased as they started climbing up the hill. Ravi tied his headscarf tighter. As the winds dove into the creek, its howling reverberated in the hills.

At the water source, Ravi expected a discussion about the creature they had been shouting at earlier, so he was surprised that no one brought up the topic while cooking or eating, or even later when they were resting. It wasn't the first time this had happened. Ravi had noticed that such topics were rarely brought up.

For him, facing the panther head on was a major incident. Confronting the hyena or the bear were also incidents that he wanted to share with others many times. But for these shepherds, it was just another happening. There was nothing special about it. Some of them would probably laugh at his reactions and thoughts. Ravi thought it was probably his naivety. Would predators not attack if they found a flock of sheep grazing in the hills, he asked himself. Would they not snarl and bare their fangs? Would the predators welcome the prey with garlands? He smiled at the thought.

However, Ravi had observed that whether at the camp in the mornings or evenings or when they gathered at a water source in the afternoon, the shepherds usually exchanged bare pleasantries, and their conversations were strictly functional. None of them showed interest in sitting as a group and talking in general about the world or other matters. They preferred sitting and lying down the moment they got some respite. Each day, all they did was walk with the sheep, eat a roti or two and then go to bed near their flock.

The difficult situation with the wood smugglers was a bit of a novelty, but once that danger had passed, it was back to inertia and stoicism. The forest had become as familiar to Ravi as the fields and groves near his village. He knew all the barren stretches of sandy and loamy soil, the hillocks and meadows, the rivulets and brooks. While herding the sheep, it seemed to Ravi that he had himself become just another sheep in the flock. A man could be extremely smart, but once he starts walking with the sheep, he becomes a sheep himself. Ravi's amusing train of thought continued.

To him, the forest was exquisitely, ethereally beautiful. The blooming trees made the valleys seem like a river of greenery. The creeks and brooks flowed with water tinged by medicinal and aromatic leaves and herbs, slithering down the mossy stones like a vine snake. What freshness in that vista, he thought. Once his fear was gone, the boulders and stone plates that were scary before now seemed majestic and mystical. The dark little caves and caverns now invoked curiosity and the hanging creepers, thick as a man's thigh, no longer resembled snakes. He could swing on them and have a good time.

The wind became wilder that day. The trees swayed like the tresses of a madwoman.

'This is the time of the red gusts,' said Pullayya. 'These are winds that bring up the dust, muck and dry leaves from barren lands and shower it on the houses in the villages. Nowadays the farms stretch up to the hills, so we are not able to see this wind. Earlier, whenever the sky was overcast, this wind would join the clouds with the soil and lash the villages with red dirt, the rascal!'

'See the wind?' Ravi interjected in surprise.

Ignoring Ravi's question, Gurappa added, 'When these hot gusts came, rice grain lifted off from the barns and lost their starch. We digested our food in less time than it took to eat it. Hunger pangs drove us crazy, and we felt like eating whatever we could lay our hands on.'

'Yes, we should cook more than the usual quantity of rice today,' Pullayya agreed.

Ravi asked again, 'You said one could *see* the wind?'

'It is true, son!' said Pullayya, explaining with his trademark dramatic flourish. 'These hot winds blow just before the first monsoon rains. They come down from the hills, cut across the flat loams and rise up as a red twisting mass of dirt and crash into the homesteads of the villages.'

'How can one see air?' protested Ravi. 'It is shapeless!'

'Can't see the wind?' shot back old Pullayya. 'Oye Gurappa! How many times have we fought shoulder to shoulder against its rage? It gave us a hell of a time when we herded the sheep along the levee of the village tank, remember? Did it allow me to close the gate of the sheep pen? I would shut it, and the wind would crash it open right away. Why does this guy say one can't see the wind?'

Gurappa guffawed. 'This wind is nothing compared to that one, mama!' he exclaimed. 'Back then we would stagger to stay upright when it blew.'

Ravi wanted to tell them that air or wind is shapeless. The form they saw was the dirt, smoke and particulate matter it carried, and its strength was simply air pressure. But before he could open his mouth, they heard a scream come from the hills.

The sound came in waves, a repeated yelling by someone who wanted to attract attention. The hills continued to reverberate with the shouts. The shepherds wondered if people had lost their way in the hills and were shouting for help. The voices came from neither the Ramapuram side nor the Obulam side. It came from near the area they were in.

Gurappa looked at Pullayya. 'Maybe they want to confirm if they are within hearing distance of other men in the hills,' said the old man. 'Go ahead and respond!'

Gurappa stood up and hollered 'Ohoy!' in response to the next shout. His voice echoed in the hills and seemed to have been heard by the other group, because a loud whistle came in response. Ankayya responded with a similar whistle so loud that Ravi felt his ears ring.

The shouts and whistles stopped from the other side. A few minutes later, they began again. The shepherds looked up and found three men standing on the hilltop. From that distance, they appeared like dolls clad in white clothes. The group below sent up a series of whistles to indicate their location. The men on the hill waved their scarves to signal that they had noticed and started descending into the valley.

The shepherds recognised them while they were still some distance away. It was Ramachandra and a couple of Ramayya's relatives. One of them was called Siddayya. He was Ramayya's wife's uncle. The third person was Obayya, Siddayya's friend.

The shepherds welcomed the visitors and enquired about news from the village. Ramachandra went straight to his flock to check on the sheep. Some food was quickly cooked for them, but it was still not clear why they had undertaken the backbreaking hike across the hills and forests to visit the camp.

After the meal, the visitors distributed beedis among the smokers in the group. They even passed around betel nuts and dried tobacco stems they had brought from the village and chatted about general topics. But they did not open up about the reason for their visit. Apart from the initial greeting, Ramachandra did not join the conversation. He declined the beedis and betel nuts and quietly tended to his flock.

Pullayya felt that the men accompanying him had come on an important errand but were wondering how to bring it up. Hesitant, they were beating around the bush. 'Siddayya!' cried the old shepherd. 'I am so happy to see you in these Obulam hills, so far away from our village. I wonder how you managed to dash across the hills and reach here by mid-afternoon. An urgent and reckless walk indeed! I have never seen such considerate people, coming all the way to enquire about our welfare and commiserate with our troubles! I see that you and Obayya have great affection for us.'

Pullayya did not hide the sarcasm in his voice and Gurappa did not control his laughter.

'Enough of the wit already,' retorted Siddayya. 'Grey hair on the head and down below, but no let-up in your cocky banter.'

'Oh, then you didn't come to see us?' shot back Pullayya. 'My fault. I assumed that was the purpose of your visit. Then you must have come to visit the deity of Ahobilam! You have to cross that hill over there to reach it . . .'

The shepherds sitting around were all laughing now.

Siddayya folded his arms and said in a low voice, 'There is a fire raging in the village. Houses are burning down.'

'Why are you here then, instead of helping douse the fire?'

'We came here to douse the fire.'

'Are you a Malayali tantric that you'll pour some water here and douse a fire in the village?' Pullayya was in full flow.

'The fire won't be extinguished until we take our Ramayya to the village,' Siddayya said, finally giving an indication of why he was there. But none of them understood what he meant by it.

'When did he learn the art of firefighting—and I unaware of it?' joked Pullayya.

'Stop your witticisms!' Siddayya almost yelled in his raspy voice. 'She has finalised an alliance for his daughter!'

'Who has?'

'Who else? Ramayya's wife!'

'She's your niece, right?'

'Oh God!' Siddayya cried and held the old man's chin. 'I did not poke my finger at all into this business. Don't frame me. I am a weakling!'

'Then who was it?'

'She did . . . along with her elder brother . . .'

'Who's the groom?'

'The brother's son,' declared Siddayya. 'It is Sunday today. The marriage has been fixed for next Saturday.'

Pullayya jerked away in surprise. 'Orey, orey . . . what is this?' he cried. 'Ramayya might be meek and soft-spoken, but he is her father! How can a girl's marriage be fixed without the father being aware of it?'

'I don't know. The brother and sister duo decided on it.'

'This is quite unfair!' interjected Gurappa. 'The rains will be here in another month or so, and then we'd all be home . . . why the hurry?'

'Couldn't delay it any further,' said Obayya.

'Not sure I understand the need for urgency. Is it a seed that would dry up and shrivel if we don't water it on time?'

'Yes! It is the seed indeed!' exclaimed Siddayya. 'It fell on fertile soil and has started germinating . . .'

Then they all understood the situation. Silence ruled for a few minutes.

'Well, why don't you just tell him then,' sighed Pullayya. 'This whole mess is like the saying, "Searching for a nest after laying an egg."'

'I was hoping that you could be the one to inform him,' said Siddayya with a groan.

'It won't matter who conveys the news,' said Pullayya. 'He's such a docile character anyway.' He looked around and shouted for Ramayya.

'Why are you shouting when he's sitting right there,' said Pichchanna.

'Where?'

'Look over there. He's sitting by the red polike tree.'

Pullayya turned towards where Pichchanna was pointing. Ramayya was sitting there with his head between his knees.

'Orey, orey!' Pullayya cried. He went over and tapped him on the head but Ramayya did not look up.

'Whether it is for good or bad,' said Pullayya, 'something is gathering momentum. It won't stop even if we try to halt it. The other day, with so many of us around, were we able to prevent the sheep's neck from being grabbed by the big fox? It is all fate, that is all. It has been ordained that the girl shall marry her cousin. We can only accept it and move on.'

The old man kept his hand on Ramayya's shoulder and tried to reason with him until he finally opened his mouth and mumbled, 'If it was ordained by God, one could accept it. But this is fate drawn by her mother . . . with an oven poker.'

'He is not a stranger, right? Your own brother-in-law's son! The girl seems to like him too . . .'

'Still a little girl. What does she know! It was my wife, the bitch . . . she brought her nephew home and set this up . . .'

'Orey, orey . . . why go to that extent? It was written in the girl's fate . . . that is all!'

'You don't know! This was all a plan. She did this to prevent the alliance with my sister's son—'

'Don't resort to useless talk, Ramudu!' cut in Gurappa.

'I did speak to them about the alliance, bava! They were being offered ten lakhs in dowry, but I settled the deal for three. The boy has a job in the army. I was hoping my daughter would have a settled, comfortable life . . .' Ramayya's voice went hoarse with emotion.

'Three lakhs? How were you planning to arrange so much money?'

'See, if we sell this flock, the owner and I would get a lakh each. I also have four acres of black regur land. I can get two lakhs if I sell two acres. And then I was hoping to borrow another lakh to spend on the wedding . . .' Ramayya whimpered as he spoke.

'If you sell the sheep and the land, what will your son survive on?'

'He will still have two acres of land, no? And would I remain idle? I'll ask the sheep owner to lease a flock. I am honest and work hard. Anyone would give me sheep to rear.'

'Your calculation is all correct,' conceded Pullayya. 'It did not work out that way, but that is okay . . .' He spoke in a consoling tone.

'She would never allow my plans to work out, ayya! She has always rejected all the proposals I have ever made. I saw it right from our wedding day! I had put a handful of turmeric rice on her head as per the ritual. She responded by dumping a whole plate of rice on my head! I knew right then and there that I wouldn't be able to handle her, that she would be the man of the house. And now, finally, she has destroyed my daughter's life . . .' Ramayya put his head down again and started weeping.

Pullayya found the situation painful, but there was nothing he could do. The visitors wanted to take Ramayya back with them, but he did not go. They stayed for the night and left at the crack of dawn. While leaving, the two men left a final message for Ramayya: 'The wedding will happen even if he doesn't show up. Tell him to come and bless the couple. He would at least be doing some justice to his position as the father of the bride.' Pullayya promised them that he'd try to convince Ramayya and send him to the village in time for the wedding.

Ramayya was distressed. He had not eaten anything the previous night and did not open his bag of rations even in the morning.

'Orey Ramudu, this is not looking good,' appealed Pullayya. 'The one who made the mistake, your daughter, is not skipping her meals. Her mother, who made her commit the mistake, is not fasting either. Is the groom or his father not eating? Why do you alone have to suffer? You foolish fellow! Come and eat!'

'I don't feel like eating.'

'You have to eat, son. Our lives are not so privileged that we can fast and grieve about things. Only those who are fortunate enough to lead a comfortable life can afford to lie down on a soft mattress, skip food and cry for four days. Ours is a different fate. The wick will burn only if there is some oil. We need to eat and then walk behind the sheep. This is the season of hot gusts; you will feel faint if you miss a single meal. You should eat more than us, in fact, because you will need extra energy to weep as well.'

'I said I don't feel like eating. Don't force me.'

Pullayya pleaded with Ramayya for some more time, and then Gurappa and Pichchanna tried to reason with him to eat as well. But Ramayya was stubborn.

Pullayya finally lost patience with him. He stood up and firmly said, 'Likes and dislikes don't work here! You must eat your normal quota of food at mealtime and do your work every day. There is no other option! If you starve and then faint from weakness, who will carry you around? Who will take care of your sheep? In your famished condition, if you stop being alert and some animal attacks the flock, who will be responsible? We all have to bear the cost equally, irrespective of whose sheep is picked up by the fox. You not having food is just not acceptable. Carrying our own rations is already a burden. No one has the free time or surplus energy to also carry you and your rations.'

Ramayya remained silent.

'All of us have issues at home,' said Pullayya in a softer tone. 'Pichchanna has them, Gurappa has them, Tiripalu, Ankayya . . . everyone. As the saying goes, "Anyone who has a nose can catch a cold." One can't cut off one's nose just because one has caught a cold!'

Ramayya was unmoved.

'Orey Ramudu!' Pullayya said finally. 'This is my final word. Stay here if you agree to eat properly and take care of the flock. Else go home. Fasting is not allowed here.'

The others supported him. In response, Ramayya threw his blanket over his shoulder and started walking in the general direction of the village.

'Your bag of rations!' shouted Gurappa.

'Keep it,' said Ramayya in between sobs. 'You all can devour it.' He did not turn around. After a while, the shepherds saw him climbing up the first hill on the trail to the village. However, they could not see him on the next hill. They assumed that he had taken the valley route.

The shepherds were happy to see Ramayya head home. They had to be firm and speak harshly to him, but it was necessary. They merged Ramayya's sheep with the flocks of Bala Rangayya and Gangayya.

Ravi had been listening to the difficult conversations that had been taking place since the visitors arrived the previous day. From the time that he could remember, he had been observing the shepherding way of life. It had been a family profession for many generations. Yet he'd never imagined there would be so many unknown facets to the lives of the shepherds.

He remembered playing with baby lambs as a child and roaming around with the sheep. He thought shepherding was just another type of work, similar to farming and construction. Once, he skipped school and went grazing with the elders of his family. He remembered that he walked behind the flock till the evening. At the end of the day, he had been exhausted and covered in dirt. There hadn't been enough water to drink nor any decent food to eat. That was when he understood how tough a shepherd's work was. He gained a new appreciation for the hard work put in by his father and grandfather to feed the family.

Ravi knew that the shepherds took their sheep on hill-grazing expeditions during the drought season, when they couldn't find enough feed and water for the flocks. Now that he had joined one such expedition, Ravi truly understood the hardships and dangers involved. Protecting the sheep while risking one's life—one had to survive not only wild animals but also viral fevers.

He had experienced the various kinds of difficulties that are faced by a hill-grazing shepherd. But he could not have imagined the range of familial situations that the shepherd might have to deal with even when hill-grazing. An alliance for a girl being fixed without her father being aware of it and the family proceeding with the wedding even if he doesn't attend it; dowry money being demanded with interest; a father refusing to allow one's daughter to marry a farmer; a shepherd readying everything for his own funeral before committing suicide—he'd never seen these aspects of rural life.

Once he had given it some thought, it seemed to Ravi that it was the womenfolk who controlled the household affairs in golla families. With the man running behind sheep most of the time, the decisions on how to manage the family and household fell upon the woman of the house. He understood then why a married man in his village was referred to with his wife's name—always 'the husband of so-and-so'.

Even Ravi's own household was known by his grandmother's name. It was called 'Rosamma's'. Their identity was connected to the senior woman of the house. People referred to his father as 'Rosamma's son Gurappa'.

That afternoon at the water source, Ramayya's ration bag once again reminded the shepherds of his plight. His helplessness made them sympathise with him as they ate. The wind was much fiercer in the valleys now than on the hilltops. It made its presence felt when it blew from the hills into the creeks and ravines.

It grew stronger by the evening and was running wild through the valleys. They managed to get to the top of the hill before sunset. The wind pressed down the branches on the slopes of the hill as it descended into the valley, moving through the trees like flowing green waves. As it moved rapidly towards them, Ravi was finally able to discern its shape and could clearly sense its moving presence. It was taking the shape of the entities that fell and rose under its force.

Yes, Ravi realised, one could see the wind. Another spellbinding feat of nature, one that opened up all the other senses through the sense of sight.

The milky moonshine of panchami night spread itself through the forest like thin butter paper. When one looked down at the forest from atop a tall hill, it seemed to be inviting one to jump down on the green mattresses that it had spread all over or to fly over it like a bird. The forest hid the hunger and cruelty of predators under its green carpet. It also covered up the bone-chilling fear felt by the prey of these nocturnal hunters, and their struggle for survival that lasted till the morning. The forest used its silence and cool darkness to mask these aspects of itself. Instead, it tried to appear beautiful and seductive.

The shepherds ate their rotis in silence and lay down at their respective sleeping spots. But Ravi kept pacing around, eventually annoying Pullayya. 'Who is loitering?' he shouted after a while. 'Go to sleep!'

Ravi did not heed the order. He walked a little distance away from the herds and found a vantage point to gaze at the crescent moon. The moonlight became faint as the temperature fell. The night breeze felt pleasant on his body.

The thick silence that enveloped the huge trees blessed the forest with a magical beauty. The silence was ready to transform the sound of a bird or an animal in the valley into a mystical note of music. If a light breeze moved the leaves, the deep silence converted that rustle into a pleasant melody.

Ravi eventually went back to lie down for the night. Before he could fall asleep, he heard a roar. It rebounded off the rocks and produced a metallic clink along with an echo. Ravi sat up. He heard the sound again, resounding from the boulders below. It seemed to have come from the valley beyond the hills to the east. He had heard this roar before. It was the same tiger that had clashed with the wild boar in the Manti hill region. The same fear-inducing roar . . . the voice of a mature adult tiger.

Ravi looked towards the western sky. The moon had begun its descent into the hills. That meant it was around ten. He lay down again and slipped into a deep sleep.

In the morning, Ravi asked Pullayya about the tiger's roar.

'The big fox is nearby,' replied the old shepherd. 'It will come to us or we will go towards it. Either way, we will come face to face at some place or the other. If it is wary of us, it will hide behind rocks or trees and make its way towards the flock, grab a sheep by the neck and disappear in the blink of an eye. If it isn't, it won't care about our presence. It will attack the herd directly, pounce upon and pin down a sheep, look at us with a calm arrogance and slurp the blood of its prey. If we try to hinder it, it will leave the sheep and leap at us. Be careful . . . observe its behaviour and act accordingly.'

Pullayya's grim words frightened most of the shepherds.

'Why should we stay here, when we are in so much danger?' asked a visibly shaken Bala Rangayya. 'Let us divert the herds and move towards the hills in our area.'

'Wouldn't we find tigers there too?' retorted Pullayya. 'We can't be shepherding if we are scared of the foxes. Stay sharp and watchful. If it is a small fox, we should chase it away. If it is a big fox, we should simply let it take its share and leave. Didn't we give a sheep as a fee to the person who allowed us to access his well for a month? Now calculate how many animals we owe the forest for providing so many flocks with water and plenty of nourishing grass. Consider the sheep taken away by the tiger as the toll we pay to the forest.'

No one uttered a word after his explanation.

17

IT HAD BEEN TWENTY-FIVE days since they had entered the forest. Because they had arrived at an auspicious time, Pullayya said, it had all worked out well for them. Yes, they had lost two or three animals and one man had caught hill fever, but on the whole, the hill-grazing had gone well as far as the old shepherd was concerned.

It was because in the previous years, on an average, they lost one or two sheep in each ration period of eight days. Either they would become prey to wildcats or pythons or fall to their deaths. In that same period, at least one shepherd would come down with hill fever and had to be carried home by the ration-bearers.

The group had moved through all the grazing spots in a fifteen-kilometre stretch from the east to the northeast of the Obulam hills. They camped on the elevation at Basayya heap and the herds stomped over Jowar mound, a hilltop covered with fine white stones that resembled mounds of jowar grain.

The shepherds then led the flocks through the Mead of the Bald Oxen, before ascending the paradoxically named Rommana trench. The local saying was that climbing the hill would crack the bones of the chest, alluding to the steepness of the ascent.

The long tails of the hills in that area had acquired unique names over the years. The flocks walked along tail ranges with names such as Bulbul, Soapstone and Trunk—which referred to an elephant's anatomy—among others. They crossed the Springs of the Eternal Souls and the Sheep meadow, before grazing in the grassland near the Om hill. That grassland was a five-acre stretch between the southern and northern hills of the Om hill complex. It was surrounded by caverns and grottos in the sides of the hills.

The local legend was that in the olden days, rishis lived in these environs, and even today blessed souls can hear the chant of 'Om' at a certain time of the night.

When the herds were at the Jowar mound, sheep that were grazing in the stretch between the narrow boulder canyons suddenly jumped sideways. The commotion had subsided by the time the shepherds reached the spot, but the sheep were still stiff and staring wide-eyed at a gap between the boulders.

That gap was actually a deep ravine. Trees, bushes and creepers criss-crossed the streambanks below, making the streambed seem like a cavern. They thought they heard the bleat of a sheep, but there were no other sounds. If a python had caught a sheep, it would have made some struggling noises. No such sounds came from the gap. If it were a tiger dragging a sheep by its neck along the stream, the sheep would have screamed or at least the trees and bushes would have moved.

The shepherds couldn't discern any such movement, so they stepped into the gap and looked into the ravine, wondering if they'd see the tiger's eyes glowing like fireballs in the pitch-dark interior. The thick vegetation did not give them any glimpse into the world beneath, so they even walked along the streambanks to find any indication of a sheep kill along the watercourse. They agreed it was unsafe to venture further into the dark ravine to investigate.

They could not ascertain whether some wild animal had indeed picked up a sheep or if the flock had just become flustered after spotting some predator. A quick attempt to count the number of sheep did not resolve the matter, as they now had to account for Ramayya's sheep along with theirs. It was not till the evening, when the herds were on a hillock near Marla hill, could they finally confirm that Bala Rangayya's flock was missing a sheep.

Pullayya declared that only a mature tiger would have the skill and cunning to steal a sheep in such a smooth manner. No other animal would have been able to carry out such a task so easily, he said. It would eat half the animal and hide the remainder somewhere in the ravine. Even the wild dogs wouldn't dare to enter such an abyss—a streambed that resembled a mineshaft. The tiger would dine on the meat for the next two days, not venturing out for another hunt until it was all gone. The flocks could take it easy for a couple of days.

As per their custom, the shepherds did a valuation of Bala Rangayya's sheep to calculate the loss to be borne by each shepherd. Then they retired for the night.

*

The next morning, the group moved east. The sheep grazed on the Pile of Bean Creepers, which was a grassy knoll but with no bean plants to justify its name. Nearby, they found a water source, the Manneru stream, and halted there for the afternoon. The yaanadis showed up as they were cooking.

Ravi was happy to see them again. The yaanadis used their own vessels to cook rice for their group. Ravi and Bhaskar took Narsimhulu aside to enquire about the red sanders thieves. They were impatient to learn about the aftermath of their little adventure.

'We are not even lying down with our heads in that direction, swamy!' exclaimed Narsimhulu. 'We are feeling quite scared. No one is venturing into those hills now. But our youth have been released from prison and are back home. I heard the police got to know about the tractor being burned down. Police jeeps and forest department vehicles are now patrolling those routes quite frequently. They even visited our homes and questioned us for a long time. To avoid all this hassle, we have been staying put at the Jyothi ashram. We only enter the forests for our livelihood.'

Ravi thought that it was a positive update. He hoped that the wood smuggling would stop at least for some time. The leaders of the smuggling gangs might want to wait until they had a clearer idea or more intelligence about the attack they had endured.

While they were having lunch, Narsimhulu mentioned that they had seen one of the gollas on the Lingala hill. Pullayya looked confused. 'Why would one of our men be there?' said the old shepherd. 'You must have seen someone else and thought he's from our group.'

'No, ayya, we recognised his face,' said the tribal. 'We had seen him in your group when you were on that side of the forest. He is quite slim and has a dusky complexion. About my height. Has a wart near his eye.'

The description matched only one person—Ramayya. But he had supposedly headed home. What was he doing near Lingala hill? It was a surprising piece of news, and a matter of concern too.

'When he saw us, he walked away,' added another of the yaanadis. 'We tried hailing him, but he did not respond. We thought that maybe he had his flock nearby, but we did not see any sheep.'

The shepherds were confused. It had been three days since he left the camp. He did not carry any food with him. Was he starving himself? The group had forced him to leave, assuming he would head straight to the village. They did not think that he would be so stubborn as to head into the hills without rations.

The sin of making Ramayya go hungry would be borne by all of them. After hearing the yaanadis speak, Pullayya could not finish his meal. His guilt had robbed him of his appetite. 'Gurappa,' he said with a heavy heart. 'Finish eating and then go on a short walk.'

Bhaskar, Ravi and Ankayya joined Gurappa as he left in search of Ramayya. They carried his bag of rations along. They would have to hike through nearly ten kilometres of hilly terrain to get to Lingala hill, passing Mango Tree hill and Red Metaka rise on their way.

They walked in silence, and it did not take them long to reach their destination. But even after looking all over Lingala hill, they did not see anyone. Then they went to the area which had the Shiva lingams that gave the hill its name. There were scores of them in that place. Some of them had elaborate designs but others were quite basic, with just a few stones put together to form the phallic shape.

Between the lingams, they found a small area cleared of rubble. There was a rough bed made of leaves and twigs and a stone slab that probably served as a pillow. It was very likely that it was Ramayya who had been sleeping there. Where was he now? They wondered if he had gone to find water or forage for some fruits and roots, which was all he could possibly find to survive on.

'Orey Ramayya!' shouted Gurappa. 'Where are you?'

The shout echoed, but there was no response. The others tried calling too and even whistled loudly.

'It is okay if you don't go home,' Gurappa called. 'At least stay with your flock.'

After waiting there for a while, they surmised that he was somewhere nearby, observing them.

'Okay, I am tying your ration bag to this tree here,' said Gurappa. 'We are camped at the end of the trail, near the Pile of Bean Creepers. Come over to the camp.'

They tied the bag tightly to a nearby sandra tree.

Ravi found it amazing that people had consecrated Shiva lingams so deep inside a forest, on such a remote hill. Gurappa said the lingams were believed to have been installed by Potuluraiah, the son of the revered saint Brahmam garu.

'Why did he have to come into these hills?' asked Bhaskar.

Gurappa told them that after Brahmam garu attained salvation, his wife, Govindamma, did not stop wearing the symbols of a married woman—mangalsutra and toe rings. When men of their caste complained about it to Potuluraiah, he confronted his mother. 'Your father has not passed away,' she told him patiently. 'He is alive in his tomb. He asked me to stay this way.'

Potuluraiah did not believe her. He angrily went to the samadhi and opened the tomb to look inside. The chant of Om was reverberating inside the chamber. The saint opened his eyes and saw the intruder. His eyes burned like charcoal fire. He cursed Potuluraiah for disturbing his meditation.

To absolve himself of the curse, Potuluraiah had to spend a certain period of time alone in the jungle. He spent some time on this hill during that period and made the Shiva lingams with his own hands and worshipped them. Ravi found the story fascinating.

They called out for Ramayya once more before deciding to head back to their camp. Pullayya sighed deeply upon hearing the search party's update. The wedding date had drawn close. Saturday was only three days away. He'd given his word that Ramayya would return to the village by then. But it didn't seem like the idiot intended to go.

The old shepherd discussed the matter with Gurappa and then called Narsimhulu over and spoke with him too. Then he took out a folded polythene bag from his pocket and pulled a hundred-rupee note from the bag. He handed it to Narsimhulu, who immediately left the camp accompanied by Obulesu. The rest of the yaanadi family slept with the herd that night.

The next day, the herd resumed walking through the pasture lands in the valley, reaching a water source just below Red Metaka rise by afternoon. The two yaanadis returned by the time the cooking fires had been set up. They were accompanied by Ramayya's wife, Durgamma, and her uncle.

Durgamma went straight to Pullayya. 'Where is that man?' she asked, her voice clear as a bell.

'He won't show up if you sound like that,' replied Pullayya. 'Don't get miffed that he made you walk such a distance. Talk to him patiently.'

'As if you and your son are personifications of patience!' she retorted. Tired from the hike, she sat down and leaned her back against a sandalwood tree. They offered her water, which she accepted. Then she took out beedis and betel leaves from her bag and handed them over to Gurappa to distribute among whoever wanted them.

'Here, anna, hand this around as well,' she added, pulling out a bag of homemade savouries. 'I am exhausted!'

'Nothing beats food cooked by a woman,' remarked Pullayya, biting into one of the snacks.

'Where is your son, appa?' she asked, leaning back further on the tree. 'Where did you hide him?'

'Relax for a while,' said Pullayya smoothly. 'Catch your breath.'

'I need to go back. Unlike all you lucky gollas . . . you are concerned only about your sheep. You don't care much for your homes, wives and children. We women have to take care of both our work and the men's responsibilities too. Come, let's go find him.'

'Eat a little first,' responded Pullayya.

'Oh, no compromise on the hospitality!' Durgamma shot back, twisting her face in rapid succession and ending with a sarcastic pout.

'Looks like your bones and joints had a thorough workout with such a long walk,' Pullayya said with a smile.

'Oh, you find this funny?' she asked in a low voice, showing her familiarity with the old man. 'You can laugh, but the wedding is day after tomorrow. After I get home today, I will collapse on the bed. Then who will take care of all the arrangements? Your mother's husband?'

Pullayya laughed and said, 'Why are you having a go at me? Go get your husband.'

After lunch, five of the shepherds joined Durgamma on the climb up the Lingala hill. They found Ramayya sleeping under the sandra tree with the ration bag next to him.

'Orey Ramayya!' called out Gurappa. Ramayya got up with a jerk and saw all of them standing there. When he noticed his wife, he looked petrified.

'What are you doing here, ayya?' Durgamma boomed, her voice ringing off the rocks. 'You ditched me and the children for the sheep. Now you have left the sheep as well and are lying here amid lingams. Have you become a monk or what?'

Ramayya stayed mute.

'What mistake did I commit?' she blazed. 'Is it a crime to get one's daughter married? You were incompetent, hence I stepped in. Didn't you weep that your nephew asked for ten lakhs and refused to go below eight lakhs? Weren't you distressed that you wouldn't be able to raise that much money even by selling your four acres of land and the sheep? Isn't that the reason why I, unable to see you wallowing, broached an alliance with my nephew? How can you behave as if the fault is mine and starve yourself here in the hills?'

'The girl made a mistake . . .' Ramayya muttered finally, without lifting his head. 'And you knew it . . .'

She stepped closer to him.

'If the girl sinned and her character was besmirched, the groom should point a finger at it and withdraw from the alliance. But the groom is fine with her conduct. It is only you, the girl's father, who is blaming her. Aren't you ashamed of yourself? Are you a father or a butcher?'

There was stunned silence from Ramayya.

'I believe your grouse is that I didn't inform you. What should I tell you? Should I come into the hills every day and sit down to discuss our problems at leisure? The time has come for her to be married, and it can't be postponed. That is why I sent a man here to let you know, to make sure that you came back at least a week before the wedding day. With so much work to do, and me, a woman, struggling through it, instead of helping, you came and sat here like a monk. The wedding is the day after . . . and you made me come all the way here today. Don't you have any compassion?' She started crying.

'You are an idiot,' said Pullayya to Ramayya. 'We believed you and thought wrongly about this woman. You are the problem, useless fellow. Go! Go with her and help organise the function. Go! I will smack you with a slipper if I find you again in the hills!'

Ramayya got up and threw his blanket over his shoulder. He handed his ration bag to Gurappa and quietly followed Durgamma and her uncle as they started walking in the direction of their village. After walking only a few metres, Durgamma stopped and turned around.

She walked up to Pullayya and pointed at the old man's face. 'What kind of a headman are you, mama?' she said. 'Is this how you resolve a problem?' She drew her head close to his and continued in a low voice, 'You were not good enough to speak a few plain words and convince him to go home. Instead, you made a woman walk through these hills. You are no good as a headman!' She poked at his head with her fingers, seemingly having the liberty to behave so with him.

Pullayya laughed. 'This wasn't a dispute that could have been resolved with my words, girl!' he shot back. 'It got settled only because you came here. Give him some attention. Don't let him cohabit with the sheep all the time. Once in a while, say every fortnight, or even once a month, let him join you on the cot. He will then be like your pet dog. No need for anyone's mediation.'

The others suppressed their smiles. The old-timer didn't hesitate in taking liberties either.

Durgamma looked him up and down. 'Your wit is still sharp, old man!' she said without a smile and turned away to join her husband and uncle on the trail to the village.

As they walked back towards the herds, Ravi reflected on Pullayya's wit. It was interesting to him that not just Pullayya but most older men his age seemed to engage in such open banter with women or even with girls the age of their grandchildren.

'If he follows her words, eats what she feeds him and quietly roams behind the sheep, his life would be fine, with no complications,' remarked Pullayya as they were about to reach the camp. 'Else he will have a dog's life.'

'Why so?' asked Gurappa.

'Even if he works his ass off and herds sheep till his last breath, would he ever save three lakh rupees? Look at that woman . . . how cleverly, without spending a single rupee on dowry, she's getting her daughter married. Saving the eight lakh rupees that this idiot was thinking of giving his nephew for the same thing. Don't you agree? This fool should have remained servile, like the slipper on her foot. Instead, he tried to show off, the windbag!'

Pullayya's analysis sounded reasonable to all of them. Durgamma's tact, competence and communication skills had impressed them a lot. She was the topic of conversation among the shepherds for the rest of the day.

*

The next morning, they turned the herds around instead of moving ahead towards the northern hill farms. They had decided to proceed to Jyothi for the remainder of that ration period. If the rains did not arrive by the time they had to pick up fresh rations, their only option would be to drive the herds through the grasslands to the east of Jyothi. From Tiger Cage area through Korrapati tamarinds and Bungalow regions, they would need to move uphill towards the southern sector. They had to keep moving the herds from one place to the other until it rained.

On some of the rocky flats, grass had grown thick and was almost half a metre high. The grass stalks were dark green. The stretch was full of the sheep's favourite rottler grass. But it was not as fresh as it had been the previous week. The stalk had become coarser and other types of grass such as kasi, dabba and peechu had merged with the rottler.

The shepherds saw four sambar deer on a hillock opposite the grassland where the sheep were grazing. The deer were standing leisurely under an oilcake tree and nibbling at the thick grass. Bhaskar hollered at them. He wanted to give them a mild scare and see them pronk away. Ankayya followed with a shrill whistle. Their ears pricked up, but the deer did not move an inch. They did not respond to any playful sounds the shepherds made either.

The area also abounded with trees bearing wild fruits, mostly plums and berries. There was lots of fruit that had fallen from the trees, including the dark pearl-sized movi plums, darker and bigger java plums, hill palm fruit, tooky fruit and ripe wood apples. The trees appeared in clusters on the mounds, streambanks and at places where herds may have camped in the past years.

They could see cart tracks here and there running through the gaps between hills, along the tail ranges and through grassy knolls with rock outcroppings. The tracks gave an indication of the struggles of previous generations, when they travelled by their ox-drawn carts. Near the cart tracks, one could see a proliferation of huge tamarind trees. Colonies of langurs occupied those trees.

For ages, travellers in these lands carried pickled tamarind in their rations as a side dish. The tamarind pickle was probably one of the earliest dishes of the region. The spicy and tangy mixture made by pounding tamarind with a bit of salt and red chilli powder could be mixed with rice or eaten with rotis. The tamarind seeds spat out by the travellers on either side of the cart tracks had over centuries grown into those huge trees.

At the water source that afternoon, Pullayya began expounding on his theories of existential philosophy on life in the hills.

'I haven't seen a single person who made it big by cutting down the hill forest,' he said. 'I have been observing the lives of these people in the villages at the foot of the hills. I have seen it happen over my long life. They go into the hills, cut down a tree, make something or the other with the wood and sell it . . . this has been their business. While it did seem as if they earned quite a lot, none of their families prospered. They remained as they were, always clamouring for some more porridge.'

'Well, this is an old-timer's talk,' remarked Ravi. 'There are people who have earned crores by cutting down red sanders trees illegally from these hills.'

'That is all an illusion!' responded Pullayya with deep conviction in his voice. 'If you cut down a tree unnecessarily, it is akin to the sin of taking a life . . . that sin keeps spinning around you. It casts a curse on you. They might feel that the crores of rupees they have earned is wealth. No, it is bad karma . . . they will have to bear the consequences eventually!'

Ravi wanted to tell him that it wasn't just the felling of trees. There were people who destroyed forests by mining. They too became wealthy. But their conversation was cut short when two strangers arrived at the camp.

'Who are you?' Pullayya asked sitting up and looking at them with suspicion.

'Don't you know us?' replied one of them. 'We are the brothers-in-law of the deity of Ahobilam, younger brothers of his consort.'

Pullayya understood who the strangers were.

'Obula Narasimha is our son-in-law,' the man continued. 'Chenchu Lakshmi is the daughter of our clan.'

'I see,' said Pullayya. 'You guys are the chenchus of Ahobilam.'

'That is right,' responded the other man. He was the taller of the two. 'For the last week or ten days, your flocks have stomped through our lands, and we only just found out. We were busy serving our son-in-law and did not come to this side of the forest. You crossed the hills without meeting and greeting us. I believe you touched the Iron Pillar of our brother-in-law. Passed through the creek named after our sister. You crossed the area without paying tax. Don't you know that eons ago, our Obulesu gifted us all these hills? You should have paid the toll when you approached Eagle hill. You did not. You could have paid when you passed through the canyon near Squirrel hill. Finally, you had the chance to pay at Merava hill. You skipped that too and made us come here searching for you.'

'How much is your toll?' asked Pullayya.

'Don't you know? Are you grazing in the hills for the first time?'

Pullayya looked at him and then put his hand inside the inner pocket of his shirt, took out two hundred-rupee notes and offered them to the strangers.

'What, what is this?' the taller one exclaimed. He took a step backwards. 'We thought you are the headman. And this is what you do? Have we ever touched paper?'

'Then what do you want?' asked Gurappa.

'You need to pay tax. Give us some of the animals that ate the grass in these lands . . . tax is in the form of animals. What will our bava do with paper? If it is animals, he will accept the sacrifice.'

Pullayya put the currency notes back in his pocket. 'How many animals does your bava want?'

'One per flock.'

Pullayya leaned back on a tree and stretched his legs. 'But we did submit some animals to your bava already,' he said casually, in a matter-of-fact tone.

'Who did you give the animals to?' the man asked with some concern. 'Who is it that collected the animal tax without our knowledge?'

'What do you mean? It was none other than your deity! He personally came by and took one sheep near the Manti hill. Near Raasala pasture, he sent his rock python, the one who forms an umbrella over his head, as his emissary to collect one more sheep. Near Balappa's well, he fought with a wild boar, killed him and dragged the body away. At Bayakka mound, he took a cow. Just the other day, near Jowar mound, he grabbed a sheep from the flock and went away. Every time we shifted the grazing area, your brother-in-law ensured that his tax was paid promptly!'

'Oh, so our bava stepped out of the temple and stole your sheep away?' the man retorted with a touch of anger, having understood only some of Pullayya's sarcasm.

'Why wouldn't he?' shot back the old shepherd, his satirical tone now hard to misunderstand. 'He'd gifted all these hills to you and asked you to collect the toll fee. You guys have been taking animals from people like us but feasting on them yourselves. You did not serve him a single piece of mutton. Just because you are his brothers-in-law, will he just let you take all the tax while he starves himself? Go away, because we already gave him around ten lives. Who knows how many more he will demand?'

'How can the lives lost to wild animals be counted as our bava's tax?' the chenchu almost shouted in anger. 'You don't seem to give a damn about us!'

'Those wild animals protect the forest to some extent at least!' retorted Gurappa. 'That's why we don't mind paying tax to them. You men look as strong as oxen. Can't you do some work for a living?'

'Your words are crossing the limits,' raged the chenchu. 'You don't know us. Don't assume that you are safe just because you have crossed the Obulam region. If we go back to our lands with empty hands, your flocks will end up following right behind us.'

Ravi had been listening to this conversation from a distance, but now he stepped closer and addressed the chenchus.

'Anna, we don't know who you are,' he said in a stern voice. 'I don't understand why our sheep will follow you. These hills belong to all of us. The forest is not your father's property. Go away, anna, go back to your lands. Forget the sheep, even their fur won't follow you. We are risking our lives to rear them. We even confronted a tiger to save one of them . . . why would we be scared of you, anna? You need to take all our lives to lay a hand on these flocks. Go away, or do what you can!'

Ravi's outburst made the chenchus back away. They turned back to Pullayya and asked, 'What will it be?'

'Get out!' said the old man. 'You guys are fools . . . you just lost two hundred rupees.' Pullayya gestured with his hands for them to leave.

The chenchus took the trail into the hills. After they climbed the rise, they stopped and shouted: 'That's why people call you gollas dumb. You could have got rid of us by offering a single sheep. The archers will come tomorrow, and they will divert an entire flock across the hills. Reconsider now!'

The younger shepherds were incensed at that statement. Bhaskar removed the sling from his waist.

'Oye Gurappa!' said Pullayya. 'What do you think? Looks like these rascals will complain to the sugaalis and bring them along tomorrow. Drunkards, the lot . . . all this drama is just to eat some meat and drink some booze. Shall we throw an old and bony sheep in their face? Let us just assume a fox took one more . . .'

While he was saying this, Bhaskar had placed a plate-sized stone in his sling. He swirled it and released. The stone whizzed past the tribals' heads and hit a tree with a thud. The chenchus had to jump sideways to avoid the ricochet.

'Will your arrows travel farther than this?' shouted Bhaskar. 'We are not alone either. There is another group of shepherds in the Jyothi hills. They will join us too. We all have slings. Come back if you dare!'

'Orey, orey,' Pullayya cried, trying to get Bhaskar to pipe down. Instead, Bhaskar slung another stone in the direction of the tribals. The chenchus did not utter another word and vanished into the hills.

'If this had happened around Potagiri or Merava hill, they would have had the upper hand,' said Gurappa. 'They would have returned with more men, and even women, children and the elderly. All of them would have charged at us.'

He then looked at Bhaskar and said, 'Your father was just like you. He never cared who the opponent was. Him from our village and Kurra Chennaiah from Pareddy Palli—if these two were around, no one dared to look at our sheep.'

'Just in case, let's drive the herds east across another set of ranges,' suggested Pullayya. 'Better to escape and mock them than get trapped and muster up an ingratiating smile.'

The shepherds took his advice. The herds were made to climb up the tallest hill in the region by nightfall, giving them a vantage point that allowed both offence and defence in case of an attack.

It was a waxing crescent moon that night. It rose to the centre of the sky quite early. For some reason, Pullayya seemed to be in a good mood that night. Looking at the moon as he ate, he remarked, 'As the saying goes, "The moon is sitting like a child up there, laughing." Wonder what he saw to make him laugh so much.'

'Why would he not laugh?' Gurappa responded as he ate his roti. 'He is the king of the night sky, isn't he? He laughs all the time, whether he's shaped like a thin sickle or when he's round and full like a pot of buttermilk.'

Gurappa then reminisced about moonlit nights from his childhood. 'This moonlight makes me remember the days when I was a kid, and you were all young men twirling your moustaches,' he said. 'On moonlit nights, we used to draw lines outside the sheep pens and play games like kabaddi, dolu patte and sirri patte. These days, the youth have become bland, mama! There are around six people in our group who were married less than five or ten years ago, but do you see even one of them pine for home? In my youth, we used to struggle to bear the difficulty of separation during hill-grazing, even for one ration period. We used to come up with some excuse or the other and run home.'

'Orey, don't say that aloud,' cautioned Pullayya. 'These guys have adjusted nicely to the hills. It will be a nuisance if they start to feel homesick!'

'I am not asking them to go home, mama. Even if they don't express their feelings openly, on the inside they should wish to be home. They simply don't seem to be missing their women, that is my point.'

'How do you know that?'

'For instance, the other night Subbi was talking in his sleep,' explained Gurappa. 'He was muttering loudly: "Wow, wow . . . what rains . . . so much grass . . ." It appears as if these fellows don't think of their wives and children, not even in their dreams.'

Pullayya was silent.

'Then that fellow Jayaramulu was shouting in his sleep, "My ash-coloured sheep is pregnant! The spotted one delivered twins!"' added Gurappa. 'And what can one say about Venkatesham? In his somniloquy, he spoke about herding his sheep after the rains. Not one of them dreams about flirting with his wife or playing with his children.'

'Yeah, I heard that too,' said Pullayya. 'They want the rains to arrive. Rain is what they dream about. They wish for such heavy rain that the rocky and barren lands are transformed into a green carpet. They want to see the streams and drains overflow with water. Only when it starts raining can they go home and end this period of separation from their wives and children. The desire to see them is the reason they dream about rains.'

Gurappa did not continue the conversation. He went to his sleeping spot and lay down on his back. Looking up at the sky, he thought the moon was chortling. He wished for a cloud puff to cover up the crescent. Let the handbasket-sized cloud grow as big as a blanket, he thought. Growing even more, let it become as big as a pond and then as big as the Porumamilla reservoir. Let the cloud connect the sky to the earth and start a torrential downpour, lashing down without a stop. It would be a lovely sight. Yes, dark clouds would be more beautiful than this moon.

The younger shepherds kept an eye on the Obulam hills that night. They were confident that no dangers would arise from that direction. And yet, they were vigilant. If they woke up during the night, they sat up for a good look at the western hill ranges. They observed the gaps between trees, the streambanks and hill slopes to confirm that there were no signs of any impending danger. Only then did the shepherds go back to sleep.

18

THE FOLLOWING MORNING, PULLAYYA addressed the group during breakfast.

'Everyone takes the gollas lightly,' he said. 'One could abuse a golla or even beat him up, but the golla would walk away with his head down. Yes, to protect the lives under our care, we let go of that little bit of shame and dignity. Sometimes when we herd the flock alongside a cropland, some of the sheep bite off a few stalks from the crops. The farmer swears at us, but we have to bear it. We need to shrug it off for the sake of the few grains the sheep eat. Sometimes, an incensed farmer might even use his fists on us. There is even a proverb about shepherds getting beaten and buffalo herders being abused. None of this is for our own sakes. It is for the sake of the sheep. And now, even in these hills, we have become an easy target for folks we have no dispute with. We do need to be afraid of everyone because our job is to protect these dumb animals. Be careful when we are at the water source. We will be at the lower level with the sheep occupying the heights.'

His sermon made them thoughtful. As they moved towards the eastern hill ranges, they ensured that none of the sheep wandered out of sight. They did not allow the herds to descend into the valleys and kept them moving along the ridges and hill slopes. When they halted at the water source, a group of four young shepherds climbed the tallest hill in the area to keep a watchful eye on the western ranges.

Over lunch, Pamuleti said, 'Once we get back, my son-in-law will anyway sell the flock to collect his dowry dues. Let the chenchus come. We can offer them a sheep from my flock and another from Gangayya's. Why do we need to fear them so much?'

'I understand your situation,' said Pichchanna. 'But why one from Gangayya's flock?'

'Who will he pass his sheep to?' Pamuleti retorted. 'Does he have anyone to cry for him? Or take care of him?'

'His younger brother does have children, right?' asked Gurappa.

'Gangayya's wife does not even allow them to visit their home.'

'Her brother has children, no?'

'Gangayya won't give even a rupee to them.'

The people around them laughed at Pamuleti's expression.

Gurappa too laughed and said, 'Looks like husband and wife have locked all the doors to their house.' Addressing Gangayya, he added, 'Orey Gangadu, till you have strength in your body, it will seem all right. The two of you can stay locked up at home and eat to your heart's content. But think about the time when you are both older. There won't be any one to talk to and no one to give you a morsel. Nobody will enter your home, even if you open all the doors.'

'It is all humbug, bava!' responded Gangayya, glaring at Pamuleti. 'My brother's sons visit my home, and my brother-in-law's children too. All this guy does is talk frivolously.'

Pamuleti smiled at Gangayya's reaction. The others had a good laugh. The afternoon rest period passed uneventfully. There was no sign of the chenchus.

The sheep's tastebuds seemed to have gone bland again. They were not grazing properly. Some sheep were even trying to lick their masters' bodies.

That night, someone brought up the topic of Ramayya's daughter. The wedding was to happen the next morning. While some shepherds sympathised with Ramayya's struggles, others cracked jokes.

*

The next day began with an overcast sky and stayed that way. The wind picked up as well. The clouds looked busy, moving briskly across the sky from the west to the east. Just below the dark clouds, they could see eagles flying with their wings fully extended. They looked like paper kites.

'A depression may have formed over the Bay of Bengal,' suggested Ravi. A depression would suck up the surrounding air, including the clouds. As it grew bigger, it would become a cyclone and move into the coastal areas, where it would descend upon the land as gusty rain. If the cyclone made landfall near Nellore, the Nallamala region would receive heavy downpour along with powerful winds. If the cyclone crossed the shore in Tamil Nadu or northern Andhra or Orissa, their area might not even get a drizzle.

The day remained pleasant, with cool winds blowing and the cloud cover masking the sun's heat. The shepherds turned towards Obulam and Jyothi, offering prayers for the rains to arrive. By evening, the winds were blowing strongly. As the winds blew from the top of the hills into the deep valleys, the swaying, heaving trees resembled a green waterfall. And in the valleys, it flattened the trees and other vegetation, surging forward like a fast-flowing, levee-breaking green river.

The sound of the wind whooshing through the bamboo groves reminded them of the noise made by rainwater as it filled up ponds and flowed rapidly over muddy embankments. The tall bamboo stems bent and released by the wind looked like a thousand whips cracked at once. Then the winds lashed the stone plates and twisted through the boulders and canyons, sounding like a harvesting machine at full throttle. The noise rang in their ears.

The rations were due to arrive the next morning. Some lucky shepherds would get replacements and get to go home. The ration-bearers had to be met at Jyothi and brought to the camp. Ankayya suggested Ravi and he go to Jyothi together in the morning.

Ravi asked if he was expecting his wife to come again with the rations.

'Yes, I think she will come,' replied Ankayya. 'It has been two ration periods since she last came.'

The following morning, they set out at four accompanied by Bhaskar. It took them two hours of brisk walking to reach their destination. By then, the ashram was already bustling with activity. They bathed with their clothes on like last time and stayed in their wet clothes. Then they bought coconuts and camphor sticks to pay obeisance to the deity Narasimha Swamy and the saint Kasi Nayana at their respective shrines.

As they stepped out of the ashram, an overloaded autorickshaw came chugging down the road. Around ten of the people on board were from their village, including Ankayya's wife and son. Subhadra got out of the autorickshaw with the little boy. She had a ration bag slung over her shoulder.

Ravi had a knowing smile on his face. Bhaskar looked surprised. Ankayya hurried towards his wife and offered to take the heavy load from her. She handed him the boy instead. Ankayya held the little boy to his chest and planted kisses on his head, his eyes growing moist.

Ravi observed the scene intently. He was probably the only one around who could sense the emotions welling up in the husband and wife. Subhadra's gesture of handing her husband the symbol of their love instead of the heavy bag stirred Ravi's heart. He felt his eyes too getting tearful.

Ravi turned his head to Bhaskar and saw that he was talking to Ramayya, who had also come by the autorickshaw. 'You're glowing!' Bhaskar said. 'You've put on some flesh in just four days! Is that a new shirt bought for the wedding?'

'It is an old shirt,' Ramayya shyly explained. 'I only wear it on special occasions. It has been ironed and so looks new.'

'No credit to him! Thank the washerman for the crisp white clothes and the barber for the smooth-shaven look,' said Balayya, who had come along for the trip. 'Let him walk around the hills for four days and the dirt won't go away even with a lime wash.'

'Yeah, that's right,' murmured Ramayya, sending the others into peals of laughter.

The sky was entirely covered by dark clouds that looked like crazed buffaloes with their tails up, ready to snap into a dusty stampede. The other shepherds left Ravi and Ankayya at the ashram and started for the hills.

Ravi walked to the Narasimha Swamy temple. The temple faced south and had an ornate flagpole. There was a statue of the sacred bull Nandi in front of the flagpole. Ravi thought it quite unusual to see a statue of Nandi, the vehicle of Shiva, in front of a Vishnu temple.

He sat at the temple for a long time, taking in the environs. Then, hoping to find the yaanadis, he walked around the ashram precincts.

After an hour, he heard Ankayya call his name. 'Let's go,' he said as he settled his son back in his wife's arms.

Once they were on the trail, Ravi said, 'Why don't you go home for a couple of days? We could take care of your flock.'

'No, we are on jungle duty,' replied Ankayya. 'There are some rules and etiquettes to be followed. It is not right for a shepherd to go home midway and get a replacement. The flock needs the same shepherd throughout the expedition. If the shepherds keep changing, the newcomer wouldn't know which sheep did not eat well the previous day or which one was showing symptoms of illness. If he assumed that the previous shepherd had already treated the ill-looking sheep, the illness could become acute by the next morning. A golla who has been herding a flock from the beginning of the expedition would remember little details like which sheep had been frightened by a tiger and which one was feeding from a different mother, and he would tend to all their needs better.'

The wisdom of Ankayya's response surprised Ravi.

'I wanted to see the little one,' Ankayya added. 'She brought him here so that I could see him. But I have asked her not to come again. Why should I alone indulge when the others cannot? I should walk the same path as all of us.'

'Tell me the truth, anna,' Ravi said. 'Did you come to see the little boy or my sister-in-law?'

'You will know the answer when you get married!' replied Ankayya. They chatted all the way to the camp, which they reached just after nine.

Among those who brought the rations, Seetharamayya and Gurumohan settled into their old places. Balayya replaced Sreenu, and Raju took the place of Venkatesham. Sankar was there too, and he asked Ravi to go home and rest. But Ravi was firm that he would only return with the flock.

'Why do we need these dogs here?' asked Bala Rangayya. 'We have to carry rations for them too! Shall we send them back?'

'Yes,' agreed Balayya. 'It has been over a month, and these dogs have not made themselves useful even once.'

'Oh, they were useful all right,' said Tiripalu, his voice dripping with sarcasm. 'If they shoved their tails between their legs and came close to us, it warned us that a python, a panther or a hyena was nearby. If they hid deep within the flock, it meant that they had smelled a tiger in the vicinity!' This triggered loud guffaws from the others.

'Well, what about our Gurappa's dog?' asked Balayya.

'He is a king, of course,' responded Tiripalu. 'The flock may be visited by a small fox or a big fox . . . it doesn't matter to him. He gets up, languidly stretches his entire body, holds the pose for a few moments, puts his tongue out and pants. Then he turns around in a circle, kicks away any small stones or pebbles and lies down for a reverie till its master announces that the meal is being served. He's careful not to expend any energy in unnecessary barking!'

Tiripalu acted out all the dog's movements, making the shepherds roll with laughter.

*

The ones heading home left after a while. The gollas spread salt on the flat rocks and let the sheep lick them dry. Then they got the flocks moving and set out in that pleasant weather. With their tastebuds active again, the sheep pounced hungrily on the grass, gobbling mouthfuls at a time.

The little white lamb was racing its step-sister, the red lamb. Some of the younger sheep were biting the grass in a hurry, while the older ones were grazing peacefully and moving at a steady pace. The eagles kept circling high in the sky. Various species of sparrows or other sparrow-sized birds flew around, making strange noises.

When they stopped for the afternoon break at a water source, Ramayya handed around laddus and savouries.

'Why didn't you distribute these in the morning?' queried Munayya.

'Did not want you all to get thirsty,' replied Ramayya. 'Now you can eat them with lunch, drink water and then relax for a bit.'

In the morning, there had been just enough time to exchange greetings. The group was now ready to know all the details of the wedding.

'I believe it was your show all the way at the wedding?' joked Ramachandra. 'Heard that you organised the whole function singlehandedly?'

Ramayya just smirked.

'They said that you received more attention than even the groom,' said Jayaramulu. 'Is that right?'

Ramayya responded with a smile.

'New clothes, new footwear, a new ring on your finger . . . it seems you were shining brighter than anyone there!' exclaimed Ramanayya.

Twirling his moustache, Ramayya threw him a sideways glance and then said, 'I went home fearing the amount of work that would be needed to get the wedding organised. Believe it or not, they did not let me do a single task. They treated me like a king and did all the work themselves . . . the only task I had to perform was the feet-washing ceremony. I can do a hundred weddings if that is all I have to perform.'

'Foolish fellow,' murmured Pullayya. 'They must have feared he would take the hill path again. That is why they gave him special treatment until the ceremony was over.' Those who heard him laughed in agreement.

Then the old shepherd spoke up. 'I had given some advice to your wife when she came here. Did she follow it or not?'

'What advice?'

'Yes, why would you remember it? Did she allow you to climb into her cot at least on one night?'

'Why would I be desperate to be in her cot?' responded Ramayya. 'It was she who was coming every night to sleep on my bed. Fearing that others would see us, I tried not to give her any space on the bed. But she pushed me to a side and slept next to me.'

'See how this fellow is bragging away!' mocked Gurappa.

'The truth is always hard to swallow,' shot back Ramayya. 'In fact, her grandmother scolded me the other morning. Do you know why?'

'Why?'

'She said, "I needed to wake her up, but you were asleep holding on to her. If she doesn't get up, how will the work get done? You should have stayed in the hills, you idiot!"'

They all laughed at that.

'I am a lucky man,' said Ramayya. 'I did not spend a single rupee and yet got my daughter married in a lavish ceremony.'

'Have some shame, you idiot!' snarled Pullayya.

'Shame?' Ramayya's voice changed suddenly. 'I lost my shame and dignity. That's why I came back smiling. Else, I would have had to drink some poison and die.'

Ravi shot him a startled look.

'I lost everything of value as soon as I saw my daughter,' said Ramayya. 'When I stepped inside the house, my eyes did not look at her face . . . they looked at her belly. She understood the meaning of my look and wept inconsolably. Until then, my head was full of—what did you say—shame, honour and false dignity. Those useless attributes, and my conditioning, that wished to see my daughter suffer, none of them found a place in my heart anymore. They melted away in tears. I wondered why I couldn't think about my daughter the way her mother did. I finally saw the events from my wife's perspective . . . and then I did not have to beg her to allow me in her bed. She fought for a space on my bed.'

Having said that, Ramayya leaned back on a tree trunk. Silence reigned for a while.

'How they respected me!' Ramayya said suddenly. 'Consulted me about every little thing. "Is it okay for the pandal to be here? Happy with where the cooking fires are being setup? How many chairs do you think we will need? Any suggestions on the catering contract? Recommendations for the wedding feast menu?" I think they had decided on all these things already. They still put up a show of getting my approval for every decision. It is not as if I was unaware of all this; I am not that naive. My wife's brother, he is my daughter's maternal uncle as well as her father-in-law now. He was worried that his niece's father would vanish into the hills and bring a bad name to the family; worried that his niece would become a laughingstock if her father doesn't show up at her wedding. With noble hearts, he and his sister, that is, my wife, gave me the position of the head of the family. I did not have such a noble heart. The bride's father did not show as much love to her as her maternal uncle did. The more they treated me as a special person, as the head of the family, the starker became my realisation of how much of an imbecile I had been. I wilted with shame. I held my wife's feet one night . . . no, not what you think . . . just to convince her that I have changed and that she could trust me now.'

Ramayya's voice went hoarse. There was nothing anyone could say.

Ramayya continued pouring his heart out. 'They say that no one recognises their own faults,' he said. 'But the errors in my thinking and behaviour became very apparent to me—like a mirror to my character—as I looked back at the events of the wedding. You know the ritual when the groom's side formally requests the bride's family to bring out the fully bedecked bride? Before we brought her out, her mother and I had to give her our blessings. She was standing in a corner near the altar. She placed the betel leaves and areca nuts, symbolizing the change in her status, in my open palms and bent down to touch our feet. We blessed her and waited for her to get up. She stayed down there, crying silently, not letting go of my feet. Maybe she wanted forgiveness from me. Tears fell on my feet. My heart fluttered and a deep emotion burst through me. "What a sinner I am, to have caused so much suffering to such a sweet girl," I thought. I tried to pull her up by the shoulders. My tears fell on her back, silently communicating my feelings of remorse. "I am the sinner, amma! Not you!" my teardrops were saying. My wife finally got her to stand up. She was crying too. The wickedness in my heart died when I hugged my daughter. I wiped away the girl's tears. As she walked out of the door, she turned around when she crossed our threshold and put kumkum on the wooden doorstep. She prayed, expressing gratitude to the home that had sheltered her all these years. Looking at her bidding farewell in tears, I could not control my weeping. I am a sinner, brothers!'

Ramayya finished speaking and closed his eyes. The shepherds remained mute.

Suddenly, the langurs on the trees near the stream started screaming in fright, jumping from one branch to the next. Pullayya sensed the danger immediately. 'Orey, orey!' he shouted. 'A really big fox seems to be headed this way! Start yelling!' He started them off with a loud 'Thoi!'

The gollas on cooking duty started screaming loudly and whistling at a high pitch. The ones near the flocks took over the screaming routine. The sheep looked on in dumb fear with ears pricked up. Within a few moments, they saw a wild pig running down the valley. Right behind it, the bushes shook violently.

Stones rained from the shepherds' slings in the direction of the pig accompanied by bloodcurdling cries from their throats. A few stones hit large rocks and splintered into pieces. Some hit the low branches and bushes, shaking them up. A couple of stones seemed to hit the pig too, making it change direction. Instead of coming towards the water source, the pig climbed up the hillock. In less than a minute, it found a gap in the hill and crossed to the other side.

The predator followed right behind, and that's when they saw it. It was a fully grown tiger with a heavy body covered in curved stripes. Almost three metres in length, its body was all strong muscle and sinew. Pullayya stopped the gollas from hurling stones at the tiger.

A few moments later, they heard the visceral death cry of the pig, followed by some low growls. The tiger had landed its kill.

If the gollas had not hit the pig with stones, it would have come straight into the camp. Would the tiger have attacked it even then? The shepherds asked Pullayya whether the presence of so many humans slinging stones and screaming battle cries would have scared the tiger away.

'It didn't look like it would get scared,' replied Pullayya. 'It was a mature tiger. Fearless. You did a good thing scaring the pig away. If it drags the body to its den, we can breathe easy for at least a couple of days. However, if the tiger has a mate and cubs, they will finish the meat in a day.'

The langurs were still making a ruckus. The slings remained in the hands of the shepherds. The two cowardly dogs were lying low somewhere in the middle of the herds. But Gurappa's dog was standing near its master. It wasn't clear whether it was from courage, loyalty or just plain inertia.

Pullayya decided that it was not safe for the herd to stay on in that area after lunch. The flustered sheep had already moved halfway up the hill. The tiger had hunted the pig down in the space between the two hills or a little beyond. From that position, it could possibly see the flocks. One couldn't assume anything about its intentions. It was best to move the flocks out of its sight.

They made the sheep ascend the hill. Then the shepherds each took their flocks in different directions before eventually meeting again on a flattish elevation above a hill slope. The gollas lit fires at a few spots around the camp and took turns to ensure that the fires kept burning through the night. The moon sank into the western hills around three in the morning.

BOOK 3

Courage

19

HAVING SEEN THE TIGER with his own eyes, Pullayya had assessed its recklessness and strength. It made him feel quite agitated. The unease kept gnawing at him. He could sense his anxiety increasing, whether he was walking beside the flock, resting at night, talking to his fellow shepherds or simply observing the valleys from atop a hill. He could not fathom the true nature of this big fox. The tiger's attitude and dexterity made the old shepherd feel that it would not hesitate to attack humans.

Pullayya worried that the younger shepherds, especially Ravi, would not back away if the tiger confronted them. It was an animal that was fully aware of its canines, he thought, and it would fight without caring for its own safety. What if they lost one of the young men? His anxiety was turning into fear.

Since he was not a man who bottled up his anxieties and suffered alone, Pullayya shared his fear with Gurappa. They decided to talk to the yaanadis. When the tribals showed up at the water source that afternoon, Pullayya and Gurappa called them to the side.

'There is a mature tiger in this area,' Pullayya said. 'Did it cross your path?'

'Many times, swamy!' responded Narsimhulu. 'Whenever we come to this area, we see it somewhere or the other, usually near the creeks or the boulders.'

'We saw it yesterday near the limestone hill,' said one of the children.

'Yes, it was dragging a carcass,' said Narsimhulu. 'See that tall hill over there? Just below it, there are some limestone caverns. Its den is there. The tiger's mate gave birth to cubs recently, I think.'

'When it finds you on the path, does it growl at you or show signs of making an attack?' asked Gurappa.

Narsimhulu scratched his head. 'The signs are there, swamy!' he responded eventually. 'Usually, any animal would be frightened if it saw a group of humans and would get off the path. But this one has no fear of men. Instead of moving away, it stands firm and stares at us. It does look like it might attack humans. If you bend down, it might jump on you. If you show your back and run away, it would probably chase you. Just yesterday, my wife held on to the children and wept, pleading with us not to venture into this side. But if we go towards the south, we have to contend with the sandalwood thieves. And on this side, we now have to deal with this new fear. We are stuck, with our lives in danger every day.'

Narsimhulu held his head in both hands and looked at the ground. Pullayya knew his fears were not baseless.

'But why would it attack a man when there are so many sheep around, swamy!' added Narsimhulu. 'Just don't come in its way if it grabs a sheep in its jaws and drags it away. Let him have it. It is not a young cub; it won't get frightened by shouts and rocks.'

Pullayya looked at the other shepherds to ensure that they were paying attention to the yaanadi's cautionary words. He looked specifically at Ravi and raised his eyebrows.

'We need at least three days to get out of this sector,' said the old shepherd to the rest of the gollas. 'Till then, don't let your guard down no matter where you are. Don't invite any trouble.'

Later, Ravi spoke to the yaanadis for a while. There were no updates from them about the smugglers. After a while, the yaanadis went on their way.

Bhaskar loosened the wooden handle from the iron head of his axe. He then sprinkled some water on a stone of rough texture by the stream and started sharpening the blade from toe to heel. Ravi began doing the same with his axe. Ramachandra, Balayya, Gurumohan, Raju and other young shepherds followed suit. They were taking turns using the same rough stones by the stream to sharpen their axes till they were satisfied.

Pullayya observed this activity and suspected that something was afoot.

'Why do you think these fellows are polishing their axes?' he asked Gurappa.

'Maybe they have gone blunt,' answered Gurappa. 'We haven't maintained them well since coming to the forest.'

'Why do we need them to be sharp? Are we herding goats that we need to cut down branches and creepers for their feed? We are herding sheep.'

'Let them do it, what's the harm?' said Gurappa casually. He asked Bhaskar to sharpen his axe too.

'Once an axe is sharpened, the hands holding it become restless,' contemplated Pullayya. 'One feels like hitting a tree trunk with it to see how deep it can cut. The mind can sometimes lead one astray.'

Gurappa did not reply.

'Each one of them is polishing his axe as if they arrived at a consensus,' continued the old shepherd. 'I suspect something, Gurappa. Are they planning something because I warned them about the big fox?'

Gurappa dismissed the idea, making Pullayya respond loudly with a harsh edge to his voice: 'If one steadies the heart and stands firm, it is possible to cut down a tiger. But by then, it would have fatally bitten or clawed two or three people. We did not come into the hills to lose lives. Ask them to stop their childish behaviour. Especially your son and that fellow Bhaskar.'

They turned around at Pullayya's agitated tone.

'What's with you, ayya?' said Ravi. 'Do you think we are so brave that we would confront the tiger?'

'Some of the axes have gone completely blunt,' explained Bhaskar. 'A few have become dull at the edges. We are just polishing them.'

Pullayya glared at them. 'We have come here to protect the lives of our sheep, not to lose the lives of our men!' he shouted. 'It is better to sell the sheep to the butcher. We should all be able to return home with no one getting even their toe injured. Let the big fox pounce on the herd and bite the necks of a few sheep if it has to. Don't come in its way. No one shall bother the tiger!'

His words were spoken as the firm order of the leader of the group. Gurappa backed him too. No one spoke after that. They got the herds up and moving and continued on their way.

*

The morning's thick cloud cover had disappeared by evening. The clouds that had been moving eastward did not return with rain. Not a single drop fell.

As the sun started going down near the western ranges, they saw two chital deer going up the slopes of a hill towards the east. One of them had twisted antlers while the other had none. They were a pair. With plenty of blackbucks, antelopes, chital deer, wild pigs, sambar and wild sheep in these hills, the area had become the natural habitat of tigers. The flocks of sheep that visited for hill-grazing every summer provided them an additional source of food.

Even by sunset they could not find a hill with a peak wide enough to host all of them. They made the sheep climb a hill with a steep slope and then settled them down on both sides of the hill, from the top to about halfway down. The hill began to resemble a festive bull decorated with a red quilt.

Two shepherds positioned themselves at the north end of the herd, and two were stationed at the south. The others descended to the slopes and found spots to lie down near their respective flocks. By the time the sheep had settled down for the night, it was around eight. The moon was already high in the sky, with the sheep and men on the eastern slope drenched in moonshine. Those on the western slope were in darkness. Soon, the men and their animals all fell asleep.

By midnight, the moon had moved further westward and was no longer in the centre of the sky. The valley to the west of the hill was now bright with moonlight. With not a single cloud above them, it was an uninterrupted stream of silvery light falling on the tops of the trees—which seemed to be conversing with each other in silence, no longer vexed by the incessant noise made by the various animals and birds during the day.

Then, from somewhere in the valley, a wild fowl uttered a cry. This was immediately followed by what sounded like a man's whistle.

When the whistle sounded again, Pullayya woke up. For a moment, he was not sure if he had only heard the sound in a dream. The old shepherd sat up. Controlling the urge to light a beedi, he sat in silence, listening. Was it really someone whistling?

Hardly ten minutes had passed when he heard the whistle again. Yes, it was the same sound. It was not a shrill, ear-splitting whistle, but a more delicate one with a specific note that would only be recognisable to a person waiting for it. It had come from the valley. To Pullayya, it seemed to have come from the groves towards the south.

'Who is it?' he wondered aloud. 'Chenchus? Sugaalis?' The young men might be sleeping like logs, he thought, but at least Gurappa would have woken up by it. The old man stood and picked up his axe. He knew that Gurappa was sleeping further down the hill slope and set off in that direction.

He had only taken a couple of steps when he saw Gurappa coming towards him, walking under the shadows cast by the moonlit trees.

'Heard the sound, mama?' asked Gurappa as he came closer.

In a low voice, Pullayya confirmed that he had. 'I could not figure out what it was and thought of checking with you,' he added. 'What are these whistles for at this time of the night?'

'Shall we wake up our people?'

'Give it a few minutes—' Pullayya began and stopped when they heard the whistle again.

This time, there was a whistled response from the northern part of the valley. The two seasoned gollas were confused. They wondered if there were two groups or just two people. Or did one person get separated from the others in the jungle and was trying to locate his comrades? Or were the signals in preparation for an attack on the camp?

This time, the whistle from the south was followed immediately by a shrill whistle from one of the shepherds stationed on the other side of the hill. It triggered a response from the northern side and then one from the south again. Both whistles sounded exactly the same, identical in pitch and tone.

That was when it struck Gurappa. 'Mama!' he said, turning to Pullayya with a concerned look. 'It is the whistle of a snake, mama! A female python in heat calling out for a mate! Not very far off from here. A male python had responded, but now our guy on the hill whistled and messed it up . . .'

The golla from the hill's spine whistled again. By then, all the shepherds were awake.

'Why are you whistling, ra?' Pichchanna shouted from the other slope.

'Some fellow is whistling in the low-lying area to the west,' replied Balayya, who was the shepherd who had whistled.

'There is no one there!' Gurappa shouted at him before turning to Pullayya and saying, 'I am worried that this guy's whistle may have directed both the snakes to this spot.'

Pullayya knew that it was entirely possible that Gurappa was right. He'd heard stories about pythons attacking a camp at night and gobbling up a human. The old shepherd shouted instructions, asking them to stay silent and not attract the pythons in their direction.

They heard the whistle again from the south side. It seemed like the python was moving towards the hill. If it reached the hill, it would coil around a sheep or a man. It would not be easy to fight it at night.

Gurappa had a sudden idea for directing the pythons away from the camp. It was an audacious plan and difficult to implement. But it was better to give it a try than face the wrath of two pythons in the darkness. He asked Ravi, Ramachandra and Bhaskar to come along with him. Brushing aside Pullayya's objections, Gurappa and his team made their way down the hill and started walking across the valley towards a hill on the western side.

The moonlight made their walk easier. It took them ten minutes to reach the base of the hill. After climbing a little distance up one of the slopes, Gurappa whistled in the same tone and pitch as the python—a soft and controlled sound. A few moments later, he received a response from the south first, and then the north.

The whistle-and-response was repeated a few times more until Gurappa and his team were confident that the two pythons had changed direction and were proceeding to meet near the hill they were on. Then they ran through the valley and kept up a brisk pace until they reached the camp.

After around thirty minutes, the shepherds heard whistles from the two snakes that indicated they had united near the western hill. The bushes over there started shaking a few minutes later and the whistles changed to a raspier sound, which told them that the snakes had begun their foreplay of clasping each other by the tails, coiling and uncoiling. The still night carried the sounds of their hissing and the noise of their heavy bodies rolling and twisting on the ground.

It was past two in the morning when the shepherds lay down again. At four, the moon sank beyond the western hill. The mating sounds of the pythons had subsided by dawn.

The shepherds got up late that morning. When they descended into the valley in batches for their morning ablutions, some of them visited the spot where the snakes had performed their mating exercise the previous night.

On a flat stretch of sandy soil about thirty metres from where Gurappa had mimicked their whistles, they found the marks made by the pythons. The topsoil had been disturbed and the bushes around were bent and flattened. The tracks indicated that the snakes had moved north. The shepherds guessed that the pythons were probably resting under some boulders to recover from their intense session.

Ravi reflected on the strangeness of nature. A female snake from one side of the forest sends signals to the other side, looking for a male to respond to the mating call. The two snakes meet and cavort on the soft soil and the male drops its seed to impregnate the female. Then the two go their own separate ways. It was a miraculous world with each species cultivating its own behaviours and rites.

*

The clouds disappeared, taking with them the hopes of even a little rain. With no wind blowing either, the heat became unbearable. None of the forest animals ventured out in the hot afternoon sun and instead rested in their respective shelters. Even the birds fell silent.

'This humid heat should result in rain, no?' said Tiripalu that afternoon while cooking near the water source.

'If it rains, will you plough your farm and sow a crop?' asked Gurappa.

'When one has a farm, one has to till or furrow the red soil, sow some seeds and make it green, right?' replied Tiripalu.

'You will become a farmer again, then!'

'I have to . . . how could I not scratch my itch?'

'You declared that you wouldn't give your daughter's hand to a tiller of the land,' exclaimed Pullayya. 'How can you go back to farming yourself?'

'Yes, my decision is firm,' said Tiripalu. 'No question of my daughter marrying a farmer!'

'If everyone thought like you, who would remain to cultivate the land and grow crops?'

'Let's not cultivate then!' retorted Tiripalu. 'Why should we do farming when there is no water? If the government wants to do good, they should pay salaries and employ the farmers. Not big salaries, mind you. Five thousand rupees per month is enough. If the government provides for the education of their children and gives them free medical treatment if they fall ill, then a regular income of five thousand will do. The salary of one government employee will cover the monthly pay of twenty farmers like me. I will work as a labourer in my field and do whatever is asked of me. If they ensure a supply of good water, fertiliser and pesticides, I will produce the best yields. I don't need bribes or other side income . . . they can take the entire yield. The labour wages would be enough for us.'

'. . . None of this is in the realm of possibility,' said Gurappa dismissively.

However, Tiripalu's argument resonated with Ravi. His tone was casual, and yet, his idea had substance. It could revive the farming sector in this drought-stricken region and be the holistic medicine to treat the chronic poverty in the villages. If the government really wanted to help, thought Ravi, they could easily implement such an idea.

The day passed by without any signs of the tiger or the pythons.

*

In the evening, they encountered a porcupine, which scared the sheep with its bristling quills. They thought of clubbing it to death, but there wasn't enough daylight left to carefully remove all the quills, cut up the flesh and cook it. As long as the stick cracked its head when they attacked it, all would be fine. But a hit on any other body part would not hurt it much. It might then charge at the men and injure them with its thorn-like quills. The injuries could take a long time to heal. They decide to wait for it to leave.

Once the porcupine had waddled its way into a hole, Pullayya picked up a couple of quills it had left behind. They were beautiful—long and fine, with jet black and lily-white stripes. Pullayya told the others about the custom of cutting porcupine quills into small pieces and stringing them together like beads on a black thread. Children would wear the thread around their waists. In the olden days, said Pullayya, people used to fit a nib to the quill, dip it in ink and use it as a pen for calligraphy.

*

It had been over a month since the last rainfall. The next day, when they arrived at a spring in the afternoon, they saw that the water level had become alarmingly low. The group had hoped that that particular water source would serve them for a week or more. Their plan had been to graze in the surrounding hills for the next five or six days and go to that spot every afternoon.

Now it seemed that even if they used the water carefully, it would only be enough for a day. There was no hope of fresh water pooling into that spring until it rained heavily and the aquifers and seeps overflowed into it. Even the little remaining water would soon evaporate.

A blackbuck was just leaving the spot when they arrived. It was a fully grown buck, almost the size of a male buffalo. It had long, twisted antlers and a dark stripe below the neck. The shepherds thought of chasing it but quickly dropped the idea. They knew that the blackbuck couldn't be outrun. Antelopes usually moved around in herds, but this one seemed to be by itself. The antelope bucks prefer being on their own in the summer, but normally stay with the herd during the winter and rainy seasons.

The gollas first filled their water cans before taking the flocks to the water. The sheep did not step into the spring; instead, the sheep bent down on their knees and sipped by lowering their mouths to the water. Meanwhile, the antelope had climbed halfway up the nearest hill and was rubbing its body against a sandalwood tree. After a while, it started bashing its horns against the tree trunk. The sound of the impact resounded throughout the valley.

'The buck starts thrashing its horns on to trees once those appendages grow too big and start itching,' said Pullayya. 'It helps to shed the horns, but it won't happen in a day.'

The old shepherd told them that bucks had to go through the painful process of losing their antlers at least once every two years. The buck could be more active and move about freely with its smaller new horns. Its troubles would begin again when those horns grew big and branched. The antlers could make it difficult for the buck to pass through narrow trails and bushes. To avoid the antlers from getting tangled with creepers or tree branches, the bucks began to prefer staying on hilltops. Walking with the herd in the valleys and the streambeds made them an easier target for tigers.

For a long time, antelope or chital antlers were a common sight in rural households. Tied to the wooden ceilings of the huts with a string, the horns were used as hooks to hang clothes or bags. However, the entry of businessmen into the forest meant that no antlers remained for use in the houses in the village.

The shepherds could hear the sound of the blackbuck thrashing against the tree throughout their afternoon break. They decided to start moving the herds again around four, which was a little earlier than usual. They needed to cover at least eight kilometres to get to the next water source. Pamuleti mapped out the route, which would see them climb the same hill that the blackbuck had, after which they'd let the sheep graze as they moved southwest.

The hill was wide, and it stretched from the north to the south. Gurappa's flock was on the southern side and was going take the lead. Once his flock started moving, the others would follow in a line. Pullayya suggested taking some of the sheep along the slopes of the hill. But just as Gurappa was about to get his flock moving, a commotion began on the hill.

They heard the sound of heavy hooves kicking stones. It was a large animal running. The sound was approaching them rapidly. Before they could understand what was happening, the horned antelope buck came crashing through the bushes at an incredible speed.

Then they saw it. A large tiger was advancing like a burning ball of fire. It was almost as fast as the buck, chasing it in a blur of movement. With a predator following it with cruel determination, the buck ran for its life. It decided to turn towards the south, because it would be able to escape the tiger if it could run past the flocks. The tiger would then give up pursuit and attack the sheep instead.

The buck headed straight for the group of shepherds and their herds. The young gollas pulled out their slings in reflex. But before the antelope could get any closer, the tops of its antlers hit a tree, causing it to stumble and fall. The tiger pounced before the buck could get back up. The momentum of the leap dragged both the animals several metres forward.

Gathering all its strength, the buck cried out and jumped even as the tiger held on to it. It landed right near Gurappa's flock. The tiger did not loosen its grip on its prey. The flocks flew into utter chaos and the sheep began running helter-skelter in fright. Most of them ran towards the north, away from the fighting animals. They rushed about madly and blindly, urinating and defecating.

The antelope made full use of its weight. Not allowing the tiger to pin it down, the buck almost heaved the tiger off its body. Then, screaming wildly, it jumped sideways, landing right in the middle of the escaping herds. That was when the gollas joined the sheep in running for their lives. There was no sign of the two cowardly dogs, but they could see Gurappa's dog had joined the sheep and was running north.

Roaring loudly, the tiger lunged at the buck. It pushed its prey down again and managed to clasp its jaws around its neck. Biting into the flesh, it steadied itself and drew blood. It had won.

Meanwhile Gurappa's flock had become completely separated from the main herd. The lead buck of the herd was dashing around in terror, and the sheep followed it, bleating and screaming. Gurappa rushed towards them, urging Bhaskar and Ravi to come with him. 'The flock is gone!' he shouted. 'Need to herd them together! Come on!'

His voice was full of fear and anxiety as he shouted while running as fast as he could. Bhaskar began running after him. 'Ravi, come on!' he shouted as he followed Gurappa.

But Ravi was fixated on the scene unfolding before him. The tiger's mouth opened wide as it loudly slurped blood from the buck's neck. It suddenly lifted its eyes and saw Ravi watching. Eyes burning bright, it gave Ravi an unblinking stare as the tip of its tail quivered a little.

The tiger looked so ferocious that for a moment Ravi felt it would leave the bleeding buck and attack him instead. The buck kicked its legs, groaning in pain. The tiger still gazed at Ravi, who did not take his eyes off the beast either even as he started to slowly step backwards.

While he walked away, he was careful not to show his back to the animal. The tiger's cruel and angry countenance sent a shiver up his spine. It did not seem to have any fear of the human, its quivering tail indicated its readiness to attack.

Ravi soon withdrew himself far enough for the tiger to not focus on him anymore. Ravi's heart raced even though he was no longer face to face with the creature. He looked around and saw that their flock was all over the place. Gurappa and Bhaskar were running behind the sheep, trying to halt their mad dash and bring them together again.

They were calling out to the animals, making sounds of admonishment and appeasement, but they knew that until the front runner—the herd's buck—was stopped, the rams wouldn't stop. However, if they could manage to get the buck to stop and then the rams, the sheep would halt behind them and crowd themselves into a flock again.

The sheep ran down the hill and then along the tail ranges, the rock beds and the valley floor. It did not look like they would snap out of their fear anytime soon. That was when Gurappa remembered his dog. He yelled for it. The dog heard him on the second call, stopped running and returned to its master.

With the dog by his side, Gurappa dashed across the valley. He was able to cut off the lead goat and make it come to a halt on a patch of soft soil. The dog then helped by running alongside the scattered sheep and barking at them to fall in line. The flock finally came to a standstill.

By then, Bhaskar and Ravi had managed to catch up with Gurappa. The three of them tried to calm the sheep down, making reassuring sounds and shouting commands when necessary. The sheep continued being flustered for a while, whining with their ears pricked up.

It took them a while to quieten the sheep and get the flock in order. Almost all the sheep had passed loose stools down their legs. They had been scared half to death. After the shepherds had patted each of them and uttered their gibberish to appease and cajole, they slowly returned to normal and bent down to eat the grass.

Then the three shepherds made the sheep climb the opposite hill, and they grazed along the way. By then, the sun had set behind the hills. The sheep had run for almost an hour, covering a distance of about eight or ten kilometres. If the other flocks had run away in the opposite direction, they could be at least fifteen kilometres apart.

It soon became completely dark, but the moon was high in the sky. By its light, they found some dry branches and twigs to build fires on three sides of the flock. Then they looked for and added a few bigger pieces of wood to the fires to make them burn brighter and longer.

Reckoning that the rest of their group would have camped on top of some hill and lit fires, they looked around at all the hilltops to the north but could not find any signs of a fire burning. They wondered if they had travelled too far to see their campfires. Or did the other sheep run to a different hill range?

It had been an unexpected series of unfortunate events, leading to a situation that none of them could have predicted. They were in a different kind of trouble from what they had faced until then. Even Gurappa's dog seemed to have been scared out of its wits. It found a spot in the middle of the flock and lay down.

The three shepherds deliberated on their next course of action as they ate rotis for dinner. Unless the other flocks returned the next day to the same water source that they had used that afternoon, they couldn't meet again. And even if they did, there was not enough water there for all the sheep.

There was also the question of the tiger. It might hide the kill somewhere near the water and later return with its mate to reclaim it. That would be an additional danger for the flock. Their own sheep would need water by afternoon tomorrow, but Pamuleti and Munayya—the water scouts in the group—were not with them. Gurappa discussed their options with the two young men. Though they had saved themselves and their flock from one tiger, the water problem was like another tiger lying in wait.

Gurappa thought that he recognised the area they were in. He had been there three years ago and remembered that there was a water source nearby. Was it a rivulet, a stream or a pool under a stone bed? He tried to jog his memory but failed to recall the details. He could not be sure of where they had ended up.

After dashing down the hill, the sheep had crossed two or three rocky outcrops and then run into the valleys between the hillocks. In the tension and anxiety of chasing the sheep and herding them back together, the gollas did not notice the direction in which they were running. They might have run south, but it could also be that they had run towards the east.

Gurappa was confused but knew that the onus of finding a water source was on him. Resting on his head was the responsibility of protecting not only the flock but also the two young men. He did not sleep much that night.

Ravi was disturbed too. He was not thinking about finding water for the sheep though. His thoughts were all about the tiger—its power and anger, its cruelty and dominance. He recalled the way it had easily and skilfully killed an opponent that was bigger and heavier.

Moonlight spread across the forest like milk cream. The silence had a music to it, and there was an aroma carried over by light breezes. Normally, it would have been a pleasant experience that turned into a sweet memory. But their minds were still shaken from the fear and anxiety caused by the tiger.

Gurappa started talking as soon as they got up in the morning. 'It was like a rebirth for all of us yesterday,' he stated. 'In all my years of hill-grazing, I have never seen such an angry tiger up close. The shiver has not left my heart yet.'

He added that if it were the poachers or the sandalwood loggers whom the tiger had frightened, they would have returned to pour some pesticide on the carcass to kill the tiger and its clan. Ravi remembered Pullayya's advice. They were visitors here and shouldn't try to subjugate the tiger in its own habitat.

Gurappa walked around the edges of the hill and observed the forest below. 'Look out for birds flying over streambeds,' he told Ravi and Bhaskar. He thought that the presence of birds would indicate a watering hole. They observed some bird movements over a ravine about three kilometres to the north.

Bhaskar went with Gurappa to scout the area. It took them an hour to return. They said that they did find water pooling under some rock plates, but it was just a trickle—enough to wet one's lips but not enough to fill their cans. Gurappa looked distraught. He knew that they had to find a water source by afternoon. Without water, the sheep would get desperately thirsty.

Gurappa gave a roti to the dog and ate one himself. Bhaskar and Ravi had eaten their rotis already. After drinking a little water, they got the sheep moving an hour earlier than they normally would. Bhaskar took the lead position, walking ahead of the flock. Ravi brought up the rear.

With his dog for company, Gurappa walked along the rim of the hill for a couple of kilometres, looking for any sign of a water source. The area was full of boulders, stone plates and hilly mounds. He also saw several streambeds, where the trees grew thick and spread downhill. Gurappa walked down into each streambed to check for water. The dog followed him, its feet making clicking sounds on the rocks. During the rainy season, these streambeds would be alive with a rapid flow of water, but were dry gullies now. Gurappa only found rocks, not a hint of moisture.

After exploring a half-dozen streambeds, Gurappa was exhausted. The dog too was tired, its tongue lolling out. The veteran shepherd sat under a yepe tree to catch his breath. He took out a polythene bag from his side pocket and extracted a folded betel leaf and an areca nut and put them in his mouth. He then took out a small box from another pocket and scratched out a line of hard lime with his finger. He then licked the finger clean.

After a while, Gurappa got up and continued the search for water with the dog. They scouted another dry streambed and the sedimentary stone plates nearby, only to be disappointed again. As they turned back, the dog suddenly started barking. It tried to lunge forward and Gurappa could only restrain it with difficulty, holding it tightly by its waist.

The dog tried to resist its master's grip. Holding the dog tight with one hand, Gurappa looked in the direction it was barking in. He reached for his axe with his other hand. Suddenly, two wild sheep jumped out from behind a bush a few metres away. They began running towards the top of the hill.

For a moment, Gurappa was tempted to allow the dog to chase them. But he knew that in their current predicament, hunting down a wild sheep would only lead to an additional burden. It would be afternoon by the time he would manage to carve and prepare the meat for cooking. They did not need mutton. What they needed was water.

Gurappa and his dog half-ran through the valley. In two of the dry streambeds they passed, he thought he saw a little water under the rocks. But upon closer inspection, it turned out to be just a patch of moisture each time. The water seemed to have dried up more than a week ago. At another stone plate, the dog barked and ran away from the spot. He bent down to see if there was water underneath. Instead, he found a python moving slowly. Gurappa sprang away and followed the dog.

He climbed back up the hill and resumed his search in the streambeds on the other side. Wherever he saw birds gathering above, he made sure to check that spot. He also inspected boulder sites because the sighting of the wild sheep could mean a watering hole was nearby. Gurappa even looked into all the deep crevices.

As the hours slipped past and fatigue set in deeper, Gurappa's agitation increased. He knew that it was very difficult to find water sources in Nallamala during the summer. Only those who had clearly mapped out water sources would know where to look. Getting lost in the hills could mean dying of thirst.

The ranges, streams and groups of boulders all looked familiar to Gurappa. But try as he might, he could not place their present area in his mental map of the hills. All his experience of hill-grazing could not help. It was a specific skill to identify water sources in the forest and map routes. Shepherds kept their eyes on their flocks and didn't usually note natural features and landmarks on their expeditions. That was the job of the water scouts.

Each group travelled with such scouts, who went on reconnaissance missions during which they stood atop the tallest peaks and divided the entire area into quadrants in their minds, memorising the visuals. They took time to note down the water sources in each area based on the unique features of the surrounding landscape—peaks, groves, deep gorges, brooks and springs, all with names and legends associated with them that made it easier to recognise and remember them. Only these water scouts would know how to follow the natural clues strewn all over the hills and forests. As the afternoon wore on, Gurappa walked briskly without conscious thought. His anxiety made him lose his usual patience. A small leopard found itself in their path. The dog started barking. Without pausing to think, Gurappa swiped at the leopard with his axe. It avoided the blow and ran away.

Gurappa immediately told himself that there had been no need to attack the animal. It would have slipped off the trail on its own once it had seen a man and his dog approach. It was uncharacteristic of the veteran shepherd to act with such impatience. He knew that it was stress that had provoked such behaviour.

He felt dismay at how bad their situation had become. The anguish of helplessness hovered over him and confusion possessed him. He had no clue what they would do if he couldn't find water. His distress was turning into despair and was about to burst out as sorrow. After rearing his sheep for all these years, he was about to end up sacrificing all their lives—so many lives—to these boulders and wild trees. The very thought burned a hole through every nerve of his being.

However, under it all, Gurappa could sense his brain giving out a weak signal. It was reminding him that he had been there before, roamed in that very area with the same flock and his fellow shepherds. But he did not have the composure to follow that signal. He began climbing up and down the hillocks and streambeds aimlessly, feeling totally alone and desperate.

'Oh God!' he found himself saying. 'Where are you, father? Kasi Nayana! You know every rock here. You know every stream. Show mercy, God!' He was shouting now, tears streaming down his face.

He heard Bhaskar calling out for him. 'Mama! Where are you?' The shout echoed in the valleys.

They probably wanted to know if he had found water, Gurappa thought. He did not respond. Bhaskar started whistling. When there was still no response, he whistled again and again. Gurappa wondered if they were worried about his safety. He finally whistled back.

Bhaskar reached the edge of the opposite hill and looked in the direction from where Gurappa had whistled. He saw the senior shepherd climbing up and felt relieved. But when he came closer, Bhaskar saw that Gurappa was in tears.

'No water anywhere, Bhaskar!' cried Gurappa. 'What shall we do? After all these years, are we going to let the sheep die in these damned hills?'

'The sheep have eaten their fill, mama,' responded Bhaskar. 'They are resting under those trees now. Let's go sit there and consider our next steps.'

'A night and almost an entire day without water,' moaned Gurappa. 'They are frail animals, Bhaskar, they can't stand the thirst!'

'I know, but what can we do, mama! We haven't had any water ourselves. We need to figure out how to get to Jyothi. Even if it is far away, we should head in that direction.'

'Where is Jyothi? We have lost our way, haven't we? It is as if we stepped on a creeper that causes amnesia. I don't seem to remember which direction we ran towards yesterday. This area looks familiar, but I am unable to place it.'

They trudged up the hill and walked to the place where the flock was resting. Bhaskar offered him the little water he had remaining. Gurappa did not drink the water himself. He poured a little on a plate and placed it in front of the dog, who quickly lapped it up. Gurappa then poured some more water on the plate, and reacted angrily when Bhaskar suggested that he should drink some too.

'With all these sheep that are parched, how can you ask me to drink?' he snapped.

Bhaskar was familiar with Gurappa's foul moods on days when the sheep didn't have enough to eat, or when he lost a sheep to disease. Ravi too knew about his father's irritability on those occasions. The two younger shepherds thought that it would be tough to handle Gurappa if the sheep went without water that day.

'I was here three years ago and walked through all these hills,' Gurappa said, his voice despairing. 'But I am unable to remember the name of even a single landmark. If I could remember, it would become easier to recognise the ranges and figure out where the trails lead. But all these hills look alike to me!'

None of them could come up with any good suggestions about the direction in which they should head. They briefly entertained the idea of retracing their steps back to the place where the tiger had killed the buck. But they were not even sure of that path. If they ended up deeper in the forest, they were certain to die of thirst.

A mild restlessness stirred among the sheep. A few began bleating softly, while some stood up and began stomping in place. Many lifted their heads, flared their nostrils and tried to sniff at something in the air.

One of the sheep approached Gurappa. Bleating feebly, it started rubbing its head against his body.

'Where is the water?' Gurappa said angrily. 'Is it in my lap? Then why are you rubbing against me? That damned animal crashed into the flock, and that is why we are facing these troubles. The tiger should have eaten one or two of you! It would have been better than this. You all ran for your life, and now our lives are at risk too. Go away or else I will bash your head with a stone. Better to die quickly anyway.'

Gurappa spoke like a man who had lost his senses.

Ravi and Bhaskar deliberated among themselves for a while and decided that it was best to head towards the south without stopping anywhere. The Obulam path ran from east to west through the hills, so they were likely to cross it at some point. From there, they could easily make their way to Jyothi, Anantarayani or Garudadri.

Bhaskar turned to looked at the sheep, because now more than half the flock was standing and stomping restlessly while making noises. He turned towards Gurappa, wanting to check if their decision was okay with him. That was when he noticed a movement on a nearby hill to the south. He peered into the distance and confirmed that it was a man.

He called Ravi excitedly. 'Look over there!' he cried, pointing at the hill that looked like a twin of the hill they were standing on. Ravi looked in that direction, and he too saw a man walking near the top of the hill. He seemed to be carrying a large bundle on his shoulder.

Bhaskar let out a loud whistle. 'O anna!' he yelled. Gurappa looked up, saw what was happening and joined in the yelling and whistling. He also took out his scarf and waved it.

The man on the other hill heard the shouts and whistles. He placed his load by a tree and whistled back. Gurappa and Bhaskar immediately set off in his direction. Afraid that the man might walk away, they kept whistling through their hurried ascent of the southern hill.

'If he is carrying so much weight, the main trails must be close by,' said Gurappa as they panted while going up the hill.

They found the man waiting for them once they reached the top. He seemed to be a woodcutter. His load was a bundle of satinwood branches that had been scraped clean of twigs with an axe. The wood was used to make cots.

'Are you gollas?' enquired the man.

'Yes, brother,' replied Gurappa. 'We lost our way. We are desperate to find a water source.' He told the man briefly about their troubles.

'There is no water in these hills,' said the woodcutter. He pointed to a tall hill further south. 'Did you look for water on the other side of that hill?'

They replied in the negative, prompting the man to react with surprise.

'You've been herding sheep in this area for so many years, but you don't know that hill?'

'I cannot remember it,' said Gurappa quietly. 'I am so worried . . .'

'That is Devarakonda,' said the woodcutter. 'The hill to the north of Jyothi.'

Gurappa looked sheepish, then hit his head hard with his own hand a few times to berate himself for his stupidity. Having established one landmark, he could suddenly identify all the surrounding hills. He also understood the route that they had taken to arrive in that area.

'Want to drink some water?' asked the woodsman. He had a plastic bottle wrapped in a thick cloth slung near his armpit. He offered the bottle to Gurappa, who took a few grateful sips before returning it. The two shepherds then thanked him profusely. The woodsman lifted his bundle on his shoulder and went on his way.

Bhaskar returned to where Ravi was waiting with the sheep. Together, they took the flock over to the other hill. As he waited, Gurappa felt ashamed. If only he had sat on a tall peak and composed his thoughts, his memory would have served him better. Unfortunately, he had not allowed himself to do that. Instead, he had run around stupidly.

They soon reached Jyothi with their herd. The sheep quenched their thirst, and the men replenished their water cans. Then they took their flock to rest near the Devarakonda foothills till the evening. At nightfall, they climbed the hill and set up camp for the night on a wide patch halfway to the top. They used some dry wood to build fires around the flock.

Now, they could let their sheep graze in the surrounding hills and use Jyothi as the water source until the other flocks arrived. This thought put them at ease. It was the most strenuous day they'd faced since entering the hills thirty-four days ago. Gurappa reflected that even if one could bear any amount of physical hardship, it became truly difficult when the mind was stressed.

20

It was still dark when Bhaskar was awoken by the call of early birds. He sat up and saw that Gurappa, who normally got up before anyone else, was still asleep with his blanket wrapped from head to toe. Bhaskar woke up Ravi, and they went together to complete their morning ablutions.

Gurappa was still asleep when they returned. That was not normal. When they went closer to where he was lying, they heard a low groan and the grinding of teeth.

'Mama! Mama!' called Bhaskar. He tried to pull off the blanket, but Gurappa had wrapped it tight. Bhaskar forcibly pulled off the blanket. 'I think I have a fever,' mumbled Gurappa. 'Let me sleep for a while.' He barely opened his eyes to look at them.

Bhaskar held Gurappa's hand and gave a start. It was like touching burning coal. Ravi examined him too, and they concluded that it was hill fever. God knows how many streambeds he had ventured into the other day, they said to each other. Perhaps he had tasted putrid water in some hole or was bitten by mosquitoes.

At any rate, he had come down with hill fever, and the sooner they got him home, the better. If they could get him to Jyothi, they could put him on a bus home. They explained the matter to Gurappa and got him ready for the trek downhill. His chills had started to become unbearable, so they enveloped him from the shoulders down in a blanket and then tied a scarf around his head, covering his ears as well.

Holding his axe as a staff, Gurappa leaned against an ash-coloured axlewood. He asked the two young men to come closer.

'Be careful,' he said, shivering as he spoke. 'You are still in the hunting zone of that demon tiger. Even if you go to the hills south of Jyothi, there is another tiger in that area. You have seen it. Wild fowl and other birds sense it first when a tiger is approaching. They make a ruckus. Langurs will jump agitatedly from one branch to the other. You should keep an eye open for such signs.'

He pulled the blanket over his nose before continuing, 'When the tiger is in your path, *do not bend down*,' he said. 'Stand straight, to your full height. If you bend to pick up a stone or a stick, the tiger will see that you have a neck too, just like the other animals. It will then know that all it needs to do is to attack that spot. Once it kills a man by biting or clawing at the neck, it will attack any other standing man by pouncing on the head. But even a tiger will fear a man standing straight. And under no circumstances should you show your back to a tiger and run away. It will give chase and then leap on you. Run only when there is enough distance between you and the tiger for you to be able to climb up to the higher branches of a tree. Otherwise don't run at all. If you are not around, it will kill as many sheep as it wants. If a human is around, it will drag just the one sheep away. Be careful, Bhaskar! Ravi!'

After giving them all the advice he could, Gurappa started walking in the direction of Jyothi. The chills were making him shiver violently. Grinding his teeth, Gurappa held his head in both hands. Bhaskar remained with the flock while Ravi went with his father, supporting him as he struggled to walk. However, Gurappa did not collapse like Veerayya had. Even with such a high fever, he trudged ahead while gritting his teeth and leaning on Ravi for support.

As they walked, he told Ravi to take good care of his dog. Once they had reached Jyothi, he repeated the advice. 'He is a loyal dog,' said Gurappa. 'Has a lot of courage and a steady heart. Some day or the other, he will put his life on the line to protect us.'

There were no vehicles at Jyothi. However, an ashram tractor was heading to the villages to pick up groceries. Ravi helped Gurappa sit inside the tractor and saw him off.

'Take care, my son!' said Gurappa and bid him farewell.

Ravi went back to Bhaskar and the herd. All the sheep were now under the guardianship of the two young men. They moved the flock within a three-kilometre radius of Jyothi, bringing them back in the afternoon for water and a rest.

*

On the second day of hill-grazing near Jyothi, a leopard tried to attack the flock while they were grazing on the western knolls. The two golla youth acted swiftly and chased it away. Yelling and whistling, they frightened the leopard, which eventually ran away after receiving a few bone-jarring hits from the stones they hurled at it.

Gurappa's dog bonded well with Ravi, who continued his father's custom of feeding it rice mixed with sheep milk. When they rested, he patted the dog's head and caressed its body to demonstrate his affection.

On the third morning after Gurappa left, Bhaskar and Ravi heard whistles from atop the Devarakonda hill. They recognised the group of men as ration-bearers from their village. Both of them responded with whistles and waved their scarves in the air. The ration-bearers made their way to the flock. They told them that Sankar had taken Gurappa to the hospital and that he was responding well to treatment.

Among them was Vakkaku Chennayya, an expert scout who knew these hills and forests very well. He no longer had sheep and had moved entirely into farming and agriculture. However, his expertise was needed to locate the scattered herds to ensure that everyone received their rations. Chennayya became the tracker to guide them through the jungle trails.

After giving Ravi and Bhaskar their rations, the ration-bearers followed Chennayya into the hills. They were back by noon, by when Ravi and Bhaskar had moved their sheep near Satyala Tippa knoll. The ration-bearers informed them that the other herds were headed their way. It would take them another two days to get to Jyothi.

Then the reunited flocks could travel together to the hill farms on the other side of Jyothi. There was another update. The other herds had been attacked by a leopard on the first day after the separation, and a tiger on the second. They had lost one sheep to each attack. Chennayya advised them to be careful.

'Gurappa spoke about this repeatedly,' he said. 'Both of you are hot-blooded youngsters. Don't be reckless.' He told them that between the two hill ranges, including the flatter rolling hills that they were presently on, there was a sixteen-kilometre stretch of valley land. Right in the middle of that land, there were smaller ranges that stretched from east to west at two spots. That entire area was the territory of the big old tiger they had encountered. It patrolled the territory at least once a week to inspect the boundaries of its estate. 'If it sees a flock of sheep in its territory, it will silently grab one and leave,' said Chennayya. 'Don't try to stop it.'

After Chennayya had shared a few more tips and precautions, the ration-bearers left for Jyothi. Their news had filled Ravi and Bhaskar with a sense of optimism. As they had already covered the nearby hills and meadows, they went a little deeper into the northern side and camped on a midsize hill for the night.

They walked together around the flock while they ate their dinner of rotis. That was the only time they could spend with each other at night as they had to guard the flock on opposite sides, sleeping by the fires they'd lit at each end.

At nine in the night, when the moon was high in the sky, Ravi found himself suddenly awake. He could not put his finger on the reason and tried to listen for any odd sound. The dog was awake, as usual. It sensed that Ravi was up and came by to check on him.

Ravi woke up again around midnight. This time, he could hear birds making agitated sounds somewhere in the valley below. He told himself that it was probably a jungle cat attacking a prey near their tree. He did not wake up again till the morning.

The next morning, the young shepherds finished their ablutions and did their routine checks on the sheep. The flock seemed to be in good health. After they had eaten and fed the dog, they set out for the day. The dale was full of axlewood and satinwood trees along with several red sanders and polike. The flock grazed through the valley as they moved northwest.

The aim was to climb the tallest hill by nightfall. From there, Bhaskar and Ravi hoped to catch sight of the herds of their fellow shepherds headed towards Jyothi. They reckoned that travelling south along the spine of the hill would get them to Velpudari. From there, they could take the flock to Jyothi via Anantarayani.

Just before the sheep began the ascent to the hilltop, they noticed a wet patch on a stone near the streambed at the bottom of the slope. It seemed as if some animal had urinated there not long ago. There was an acrid smell and insects buzzed around the spot.

'It was the big fox, I think,' said Bhaskar. He led the flock briskly up the hill. Ravi brought up the rear. Both walked on the side of the ravine, throwing stones into it and hitting the bushes with their axe handles to make noise.

The banks of the ravine were covered with amla trees mixed with some sandalwood. Ravi sensed some movement in the stream below. But the sounds were upstaged by the high-pitched calls of the birds. He stopped for a moment and focused, trying to catch any unusual sound. He could not hear anything. No animal came into view either.

Doubt pecked at him. He asked himself if he was a little jumpy because they had seen the urine patch of the tiger. He took another ten steps but stopped when he sensed movement again. However, it was still not clear . . . until suddenly, the birds atop the trees some hundred metres from the streambed rushed upwards, noisily settling down on other trees.

Ravi's suspicion now had firm roots. A sense of urgency took over him.

'Bhaskar!' he shouted. 'Take them away from the ravine. Let's get on to the hill quickly.'

They both uncoiled their slings. The bushes were shaking here and there in the streambed. The birds continued to be agitated.

The flock reached the top of the hill even as the birds rose again in fright, flapping their wings rapidly. Their movements were like a wave moving up the hill, telling the shepherds that a predator was climbing up towards them through the bushes along the ravine.

They moved the flock further away and secured their ration bags to a tree. Then they found a few big stones and hurled them with their slings in the direction of the ravine. The stones pierced the air and crashed into the bushes by the ravine's edge. They hurled more stones until their attacks gave them a quick glimpse of the animal. But it still wasn't clear if it was the tiger or a leopard.

Without giving it a second thought, Ravi and Bhaskar placed stones in their slings again and hurled them with all the power they could muster towards the spot where they had seen the creature.

The stones hit the mark, because the animal shrieked and jumped into the adjacent bushes.

It was another brief glimpse, but they were able to clearly identify the animal this time.

It was the big tiger.

The young men were still under the spell of confidence and zest that they had gained after their victory over the leopard the previous day. They decided a few more hits like that would teach the tiger a lesson too. They placed even heavier stones in their slings. The weight required them to whirl the sling using both hands. To give their missiles more momentum, they swung four or five times before releasing the projectiles.

The first stone hit a tree trunk, making the tree shake with the impact. The second one crashed into a boulder and splintered into sharp pieces that flew into the nearby bushes.

They heard the savage roar of the tiger first. It was immediately followed by the sight of the giant predator jumping from the bushes on to the bank of the ravine. Now that they could see it clearly, they were absolutely sure that it was the same tiger that had brutally killed the buck.

With eyes burning like cinders, the beast started running up the hill. It bounded over the rocks, moving like the wind. Opening its mouth wide, it roared even as it surged ahead, rushing uphill like a forest fire. Just its ferocious form could make the heart tremble and the feet give way in fear.

The flock was in terror. There was no sign of the dog anywhere. The shepherds suddenly realised that the beast's gaze and its sprint were directed not towards the sheep . . . but towards them.

'Run!' screamed Bhaskar. 'Climb a tree! We will die, Ravi!' He turned around, ran and quickly clambered up an axlewood tree.

However, Ravi stood his ground. As the tiger bounded up the hill astonishingly fast, there was no time left to run away.

The tiger's claws would tear into his flesh. Its fangs would pierce his neck.

Death was certain . . .

Then, what was the point of being scared?

That thought was the spark that flushed the fear out of his body.

Ravi picked up his axe. He braced himself on the hard ground, stood tall and held the axe tight with both hands. He then raised it and assumed a posture of attack with a high backlift. Giving himself as solid a base as possible, he readied himself to make an an almighty swipe at the tiger when it pounced.

Bhaskar was screaming wildly. His shrieks were not the normal cries a shepherd made to scare off an animal. They were primal screams of terror. He first shouted at Ravi, imploring him to run away, to escape. Then he shook the branches of the tree, hollering at the tiger to go away. Finally, realising that he was about to witness Ravi being ripped to shreds by a tiger, his cries became a mix of grief and helplessness.

When the tiger was ten metres from Ravi, it crouched low and roared, preparing to lunge. Ravi's plan was simple but almost impossible to execute properly. Before its claws reached him, he intended to swing his axe at the tiger while simultaneously jumping sideways.

Just as the tiger was about to jump into the air, something entirely unexpected happened. It was a bizarre twist that no one could have even dreamt of.

Gurappa's dog suddenly flew out from among the flock and rushed to attack the tiger. Without any hesitation, the dog slipped in between the tiger's legs and bit into the predator's testicles. The tiger cut short its intended leap, utterly confused. Before it could understand what had happened, the dog had firmly gripped the tiger's balls in its mouth.

Growling in pain, the tiger turned around swiftly. The dog, hanging on to the beast's gonads for its dear life, moved with the tiger. The tiger roared at full pelt and then it shrieked violently. Unable to bear the pain, it kept swivelling this way and that. The dog held on firmly, ensuring that it remained behind the tiger even as the bigger animal tried to rid itself of the excruciating pain.

The tiger tried to land a paw on the dog's body by twisting itself, but the dog remained out of reach. It bit further into the tiger's testicles with a wild desperation even as it was swung around like a rock tied to the tiger's tail.

For a few moments, Ravi was transfixed by the scene playing out in front of him. He had thought that the dog had hid its tail between its legs and merged into the thickness of the flock to escape from the tiger. Instead, it had emerged with an utterly clever, courageous and unexpected intervention.

Ravi recovered from his shock and realised that if the tiger rolled on the ground a few times, it would manage to reach the dog eventually. A single smack with its paw would break the dog's skull. That would be followed by its body being torn to pieces by the enraged tiger. Before that could happen, Ravi had to help the dog by somehow bringing down the tiger.

He did not hesitate any further. With an uncontrollable surge of adrenaline flowing through his body and breathing hot air out of his flaring nostrils, Ravi let out a wild cry and rushed towards the tiger. He dealt the beast's head a blow with the butt of his axe.

The heavy impact of the hard metal on its skull dazed the creature for a moment. It turned its head around slowly and gave Ravi an enraged glare. But before it could make a move, Ravi targeted the same spot on its head with the butt of the axe again. This time, it was an even heavier blow.

The tiger's skin ripped open and a fountain of blood gushed out from the wound. The tiger swayed for a moment and then swooned. It was not clear if the blows had cracked its skull, but the tiger collapsed to the ground and lay there, immobile.

The dog was lying behind the tiger, as if dead. Sweat was trickling down Ravi's body. He could hear the sound of his heart beating wildly. The sheer incredulousness of the situation overwhelmed him. With some effort, he composed himself and took a look at the dog.

It was lying on the ground with its eyelids half-open. Its mouth was still firmly clasped around the tiger's balls. Ravi approached the dog and called for it, making reassuring sounds. He asked the dog to open his eyes and come to him. The dog remained still.

The tiger was almost three metres long. Ravi walked around it with trepidation and reached out to touch the dog. He patted the dog and called to it again. The dog opened its eyes slowly and looked around. It hesitated for a few moments, checking to see whether it was safe to let go of its grip on the tiger's balls.

Then it saw the beast was lying unconscious. And there was its master, standing nearby, unharmed. Still, the dog kept its jaws locked on the tiger's testicles for a while longer as its fear drained away slowly. Then it opened its mouth, got up and stepped away from the tiger. It walked unsteadily towards Ravi and collapsed on the ground in front of him.

Ravi sprinkled some water on the dog's face and then poured some water into its panting mouth, red from the tiger's blood. Ravi patted and caressed its body, trying to drive away any remaining fear. Meanwhile, Bhaskar had climbed down the tree and was approaching the tiger.

Ravi saw that Bhaskar was going to strike the tiger with his axe. Pullayya's words came back to him, and he reminded himself that they had entered the tiger's kingdom to eat the produce from its territory. They did not have the right to kill the tiger. He gestured for Bhaskar to stop.

Ravi was confused about the tiger's condition. He approached the beast. Its eyes were open. Blood was dribbling from the wound in its head. Ravi sprinkled some water on the tiger's face. Bhaskar trembled. His mind told him that Ravi was doing the wrong thing.

The tiger's eyeballs moved. Its face twitched and its eyes closed and opened. After a few minutes, it slowly shook all of its body.

Ravi started to step backwards. Bhaskar got ready to climb a tree again. The dog stood behind a tree and watched.

The tiger moved.

The axe tightened in Ravi's hands.

It tried to stand up, but its legs gave away. It tried again and then again, succeeding after a few attempts. Then it turned its head and looked at them. Its eyes were like the last embers of a dying fire.

The beast gingerly took two steps forward but swooned and fell. After a few moments, it stood up again. This time, it could walk. It started heading back down the hill with measured steps, trying to protect its bloody hindquarters. The blood was from its testicles, which resembled a red wound between its legs. The dog had bitten deep into them.

At the bottom of the hill, the tiger turned around once. It gave Ravi a steady, emotionless look, then laboured away with heavy steps.

Once it had left, Ravi's pent-up emotions burst out like a bubble. He fell to the ground and lay on his back. The dog came over and snuggled close to him. Bhaskar was still in a state of disbelief about what he had witnessed. However, he understood that Ravi was mentally and physically exhausted, so the responsibility of getting the flock back together was now only his. He quickly moved in the direction he had seen the sheep run.

Ravi reflected on the moment when he had pounced on the tiger. It had caused a change in him, unleashing a strange emotion. It seemed like limitless cruelty, rooted in macabre violence, as animal-like as the blood-drenched teeth of the tiger.

Any man would have hit the tiger in that situation. Lest the tiger pounce on him, he would have used the sharpened blade of the axe to slash at the tiger. But then the axe would have got stuck in the tiger's skull. One could only imagine what would have happened next.

However, not many would have tried to use the butt of the axe. What Ravi found strange was the belief that had engulfed him at the time—that he could wield an axe with such demonic power that it would bring down a tiger with a blunt hit. He had felt intoxicated; it had made him feel like his body was made of steel.

He had been unable to handle the violent mental jolt caused by that state of heightened excitement. He was grateful he had come out of that spell after he had clubbed the tiger the second time. A third hit would have broken the tiger's skull, killing it immediately.

He was not sure if the tiger would live or die. If its skull was cracked, it would be difficult for the tiger to survive for long. Its remaining life would be short and painful if the wound festered and attracted worms. However, if the skull had not cracked and it could get home to its mate, the tigress would lick the wound till it healed.

Ravi was quite distressed by these thoughts. He found it distasteful that he had entered the tiger's abode and punished it so severely. He gazed at his palms and was aggrieved at the circumstances that had turned him into a killer.

If they had not attacked the tiger with stones, it may have just grabbed a sheep by the neck and gone away. The tiger attacked them only because they hurled stones at it and prevented it from getting food. It had the right to hunt according to the jungle's way of life. Ravi reasoned it was wrong to enforce rules of civilisation in a forest.

His thoughts went in many directions after that, but through it all, he hoped the tiger would survive. After a while, he sat up. His body felt weak. He heard Bhaskar's voice in the distance. He must have managed to herd the sheep together.

Ravi stood up. His head swam, and he held on to a tree branch for support. Slowly, he removed his ration bag from the branch he had hung it on. He slung it over his shoulder and then picked up his sling lying on the ground and tied it around his waist. With his axe in his hand, Ravi looked at where he and the dog had fought the tiger and noticed the streaks of blood on the ground where the tiger had fallen. The tiger's blood on his hands made him feel miserable.

The thought of life as a harsh and cruel experience flustered him. He moved towards the flock, which had returned with Bhaskar. They walked back together towards Jyothi. On the way, Ravi felt faint and weak. His body felt unable to tolerate the after-effects of such a heavy dose of excitement and emotion, and he desperately wanted to lie down for a while.

He somehow made it to Jyothi, drank some water and then collapsed to the ground. He did not respond when Bhaskar asked him about his appetite. The dog lay down next to Ravi.

Bhaskar did not cook for himself. He thought that they could get some food from the ashram once Ravi felt well enough to eat. He kept minding the sheep only because there was no other option. If there had been anyone else around, Bhaskar would have left the flock and fled home. The reason was that he could not bear the shame he felt at how he had acted when the tiger had attacked.

His fear had turned him into a coward, a deserter. Leaving Ravi at the mercy of the tiger, he had sprinted to the tree and climbed it as fast as he could. The scene refused to leave his mind and was haunting him. Bhaskar thought despondently about what he considered to be dastardly and selfish behaviour. He felt too ashamed to even directly look at Ravi.

Once the others heard about it, they would despise him as a traitor and look down upon him, he thought. It made his heart well up with sadness. Bhaskar sat dejectedly by Ravi's side, moping about his situation.

Ravi finally sat up after a couple of hours. He seemed to have regained some energy. They broke some coconuts and drank the water and then ate a meal of rice with buttermilk. The dog was given as much rice mixed with sheep milk as it could eat.

That night, they camped near the Anantarayani hill. By then, Ravi had understood the reason for Bhaskar's strange demeanour and tried to normalise things between the two of them. However, he only succeeded in making matters worse.

'In your place, anyone would have done the same thing,' said Ravi. 'I was the one who made a mistake. The dog saved my life.'

Those words made Bhaskar feel worse.

Once they had retired for the night, Bhaskar let himself be overcome by sorrow. He wept for a long time. The tears flushed out his feelings of grief and shame. It took him a while to become calm enough to fall asleep.

21

THE NEXT MORNING, THE clouds started gathering again. It had now been forty days since the start of their expedition. Bhaskar and Ravi took the sheep to graze on a hill to the south of Anantarayani.

Just before noon, Bhaskar saw the other herds from their village on the Velpudari hill to the north. They resembled red ants as they came down the hill. He yelled in delight. They both stepped out of the grove, climbed a tall boulder and started waving their scarves and whistling.

The gollas on the Velpudari hill noticed them and responded with whistles that reverberated through the hills. The two groups expressed their happiness at the impending reunion with whoops and whistles until they finally met at Jyothi.

Eight days had passed since the herds had been separated. As soon as they were close enough, Ramachandra came running and lifted Bhaskar. Ankayya held Ravi by the waist and swung him around. Happiness coursed through the group like a flood during the joyous reunion.

*

The cloud cover meant that they weren't exposed to the sun's heat that day. Even the winds were not as warm. Pullayya reckoned that they had moved into the Mrigasira Karti season, which usually began in the first week of June.

During lunch, they exchanged stories of their trials and tribulations over the last week. The other shepherds expressed their concern at Gurappa coming down with hill fever and having to head home.

Ravi did not bring up the fight with the tiger, but Bhaskar could not hold himself back and told them every detail. They all looked at Ravi and the dog in amazement. The story was scarcely believable. It had indeed been a miracle. A festive atmosphere spread through the group.

Pullayya gave Ravi a look before asking him to come closer. The old man pressed Ravi's biceps and said, 'These are not muscles, my dear! These are lumps of steel.' He then tapped Ravi on the chest, and said, 'Heart of steel.' Finally, touching Ravi's upper lip with his finger, he bellowed, 'Twirl your moustache, my boy!'

Ravi smiled a little but did not say a word in response. The dog had been sitting next to Ravi, but Pichchanna suddenly lifted it up and placed it on his shoulders. The dog moaned and tried to get off, which it managed to with Ravi's help.

Pichchanna had always mocked that dog for being good at nothing else but eating and lying down. He now squatted in front of the dog and ritually slapped his own cheeks in a gesture of apology. His actions sent ripples of laughter through the group.

Pullayya had, however, always remarked on its fearless nature, but no one had believed him. They now acknowledged that he had been right all along about the dog's bravery.

That night, the reunited group camped on the Janku Janthala hillocks to the south of Jyothi. Before lying down for the night, Pullayya called Ravi over and congratulated him again.

'You are a tiger yourself, my boy!' he said.

'Don't praise me, thatha,' protested Ravi. 'I am unable to bear it. I feel sad that I had to become a demon. And now you are calling me a wild animal.'

'What are you saying, son?' Pullayya asked, confused.

'I entered the tiger's kingdom and tried to kill it, thatha! You too had said that killing a tiger is not the right thing to do. And now, you are praising me . . .'

'True! It is wrong to kill it,' agreed Pullayya, scratching his head. 'But to confront such a wild animal and club its skull with an axe . . . has there ever been a man who has done that? How can we not praise such courage, son?'

'No, thatha,' responded Ravi. 'Please don't make me a butcher.'

Ravi walked back to his flock, leaving Pullayya puzzled.

When they woke up the next morning, heavy clouds covered the sky. A cold wind was blowing. 'As the saying goes, "Mrigasira cools down the front porches,"' said Pullayya. 'Not sure about the villages, but the forest has definitely become cooler.'

Soon, thunder and lightning followed. The sheep began stomping their feet, raising their necks towards the sky and jumping on the spot. The impending rains seemed to have excited them. The gollas understood the signs. Animals like sheep notice changes in the moisture content of the air and sense the rain before its arrival.

A light drizzle began by the afternoon. The flocks were moved to the spine of the hill. The drizzle continued but did not change in intensity. The clouds moved along in clusters without bringing a downpour. The stones became wet, but there was not enough rain for the water to run down the stones into the ground.

The shepherds did not even need to bring out the plastic sheets that served as their raincoats. The spray just tickled the skin and dried up soon. If even men did not get wet in this rain, thought Pullayya, how would the soil?

The same weather pattern continued through the night. The sky remained covered in clouds, with no moon visible during the night, just like the sun wasn't seen during the day. The next day, the clouds were darker still and so low that they looked like they would touch the trees on the peaks. The birds that hid themselves in the trees and branches during the hot season were performing acrobatics in the sky. The trees too seemed to have imbibed a jolt of fresh energy and were shining again in new green clothes.

The herd's delight was apparent. Not just the little ones, but even the adult sheep were cavorting in feverish anticipation of the rain. It started raining properly by the evening. Raindrops the size of tamarind seeds pattered down streambeds and tree branches and steadily drummed on the plastic raincoats of the gollas.

The shepherds moved the flocks on to the hard ground near the hill's edge. Then they hacked off the branches of some buttercup trees to build rudimentary cots for the night. The buttercup tree was chosen because its soft wood made it easier to chop it.

Two long branches were placed lengthwise and other smaller branches and bamboo shoots were placed across them to form a wooden frame, raised a little above the ground. Dry grass stalks were then used to cover the wooden frame, forming a rough bed of sorts. The gollas slept on these grassy mattresses with their plastic sheets covering them. Rainwater flowed under the wooden cots they had made, but the gollas were fully covered and managed to remain dry by staying off the ground.

The rain continued through the night. There was no respite from lightning and thunder either. The hills seemed to play music as the flowing rainwater converted the rocks and boulders into instruments, and the sky seemed to shower its blessings through lightning and applause through thunder.

The sheep stood on their legs the entire night. They shifted their weight, stretched their bodies, sneezed and bent their heads in submission to the rain.

When the sun came up from behind the clouds the following morning, it seemed to carry only light but no heat. A steady drizzle continued to fall without a pause. Though the shepherds had saved themselves from being drenched overnight, sleeping with their legs tucked in under the makeshift plastic tents left them with body aches.

However, they were in good spirits. The onset of monsoon acted as a balm, making them forget the aches in their bodies. The gollas took in the panoramic view of the hills and valleys, their hearts filled with happiness and gratitude for the rains. The hills that were covered with dry leaves and ash until then were now glowing after a thorough scrub.

Every hill around them was full of newly reborn watercourses. The streams and ravines came to life, with water flowing between the stones and pebbles like pythons. The brooks and rivulets reunited in the valleys, forming larger streams. Leaving the silence of the hot season behind them, the watercourses noisily rushed through the forests and sped towards the plains. The rainfall made the birds and animals quiet while giving voice to the hills and streams.

Though the shepherds were confident that the villages had also received rainfall, they could not confirm it despite being atop one of the tall peaks that overlooked the villages beyond the forest. The rain formed a dense curtain, reducing visibility beyond the surrounding hills.

For Ravi, the change in the forest after the rains was another novel experience. Till yesterday, the forest had seemed still and silent to him. It now seemed that it was showcasing its divine musical talent. The heat and thirst had been replaced by fragrant shadows and flowing water.

The rain continued throughout the day. When there was a brief respite from the downpour, the sheep were taken to graze. The shepherds ate rotis for breakfast and dinner as usual but went down to Jyothi ashram for their midday meal instead of cooking. The downpour became lighter at night.

By the following morning, the rains had subsided completely. The hills were gleaming under the bright sun. The gollas climbed the tallest peak around and looked in the direction of their village. They could see the lands beyond the hills and forest all the way to the Sagileru stream and noticed quadrangular and semicircular shapes shining like mirrors in the sunlight.

It did not take the gollas long to identify them as ponds and water tanks that had filled to the brim and were even overflowing at places. They could even recognise some of the water bodies. The realisation that their region had also received the same rains made the shepherds jump around in delight. They celebrated with ear-splitting whistles and primal cries of unbridled and childlike joy. Some even made funny noises by covering their mouths with their hands.

This torrential downpour had arrived after a gap of six years and had merged the brooks and streams with the ponds and tanks, connecting the elevated areas with the low-lying ones. The Sagileru stream was in full flow, appearing white in colour when seen from a height as it twisted through its course like a hill python.

The shepherds were bursting with excitement. The celebratory mood of the trees, sheep and the birds in the sky pulsed through the men as well. Their jungle sentence was coming to an end. They could leave the harrowing experiences of the hills behind and head back to their own lands.

After breakfast, the gollas drove the flocks down the eastern slopes of the hill into the valley below. They had a spring in their step. Some whistled a favourite tune, while others sang verses from puranic dramas. A few shepherds even began practising their repertoire of folk songs and devotional bhajans. Conversation and banter abounded.

Pullayya observed the behaviour of his fellow shepherds. Since Gurappa was not around to deliberate with on the matter, he called Pichchanna to his side.

'As the saying goes, "While the groom got miffed and waited outside the village, the tiger readied him for the ritual shower and took him away,"' said the old man. 'All of you are distracted by your thoughts about home and are assuming that we have left the forest and its associated troubles behind. But any negligence now would extract a great cost. It has rained non-stop for four days. The foxes would have been sheltering in the caves beneath the boulders. They would be ravenously hungry by now. The rains have stopped, so they will emerge and hunt for prey. Ask them to be extra vigilant these last two days of us being here.'

Pichchanna passed on the leader's warning to all the other shepherds. After lunch at the Jyothi ashram, they corralled the flocks and did not venture too far into the jungle. In the evening, they took the herds to the grasslands near the wellsprings. The hills sported a new look after being soaked for four days.

The water gullies were still bringing rainwater down from the hills. The streams flowed full and fast. The men and the sheep had been desperate for a little clean water all these days and were now enjoying the abundance of it even as their feet got stuck in the ankle-deep mud near the brooks and streams. The surrounding rocks shone bright after all the dirt had been washed away by the rainwater, while the bark of trees had turned dark after being soaked by the rain.

All around them was the incessant chirp of insects, and even the birds called to each other in delight. Scrubbed clean by the rain, with shiny tender green shoots, the tree trunks resembled a group of children standing fresh in their new clothes after the ritual bath on a festival day. The trees were surrounded by the slush of dry leaves whipped up by the wind and rain. The fallen wings of fireflies stuck to twigs on the ground, with birds creating a ruckus as they tried to pick them up.

As the flocks moved uphill, the shepherds noticed columns of wild ants leaving their crumbling anthills in search of a dry place to build a new home. Then they came across a herd of cows noisily hoofing their way down the hill. The cowherds' shouts could be heard in the distance.

The cows belonged to the Jyothi ashram. They had been donated by devotees to fulfil vows or as tokens of gratitude for the blessings of the saint. They crossed the trail and walked towards the northern foothills just as the cowherds came into view. They exchanged pleasantries with the shepherds and shared some of their stock of betel leaves and beedis.

*

That night, the gollas moved the flocks up the eastern slope of a tall hill to a rocky spot where there was no mud. The waning crescent meant that the moonlight was dim. The lights from the surrounding villages were visible through the gaps between the ranges. The sight made the shepherds long for home and their loved ones. They eventually lay down to rest at their usual spots beside the flocks.

The ground was moist, so the shepherds were forced to sleep on wide rocks. They had all been sleeping wherever they could for the past forty-five days and had become impatient for the comforts of home. Sometime during the night, a tiger's roar echoed in the valley below. The shepherds were jerked awake from their slumber. No one spoke, but most of them made a noise—coughing, clearing of throat, noisily turning around—to indicate that they were awake and alert.

The moon began its descent around three in the morning. As soon as dawn broke, the gollas walked down to the brook at the base of the hill. Fresh water flowed steadily. It was clear, without any rotten leaves floating in it nor any mosquitoes buzzing around. They completed their morning ablutions using the brook's water with no fear or hesitation.

Ravi thought that they had all gained courage from the knowledge that they were headed home soon. Yes, just one more range to cross, and they would be out of the forest. He walked a little distance from the brook to take a look at the tall hill they were camping on. It seemed like a border outpost of the dense jungle.

Exiting the hills felt like stepping out of a wondrous, marvellously evocative world. It was like leaving a world of silence and entering one full of sounds. From a lonely, fearful life back into the safety of community. He thought of the number of novel experiences the forest had given him. He would remember them for the rest of his life, the sensations remaining fresh in his heart. He couldn't wait to regale others with all the stories from his sojourn in the hills.

By the time they got the sheep up and moving, it was past ten in the morning. The sun was bright, though the weather remained cool and pleasant. The flocks had crossed the Spring hill, Creeper trail, Rocky knolls and Black hill the previous day. Now they were headed south, over the Big Stream hill and the Little Stream hill.

Even though the fresh green grass was abundant, the sheep were not grazing with any vigour. Their mouths touched the stalks without biting into the grass. The sheep soon began to move without stopping to graze at any spot. The shepherds understood that their taste buds had gone bland again. The sheep needed to lick some rock salt, which would arrive with the rations that were due the next day.

There was no need to go anywhere in search of water. It was available wherever one looked. Thin gullies ran through the tracts, their water the colour of the red soil underneath. The gollas dropped to their knees to sip the water just like their sheep did. Pullayya suggested that they take the flocks south to the Mallalamma hill and stop at the Varikuntla pond for the night. The others agreed with his suggestion, as the herds were moving at a good pace without meandering to graze.

Clusters of axlewood, sandra, amla and daadira trees dominated the area. From where he stood on a hill slope, Ravi noticed a small pond. It was more of a water pit than a pond, with red-coloured water gleaming under the sun. He realised that it was not natural but manmade, dug by a kind soul so that the forest animals and cattle could have a watering hole in the area. Ravi wanted to take a closer look at it and drove the flock towards the pool.

On the way, he heard some animals coming through the grove. Catching glimpses of white bodies moving through the trees, he first thought that they were cows. As they entered the open meadow, Ravi saw that they were oxen. Pichchanna recognised the man herding the oxen. 'Narayana!' he called. 'Why have you brought the oxen to the hills?'

'Who is that . . . oh, Pichchanna!' responded the man. 'Yes, the lands near the village haven't turned green yet. At first, I thought of tying them up in the shed and feeding them dry grass. But it is muddy everywhere. I had nothing to do for a few days, so I brought them on a trip to the hills.' Then his tone became anxious. 'Don't take the sheep up the rise beyond this pool,' he warned. 'Don't even venture that side. Cross this range through the knoll.'

'Why?'

'I saw a big one. A mature tiger. Seems it had waylaid a cow and eaten a hearty meal. I saw it standing on the hillock over there with its body covered in blood. The king did not bother with my oxen; he ignored my presence too. He did not move or even twitch when he saw us. Don't go that side.'

Narayana left the shepherds with his warning, taking his cattle through the meadow to the next range. Pichchanna changed the direction of his flock towards the knoll. He whistled and cautioned nearby shepherds to do the same. His information was passed on to the others within minutes.

However, Ravi felt like seeing the tiger. He wanted to know what a tiger that had just eaten a heavy meal would look like in its satiated, lazy arrogance. He asked another shepherd to mind his flock and moved towards the rise. Bhaskar, Ramachandra, Sreenu and Ankayya followed him.

'It has a full stomach, but it'll be looking for a place to hide the leftover carcass,' Pichchanna shouted at their retreating backs. 'Don't interfere in its work!'

As they walked through the grove, they came upon a cart trail that led to Nayanapalle village. They walked cautiously along the trail, heading west. They maintained a slow pace, peering into the bushes by the banks of the pool and behind tree trunks in the grove.

They finally spotted the tiger after turning around a bend in the trail. It was standing on an elevation under a daadira tree. Its three-metre-long body glistened in the sun as it stood silently, shaking its head every now and then. Ravi noticed that the tiger kept opening its mouth and then snapping it shut and chewing something.

Looking closer, Ravi saw the scores of hill flies buzzing around the tiger's face and body. The flies were crowding on the blood-splattered areas, not moving away even when the beast shook its head vigorously. The flies were so thick around its face that the tiger was unable to open its eyes properly.

The big predator was getting irritated by the pesky mob of flies, but it knew that unless it retired into a dark cave, it couldn't get rid of them. The infuriating hum of the flies made the tiger deaf to its surroundings. It did not notice the shepherds. Even if it had sensed them, it was not thinking of another kill, having already had its meal.

The young gollas turned around and slowly made their way back to the flocks. Ravi wondered about the hill flies. He had been walking through the rocky grasslands near the hills when some hill flies had begun milling around his head and face. This happened to many a traveller in those parts, and when it did, the flies would follow the person back to their village. Even running fast couldn't help in shaking them off.

The flocks and shepherds passed through the ranges and camped on the stony embankment of Varikuntla pond for the night. They were now out of the forest. As he lay down to sleep, Ravi's thoughts turned towards the tigers he has seen during his expedition, especially the one he and the dog had fought with and subdued.

Today, they had seen another big tiger, just as they were about to exit the forest. He imagined a king bidding farewell to the guests of his kingdom. Did the tiger come to bid them farewell? Maybe it had walked till the edge of the forest and stood on the last hillock for their benefit?

The notion touched him delicately somewhere deep in his heart.

22

The rations arrived early next morning. Four gollas in the hill-grazing group were replaced and the substitutes settled down with their flocks. Some of the rock salt included with the rations was spread on a dry stone for the sheep to lick. Then they all headed out to graze the sheep.

The Varikuntla pond was brimming with water. The streams that fed the pond were full too. Excess water flowed down the embankment stones. The shepherds saw groups of people walking along the levee to the place where the water overflowed. The women bore pots striped with lime and red soil. It seemed the entire village of Varikuntla was gathering at the pond to show their gratitude to Gangamma, the local goddess of fertility and prosperity, with an offering of sweet rice porridge.

The flocks turned south, towards the rocky pasture lands. It was acres of flat land interspersed with some bushes but no big trees. It was cultivated in the past. The first year, they would clear the land of the wild bushes and small thorn trees and then plough it. In the second year, they would sow horse gram, followed by kodo, foxtail and little millets in the third year.

After three or four years, the land would be left to regain its fertility. The farmers would scout for a similar piece of flat land elsewhere. This practice of shifting agriculture led to higher crop yield as the lands would always be fertile. Even if rabbits, deer, antelope and sambar feasted on the millet crop, other crops could give a high yield.

The recent rains had helped the grass seeds germinate again, making the place look like a green carpet. Ravi saw some scattered plants shining greener than the rest. They were as long as onion shoots, taller than the other grasses in the area. Their stalks were thick and the leaves bent backwards. The sheep ate those leaves.

Ravi looked at the plants with suspicion. Pointing at them, he asked Bhaskar, 'Aren't those bindweed leaves? Wouldn't the sheep fall sick after eating them?'

While Bhaskar was examining them, Pamuleti passed by with his flock. 'Those are kuchche leaves. They look exactly like bindweed but are harmless. It too has tubers in the ground.'

Pullayya addressed them all during the lunch break.

'We spent six ration periods in the forest and lost only six sheep,' said the lead shepherd. 'Now that we have crossed the forest, there is no longer any danger from the foxes. But the recent rains may have caused bindweed plants to sprout throughout the meadows. Having eaten the kuchche grass in the hills, many sheep might graze on bindweed leaves because they look similar. It'll make them sick. These plants look harmless but are as dangerous as the big fox . . . in fact, we can't scare them with our shouts nor chase them away with slings and stones. We can't even detect that a sheep has eaten the leaves till it crashes to the ground with dilated pupils. We need to keep a close eye on them. The skills of a shepherd will be tested in these situations. Returning safely from hill-grazing alone does not make one a hero. Only the one who brings his flock back without losses can be considered a true winner. The pearl millet stalk stands tall and proud only to be targeted by birds. However, the foxtail stalk bends a little and escapes the birds. Don't strut around proudly looking at the sky as if you have all participated in a heroic battle by crossing the jungle. Stay humble and keep your eyes on the ground.'

The shepherds discussed how to prevent the sheep from eating bindweed. Someone said that when the bindweed plants grow bigger, the sheep notice the coarse texture and bitter taste of the leaves and avoid eating them. Therefore, it was better to spend the next four days in their present location and wait for the bindweed to grow. They decided to remain in the lower parts of the hills for a few more days.

*

Around nightfall, the shepherds settled the sheep down near the embankment. Pullayya noticed that Ramanayya, Jayaramulu and two other young men were discussing something in low voices and good spirits. The old man observed their behaviour. Since Gurappa was not around to look into the matter, he hailed Pichchanna.

'What are they smirking about?' he asked when Pichchanna came over.

'See, if they climb this heap of rocks, they can see our village,' explained Pichchanna. 'The barns, the houses, the neem trees outside the houses . . .'

'So what?'

'They say that their bodies feel dirty and the rain has added to the itchiness and stink. Unless they go home and have a hot water bath, they won't be able to bear it, apparently.'

'There are twigs around, and we have vessels,' countered the old man. 'Let them boil some water and do their clean-up here.'

'Who will scrub their backs?' Pichchanna asked, trying hard to suppress his smile.

'They can scrub each other's backs!'

'They say that it is not proper for a man to brush and scrub another man's back. Only bangled hands should do that . . . it seems.'

Those listening to this exchange burst into laughter. Even Pullayya could not hold back his smile.

'Hot water, my foot!' Pamuleti interjected. 'They want to douse the heat in their bodies, that is all. Let them be, the poor fools.' Having it spelt out made the listeners laugh again.

Pullayya did not object to the request as there was no danger from tigers now. Four young men hurried home that night.

Three of them rejoined the camp before dawn, but Jayaramulu did not show up. Before setting off for the camp, they had knocked on his door, the other three said, but he hadn't been home.

'Where did he go?' asked Pichchanna.

'His wife went to her parents' village two days ago, we were told.'

'So he went to his in-laws' village at that time of the night to get his back scrubbed clean?' Pichchanna's words drew laughter from everyone around, including Pullayya.

Jayaramulu arrived just as they were about to move the herds out for the day. His eyes were bleary and red, which told them that he could not get much sleep the previous night, what with having to walk to his wife's village and back. Pullayya looked at the young shepherd's eyes and his sleepy face. It brought back some memory in his mind, making him laugh.

Jayaramulu's struggles through the rest of the day caused a lot of mirth. The moment he found a tree to lean on, he'd close his eyes and take a nap. At other times, he would sit on a stone slab, put his head down on his knees and drift off. He even dozed while standing, keeping the wooden staff under his chin for support. In the afternoon, he placed the vessel of rice to cook on the fire and then seconds later he was snoring on the ground.

After lunch, Ravi sat next to Ankayya and said, 'You could have gone home too last night, anna.'

'Why would I go?' asked Ankayya.

'Well, for the same reason all these guys went home . . .'

'I don't like it, brother!' interjected Ankayya, confusing Ravi.

When there was no opportunity to go home, Ankayya was desperate to see his wife and child. But now that there was an easy chance to visit them, he said that he didn't want to. Ravi found it baffling until Ankayya explained.

'Arriving suddenly late at night, waking her up and asking her to get out of bed to boil water for a hot bath and then cook a meal . . . is that reasonable?' said Ankayya. 'And then, after eating, putting out the lamp to quench the body's heat quickly and secretively . . . but leaving almost immediately after that to return before dawn . . . that is not how I like to do things, brother. If there is someone to take care of my flock during the day, I don't mind visiting the village to spend a little time with my wife and kid.'

That night, a few more shepherds paid a quick visit to the village.

'Orey Ramudu!' called Pullayya to Ramayya. 'You too can go home if you wish. Just come back in the morning.'

'Who, me?' Ramayya looked at the old man in surprise. 'Who will even care if I go home?'

'Didn't you say that they pampered you when you went home for the wedding?'

'Yes, till the ceremony was complete, my wife did give me attention. If I go home now, I doubt whether she would even open the door. I would end up spending the whole night pacing around the street like a dog. My wife is now only interested in taking care of our daughter and son-in-law.'

Pullayya laughed. 'You speak the truth!' he said. 'As the saying goes, "Whether you hit someone with a stone or with your hands, the mark should remain." Your wife is an expert markswoman!'

*

Before the shepherds had finished breakfast the next morning, four men arrived at the camp on two motorcycles. They parked their vehicles near the levee and walked from there to avoid the thorn trees. The shepherds recognised Pamuleti's son-in-law, Naga Sekhar, once they came closer. Two of the other men were introduced as buyers, and the fourth man was a broker.

Pamuleti knitted his brows as soon as he saw them. He did not open his mouth while the others exchanged pleasantries with his son-in-law, not even to ask about the well-being of his daughter.

'Where is our flock?' Naga Sekhar asked Sreenu, who pointed it out to him.

The four men went to the flock and counted the various animals—the lone buck, the rams, the adult sheep and the lambs. Then the broker came and sat in front of Pullayya. The two buyers lit cigarettes. Pushing their dhotis between their legs, they arranged stones under their ankles and squatted on them. Naga Sekhar remained standing.

'There are twenty-four pairs of animals,' began the broker. 'Two rams and one buck. Ten of the sheep have offsprings.' He turned towards Naga Sekhar and asked, 'Will you mention the price, or will it be your father-in-law?'

Naga Sekhar replied after a moment's silence. 'Let him set the price.'

'Okay, good,' said the broker. He then turned to Pamuleti. 'Tell me the price, anna. Give one rate for the sheep with lambs. Let the rams and buck have their own price, and you can state another price for the rest of the sheep. Give me separate prices for all three groups . . . or, if you wish, state an overall price for the whole flock.'

Pamuleti stood with his eyes closed and did not say a word in response.

The broker looked at him for a moment. 'What do you say, anna? State your price!'

Pamuleti remained silent.

'You can't stand there like a dumb ox!' interjected Pullayya. 'How will the deal get finalised unless you state a price? Or will you remain mute like a numbered pillar? Is there any difference between you and a tent pole?'

Pamuleti opened his eyes and looked at Pullayya.

'Have I ever sold the entire flock in one go?' he finally said. 'Once in a while, I may have sold a ram or two to meet some immediate need. That's all.'

Pullayya understood his anguish. He turned towards Naga Sekhar.

'We have been hill-grazing for a month and a half,' said the old shepherd. 'Pamuleti managed to get through it without losing even a single sheep. Were you worried that a big tiger would come by and bite their necks in the last two days, after we had left the forest? You brought the buyers here into the hills. Couldn't you have waited for two more days?'

'The flock has to be sold anyway,' replied Naga Sekhar. 'Selling it now would save him two days of hard work, right?'

The son-in-law was talking about two days of work, but for Pamuleti it meant getting to be with his flock for two more days. Pullayya understood the situation, and his heart became heavy with emotion. Pamuleti walked away and went over to his flock.

After a bit of discussion, Naga Sekhar stated a price. The broker began negotiating with him.

'Orey Pamuleti!' Pullayya shouted. 'Come over here! How can you not be around when the deal is being discussed?'

His call elicited no response from Pamuleti.

'The deal is getting finalised!' Pullayya shouted again.

'Let him close the deal and sell them off,' Pamuleti shouted back, not leaving the flock's side. 'Will they keep quiet while I owe the dowry money? If I object, they will push me away and sell the flock anyway. Let him sell it and consider my debt cleared.'

He suddenly walked briskly over to the others and announced: 'There are four sheep that birthed this flock. All the other sheep are their offspring. I want those four sheep and their lambs. He can sell the rest!' Pamuleti went back to his flock.

Pullayya knew that if Pamuleti's entire flock was taken away, he would not be able to to buy even a single sheep. And he couldn't live without sheep. He didn't know any work other than shepherding. That is why he wanted the four sheep to remain with him. He could hope to revive the flock with their help, and, by working his backside off, he could hope to become a golla again.

One of the buyers understood the situation. 'What use is the flock without the mother sheep?' he said.

Naga Sekhar did his calculations and determined that unless the entire flock was sold, he would not collect his full dowry money. He became infuriated with his father-in-law's grumbling and stalling.

'Don't bother about him,' he said harshly. 'Discuss the deal for the entire flock. If he wants, he can get some sheep on lease.'

As the deal was being closed, Pamuleti was overcome by helplessness and frustration. He could not restrain himself for long.

'Sell them off and take them with you!' he hissed. He set off in the direction of the village with his ration bag slung over his shoulder. They shouted for him to stop and come back, but he did not listen.

The shepherds looked on at the strange situation while Naga Sekhar grumbled about his father-in-law not clearing the dowry debt even after so many years. The deal was finalised. The buyers said that they would take the flock away two days later.

Pullayya objected as there was no one there to take care of the flock until then. He was firm that without the owner being around, they couldn't take responsibility for the sheep. If they fell sick or were taken by a predator, who would bear the liability?

Naga Sekhar was in a quandary. He thought about it for a few minutes and then followed the buyers and the broker as they headed back to their motorcycles.

'How can you leave the flock, son?' Pullayya shouted at him.

'My father-in-law will come!' Naga Sekhar shouted back.

Pamuleti did indeed return after an hour. He was weeping. Pullayya asked him what had happened.

'He threatened to send my daughter to look after the sheep,' Pamuleti replied, wiping his tears. 'It was either me or my daughter . . .'

Pamuleti believed that his son-in-law was capable of carrying out his threat and sending his wife to herd sheep. The others felt sorry for Pamuleti, who kept wiping tears from his face throughout the rest of the day.

While walking behind the sheep, he would suddenly break into sobs and share his anguish with the trees, bushes, birds and animals, wailing loudly that he wouldn't know how to live without the sheep after they were taken away. He held each sheep and poured out his pain in words and tears. Pamuleti's anguish touched the hearts of all the other gollas.

*

That night, some of the gollas went to their homes in the village again. Jayaramulu was among them. However, he went in the direction of his in-laws' village, assuming his wife was still there. In the morning though, Jayaramulu came back with the other shepherds. If he'd gone to his in-laws' village, he should have returned alone. This was noted with surprise by the ones tending the sheep at the camp.

Seetharamulu revealed what had happened. Apparently, Jayaramulu's wife had expected her husband to visit again and had gone back to their home to reduce the time and effort it would take him to come see her. So, Jayaramulu ended up spending most of the night walking from the camp to his in-laws' village, and from there to his own village. Then, after a brief stay, he had to quickly join the others on the return journey to the camp.

Hearing Jayaramulu's travails caused the others to break into guffaws. The banter and jokes that followed helped them in passing the day in merriment.

23

THE SHEPHERDS AND THEIR sheep finally set out on the trail back to their village. Once they had passed Varikuntla and Nayanapalle, they saw hectic activity in the red soil fields. They were full of people, with entire families, including children, engaged in farming activities. Some were tilling the land with tractors or oxen, others were removing the stubble and another group of people were burning it.

Ravi wondered about the change wrought by one good rainfall. The rains had transformed the parched, barren soil into wet, sticky mud resembling cooked millet. Dry, dusty trees now looked fresh and green, with birds busy hunting insects that emerged from the soil. One decent downpour had led to so much change, bringing a close to water disputes in the villages and quenching the thirst of the animals. The rain had germinated hope in the hearts of men, filled the minds of farmers with dreams about crops, yields, grains and money. Just one rainstorm and so much change!

In the ploughed lands, the soil felt soft underfoot. Ravi removed his footwear and walked barefoot through some of these farms, enjoying the ticklish feeling on the soles of his feet. He felt one could lie down on the soft red soil and sleep comfortably. There were no stones in it. After sleeping on hard rocks for the last few weeks, this ground seemed like a cotton mattress in comparison.

They saw an old man gamely trying to hack down a tough thorn tree with his axe. He wore an elaborate turban on his head, the tail cloth of which hung around his shoulder. The broken straps of his slippers were held together by pieces of string. His spectacles too were broken and hooked around his ears with a piece of cloth. His axe was small, and he did not have energy to take more than two swings at a time.

Panting from exertion, the old man stopped his work when he saw the herd approach. As a sheep passed him, he caressed its back. He then hailed Bhaskar, who was standing under a berry tree a little distance away. Ravi joined Bhaskar as he went up to the old man.

'What's up, thatha?' asked Bhaskar.

'Have you all returned, my son?' said the old man affectionately. 'The rains have arrived, my boy! It had been such a long time . . . all it needed was for God to open his eyes. Such a heavy downpour . . . I wanted to see it with my own eyes, but most of it fell at night. The next day was one long drizzle, and it was the downpour again at night. I couldn't see it, but I heard its thunder and clamour. The rain God did not come down from the sky for those of us who play board games during the day and snuggle in our beds at night. The rains have come for you, because of you shepherds. You took a stubborn vow that you wouldn't return to the village until it rained. Your hard penance in the jungle melted the clouds and delivered the rain. You brought us all this rain!'

The old man became emotional. His evocative and effusive words warmed Ravi's heart. He felt a shiver of excitement, and his eyes became moist. The old man's words felt like a balm for the fifty days of hard labour and the dangers that they had faced in the hills.

The effects of the emotion persisted within him until dusk, when they finally reached their village. All the villagers were waiting to welcome the group returning from the hill-grazing expedition. The old and young, women and children—all stood by to shower affection and care on the herdsmen and their animals.

The sheep were feted as brave survivors and led to their pens, which had been prepared with barbed-wire fences near the village barns. The men were relieved of their ration bags, staffs, axes and blankets by their family members. Each shepherd's luggage was carried by someone from their family as they were escorted home. A celebratory mood spread through the village that evening.

However, Guramma was heard grumbling. 'Used to look like a turmeric bar, he's now the colour of regur soil,' she mumbled in a low voice, wiping the tears from her eyes as she placed a big bucket of hot water in the bathroom. 'Used to resemble a fresh betel leaf, now looks like a hardened thorny okra.'

Ravi had a bath with that hot water, getting rid of fifty days of accumulated dirt. After changing into clean clothes, he began to feel the sweet intoxication of sleep come over him. However, he knew that he had to eat something first. It was a tradition in golla families to serve horse gram lentils and soup as the first meal after a family member returned from hill-grazing. Those foods were believed to remove the various infections or ailments people might carry back home after a stay in the forest.

Guramma added jaggery to boiled horse gram lentils, mashed the mixture into a pulp, added ghee to the pulp and then shaped it into laddus. She made Ravi eat a palm-sized laddu and then served him ulava charu, or horse gram lentil soup, with piping hot rice.

Once he was done eating the ulava charu, Ravi felt that he would fall asleep right there. He hit the cot and immediately fell into a deep sleep. He was asleep even after nine the following morning. Guramma became concerned when her son did not have his breakfast. Praveena brushed his nose and cheeks with a hen's feather to tickle him into wakefulness.

Ravi opened his eyes, but they still felt quite heavy. The inebriety of sleep had not left his head yet. Ravi wanted to sleep till the exhaustion of the hill-grazing expedition left his muscles; his body screamed for more recovery time. But his mother's grumbling made him get up and have a meal. He went back to sleep right after. He slept through the day and the following night, only getting up once for another light meal. He slept for so long that he lost all sense of time.

Having heard about Ravi's epic fight with the tiger, many villagers came by to meet him while he slept. Though they said that they just wanted to take a look at him, and wouldn't disturb his sleep, Guramma did not allow most of them in. Those given permission to enter were allowed to go up to Ravi's bed, but Guramma refused to let any of them wake up her son.

The kapu lady Subbamma had given Guramma some yellow lentils as part of a barter before the hill-grazing group headed out, requesting a wooden ladle in return. She had now come over to collect the item. When Guramma went into the backyard to get the teak ladle, Subbamma approached Ravi's cot and closely gazed at every inch of his body.

When Guramma returned, Subbamma commented, 'They say he fought with a tiger. But I don't see even a scratch on his body.'

Guramma did not reply. She had thought the same thing after she had examined Ravi's body and found no signs of an injury. Her concern did not diminish though. Maybe the wounds had healed, she thought, her mother's heart wincing in pain.

*

The next morning, Ravi was awoken from his long slumber by the sound of his grandfather's booming voice. The voices of old men talking loudly on the stone bench outside the house reached Ravi's ears. He slowly walked outside to see what was happening. His grandfather was throwing a challenge at someone. When he saw his grandson, he proclaimed, 'See there, he has come, our tiger!'

The folks on the stone bench gaped at Ravi. People on the street started gathering around him, shouting out questions about the fight and enquiries about his well-being.

'Heard you got into a wrestling bout with it! Didn't you get scared of its power?'

'Did the fangs cause any injury?'

'It would have tried to tear you apart with its claws! How did you counter it?'

'You are a real man, son! Never heard of such courage!'

The crowd was getting bigger by the minute. They were all looking at him in a new way. The women covered their cheeks with their palms to express their wonder and disbelief. It was the same old Ravi they used to see every day. But now, he appeared like a new man, almost a stranger. It was in the nature of rural life that whether it was a happy occasion or a sad one, the villagers needed to see it with their own eyes to be satisfied. That is why even people who knew Ravi well wanted to come and take another look at him.

Ravi thought it was perhaps similar to how the girl people saw every day became a temporary celebrity when she stepped out in her bridal finery. Or how the ox that just stood around the farm became the cynosure of all eyes on the day it left the homestead after being sold. However, he could not deal with the reactions from the villagers. He felt embarrassed at the attention.

As soon as he could, he escaped the crowd and went back inside the house. Climbing back into his bed, he covered himself with a blanket. Guramma turned away any other people who arrived eager to have a look at Ravi and maybe have a word with him. But Ravi could not sleep. The reception from the public gave him goosebumps.

A smile played on his lips when he thought about the tiger, the reason for all this excitement. He remembered the tiger, beaten close to death, walking away with its backside hunched. He wondered if it had survived. Perhaps it was struggling between life and death in the dark corner of some cave. Or did it die?

All those who heard about the incident sounded confident that the tiger would have died of the injuries to its head and testicles. 'Walking away from its prey with its head down can mean only one thing—the tiger saw death coming for it,' theorised the shepherds. 'A man would run away due to cowardice or fear of death. A tiger is different. Death is its only defeat.'

When the villagers heard the story, not a single person said the tiger might have survived. If a single person had said that the beast had a chance of recovering from its injuries, Ravi would have drawn some hope from the statement. It would have given him some relief from the guilt he was feeling.

People were seeing the death of the tiger as a symbol of Ravi's heroism. Their praise and adulation frightened him. He thought that if he didn't get a job offer soon, there was no way to predict how the sentiment of the people would turn. However, he felt an unfamiliar courage when he thought about his hunt for a job. The feeling washed over him in waves as he sensed a mature understanding of his own self taking root and growing in his heart.

As he thought about the fears he had faced till then, Ravi found himself surprised at the change within. He felt ashamed of the cowardice of his past self and felt a little frustrated as well. It was not a lack of knowledge or skills that was preventing him from getting a job. The main reason that he had not got a job offer yet was quite simply his timidity. He could see it clearly now. And he wanted to wreak vengeance on his fearfulness the next time.

There was another jungle awaiting his arrival. He'd lived a terrified life in that forest, like a deer counting each day it survived the predators. Ravi knew that he now needed to re-enter that forest in his new avatar. He wanted to go back to the city. He drifted off to sleep thinking about that desire.

*

Sankar arrived home that evening. He had decided on the location for the business he was setting up with his brothers-in-law and told them that he needed to move to Bangalore soon. That meant that Gurappa would have no company for his shepherding. Guramma suggested selling off half the flock, but Sankar felt that the entire flock should be sold.

'Till the younger boy gets a job and the girls are married, how can we not rear sheep?' countered Gurappa.

'I will take care of those expenses,' replied Sankar.

'I still have strength in my body, son!' said Gurappa firmly. 'Let me handle this guy's education and their weddings. If I can't bear the load, you can step in to help.' He walked away, allowing no further discussion.

Ravi informed them at dinner that he was leaving for Hyderabad the next day.

'What's the hurry, sinnoda?' said his mother. 'Can't you stay for two more days?'

'Why, ma?'

'At least let the sleep-talking stop, child! You are still herding sheep and screaming at foxes in your sleep. Thank God you are at home. If you did that in the city, wouldn't your friends laugh at you?'

Ravi's sisters laughed.

'Am I talking in my sleep?' Ravi asked awkwardly. 'In the city, once I am back at my studies, I wouldn't be thinking of all these things, ma!' he added after regaining his composure.

When he stepped out after dinner, the stone benches in front of the houses were full of people chatting about all things under the sun. Ravi's grandfather was there too. Within a few minutes, the old man turned the conversation towards his grandson's heroic fight with the tiger.

Ravi overheard another old-timer talking to his grandfather. He was a farmer by the name of Rami Reddy. He was speaking slowly in a quaint fashion and taking time to make his point.

'Keep the fight with the tiger aside,' Rami Reddy was saying. 'An educated young man who had never roamed much in the sun, who is not used to walking amid thorny bushes, trees, rocks and boulders, who couldn't stand going a single day without a bath . . . I can't believe that he managed to stay hill-grazing for six ration periods. What did he like so much in the hills? Who or what entrapped or ensnared him? Was it the sheep? The hills themselves? That he refused a replacement says something—he liked it there. I wonder what this boy liked so much in the forest.'

When Rami Reddy saw Ravi standing there, he got off the bench and came straight to him.

'Tell me, son, what hooked you?' the old farmer asked, looking straight into Ravi's eyes.

Ravi did not know what to tell him. He thought about the question while the old man kept staring at his face. After a few moments, Ravi said, 'The drought had been around for six years. Seeds sown in the soil would germinate and then die due to the heat and the lack of water. Still, you continued to plough and sowed a crop every season. Tell me, what hooked you, thatha?'

The old man laughed at his response. He turned around and went back to his spot on the bench.

Ravi had managed to avoid giving the old man a direct answer, but he could not get the question out of his mind. It haunted him when he went to bed that night. Who or what had ensnared him? The days spent hill-grazing flashed through his mind as he searched for an answer.

Ravi had gone to the forest under unavoidable circumstances, but within a few days, he had grown used to the life there. Soon, he even became fond of it. He then started to feel a desire to take care of the sheep and protect the flock. Without being aware of it, he had fallen in love with the sheep. It probably began with the little white lamb. The love he felt for them made him forget his home, studies, friends . . . he did not think about any of those things. The sheep occupied his mind completely. His thoughts were only about what he had to do to find them food and water and ensure their safety.

Yes . . . it was the sheep that had entrapped him. They were the reason that he lost his fear. It was for their sake that he became committed to his shepherding duty. The sheep made him relish the hard physical labour. There was no doubt in his mind, now that he had given it some thought—it was the sheep that had ensnared him.

Ravi felt like going to Rami Reddy's home right then to give him his answer. Even as he thought about it, his eyelids grew heavy with sleep. Various scenes flitted in front of his eyes. Sleep was trying to conquer him by throwing nets of memories and dreams, all mixed up.

Suddenly, he remembered what his mother had told him about his sleep-talking. Ravi opened his eyes. He tried to remember the scenes that had played in his mind till then. He could recall some of them, the recent dreams from a few moments ago when he was just falling asleep.

All the scenes were related to his days in the hills and the forests and the lessons he had learned from the sheep, the trees, the grass and the watercourses. Lessons from nature. Lessons from the tiger.

Walking behind the sheep, driving them through the hills and valleys, facing off against wild animals . . . he experienced the same images and sensations. He realised why he was talking in his sleep and what he was talking about.

The moment he closed his eyes, he was transported back into the hills.

The forest hadn't left him just yet. And he didn't want to let go of the forest either.

24

RAVI AWOKE WITH A start.

Unsure of the time, he sat up, rubbing his eyes. He could hear some dogs barking.

He was on his cot on the veranda of his home—not beside the flock on the Velpudari hill. The dogs were barking in the street, not the hills.

In Ravi's dream, a tiger had roared in the valley north of the Velpudari hill, and his father's dog had responded with its vicious bark.

He lay down again and closed his eyes but was unable to sleep. The room felt hot and stuffy. He had not felt any discomfort during the first two days after returning from the hills. Though there was no discernible difference in the weather, he was beginning to feel the heat. He understood that the change was within him. His body seemed to have had enough rest, and he was beginning to notice the difference between the weather in the hills and the village.

Ravi got up and went out of the house to lie down on the stone bench. It felt a little cooler. Eyes closed, he stretched, twisted and turned but could not go back to sleep. He began to wonder if he would sleep better if he lay down near the sheep. The smell, the sneezes and the stomping might lull him into sleep. His thoughts turned towards the flock.

He had brought the sheep back from the hills and left them near the pen. But for the past two days, he had not bothered about the sheep, his father's dog, the little white lamb or the infant lambs in the pen. Nor had he enquired about who was taking the sheep out to graze or who was attending to their needs in the pen. He had not thought about any of this.

With Sankar not around, who was doing all this work? Was it his father, who was still recovering from a serious illness? Ravi sat up. He had behaved as if his work was done once the flock was home from the hills. Like an employee who leaves behind all thoughts of work once he leaves the office.

Their flock's size required two full-time shepherds. It was not an office job where one could finish a given project and then wash one's hands of it. A shepherd's job was to handle lives. The person doing it became responsible for taking care of the hunger and thirst of living beings. Unlike files stored in an office cabinet, the sheep couldn't remain in the pens without feed and water.

Ravi felt ashamed. A true shepherd was one who would sleep beside the flock, even if they had just returned from the hills. He stepped off the stone bench, put on his slippers and walked to the sheep shed near the barns. The dog greeted him halfway to the shed. Unlike Ravi, it had been doing its duty by staying awake through the night and guarding the flock.

Ravi found his father asleep on the cot outside the shed, covered in a thick blanket. Gurappa did not get up when Ravi went closer. He did not stir or lift his blanket even when Ravi walked around with heavy steps. Ravi understood that his father had still not fully recovered from his illness. Had he been fine, he would have surely sat up if he heard footfall.

Ravi decided not to make any more noise lest he woke up. Seeing his father, he had understood the meaning of commitment to work, including where he needed to improve his own approach. He went back home and got some sleep.

*

In the morning, he learned from his mother that Sasi had been accompanying Gurappa to help the flock graze. And his mother was taking care of the feed and water for the lambs in the mornings and evenings. Ravi told Sankar to find some excuse and get his father to sell off at least half the flock.

He went to Porumamilla at eight in the evening and boarded the bus to Hyderabad. As he reclined in the seat and closed his eyes, his mind travelled back to the hills. Till Giddalur, the road went through the wide valley between two hill ranges. When he got off the bus at Giddalur to stretch his legs, Ravi looked up at the sky. To the west, the panchami moon was rolling slowly down to the Nallamala hills. It looked like a flat piece of broken limestone, off-white in colour. The milky light on the hills looked pleasant.

Ravi got back on the bus and closed his eyes when it resumed its journey. The windows were open just a crack. Cool breeze blew in, lulling him to sleep. But each time he drifted off to sleep, the bus's jerks and jolts on the bumpy ride kept waking him up. He had a troubled sleep, even though the other passengers all seemed to sleep soundly.

The bus was travelling fairly fast when Ravi woke up suddenly. The breeze from the window had brought a different, yet familiar, smell to his nostrils. He recognised it immediately. It was the hill breeze, one that he had breathed in and got used to over the course of one and a half months. The breeze that caressed the leaf buds of axlewood, sandra, red sanders, yepe, bamboo and other such trees and aromatic plants as it flew across the hills.

It filled him with excitement, making him fully awake. He sat up. The bus was travelling on the curvy ghat section through the Nallamala hills. That area was known as the Stream of the Flame-of-Forest. It was about thirty to forty kilometres from where they had done their hill-grazing. The crescent moon floated above the peaks on the western sky, adding a supernatural beauty to the forest. Sleeping with their green blankets on, the hills looked innocent and delicate.

Ravi thought about how he had been fearful of the movements of wild animals by the streams and rivulets, under the trees, behind the bushes, at the water sources and where the trails met. He had then learned about the tame and meek animals that lived in constant fear of predators, and how, driven by the urge to live and thrive, they would head into the territory of a fierce tiger to drink some water or forage for some food. Ravi had also witnessed the motherly nature of the forest, which gave succour and shelter to innumerable varieties of plants and animals.

While travelling in a bus through this area, one could observe how the hills closer to the human habitats had been denuded of their greenery and had started to resemble a heap of rocks. Some of the hills had been turned into the gravel that covered the roads leading into the hinterland of human settlements. Yet, Ravi thought, the five or six districts surrounding Nallamala were able to survive only because of these hills.

If one could revive the bald hills that had lost their green cover, the surrounding farms and villages would be rejuvenated too and become prosperous. If the government was unable to conserve the hills, it could at least encourage voluntary organisations that are passionate about saving these hills.

The people and organisations that succeed in regenerating the ecosystem of a hill deserve accolades. Awards like the Padma Bhushan and Padma Shri—so often handed to actors, sportspeople, musicians and artists—should also be given to those who contribute to saving the environment, thought Ravi.

The bus crossed the Nallamala hills and Ravi eventually drifted off to sleep by the time it reached Nandyala. It pulled into Hyderabad at around six in the morning. He got off the bus and went to the flat that he shared with his friends.

25

After his sojourn in the forest, Ravi needed time to readjust to the rhythms of the city. It took him four days to go back to the coaching centre. There, his new self-confidence was soon evident. There was no more fear, reticence or dithering. One of the tutors patted him on the back and declared, 'This time you will nail any interview. You will land a job with a good salary package.'

Even Ravi's flatmates noticed the change in him and were surprised. Three months ago, he had gone home full of despair about his failures and anxious about his future. But he had returned looking so assured and confident. It was a bit confusing for them. What soft skills could he have acquired in his village? Which spoken English course was available in that hamlet? Compared to the city, the village lagged behind by a generation. In such a village, who could have crafted this change in Ravi?

They peppered Ravi with the same questions.

'I just learned my family profession,' replied Ravi.

'What is the link between shepherding and software programming?' they asked with a tinge of sarcasm.

'I understood how to work with passion and commitment,' explained Ravi. 'From my experiences, I learned what it meant to be immersed in work and take ownership of it. I am no longer afraid of those who question me about how I work.'

'But no one will ask you about herding sheep.'

'Work is work. When I saw work as something other than my essential nature, I was scared of the work. Once I became one with work, I lost my fears.'

His friends could not understand his words. And yet, they could not disregard the changes they saw in him. In any case, they thought, something had happened, and they could see the difference in Ravi.

Ravi had worked hard for the past four years to get a job in the software sector. He had struggled both physically and mentally. Now that he was confident about his success, he started visualising the life of a software professional. He tried to imagine his life: he would sit in front of a computer, always in an air-conditioned room and try to solve problems with his intellect. He concluded that his life would remain restricted indoors and computers would gradually dominate every aspect of his being.

Gradually, he stopped attending the coaching classes. Instead, he began watching movies and reading novels and short fiction. He stopped bothering with books related to cracking job interviews. Ravi's flatmates could not comprehend his behaviour. Was it a display of self-confidence? Or something else? When he was so close to achieving his goal of getting a job, why this change in attitude?

'Your conduct is not right,' they advised him once. 'You are going in the wrong direction.'

Ravi smiled and replied, 'I am finding my path.'

'What do you mean?'

'I have decided that software engineering does not suit me.'

His friends looked at him in surprise.

'I can't cohabit with lifeless computers, imprisoned within four walls throughout my life,' he explained.

They could not understand him.

'I need people,' Ravi continued. 'I need trees and plants, I need animals. I need a world full of life. And I want to work in that world. I cannot work among non-living things.'

His words stunned them. They looked at him as if he was a lunatic.

'Have you gone mad?' asked one of his friends. 'Software is what you have studied all these years. This is the field you have strived so hard to get into. And now you want to shift to a different field and struggle again for four or five years without a job? Will you keep doing rounds of coaching centres throughout your life?

'I don't like this field, that's all!' countered Ravi. 'There are lakhs of people available to work as software engineers. But there is another field that needs more people—people like me.'

'Oh, a job just happens to be waiting for you, is it?' said another friend, sounding frustrated by Ravi's words.

'Yes!'

'And what would that be?'

'District forest official.'

They gave him a puzzled look.

'A job in the forest department would have close links to my family's profession,' elaborated Ravi. 'I have the experience for it, and the job needs people like me. It would give me a sense of fulfilment.'

Though he spoke with conviction, his friends just shook their heads in confusion and gave up on him.

*

Ravi soon moved out of that apartment. He changed his coaching centre and the books he read. He reviewed his decision and progress many times, and each time he concluded that he was moving in the right direction.

It was the forest that had changed him profoundly and filled him with confidence. The forest had taken him into its lap like a mother. He'd stepped into the forest steeped in cowardice and fear, worried about his future and unable to trust his own abilities. The forest had welcomed him and held him close. By doing so, it had infused in him self-belief as durable as the trunk of a sandra tree.

The forest had nurtured in him the strength to face challenges and unlocked courage in him to confront even a life-threatening situation with equanimity. The forest had transformed him into a complete human being and only then sent him back to human society.

Yes, it was the courage instilled in him by the forest that had shaped his decision to quit looking for a software job. He was no longer scared of written and oral examinations. He felt as if he was a few rungs above such tests. The forest department was his priority now. His aim was to become a district-level forest official.

'The forests I stepped into as a golla, I want to enter those forests again as an official with the power to protect them from extinction,' Ravi said to himself. 'I would like to stand in solidarity with, and offer my support to, the trees, the animals, the hills and the streams.' Ravi wrote it down as his vision. He began working hard to reach his goal. He set down the level of hard work required to herd sheep during a hill-grazing expedition as his benchmark and strove to work harder than that.

It took him two years to realise the dream. He sailed through both the competitive written exam and the final interview. In comparison to the anxiety, terror and emotional turmoil he'd faced in his fight with the tiger, the exams were child's play. Compared to the job of a hill-grazing shepherd, the hard work required to prepare for those exams was an easy task.

Ravi was successful in achieving his target of direct recruitment to the post of District Forest Officer (DFO).

Right from the training period, he could see his next goal in front of his eyes. He had read the statistics on the loss of forest wealth in different parts of the country due to unchecked smuggling activity. The illegal felling of trees continued unabated. His blood had boiled at learning about the wanton destruction of hills and forests. The knowledge had made him firm up his resolve—he was going to end the pestilence afflicting the forest.

When he first entered the forest as an official, he experienced the comfort of returning to a mother's lap. He saw himself as the younger son of the forest that sheltered him with motherly love.

*

The villagers knew a great deal about the men who illegally felled trees in the forest, and the smugglers who tempted them with large sums of money and sent them into the forest. Knowing this, Ravi kept meeting the folk living in the hamlets below the hills, socialising with them as the son of a golla.

He attended their functions, drank the buttermilk that they offered him and encouraged their children with gifts of educational material. He conducted awareness campaigns at schools, households and village squares about the ill effects of cutting down forest trees, the civic duty to conserve the forest ecosystem and the punishments for those caught breaking the law.

Ravi built a good rapport with the tribal folk. He also mingled closely with the gollas herding their flocks near the foothills and nurtured his emotional connection with the shepherds who went hill-grazing during summers. Using his connections and relationships, he built a network of informers who alerted the forest department whenever groups of people entered the forest carrying axes.

Unlike other officials, Ravi did not simply sit in his office at the district headquarters and pass on orders to his subordinates and field staff. He went into the forests himself, accompanied by not only some of his energetic staff but also the yaanadis, chenchus, sugaalis and even some of the gollas who knew the forest well.

Ravi walked on the jungle trails, and where there was no trail, he climbed over the hills. The tribals—who were children of the hills, born and raised in the forests—were surprised to see a forest officer handle the terrain better than them. Ravi would set the pace, skilfully bounding across the rocks, walking briskly along the streambeds and thorny bushes and climbing the steep slopes with assured grace and ease.

By entering the deep forests and climbing hills of the inner ranges himself, Ravi was able to put a stop to the atrocities being committed there. He confronted thieves and smugglers and caught them red-handed. He ensured that none of the criminals could escape the law by systematically collecting evidence and handing it over to the justice system. This ensured that the thugs were all sent to jail.

The reason for Ravi's success was his engagement with the locals and natives of the forest. He behaved as a local person himself and made it known to everyone that he was on their side. He did not show off his official powers like the other officers nor did he leverage the arrests of smugglers for bribes. His actions built trust among the people that everything he did was to protect the forests. Within a short period, Ravi had earned the reputation of being an honest officer.

*

Ravi—now called Ravindra Yadav by most people—married a village woman. With family in tow, he visited his village every Sankranthi and Ugadi. He also went whenever required to help his family, friends or the village itself. He never let go of any opportunity to spend a night in the homely comfort of his native place.

Ravi often told his colleagues in the forest department that it was a big relief for him to visit his village. It was a perfect break that relieved him of all his work-related tension. 'I get recharged every time I go see my mother and my mother-like village,' he said. 'Fresh energy infuses my body and soul every time I spend a couple of days in the company of my family and friends. This energy gives me the courage and strength I need to handle pressures from senior officials, threats from politicians and challenges from the smugglers. My village is my strength.'

On every visit to the village, the first thing Ravi did was visit his old friends from the hill-grazing expedition and their families. Some of them had left the village over the years for different reasons. A few remained though, including Bhaskar, with whom Ravi shared a special bond. Then there was old Pullayya, who had stopped rearing sheep a few years ago. Now he mostly stayed at home with his weak knees and bent back. And yet, he kept a single sheep and a little lamb with him at home. 'Without them, I feel empty,' he told Ravi.

Ravi was always received with a lot of affection at Ankayya's home. Subhadra would force him to eat freshly-made sweetmeats and then they would reminisce about the time she reunited with her husband at the Kasi Nayana ashram.

Gurappa continued to rear a herd, much to the chagrin of the rest of the family. They expected Ravi to support their stance and convince Gurappa to retire. But Ravi understood his father's point of view—it was better to keep oneself active than simply sit at home and get bored. A shepherd never retires as long as he is physically capable of taking care of his sheep.

*

Over the years, many things changed in the village, but some things remained the same. Among them was the inability of the village youth to find jobs and have successful careers in the cities. To address this issue, Ravi often reminded them to leverage the inherent strengths that the village life had given them. He told the youngsters that he too had faced the same issues, and then described how he had confronted and resolved them.

Ravi explained the methods that worked for him in taking ownership of his work, channelising his passion to enjoy work and making it a healthy addiction. He asked them to closely observe the fervour of a farmer to save his crop during a drought or the passion of a shepherd to nourish and protect a motherless little lamb. He advised them to study the commitment and concentration of people engaged in their family professions and exhorted them to adopt the hardworking nature of the people who laboured in the fields and forests.

An example Ravi often used was the story of a woman who removed weeds from a five-acre farm all by herself. He would ask the youngsters to consider the hard work, dedication and self-belief she must have had to single-handedly complete such an impossibly difficult job, and then he would motivate them to unlock that self-belief within themselves.

'You won't find better motivational speakers and personality development experts than your parents, siblings and fellow villagers who show dedication and passion towards their work,' Ravi said to anyone who asked him for career advice. 'You won't find people more committed and dutiful than the ones who try to sustain their families and livestock in these drought-prone lands. Get inspired by them. Study their resilience, patience and zeal for life. You will then achieve well-deserved success.'

Translator's Note

When I reread *Kondapolam* from the perspective of a translator, several challenges presented themselves to me—the local Telugu idiom of the Nallamala region, the proverbs and witticisms used by Pullayya and other shepherds, the names and customs of castes and sub-castes, the kinship terms used by the villagers to address each other (because the entire village is one big family after all), the dozens of names of places, the references to saints, gods and goddesses, the types of grasses, plants, trees and animals, the plurality of terms associated with hills, hillocks, brooks, meadows, soil and, of course, the way shepherds refer to sheep using terms that describe a bewildering variety of colours and their shades. All of this, along with the challenge of translating the essence of the novel, the poetic passages describing nature and the many Telugu words specific to the Rayalaseema region, used only by the villagers.

It has been a profound learning experience to say the least. The research involved in finding the botanical and zoological names of the flora and fauna was enjoyable, and my first draft had footnotes on practically every page. Some of the Telugu words used to refer to agricultural implements, soil types and other such things posed a bigger problem. The internet was not of much help there. That I hail from the same region as the author (also where the story unfolds) helped a bit, however. My father, who passed away during the pandemic, a month after I completed my first draft, had advised me to refer to old Telugu to English dictionaries. The classic Brown Dictionary (commissioned by C.P. Brown, an English officer and patron of Telugu language), first published in 1852, was quite useful. *Surya Rayandhra Nighantuvu*, first published in 1939 and expanded since then under the aegis of the Telugu Sahitya Academy, was another useful reference book.

The footnotes from the first version of the translation disappeared over the course of editing. So here are some explanations to help the reader gain a better understanding of the milieu of the novel.

The gollas are a Telugu-speaking pastoral community with links to other pastoral/cattle- and sheep-herding communities across the subcontinent. 'Golla' comes from Gopala (Sanskrit) or Gwala (Prakrit), and the gollas trace their lineage to the Yadavas of the Mahabharata with Krishna as their god/king. In other words, 'yadav' is the Sanskritised name for a golla. As the saying goes in rural Rayalaseema, 'When a golla becomes rich, he becomes a yadav. When a kapu becomes rich, he calls himself a reddy.'

However, it is not just the gollas who rear sheep or cattle in Telugu villages. Due to self-interest or financial reasons (lack of land ownership, non-viability of small holdings), people from other castes also take up the herding of cattle or sheep or both. They become kapu–gollas or rajaka–gollas as a result, but when it comes to marriages or village politics, they stick to their caste groups.

The village communities are like an extended family. It is common practice for people to address fellow villagers using kinship terms such as uncle, aunt, grandfather and so on, even if they are not related or are of a different caste. A friend is an elder or younger brother, and a friend's wife is a sister-in-law or sister.

Temple and deity names usually have a Sanskrit name or a Sanskritised version used by the educated and/or urban folk. The villagers shorten the names or create their own. Ahobilam becomes Obulam and the deity Narasimha Swamy is simply referred to as Swamy or Saami. The deity at Tirumala, Venkateswara, is referred as Venkanna or Edu Kondala Vadu (Lord of the Seven Hills). The names of saints are simplified too. The saint Kasi Reddy Nayana is sometimes called Kasi Nayana or even simply Nayana.

We encounter people from three tribes in the novel—the yaanadis, the sugaalis and the chenchus. They know the terrain of the hills better than anyone else and are the true people of the forest. However, whilst the yaanadis survive by hunting small animals and gathering fruits, honey, roots and medicinal plants from the forests and are also exploited by the sandalwood smugglers, the sugaalis do more hunting and poaching. The chenchus also hunt but over the years have gravitated towards shifting cultivation and learned the habits of townspeople.

In the novel, we see the chenchus referring to the Ahobilam deity Narasimha Swamy as their brother-in-law and claiming tax from the shepherds for having grazed their sheep near the temple in the hills. The legend is that Narasimha Swamy's spouse was a chenchu woman. The deity is considered the community's son-in-law and some chenchus use the legend to collect money or sheep from the shepherds by sweet-talking or some bullying. Such local ownership of a temple in the woods or hills is common across the country, especially because the communities often see the temple as an anchor for the local economy.

The golla women in the novel—Ravi's mother and grandmother, his sisters, the wives of his shepherd friends—run the household and manage the money. In the villages, golla households are known by the matriarch's name—Ravi's house is known as 'Rosamma's house'. Whilst the men decide matters related to the herd, the women are in control of the matters of the household and family. The lady of the house counts on the support of her brothers and sisters, not the husband's relatives.

It has been a pleasure translating the Telugu idiom and rural witticisms, conveying the bond between the men and the sheep and that of the herd with the forest. *Tiger Lessons* is a tale of one man discovering his inner strength and courage, triggered by the affection he develops for an orphaned lamb. It is also the tale of shepherds braving the dangers of the forest and its predators to help their herd survive the harsh summer. The unique worldview of the shepherds about humans and their place as only 'guests' of the forest is relevant to today's debates and discussions around ecology and conservation. I shall consider my job done if the essential message of the novel is conveyed to the readers.

About the Author

Sannapureddy Venkatarami Reddy retired as a biology teacher at a government school in the village of Balaraju Palle, a few miles from the foothills of the Nallamala ranges. *Kondapolam* received both critical and popular acclaim as a modern classic in Telugu literature. It was adapted into a movie in 2021.

About the Translator

Narasimha Kumar is a technology entrepreneur with a humanities background. *Tiger Lessons* is his first work of translation from Telugu to English. Kumar had earlier adapted Albert Camus's play *The Just Assassins* for an award-winning Telugu movie.